The Skipper and the Skipped

Holman Day

THE SKIPPER TELLS OF "THE GLORIOUS, FASCINATING SEA."

THE SKIPPER AND THE SKIPPED

BEING THE SHORE LOG OF CAP'N AARON SPROUL

BY

HOLMAN DAY

AUTHOR OF
"THE RAMRODDERS"
"KING SPRUCE" ETC.

ILLUSTRATED

NEW YORK AND LONDON
HARPER & BROTHERS PUBLISHERS
MCMXI

BOOKS BY
HOLMAN DAY

THE SKIPPER AND THE SKIPPED. Post 8vo . . $1.50
THE RAMRODDERS. Post 8vo $1.50
KING SPRUCE. Ill'd. Post 8vo $1.50
THE EAGLE'S BADGE. Ill'd. Post 8vo . . . $1.25

HARPER & BROTHERS, PUBLISHERS, N.Y.

1911. BY HARPER & BROTHERS
PRINTED IN THE UNITED STATES OF AMERICA
PUBLISHED FEBRUARY, 1911

The Skipper and the Skipped

I

Cap'n Aaron Sproul, late skipper of the *Jefferson P. Benn*, sat by the bedside of his uncle, "One-arm" Jerry, and gazed into the latter's dimming eyes.

"It ain't bein' a crowned head, but it's honer'ble," pleaded the sick man, continuing the conversation.

His eager gaze found only gloominess in his nephew's countenance.

"One way you look at it, Uncle Jed," said the Cap'n, "it's a comedown swifter'n a slide from the foretop the whole length of the boomstay. I've been master since I was twenty-four, and I'm goin' onto fifty-six now. I've licked every kind in the sailorman line, from a nigger up to Six-fingered Jack the Portugee. If it wa'n't for—ow, Josephus Henry!—for this rheumatiz, I'd be aboard the *Benn* this minute with a marlinespike in my hand, and op'nin' a fresh package of language."

"But you ain't fit for the sea no longer," mumbled One-arm Jerry through one corner of the mouth that paralysis had drawn awry.

"That's what I told the owners of the *Benn* when I fit 'em off'm me and resigned," agreed the Cap'n. "I tell ye, good skippers ain't born ev'ry minute—and they knowed it. I've been turnin' 'em in ten per cent. on her, and that's good property. I've got an eighth into her myself, and with a man as good as I am to run her, I shouldn't need to worry about doin' anything else all my life—me a single man with no one dependent. I reckon I'll sell. Shipmasters ain't what they used to be."

"Better leave it where it is," counselled Jerry, his cautious thrift dominating even in that hour of death. "Land-sharks is allus lookin' out sharp for sailormen that git on shore."

"It's why I don't dast to go into business—me that's follered the sea so long," returned the skipper, nursing his aching leg.

"Then do as I tell ye to do," said the old man on the bed. "It may be a come-down for a man that's had men under him all his life, but it amounts to more'n five hundred a year, sure and stiddy. It's something to do, and you couldn't stand it to loaf—you that's always been so active. It ain't reskin' anything, and with all the passin' and the meetin' folks, and the gossipin' and the chattin', and all that, all your time is took up. It's honer'ble, it's stiddy. Leave your money where it is, take my place, and keep this job in the family."

The two men were talking in a little cottage at the end of a long covered bridge. A painted board above the door heralded the fact that the cottage was the toll-house, and gave the rates of toll.

"It's Providence that has sent you here jest as I was bein' took out of the world," went on Uncle Jerry. "You're my only rel'tive. I'm leavin' you the three thousand I've accumulated. I want to leave you the job, too. I—"

A hoarse hail outside interrupted. The Cap'n, scowling, shuffled out and came in, jingling some pennies in his brown hand.

"I feel like a hand-organ monkey every time I go out there," he muttered.

"I tell ye," protested the old man, as earnestly as his feebleness would permit, "there's lots of big business in this world that don't need so long a head as this one does—bein' as how you're goin' to run it shipshape. You need brains; that you do, nephy. It'll keep you studyin' all the time. When you git interested in it you ain't never goin' to have time to be lonesome. There's the plain hello folks to be treated one way, the good-day folks, the pass-the-time-o'-day folks, the folks that need the tip o' the hat—jest for politeness, and not because you're beneath 'em," he hastened to add, noting the skipper's scowl; "the folks that swing up to the platform, the folks that you've got to chase a little, even if it is muddy; the folks that pay

2

in advance and want you to remember it and save 'em trouble, the folks that pay when they come back, and the folks that never pay at all—and I tell ye, nephy, there's where your work is cut out for ye! I've only had one arm, but there's mighty few that have ever done me out of toll, and I'm goin' to give ye a tip on the old bell-wether of 'em all. I'm goin' to advise ye to stand to one side and let him pass. He's—"

"And me a man that's licked every—"

"Hold on! He's diff'runt from all you've ever tackled."

In his excitement the old toll-gatherer attempted to struggle upon his elbow. He choked. The nurse came and laid him back with gentle remonstrance. Before he had regained his voice to talk more the minister came, obeying a summons of grave import. Then came One who sealed One-arm Jerry's lips and quieted the fingers that had been picking at the faded coverlet as though they were gathering pennies.

And a day later, half sullenly, the Cap'n accepted the proposition of the directors of the bridge company, who had said some very flattering things to him about the reliability of the Sproul family. He reflected that he was far enough from tide-water to avoid the mariners who had known him in his former state. "I'll dock and repair riggin'," he pondered. "It's a come-down, but I'll clear and cruise again when the notion strikes me."

His possessions came promptly by express—his sea-chest, two parrots, and a most amazing collection of curios that fairly transformed the little cottage where the skipper, with seaman's facility in housekeeping, set up bachelor's hall.

He grudgingly allowed to himself that he was going to like it. The sun beamed blandly warm on the little bench before the toll-house. His rheumatism felt better. People commented admiringly on such of the curios as were displayed in the windows of the cottage. And when the parrots—"Port" and "Starboard"—ripped out such remarks as "Ahoy!" "Heave to!" "Down hellum!" and larded the conversation with horrible oaths, the wayfarers professed to see great humor in the performance.

In a little while the parrots would squall as soon as a traveller appeared at the brow of the river hill or poked out from the dim depths of the covered bridge. Even when the Cap'n was busy in his little kitchen he never failed to receive due notice of the approach of persons either in wagons or on foot.

"It will be a good man who runs toll on this bridge," he mused one day, as he poked dainties between the bars of the parrots' cages. "The old 'un was a good man in his day, like all the Sprouls. He didn't have but one arm, but there wa'n't many that ever come it over him. I've been thinkin' about one that did, and that he was scart of. If there was ever a man that scart him, and kept him scart till the day he died, then I'd like to see that same. It will be for me to show him that the nephy has some accounts of the poor old uncle to square."

Up the slope where the road to Smyrna Bridge wound behind the willows there was the growing rattle of wheels. The Cap'n cocked his head. His seaman's instinct detected something stormy in that impetuous approach. He fixed his gaze on the bend of the road.

Into sight came tearing a tall, gaunt horse, dragging a wagon equally tall and gaunt. The horse was galloping, and a tall man in the wagon stood up and began to crack a great whip, with reports like a pistol fusillade.

Cap'n Sproul took three defiant steps into the middle of the road, and then took one big step back—a stride that made his "rheumatiz speak up," but a stride that carried him safely to his platform. The team roared past. The big whip swished over his head, and the snapper barked in his ear. He got one fleeting glimpse at the man who was driving—a man with a face as hard as a pine knot. His lips were rolled away from his yellow teeth in a grimace that was partly a grin, partly a sneer. A queer, tall, pointed cap with a knob on its top was perched on his head like a candle-snuffer on a taper. With a shrill yell and more crackings of his whip he disappeared into the gloomy mouth of the covered bridge, and the roaring echoes followed him.

The skipper stood looking first at the mouth of the bridge and then at the sign above it that warned:

THREE DOLLARS' FINE
FOR DRIVING FASTER THAN A WALK

"As I was jest sayin'," he muttered, as the noise of the wheels died away, "I should like to see that man—and I reckon as how I have."

He sat down under the woodbine that wreathed the little porch and slowly filled his pipe, his gaze still on the bridge opening. As he crooked his leg and dragged the match across the faded blue of his trousers he growled:

"I dunno who he is, nor where he's come from, nor where he's goin' to, nor when he expects to get back, but, as near as I can figger it, he owes me ten cents' toll and three dollars' fine-money, makin' a total of three ten, to be charged and collected, as I understand it."

When he had got his pipe to going, after some little gruntings, he pulled out a note-book and a stubby pencil and marked down the figures. At the head of the page he scrawled:

"Old Hurrycain, Dr."

"That name 'll have to do till I git a better one," he mused, and then stood up to receive toll from a farmer who drove slowly out from the bridge, his elbows on his knees, his horse walking slouchily.

"If it ain't no great output to you, mister, to tell, do you happen to know who was the nub of that streak of wind and cuss-words that jest went past here?"

The farmer bored him strangely a moment with his little gimlet eyes, snorted out a laugh, clapped his reins, and started on.

"I heard ye was a joker!" he shouted back, his beard trailing over his shoulder as he turned his head.

"There ain't no joke to this!" roared the skipper. But the man kept on.

Another patron emerged from the bridge, digging from his trousers pocket.

"You spoke it, didn't ye?" demanded the skipper. "Chain lightnin' on wheels. Who is he?"

The man grinned amiably and appreciatively.

"Quite a hand to hector, ain't ye, toll-keeper? He was goin' so fast I didn't know him, neither." He drove on, though the Cap'n hobbled after him, shouting strong language, in which the parrots joined.

"You needn't try to make me think that there ain't nobody who don't know the Kun'l," was the retort the man flung over his shoulder.

"Nice and accommodatin' class of paternage that's passin'," growled the Cap'n, kicking an inoffensive chair as he came back to his platform. "They talk about him as though he was Lord Gull and ruler of the stars. Jest as though a man that had sailed deep water all his days knowed all the old land-pirut's 'round here!"

It was a pedestrian—Old Man Jordan, bound to the village with a few pats of butter in a bucket—that the skipper finally held up.

"Oh, sho!" said Old Man Jordan. "'Course ye know him. Every one does."

"I tell you I don't!" bawled the skipper.

"Why, yas you do."

"Say, look a-here, What's-your-name, I'm goin' to give ye ten seconds to tell me the name of that critter."

He made a clutch to one side, and then remembered with a flush that he was no longer in reach of a spike-rack.

"Why, that was Kun'l Gideon Waid," faltered Uncle Jordan, impressed at last by the Cap'n's fury. "I thought ye knew."

"Thought! Thought! Why, ye never thought in your life. You only thought you thought. I dunno no more who you mean by 'Kun'l Gideon Ward' than as though you said General Bill Beelzebub."

"Why, yas you do—"

"There you go again! Do you mean to stand here and tell me I'm a liar?"

The glare in the seaman's eyes was too fierce to be fronted.

"Kun'l Gideon Ward is—is—wall, he's Kun'l Gideon Ward."

Jordan backed away suddenly at the oath the Cap'n ripped out.

"He owns more timber land than any other man in the county. He hires more men than any one else. He ain't never been downed in a trade or a fight yet. He's got double teeth, upper and lower, all the way round, drinks kairosene in the winter 'cause it's more warmin' than rum, and—and—"

"Well, what's that got to do with his runnin' toll on this bridge?" demanded the Cap'n.

"Bridge piers hold up his logs, he says, and he ain't never goin' to pay toll till the bridgemen pay him for loss of time on logs. It's been what you might call a stand-off for a good many years. Best thing is to let him run toll. That's what your uncle thought. I reckoned you knew all about Kun'l Gid Ward. Why, everybody knows—"

"Say, you let up on that string right now and here," snorted the Cap'n.

Old Man Jordan trotted away.

While the skipper was still pondering on the matter of Colonel Ward—the meditation had lasted over into the next day—there was a roar on the bridge, and the subject of his reflections passed in a swirl of dust on his return trip. He was standing up in his wagon as before, and he saluted the indignant toll-man with a flick of his whip that started the dust from the latter's pea-jacket.

"He's been over to the home place to see his sister Jane," volunteered Uncle Jordan, again on his way to the village with eggs. "She ain't never got married, and he ain't never got married. Old Squire Ward left his whole property to the two of 'em, and the Kun'l ain't ever let it be divided. He runs the whole estate and domineers over her, and she don't dast to say her soul's her own. If I was Jane I'd have my half out and git married to some nice man, and git a little comfort out'n life. He don't give her none—don't let her have the handlin' of a cent of money. She's a turrible nice sort of woman. There's risin' a hundred thousand dollars in her share, if the truth was known, and there's been some pretty good men shine up around her a little, but the Kun'l has run 'em away with a picked stick."

"Has, hey?"

"There ain't no Jack the Giant-Killers in these parts," sighed Old Man Jordan, hooking his bucket upon his arm and shambling away.

For several days Cap'n Sproul was busy about the gable end of the bridge during his spare moments and hours, climbing up and down the ladder, and handling a rope and certain pulleys with sailor dexterity. All the time his grim jaw-muscles ridged his cheeks. When he had finished he had a rope running through pulleys from the big gate up over the gable of the bridge and to the porch of the toll-house.

"There," he muttered, with great satisfaction, "that's the first bear-trap I ever set, and it ain't no extra sort of job, but I reckon when old grizzly goes ag'inst it he'll cal'late that this 'ere is a toll-bridge."

Then came days of anxious waiting. Sometimes a teamster's shouts to his horses up around the willows sent the Cap'n hobbling to the end of the rope. An unusual rattling in the bridge put him at his post with his teeth set and his eyes gleaming.

II

One day a mild and placid little woman in dove-gray came walking from the bridge and handed over her penny. She eyed the skipper with interest, and cocked her head with the pert demureness of a sparrow while she studied the parrots who were waddling about their cages.

"I never heard a parrot talk, sir," she said. "I hear that yours talk. I should dearly love to hear them."

"Their language is mostly deep-water flavor," said the Cap'n, curtly, "and 'tain't flavored edsackly like vanilla ice-cream. There's more of the peppersass tang to it than ladies us'ly enjoys."

The little woman gave a chirrup at the birds, and, to the skipper's utter astonishment, both Port and Starboard chirruped back sociably. Port then remarked: "Pretty Polly!" Starboard chirruped a few cheery bars from "A Sailor's Wife a Sailor's Star Should Be." Then both parrots rapped their beaks genially against the bars of the cages and beamed on the lady with their little button eyes.

"Well, I swow!" ejaculated the Cap'n, rubbing his knurly forefinger under his nose, and glancing first at the parrots and then at the lady. "If that ain't as much of an astonisher as when the scuttle-butt danced a jig on the dog-vane! Them two us'ly cusses strangers, no matter what age or sect. They was learnt to do it." He gazed doubtfully at the birds, as though they might possibly be deteriorating in the effeminacies of shore life.

"I always was a great hand with pets of all kinds," said the lady, modestly. "Animals seem to take to me sort of naturally. I hear you have long followed the sea, Cap'n Sproul—I believe that's the name, Cap'n Sproul?"

"Sproul it is, ma'am—Aaron for fore-riggin'. Them as said I follered the sea was nearer than shore-folks us'ly be. Took my dunnage aboard at fourteen, master at twenty-four, keel-hauled by rheumatiz at fifty-six—wouldn't be here if it wasn't for that. I ain't stuck on a penny-flippin' job of this sort."

"I should think it would be very pleasant after all the storms and the tossings. And yet the sea—the sea, the glorious sea—has always had a great fascination for me—even though I've never seen it."

"Nev—nev nevei seen salt water!" This amazedly.

"Never." This sadly. "I've been kept—I've stayed very closely at my home. Being a single lady, I've had no one to talk to me or take me about. I have read books about the ocean, but I've never had any chance to hear a real and truly mariner tell about the wonderful waste of waters and describe foreign countries. I suppose you have been 'way, 'way out to sea, Cap'n Sproul—across the ocean, I mean."

She had timidly edged up and taken one of the chairs on the porch, gazing about her at the curios.

"Well, ma'am," remarked the Cap'n, dryly, as he seated himself in another chair, "I've waded across a cove wunst or twice at low water."

"I should love so to hear a mariner talk of his adventures. I have never had much chance to talk with any man—I mean any sailor. I have been kept—I mean I have stayed very closely at home all my life."

"It broadens a man, it sartain does, to travel," said the skipper, furtively slipping a sliver of tobacco into his cheek and clearing his throat preparatory to yarning a bit. The frank admiration and trustful innocence in the eyes of the pretty woman touched him.

"I suppose you have been out at sea in some awful storms, Cap'n. I often think of the sailormen at sea when the snow beats against the window and the winds howl around the corner."

The Skipper and the Skipped

"The wu'st blow I ever remember," began the skipper, leaning back and hooking his brown hands behind his head like a basket, "was my second trip to Bonis Airis—general cargo out, to fetch back hides. It was that trip we found the shark that had starved to death, and that was a story that was worth speakin' of. It—"

There was a hoarse bellow of "Giddap!" up behind the willows. Then into sight came galloping the tall, gaunt horse of Colonel Gideon Ward. The Colonel stood up, smacking his whip.

With one leap the Cap'n was at his rope, and began to haul in hand over hand.

The big gate at the mouth of the bridge squalled on its rusty hinges.

"You mustn't shut that gate—you mustn't!" shrieked the little woman. She ran and clutched at his sturdy arms. "That's my brother that's coming! You'll break his neck!"

The gate was already half shut, and the doughty skipper kept on pulling at the rope.

"Can't help it, ma'am, if it's the apostle Paul," he gritted. "There ain't nobody goin' to run toll on this bridge."

"It will kill him."

"It's him that's lickin' that hoss. 'Tain't me."

"It's my brother, I tell you!" She tried to drag the rope out of his hands, but he shook her off, pulled the big gate shut, set his teeth, clung to the rope, and waited.

The rush down the hill had been so impetuous and the horse was now running so madly under the whip that there was no such thing as checking him. With a crash of splintering wood he drove breast-on against the gate, throwing up his bony head at the end of his scraggy neck. At the crash the woman screamed and covered her eyes. But the outfit was too much of a catapult to be stopped. Through the gate it went, and the wagon roared away through the bridge, the driver yelling oaths behind him.

Cap'n Aaron Sproul walked out and strolled among the scattered debris, kicking it gloomily to right and left. The woman followed him.

"It was awful," she half sobbed.

"So you're Miss Jane Ward, be ye?" he growled, glancing at her from under his knotted eyebrows. "Speakin' of your pets, I should reckon that 'ere brother of yourn wa'n't one that you had tamed down fit to be turned loose. But you tell him for me, the next time you see him, that I'll plug the end of that bridge against him if it takes ev'ry dum cent of the prop'ty I'm wuth—and that's thutty thousand dollars, if it's a cent. I ain't none of your two-cent chaps!" he roared, visiting his wrath vicariously on her as a representative of the family. "I've got money of my own. Your brother seems to have made door-mats out'n most of the folks round here, but I'll tell ye that he's wiped his feet on me for the last time. You tell him that, dum him!"

Her face was white, and her eyes were shining as she looked at him.

"Gideon has always had his own way, Cap'n Sproul," she faltered. "I hope you won't feel too bitter against him. It would be awful—he so headstrong—and you so—so—brave!" She choked this last out, unclasping her hands.

"Well, I ain't no coward, and I never was," blurted the Cap'n.

"It's the bravest man that overcomes himself," she said. "Now, you have good judgment, Cap'n. My brother is hot-headed. Every one knows that you are a brave man. You can afford to let him go over the bridge without—"

"Never!" the skipper howled, in his best sea tones. "You're the last woman to coax and beg for him, if half what they tell me is true. He has abused you wuss'n he has any one else. If you and the rest ain't got any spunk, I have. You'll be one brother out if he comes slam-bangin' this way ag'in."

She looked at him appealingly for a moment, then tiptoed over the fragments of the gate, and hurried away through the bridge.

"You ain't no iron-clad, Kun'l Ward," muttered Sproul. "I'll hold ye next time."

He set to work on the river-bank that afternoon, cutting saplings, trusting to the squall of the faithful parrots to signal the approach of passers.

But the next day, when he was nailing the saplings to make a truly Brobdingnagian grid, one of the directors of the bridge company appeared to him.

"We're not giving you license to let any one run toll on this bridge, you understand," said the director, "but this fighting Colonel Ward with our property is another matter. It's like fighting a bear with your fists. And even if you killed the bear, the hide wouldn't be worth the damage. He has got too many ways of hurting us, Cap'n. He has always had his own way in these parts, and he probably always will. Let him go. We won't get the toll, nor the fines, but we'll have our bridge left."

"I was thinking of resigning this job," returned the Cap'n; "it was not stirrin' enough for a seafarin' man; but I'm sort of gittin' int'rested. How much will ye take for your bridge?"

But the director curtly refused to sell.

"All right, then," said the skipper, chocking his axe viciously into a sapling birch and leaving it there, "I'll fill away on another tack."

For the next two weeks, as though to exult in his victory, the Colonel made many trips past the toll-house.

He hurled much violent language at the Cap'n. The Cap'n, reinforced with his vociferous parrots, returned the language with great enthusiasm and volubility.

Then came the day once more when the little woman sat down in a chair in the shade of the woodbine.

"I took the first chance, Cap'n, while my brother has gone up-country, to come to tell you how much I appreciate your generous way of doing what I asked of you. You are the first man that ever put away selfish pride and did just what I asked."

The seaman started to repudiate vigorously, but looked into her brimming eyes a moment, choked, and was silent.

"Yes, sir, you're what I call noble, not to pay any attention to the boasts my brother is making of how he has backed you down."

"He is, is he?" The Cap'n rolled up his lip and growled.

"But I know just how brave you are, to put down all your anger at the word of a poor woman. And a true gentleman, too. There are only a few real gentlemen in the world, after all."

The Cap'n slid his thumb into the armhole of his waistcoat and swelled his chest out a little.

"There was no man ever come it over me, and some good ones have tried it, ma'am. So fur as women goes, I ain't never been married, but I reckon I know what politeness to a lady means."

She smiled at him brightly, and with such earnest admiration that he felt a flush crawling up from under his collar. He blinked at her and looked away. Starboard, with an embarrassing aptness that is sometimes displayed by children, whistled a few bars of "A Sailor's Wife a Sailor's Star Should Be."

"I don't mind owning up to you that my brother has imposed upon me in a great many ways," said the little lady, her eyes flashing. "I have endured a good deal from him because he is my brother. I know just how you feel about him, Cap'n, and that's why it makes me feel that we have a—a sort of what you might call common interest. I don't know why I'm talking so frankly with you, who are almost a stranger, but I've been—I have always lacked friends so much, that now I can't seem to help it. You truly do seem like an old friend, you have been so willing to do what I asked of you, after you had time to think it over."

The Cap'n was now congratulating himself that he hadn't blurted out anything about the bridge director and that sapling fence. It certainly was a grateful sound—that praise from the pretty lady! He didn't want to interrupt it.

"Now will you go on with that story of the storm?" she begged, hitching the chair a bit nearer. "I want to hear about your adventures."

She had all the instincts of Desdemona, did that pretty little lady. Three times that week she came to the toll-house and listened with lips apart and eyes shining. Cap'n Sproul had never heard of Othello and his wooing, but after a time his heart began to glow under the reverent regard she bent on him. Never did mutual selection more naturally come about. She loved him for the perils he had braved, and he—robbed of his mistress, the sea—yearned for just such companionship as she was giving him. He had known that life lacked something. This was it.

And when one day, after a stuttering preamble that lasted a full half hour, he finally blurted out his heart-hankering, she wept a little while on his shoulder—it being luckily a time when there was no one passing—and then sobbingly declared it could never be.

"'Fraid of your brother, hey?" he inquired.

She bumped her forehead gently on his shoulder in nod of assent.

16

"I reckon ye like me?"

"Oh, Aaron!" It was a volume of rebuke, appeal, and affection in two words.

"Then there ain't nothin' more to say, little woman. You ain't never had any one to look out for your int'rests in this life. After this, it's me that does it. I don't want your money. I've got plenty of my own. But your interests bein' my interests after this, you hand ev'rything over to me, and I'll put a twist in the tail of that Bengal tiger in your fam'ly that 'll last him all his life."

At the end of a long talk he sent her away with a pat on her shoulder and a cheery word in her ear.

It was Old Man Jordan who, a week or so later, on his way to the village with butter in his bucket, stood in the middle of the road and tossed his arms so frenziedly that Colonel Ward, gathering up his speed behind the willows, pulled up with an oath.

"Ye're jest gittin' back from up-country, ain't ye?" asked Uncle Jordan.

"What do you mean, you old fool, by stoppin' me when I'm busy? What be ye, gittin' items for newspapers?"

"No, Kun'l Ward, but I've got some news that I thought ye might like to hear before ye went past the toll-house this time. Intentions between Cap'n Aaron Sproul and Miss Jane Ward has been published."

"Wha-a-at!"

"They were married yistiddy."

"Wha—" The cry broke into inarticulateness.

The Skipper and the Skipped

"The Cap'n ain't goin' to be toll-man after to-day. Says he's goin' to live on the home place with his wife. There!" Uncle Jordan stepped to one side just in time, for the gaunt horse sprung under the lash as though he had the wings of Pegasus.

The Cap'n was sitting in front of the toll-house. The tall horse galloped down the hill, but the Colonel stood up, and, with elbows akimbo and hands under his chin, yanked the animal to a standstill, his splay feet skating through the highway dust. The Colonel leaped over the wheel and reversed his heavy whip-butt. The Cap'n stood up, gripping a stout cudgel that he had been whittling at for many hours.

While the new arrival was choking with an awful word that he was trying his best to work out of his throat, the Cap'n pulled his little note-book out of his pocket and slowly drawled:

"I reckoned as how ye might find time to stop some day, and I've got your account all figgered. You owe thirteen tolls at ten cents each, one thutty, and thirteen times three dollars fine—the whole amountin' to jest forty dollars and thutty cents. Then there's a gate to—"

"I'm goin' to kill you right in your tracks where you stand!" bellowed the Colonel.

The Cap'n didn't wait for the attack. He leaped down off his porch, and advanced with the fierce intrepidity of a sea tyrant.

"You'll pay that toll bill," he gritted, "if I have to pick it out of your pockets whilst the coroner is settin' on your remains."

The bully of the countryside quailed.

"You've stole my sister!" he screamed. "This ain't about toll I'm talkin'. You've been and robbed me of my sister!"

"Do you want to hear a word on that?" demanded the Cap'n, grimly. He came close up, whirling the cudgel. "You're an old, cheap, ploughed-land blowhard, that's what you are! You've cuffed 'round hired men and abused weak wimmen-folks. I knowed you was a coward when I got that line on ye. You don't dast to stand up to a man like me. I'll split your head for a cent." He kept advancing step by step, his mien absolutely demoniac. "I've married your sister because she wanted me. Now I'm goin' to take care of her. I've got thutty thousand dollars of my own, and she's giv' me power of attorney over hers. I'll take every cent of what belongs to her out of your business, and I know enough of the way that your business is tied up to know that I can crowd you right to the wall. Now do ye want to fight?"

The tyrant's face grew sickly white, for he realized all that threat meant.

"But there ain't no need of a fight in the fam'ly—and I want you to understand that I'm a pretty dum big part of the fam'ly after this. Be ye ready to listen to reason?"

"You're a robber!" gasped the Colonel, trying again to muster his anger.

"I've got a proposition to make so that there won't be no pull-haulin' and lawyers to pay, and all that."

"What is it?"

"Pardnership between you and me—equal pardners. I've been lookin' for jest this chance to go into business."

The Colonel leaped up, and began to stamp round his wagon.

"No, sir," he howled at each stamp. "I'll go to the poor-farm first."

"Shouldn't wonder if I could put you there," calmly rejoined the Cap'n. "These forced lickidations to settle estates is something awful when the books ain't been kept any better'n yours. I shouldn't be a mite surprised to find that the law would get a nab on you for cheatin' your poor sister."

Again the Colonel's face grew white.

"All is," continued the Cap'n, patronizingly, "if we can keep it all in the fam'ly, nice and quiet, you ain't goin' to git showed up. Now, I ain't goin' to listen to no more abuse out of you. I'll give you jest one minute to decide. Look me in the eye. I mean business."

"You've got me where I'll have to," wailed the Colonel.

"Is it pardnership?"

"Yas!" He barked the word.

"Now, Colonel Ward, there's only one way for you and me to do bus'ness the rest of our lives, and that's on the square, cent for cent. We might as well settle that p'int now. Fix up that toll bill, or it's all off. I won't go into business with a man that don't pay his honest debts."

He came forward with his hand out.

The Colonel paid.

"Now," said the Cap'n, "seein' that the new man is here, ready to take holt, and the books are all square, I'll ride home with you. I've been callin' it home now for a couple of days."

The new man at the toll-house heard the Cap'n talking serenely as they drove away.

"I didn't have any idee, Colonel, I was goin' to like it so well on shore as I do. Of course, you meet some pleasant and some unpleasant people, but that sister of yours is sartinly the finest

20

woman that ever trod shoe-leather, and it was Providunce a-speakin' to me when she — "

The team passed away into the gloomy mouth of the Smyrna bridge.

III

Once on a time when the Wixon boy put Paris-green in the Trufants' well, because the oldest Trufant girl had given him the mitten, Marm Gossip gabbled in Smyrna until flecks of foam gathered in the corners of her mouth.

But when Cap'n Aaron Sproul, late of the deep sea, so promptly, so masterfully married Col. Gideon Ward's sister—after the irascible Colonel had driven every other suitor away from that patient lady— and then gave the Colonel his "everlasting comeuppance," and settled down in Smyrna as boss of the Ward household, that event nearly wore Gossip's tongue into ribbons.

"I see'd it from a distance—the part that happened in front of the toll-house," said Old Man Jordan. "Now, all of ye know that Kun'l Gid most gin'ly cal'lates to eat up folks that says 'Boo' to him, and pick his teeth with slivers of their bones. But talk about your r'yal Peeruvian ragin' lions—of wherever they come from—why, that Cap'n Sproul could back a 'Rabian caterwouser right off'm Caterwouser Township! I couldn't hear what was said, but I see Kun'l Gid, hoss-gad and all, backed right up into his own wagon; and Cap'n Sproul got in, and took the reins away from him as if he'd been a pindlin' ten-year-old, and drove off toward the Ward home place. And that Cap'n don't seem savage, nuther."

"Wal, near's I can find out," said Odbar Broadway from behind his counter, where he was counting eggs out of Old Man Jordan's bucket, "the Cap'n had a club in one hand and power of attorney from Kun'l Gid's sister in the other—and a threat to divide the Ward estate. The way Gid's bus'ness is tied up jest at present would put a knot into the tail of 'most any kind of a temper."

"I'm told the Cap'n is makin' her a turrible nice husband," observed one of the store loungers.

Broadway folded his specs into their case and came from behind the counter.

"Bein' a bus'ness man myself," he said, "I come pretty nigh knowin' what I'm talkin' about. Kun'l Gid Ward can never flout and jeer that the man that has married his sister was nothin' but a prop'ty-hunter. I'm knowin' to it that Cap'n Sproul has got thutty thousand in vessel prop'ty of his own, 'sides what his own uncle Jerry here left to him. Gid Ward has trompled round this town for twenty-five years, and bossed and browbeat and cussed, and got the best end of every trade. If there's some one come along that can put the wickin' to him in good shape, I swow if this town don't owe him a vote of thanks."

"There's a movement on already to ask Cap'n Sproul to take the office of first s'lec'man at the March meetin'," said one of the loafers.

"I sha'n't begretch him one mite of his popularity," vowed the storekeeper. "Any man that can put Kun'l Gid Ward where he belongs is a better thing for the town than a new meetin'-house would be."

But during all this flurry of gossip Cap'n Aaron Sproul spent his bland and blissful days up under the shade of the big maple in the Ward dooryard, smoking his pipe, and gazing out over the expanse of meadow and woodland stretching away to the horizon.

Most of the time his wife was at his elbow, peering with a species of adoration into his browned countenance as he related his tales of the sea. She constantly carried a little blank-book, its ribbon looped about her neck, and made copious entries as he talked. She had conceived the fond ambition of writing the story of his life. On the cover was inscribed, in her best hand:

FROM SHORE TO SHORE

LINES FROM A MARINER'S ADVENTURES

The Life Story of the Gallant Captain Aaron Sproul

The Skipper and the Skipped

Written by His Affectionate Wife

"I reckon that Providunce put her finger on my compass when I steered this way. Louada Murilla," said the Cap'n one day, pausing to relight his pipe.

He had insisted on renaming his wife "Louada Murilla," and she had patiently accepted the new name with the resignation of her patient nature. But the name pleased her after her beloved lord had explained.

"I was saving that name for the handsomest clipper-ship that money could build," he said. "But when I married you, little woman, I got something better than a clipper-ship; and when you know sailorman's natur' better, you'll know what that compliment means. Yes, Providunce sent me here," continued the Cap'n, poking down his tobacco with broad thumb. "There I was, swashin' from Hackenny to t'other place, livin' on lobscouse and hoss-meat; and here you was, pinin' away for some one to love you and to talk to you about something sensibler than dropped stitches and croshayed lamp-mats. Near's I can find out about your 'sociates round here, you would have got more real sense out of talkin' with Port and Starboard up there," he added, pointing to his pet parrots, which had followed him in his wanderings. "We was both of us hankerin' for a companion—I mean a married companion. And I reckon that two more suiteder persons never started down the shady side—holt of hands, hey?"

He caught her hands and pulled her near him, and she bent down and kissed his weather-beaten forehead.

At that instant Col. Gideon Ward came clattering into the yard in his tall wagon. He glared at this scene of conjugal affection, and then lashed his horse savagely and disappeared in the direction of the barn.

"I read once about a skelington at a feast that rattled his dry bones every time folks there started in to enjoy themselves," said the

24

Cap'n, after he watched the scowling Colonel out of sight. "For the last two weeks, Louada Murilla, it don't seem as if I've smacked you or you've smacked me but when I've jibed my head I've seen that ga'nt brother-in-law o' mine standing off to one side sourer'n a home-made cucumber pickle."

"It's aggravatin' for you, I know it is," she faltered. "But I've been thinkin' that perhaps he'd get more reconciled as the time goes on."

"Reconciled?" snapped the Cap'n, a little of the pepper in his nature coming to the surface. "If it was any one but you little woman, that talked about me as though I was death or an amputated leg in this family, I'd get hot under the collar. But I tell ye, we ain't got many years left to love each other in. We started pritty late. We can't afford to waste any time. And we can't afford to have the edge taken off by that Chinese image standin' around and makin' faces. I've been thinkin' of tellin' him so. But the trouble is with me that when I git to arguin' with a man I'm apt to forgit that I ain't on shipboard and talkin' to a tar-heel."

He surveyed his brown fists with a certain apprehensiveness, as though they were dangerous parties over whom he had no control.

"I should dretfully hate to have anything come up between you and Gideon, Cap'n," she faltered, a frightened look in her brown eyes. "It wouldn't settle anything to have trouble. But you've been about so much and seen human nature so much that it seems as though you could handle him different than with — with — "

"Poundin' him, eh?" Smiles broke over the skipper's face. "See how I'm softened, little woman!" he cried. "Time was when I would have chased a man that made faces at me as he done just now, and I'd have pegged him into the ground. But love has done a lot for me in makin' me decent. If I keep on, I'll forgit I've got two fists — and that's something for a shipmaster to say, now, I'll tell ye! A man has got to git into love himself to know how it feels."

Sudden reflection illuminated his face.

"Ain't old pickalilly—that brother of yourn—ever been in love?" he asked.

"Why—why," she stammered, "he's been in—well, sometimes now I think perhaps it ain't love, knowin' what I do now—but he's been engaged to Pharlina Pike goin' on fifteen years. And he's been showin' her attentions longer'n that. But since I've met you and found out how folks don't usually wait so long if they—they're in love—well, I've—"

"Fifteen years!" he snorted. "What is he waitin' for—for her to grow up?"

"Land sakes, no! She's about as old as he is. She's old Seth Pike's daughter, and since Seth died she has run the Pike farm with hired help, and has done real well at it. Long engagements ain't thought strange of 'round here. Why, there's—"

"Fifteen years!" he repeated. "That's longer'n old Methus'lum courted."

"But Gideon has been so busy and away from home so much in the woods, and Pharlina ain't been in no great pucker, seein' that the farm was gettin' on well, and—"

"There ain't no excuse for him," broke in the Cap'n, with vigor. He was greatly interested in this new discovery. His eyes gleamed. "'Tain't usin' her right. She can't step up to him and set the day. 'Tain't woman's sp'ere, that ain't. I didn't ask you to set the day. I set it myself. I told you to be ready."

Her cheek flushed prettily at the remembrance of that impetuous courtship, when even her dread of her ogre brother had been overborne by the Cap'n's masterful manner, once she had confessed her love.

"I know what love is myself," went on the Cap'n. "He don't know; that's what the trouble is with him. He ain't been waked up. Let him be waked up good and plenty, and he won't be standin' around makin' faces at us. I see what's got to be done to make a happy home of this. You leave it to me."

They saw the Colonel stamping in their direction from the barn.

"You run into the house, Louada Murilla," directed the Cap'n, "and leave me have a word with him."

The Colonel was evidently as anxious as the Cap'n for a word.

"Say, Sproul," he gritted, as he came under the tree, "I've got an offer for the stumpage on township number eight. Seein' that you're in equal partners with me on my sister's money," he sneered, "I reckon I've got to give ye figures and prices, and ask for a permit to run my own business."

"Seems 'most as if you don't enj'y talkin' business with me," observed the Cap'n, with a meek wistfulness that was peculiarly aggravating to his grouchy partner.

"I'd about as soon eat pizen!" stormed the other.

"Then let's not do it jest now," the Cap'n returned, sweetly. "I've got something more important to talk about than stumpage. Money and business ain't much in this world, after all, when you come to know there's something diff'runt. Love is what I'm referrin' to. Word has jest come to me that you're in love, too, the same as I am."

The gaunt Colonel glared malevolently down on the sturdy figure sprawling in the garden chair. The Cap'n's pipe clouds curled about his head, and his hands were stuffed comfortably into his trousers pockets. His face beamed.

"Some might think to hear you talk that you was a soft old fool that had gone love-cracked 'cause a woman jest as soft as you be has showed you some attention," choked the Colonel. "But I know what you're hidin' under your innocent-Abigail style. I know you're a jill-poke."

"A what?" blandly asked Sproul.

"That's woods talk for the log that makes the most trouble on the drive—and it's a mighty ornery word."

"Er—something like 'the stabboard pi-oogle,' which same is a seafarin' term, and is worse," replied the Cap'n, with bland interest in this philological comparison. "But let's not git strayed off'm the subject. Your sister, Louada Murilla—"

The gaunt man clacked his bony fists together in ecstasy of rage.

"She was christened Sarah Jane, and that's her name. Don't ye insult the father and mother that gave it to her by tackin' on another. I've told ye so once; I tell ye so—"

"Louada Murilla," went on the Cap'n, taking his huge fists out of his pockets and cocking them on his knees, not belligerently, but in a mildly precautionary way, "told me that you had been engaged to a woman named Phar—Phar—"

"Oh, give her any name to suit ye!" snarled the Colonel. "That's what ye're doin' with wimmen round here."

"You know who I mean," pursued Sproul, complacently, "seein' that you've had fifteen years to study on her name. Now, bein' as I'm one of the fam'ly, I'm going to ask you what ye're lally-gaggin' along for? Wimmen don't like to be on the chips so long. I am speakin' to you like a man and a brother when I say that married life is what the poet says it is. It's—"

"I've stood a good deal from you up to now!" roared Ward, coming close and leaning over threateningly. "You come here to town with so much tar on ye that your feet stuck every time you stood still in one place; you married my sister like you'd ketch a woodchuck;

you've stuck your fingers into my business in her name—but that's jest about as fur as you can go with me. There was only one man ever tried to advise me about gitting married—and he's still a cripple. There was no man ever tried to recite love poetry to me. You take fair warnin'."

"Then you ain't willin' to listen to my experience, considerin' that I've been a worse hard-shell than you ever was in marriage matters, and now see the errors of my ways?" The Cap'n was blinking up wistfully.

"It means that I take ye by your heels and snap your head off," rasped Ward, tucking his sleeves away from his corded wrists. "You ain't got your club with you this time."

The Cap'n sighed resignedly.

"Now," went on the Colonel, with the vigorous decision of a man who feels that he has got the ascendency, "you talk about something that amounts to something. That stumpage on number eight is mostly cedar and hackmatack, and I've got an offer from the folks that want sleepers for the railroad extension."

He went on with facts and figures, but the Cap'n listened with only languid interest. He kept sighing and wrinkling his brows, as though in deep rumination on a matter far removed from the stumpage question. When the agreement of sale was laid before him he signed with a blunted lead-pencil, still in his trance.

"Northin' but a cross-cut saw with two axe-handles for legs," he said to himself, his eyes on the Colonel's back as that individual stamped wrathfully away. "Teeth and edge are hard as iron! It's no good to talk mattermony to him. Prob'ly it wouldn't do no good for me to talk mattermony to Phar—Phar—to t'other one. She couldn't ask him to go git a minister. 'Tain't right to put that much onto a woman's shoulders. The trouble with him is that he's too sure of wimmen. Had his sister under his thumb all them years, and thought less and less of her for stayin' there. He's too sure of t'other. Thinks nobody else wants her. Thinks all he's got to do is step round and git her some day. Ain't got no high idee of wimmen like I have. Thinks they ought to wait patient as a tree in a wood-lot. Has had things too much his own way, I say. Hain't never had his lesson. Thinks nobody else don't want her, hey? And she can wait his motions! He needs his lesson. Lemme see!"

With his knurly forefinger at his puckered forehead he sat and pondered.

He was very silent at supper.

The Colonel, still exulting in his apparent victory, said many sneering and savage things, and clattered his knife truculently on his plate. Sproul merely looked at him with that wistful preoccupation that still marked his countenance.

"He's a quitter," pondered the Colonel. "I reckon he ain't playin' lamb so's to tole me on. He's growed soft—that's what he's done."

Ward went to sleep that night planning retaliation.

Sproul stayed awake when the house was quiet, still pondering.

IV

During the next few days, as one treads farther and farther out upon thin ice to test it, the Colonel craftily set about regaining, inch by inch, his lost throne as tyrant. Occasionally he checked himself in some alarm, to wonder what meant that ridging of the Cap'n's jaw-muscles, and whether he really heard the seaman's teeth gritting. Once, when he recoiled before an unusually demoniac glare from Sproul, the latter whined, after a violent inward struggle:

"It beats all how my rheumaticks has been talkin' up lately. I don't seem to have no ginger nor spirit left in me. I reckon I got away from the sea jest in time. I wouldn't even dare to order a nigger to swab decks, the way I'm feelin' now."

"You've allus made a good deal of talk about how many men you've handled in your day," said the Colonel, tucking a thumb under his suspender and leaning back with supercilious cock of his gray eyebrows. "It's bein' hinted round town here more or less that you're northin' but bluff. I don't realize, come to think it over, how I ever come to let you git such a holt in my fam'ly. I—"

The two were sitting, as was their custom in those days of the Colonel's espionage, under the big maple in the yard. A man who was passing in the highway paused and leaned on the fence.

"Can one of you gents tell me," he asked, "where such a lady as Miss Phar"—he consulted a folded paper that he held in his hand— "Pharleena Pike lives about here?"

He was an elderly man with a swollen nose, striated with purple veins. Under his arm he carried a bundle done up in meat-paper.

There was a queer glint of excitement in the eyes of the Cap'n. But he did not speak. He referred the matter to Ward with a jab of his thumb.

"What do you want to know where Miss Pike lives for?" demanded the Colonel, looking the stranger over with great disfavor.

"None of your business," replied the man of the swollen nose, promptly. "I've asked a gent's question of one I took to be a gent, and I'd like a gent's reply."

"You see," said Cap'n Sproul to the stranger, with a confidential air, as though he were proposing to impart the secret of the Colonel's acerbity, "Colonel Ward here is—"

"You go 'long two miles, swing at the drab school-house, and go to the second white house on the left-hand side of the road!" shouted Ward, hastily breaking in on the explanation. His thin cheeks flushed angrily. The man shuffled on.

"Why don't you print it on a play-card that I'm engaged to Pharlina Pike and hang it on the fence there?" the Colonel snorted, wrathfully, whirling on the Cap'n. "Didn't it ever occur to you that some things in this world ain't none of your business?"

The Cap'n sighed with the resigned air that he had been displaying during the week past.

"Lemme see, where was I?" went on the Colonel, surlily. "I was sayin', wasn't I, that I didn't see how I'd let you stick yourself into this fam'ly as you've done? It's time now for you and me to git to a reck'nin'. There's blamed liars round here snick'rin' in their whiskers, and sayin' that you've backed me down. Now—"

Another man was at the fence, and interrupted with aggravating disregard of the Colonel's intentness on the business in hand. This stranger was short and squat, stood with his feet braced wide apart, and had a canvas bag slung over his shoulder. His broad face wore a cheery smile.

"I've beat nor'west from the railroad, fetched a covered bridge on the port quarter, shipmates," he roared, jovially, "and here I be, bearin's lost and dead-reck'nin' skow-wowed."

"Seems to be your breed," sneered Ward to the Cap'n. "What's that he's sayin', put in human language?"

"I'm chartered for port—port"—he also referred to a folded paper—"to port Furliny Pike, som'eres in this latitude. Give me p'ints o' compass, will ye?"

Ward leaped to his feet and strode toward the fence, his long legs working like calipers.

"What do ye want of Pharline Pike?" he demanded, angrily.

"None of your business," replied the cheerful sailor. "If this is the way landlubbers take an honest man's hail, ye're all jest as bad as I've heard ye was."

"I'm a mind to cuff your ears," yapped the Colonel.

The other glanced up the angular height of his antagonist.

"Try it," he said, squaring his sturdy little figure. "Try it, and I'll climb your main riggin' and dance a jig on that dog-vane of a head of yourn."

This alacrity for combat clearly backed down Ward. In his rampageous life his tongue had usually served him better than his fists.

"Avast, shipmate!" called the Cap'n, in his best sea tones. The sailor beamed delighted recognition of marine masonry. "The fact of the matter is, my friend here has some claim—the truth is, he's—"

"You go 'long two miles, swing at the drab school-house, and then take the second house—white one—on the left-hand side of the road," bawled Ward, "and you go mighty quick!"

The sailor ducked acknowledgment and rolled away.

"If you'd unpinned that mouth of yourn fur enough to tell that tramp that I'm engaged to Pharline Pike," growled Ward, returning to the tree, "I'd 'a' broke in your head—and you might as well know it first as last."

"Ain't you engaged to her?"

"You know I be."

"Well, I've allus told the truth all my life—and I reckon I shall continner to tell it. If you're ashamed to have it knowed that you're engaged to Pharlina Pike, then it's time she heard so. I'd jest as soon tell her as not."

"I started to say to you," raged Ward, "that you'd stuck your finger into my pie altogether too deep. I ain't killed as many sailors as you're braggin' on, but there ain't no man ever licked Gid Ward, and—"

"Near's I can tell from what I hear about you," retorted the Cap'n, "built on racin' lines as you be, you've never let a man git near enough to lick ye."

Again the Colonel noted that red vengefulness in the skipper's eyes, and recoiled suspiciously.

"Oh, my rheumaticks!" the seaman hastened to moan.

Ward had his back to the fence.

"I cal'late as how there's another party that wants his bearin's," suggested Sproul.

A rather decayed-looking gentleman, wearing a frock-coat shiny at the elbows, and a fuzzy plug-hat, was tapping his cane against one of the pickets to attract attention.

"I am looking for the residence of Miss Pharlina Pike," he announced, with a precise puckering of his lips. "I'll thank you for a word of direction. But I want to say, as a lowly follower of the Lord—in evangelical lines—that it is not seemly for two men to quarrel in public."

Ward had been gaping at him in amazement.

"I can tell ye right now," he cried, "that Miss Pharline Pike ain't hirin' no farm-hand that wears a plug-hat! There ain't no need of your goin' to her place."

"My dear sir," smiled the decayed gentleman, "it is a delicate matter not to be canvassed in public; but I can assure you that I shall not remain with Miss Pike as a menial or a bond-servant. Oh no! Not by any means, sir!"

Ward scruffed his hand over his forehead, blinking with puzzled astonishment.

"I'll thank you for the directions," said the stranger. "They were not able to give me exact instructions at the village—at least, I cannot remember them."

"I ain't no dadfired guide-board to stand here all day and p'int the way to Pharline Pike's," roared Ward, with a heat that astonished the decayed gentleman.

"I don't want no elder to go away from this place and report that he wa'n't used respectful," said Sproul, meekly, addressing the stranger. "You'll have to excuse Colonel Ward here. P'r'aps I can say for him, as a pertickler friend, what it wouldn't be modest for him to say himself. The fact is, he's en—"

The infuriated Ward leaped up and down on the sward and shrieked the road instructions to the wayfarer, who hustled away, casting apprehensive glances over his shoulder.

But when the Colonel turned again on the Cap'n, the latter rose and hobbled with extravagant limpings toward the house.

"I don't reckon I can stay out here and pass talk with you, brother-in-law," he called back, reproachfully. "Strangers, passin' as they be, don't like to hear no such language as you're usin'. Jest think of what that elder said!"

Ward planted himself upon a garden chair, and gazed down the road in the direction in which the strangers had gone. He seemed to be thinking deeply, and the Cap'n watched him from behind one of the front-room curtains.

Two more men passed up the road. At the first, the Colonel flourished his arms and indulged in violent language, the gist of which the Cap'n did not catch. He ran to the fence when the second accosted him, tore off a picket, and flung it after the fleeing man.

Then he sat down and pondered more deeply still.

He cast occasional glances toward the house, and once or twice arose as though to come in. But he sat down and continued to gaze in the direction of Pharlina Pike's house.

It was late in the afternoon when a woman came hurrying down the slope through the maple-sugar grove. The Cap'n, at his curtain with his keen sea eye, saw her first. He had been expecting her arrival. He knew her in the distance for Pharlina Pike, and realized that she had come hot-foot across lots.

Sproul was under the big maple as soon as she.

"For mercy sakes, Colonel Gid," she gasped, "come over to my house as quick's you can!"

She had come up behind him, and he leaped out of his chair with a snap like a jack-in-the-box.

"There's somethin' on, and I knowed it!" he squalled. "What be them men peradin' past here to your house for, and tellin' me it ain't none of my business? You jest tell me, Pharline Pike, what you mean by triflin' in this way?"

"Lord knows what it's all about! I don't!" she quavered.

"You do know, too!" he yelled. "Don't ye try to pull wool over my eyes! You do know, too!"

"It's a turrible thing to be jealous," cooed Cap'n Sproul to his trembling little wife, who had followed at his heels.

"I don't know, either," wailed the spinster. "There's one of 'em in the settin'-room balancin' a plug-hat on his knees and sayin', 'Lo! the bridegroom cometh'; and there's two on the front steps kickin' the dog ev'ry time he comes at 'em; and there's one in the kitchen that smells o' tar, and has got a bagful of shells and sech things for presents to me; there's one in the barn lookin' over the stock—and I s'pose they're comin' down the chimbly and up the suller stairs by this time. You're the only one I've got in the world to depend on, Colonel Gid. For mercy sakes, come!"

"What do they say—what's their excuse?" he demanded, suspiciously.

"They say—they say," she wailed—"they say they want to marry me, but I don't know what they've all come hov'rin' round me for— honest to Moses I don't!" She folded her hands in her apron and wrung them. "I'm pretty nigh scart to death of 'em," she sobbed.

"I reckon you can give 'em an earful when you git down there," said the Cap'n, "when you tell 'em that you've been engaged to her for fifteen years. But it ain't none surprisin' that men that hear of that engagement should most natch'ally conclude that a woman would like to git married after a while. I cal'late ye see now, brother-in-law, that you ain't the only man that appreciates what a good woman Miss Pharlina Pike is."

"You come along, Pharline," said the Colonel, taking her arm, after he had bored the Cap'n for a moment with flaming eye. "I reckon I can pertect ye from all the tramps ever let loose out of jails—and—and when I git to the bottom of this I predict there'll be bloodshed—there'll be bones broke, anyway." With one more malevolent look at the Cap'n he started away.

"It's only a short cut through the maple growth, Louada Murilla," said Sproul. "My rheumaticks is a good deal better of a sudden. Let's you and me go along."

As they trudged he saw farmers at a distance here and there, and called to them to follow.

"Look here, I don't need no bee!" howled the Colonel. "This ain't nothing to spread broadcast in this community."

"Never can tell what's li'ble to happen," retorted Sproul. "Witnesses don't never hurt cases like this."

He continued to call the farmers, despite Ward's objurgations. Farmers called their wives. All followed behind the engaged couple. As usually happens in country communities, word had gone abroad in other directions that there were strange doings at the Pike place. With huge satisfaction the Cap'n noted that the yard was packed with spectators.

"Where be ye?" bellowed Colonel Ward, now in a frenzy. "Where be ye, ye scalawags that are round tryin' to hector a respectable woman that wouldn't wipe her feet on ye? Come out here and talk to me!"

The neighbors fell back, recognizing his authority in the matter; and the men who were suing this modern Penelope appeared from various parts of the premises.

"I desire to say, as a clergyman along evangelical lines, and not a settled pastor," said the man in the fuzzy plug-hat, "that I do not approve of this person's violent language. I have seen him once before to-day, and he appeared singularly vulgar and unrefined. He used violent language then. I desire to say to you, sir, that I am here on the best of authority"—he tapped his breast pocket—"and here I shall remain until I have discussed the main question thoroughly with the estimable woman who has invited me here."

"It's a lie—I never invited him, Colonel Gid!" cried the spinster. "If you're any part of a man, and mean any part of what you have allus said to me, you'll make him take that back."

For a moment the Colonel's jealous suspicion had flamed again, but the woman's appeal fired him in another direction.

"Look here, you men," he shouted, his gaze running over plug-hat, swollen nose, seaman's broad face, and the faces of the other suitors, "I'm Gideon Ward, of Smyrna, and I've been engaged to Miss Pharline Pike for fifteen years, and—"

"Then I don't blame her for changing her mind, ye bloody landlubber!" snorted the seaman, smacking his hand upon his folded paper.

"Being engaged signifies little in the courts of matrimony," said the decayed-looking man with dignity. "She has decided to choose another, and—"

Colonel Ward threw back his shoulders and faced them all with glittering eyes.

"I'd like to see the man that can step into this town and lug off the woman that's promised to me," he raved. "Engagements don't hold, hey? Then you come this way a week from to-day, and you'll see Gideon Ward and Pharline Pike married as tight as a parson can tie the knot. I mean it!" The excitement of the moment, his rage at interference in his affairs, his desire to triumph thus publicly over these strangers, had led him into the declaration.

The spinster gasped, but she came to him and trustfully put her hand on his arm.

"P'raps some can be put off by that bluff," said the man with the swollen nose, "but not me that has travelled. I'm here on business, and I've got the dockyments, and if there's any shenanigan, then some one's got to pay me my expenses, and for wear and tear." He waved a paper.

Ward leaped forward and snatched the paper from his grasp.

"It's about time for me to see what you're flourishing round here promiskous, like a bill o' sale of these primises," he snarled.

"You can read it, and read it out jest as loud as you want to," said the man, coming forward and putting a grimy finger on a paragraph displayed prominently on the folded sheet of newspaper.

The Colonel took one look and choked. An officious neighbor grabbed away the paper when Ward made a sign as though to tuck it into his pocket.

"I'll read it," said the neighbor. "Mebbe my eyesight is better'n yourn." Then he read, in shrill tones:

"NOTICE TO BACHELORS

"Unmarried maiden lady, smart and good-looking, desires good husband. Has two-hundred-and-thirty-acre farm in good state of cultivation, well stocked, and will promise right party a home and much affection. Apply on premises to Pharlina Pike, Smyrna."

"I never—I never—dadrat the liar that ever wrote that!" screamed the spinster.

"You see for yourself," said the man of the swollen nose, ignoring her disclaimer. "We're here on business, and expect to be treated like business men—or expenses refunded to us."

But the Colonel roared wordlessly, like some angry animal, seized a pitchfork that was leaning against the side of the spinster's ell, and charged the group of suitors. His mien was too furious. They fled, and fled far and forever.

"There's some one," said Ward, returning into the yard and driving the fork-tines into the ground, "who has insulted Miss Pike. I'd give a thousand dollars to know who done that writin'."

Only bewildered stares met his furious gaze.

"I want you to understand," he went on, "that no one can drive me to git married till I'm ready. But I'm standin' here now and tellin' the nosy citizens of this place that I'm ready to be married, and so's she who is goin' to be my companion, and we'll 'tend to our own business in spite of the gossips of Smyrna. It's for this day week! I don't want no more lyin' gossip about it. You're gittin' it straight this time. It's for this day week; no invitations, no cards, no flowers, no one's durnation business. There, take that home and chaw on it. Pharline, let's you and me go into the house."

"I reckon there's witnesses enough to make that bindin'," muttered Cap'n Sproul under his breath.

He bent forward and tapped the Colonel on the arm as Ward was about to step upon the piazza.

"Who do ye suspect?" he whispered, hoarsely.

It was a perfectly lurid gaze that his brother-in-law turned on him.

What clutched Ward's arm was a grip like a vise. He glared into the Colonel's eyes with light fully as lurid as that which met his gaze. He

41

spoke low, but his voice had the grating in it that is more ominous than vociferation.

"I thought I'd warn ye not to twit. My rheumaticks is a good deal better at this writin', and my mind ain't so much occupied by other matters as it has been for a week or so. When you come home don't talk northin' but business, jest as you natch'ally would to a brother-in-law and an equal pardner. That advice don't cost northin', but it's vallyble."

As Cap'n Sproul trudged home, his little wife's arm tucked snugly in the hook of his own, he observed, soulfully:

"Mattermony, Louada Murilla—mattermony, it is a blessed state that it does the heart good to see folks git into as ought to git into it. As the poet says—um-m-m, well, it's in that book on the settin'-room what-not. I'll read it to ye when we git home."

V

Cap'n Aaron Sproul was posted that bright afternoon on the end of his piazza. He sat bolt upright and twiddled his gnarled thumbs nervously. His wife came out and sat down beside him.

"Where you left off, Cap'n," she prompted meekly, "was when the black, whirling cloud was coming and you sent the men up-stairs—"

"Aloft!" snapped Cap'n Sproul.

"I mean aloft—and they were unfastening the sails off the ropes, and—"

"Don't talk of snuggin' a ship like you was takin' in a wash," roared the ship-master, in sudden and ungallant passion. It was the first impatient word she had received from him in that initial, cozy year of their marriage. Her mild brown eyes swam in tears as she looked at him wonderingly.

"I—I haven't ever seen a ship or the sea, but I'm trying so hard to learn, and I love so to hear you talk of the deep blue ocean. It was what first attracted me to you." Her tone was almost a whimper.

But her meekness only seemed to increase the Cap'n's impatience.

"You haven't seemed to be like your natural self for a week," she complained, wistfully. "You haven't seemed to relish telling me stories of the sea and your narrow escapes. You haven't even seemed to relish vittles and the scenery. Oh, haven't you been weaned from the sea yet, Aaron?"

Cap'n Sproul continued to regard his left foot with fierce gloom. He was giving it his undivided attention. It rested on a wooden "cricket," and was encased in a carpet slipper that contrasted strikingly with the congress boot that shod his other foot. Red roses and sprays of sickly green vine formed the pattern of the carpet

43

slipper. The heart of a red rose on the toe had been cut out, as though the cankerworm had eaten it; and on a beragged projection that stuck through and exhaled the pungent odor of liniment, the Cap'n's lowering gaze was fixed.

"There's always somethin' to be thankful for," said his meek wife, her eyes following his gaze. "You've only sprained it, and didn't break it. Does it still ache, dear?"

"It aches like—of course it aches!" roared the Cap'n. "Don't ask that jeebasted, fool question ag'in. I don't mean to be tetchy, Louada Murilla," he went on, after a little pause, a bit of mildness in his tone, "but you've got to make allowance for the way I feel. The more I set and look at that toe the madder I git at myself. Oh, I hadn't ought to have kicked that cousin of yourn, that's what I hadn't!"

"You don't know how glad I am to hear you say that, Aaron," she cried, with fervor. "I was afraid you hadn't repented."

"I ought to 'a' hit him with a club and saved my toe, that's what I mean," he snorted, with grim viciousness.

She sighed, and he resumed his dismal survey of the liniment-soaked rags.

"Once when I was—" he resumed, in a low growl, after a time.

"Oh, I'm so glad you're goin' to tell a story, Cap'n," she chirped, welcoming his first return of good-nature since his mishap.

"There ain't no story to it," he snapped. "I only want to say that there's a place down in Africa where I put in with the *Jefferson P. Benn* one time, where they daub honey on folks that they want to git red of, and anchor 'em on an ant-bed. That's jest what's happenin' to me here in Smyrna, and my thutty thousand dollars that I've worked hard for and earnt and saved is the honey. You've lived among them here all your life, Louada Murilla, and I s'pose you've got more or less wonted to 'em. But if I hadn't squirmed and thrashed round a little durin' the time I've lived here, after marryin' you and settlin' down among 'em, they'd have et me, honey, money, hide, and hair. As it is, they've got their little lunch off'm me. I haven't thrashed round enough till—till yistiddy."

He wriggled the toe in the centre of the rose, and grunted.

"I was in hopes we wouldn't have any more trouble in the family, only what we've had with brother Gideon since we've been married," she said mildly. "Of course, Marengo Todd is only a second cousin of mine, but still, he's in the family, you know, and families hang together, 'cause blood—"

"Blood is what they want, blast 'em!" he bawled, angrily. "I've used Marengo Orango, there, or whatever you call him, all right, ain't I? I've let him do me! He knowed I was used to sea ways, and wa'n't used to land ways, and that he *could* do me. I lent him money, first off, because I liked you. And I've lent him money sence because I like a liar—and he's a good one! I've used all your relatives the best I've knowed how, and—and they've turned round and used me! But I've put a dot, full-stop, period to it—and I done it with that toe," he added, scowling at the pathetic heart of the red rose.

"I wish it hadn't been one of the family," she sighed.

"It couldn't well help bein' one," snarled the Cap'n. "They're about all named Todd or Ward round here but one, and his name is Todd Ward Brackett, and he's due next. And they're all tryin' to borry money off'm me and sell me spavined hosses. Now, let's see if they can take a hint." He tentatively wriggled the toe some more, and groaned. "The Todds and the Wards better keep away from me."

Then he suddenly pricked up his ears at the sound of the slow rumble of a wagon turning into the yard. The wagon halted, and they heard the buzzing twang of a jew's-harp, played vigorously.

"There's your Todd Ward Brackett. I predicted him! 'Round here to sell ye rotten thread and rusted tinware and his all-fired Balm o' Joy liniment."

"It's good liniment, and I need some more for your toe, Aaron," pleaded his wife, putting her worsted out of her lap.

"I'll chop that toe off and use it for cod bait before I'll cure it by buying any more liniment off'm him," the Cap'n retorted. "You jest keep your settin', Louada Murilla. I'll tend to your fam'ly end after this."

He struggled up and began to hop toward the end of the piazza. The new arrival had burst into cheery song:

"There was old Hip Huff, who went by freight
To Newry Corner, in this State.
Packed him in a—"

There was a red van in the yard, its side bearing the legend:

T. BRACKETT,

TINWARE AND YANKEE NOTIONS.

LICENSED BY C. C.

A brisk, little, round-faced man sat on the high seat, bolt upright in the middle of it, carolling lustily. It was "Balm o' Joy" Brackett, pursuing his humble vocation and using his familiar method of attracting customers to their doors.

"Shet up that clack!" roared the Cap'n.

"Hillo, hullo, hallah, gallant Captain," chirped Brackett, imperturbable under the seaman's glare. "I trust that glory floods your soul and all the world seems gay." And he went on breathlessly:

"May ev'ry hour of your life seem like a pan of Jersey milk, and may you skim the cream off'm it. Let's be happy, let's be gay, trade with me when I come your way. Tinware shines like the new-ris' sun, twist, braid, needles beat by none; here's your values, cent by cent, and Balm o' Joy lin-i-ment. Trade with—"

"Git out o' this yard!" bawled the Cap'n, in his storm-and-tempest tones. "You crack-brained, rag-and-bone-land-pirate, git off'm my premises! I don't want your stuff. I've bought the last cent's wu'th of you I'll ever buy. Git out!"

"The Cap'n isn't well to-day, Todd," quavered Mrs. Sproul. Fear prompted her to keep still. But many years of confidential barter of rags for knicknacks had made Todd Brackett seem like "own folks," as she expressed it. "We won't trade any to-day," she added, apologetically.

"Nor we won't trade ever," bawled the Cap'n, poising himself on one foot like an angry hawk. "You go 'long out of this yard."

Without losing his smile—for he had been long accustomed to the taunts and tirades of dissatisfied housewives—the peddler backed his cart around and drove away, crying over his shoulder with great good-humor:

"A merry life and a jolly life is the life for you and me!"

"I'll make life merry for ye, if ye come into this yard ag'in, you whiffle-headed dog-vane, you!" the Cap'n squalled after him. But Brackett again struck up his roundelay:

"There was old Hip Huff, who went by freight
 To Newry Corner, in this State.
 Put him in a crate to git him there,
 With a two-cent stamp to pay his fare.
 Rowl de fang-go—old Smith's mare."

The Cap'n hopped into the house and set his foot again on the cricket that his wife brought dutifully. He gritted his teeth as long as the voice of the singer came to his ears.

"I wish you hadn't," mourned his wife; "he's as good-meaning a man as there is in town, even if he is a little light-headed. He's always given me good trades, and his st'ilyards don't cheat on rags."

The old mariner was evidently preparing a stinging reply, but a knock on the door interrupted him. Louada Murilla admitted three men, who marched in solemnly, one behind the other, all beaming with great cordiality. Cap'n Sproul, not yet out of the doldrums, simply glowered and grunted as they took seats.

Then one of them, whom Sproul knew as Ludelphus Murray, the local blacksmith, arose and cleared his throat with ominous formality.

"It's best to hammer while the iron is hot, Cap'n," he said. "It won't take many clips o' the tongue to tell you what we've come for. We three here are a committee from the Smyrna Ancient and Honer'ble Firemen's Association to notify you that at a meetin' last ev'nin' you was unanimously elected a member of that organization, and—"

"Oh, Aaron!" cried Louada Murilla, ecstatically. "How glad I am this honor has been given to you! My own father belonged."

"And," continued Murray, with a satisfied smile, and throwing back his shoulders as one who brings great tidings, "it has been realized for a long time that there ain't been the discipline in the association that there ought to be. We have now among us in our midst one who has commanded men and understands how to command men; one who has sailed the ragin' deep in times of danger, and—and, well, a man that understands how to go ahead and take the lead in tittlish times. So the association"—he took a long breath—"has elected you foreman, and I hereby hand you notice of the same and the book of rules."

The Cap'n scowled and put his hand behind the rocking-chair in which he was seated.

"Not by a—" he began, but Murray went on with cheerful explanation.

"I want to say to you that this association is over a hundred years old, and our hand tub, the 'Hecla,' is ninety-seven years old, and has took more prizes squirtin' at musters than any other tub in the State. We ain't had many fires ever in Smyrna, but the Ancients take the leadin' rank in all social events, and our dances and banquets are patronized by the best."

"It's an awful big honor, Aaron," gasped his wife. She turned to the committee. "The Cap'n hasn't been feelin' well, gentlemen, and this honor has kind of overcome him. But I know he appreciates it. My own father was foreman once, and it's a wonderful thing to think that my husband is now."

"'Tain't likely that the Ancients will ever forget them dinners we had here, Mis' Sproul," remarked one of the men, 'suffling' the moisture at the corners of his mouth.

"Seein' that you ain't well, we don't expect no speech, Cap'n," said Murray, laying the documents upon Sproul's knee. "I see that the honor has overcome you, as it nat'rally might any man. We will now take our leave with a very good-day, and wishin' you all of the best, yours truly, and so forth." He backed away, and the others rose.

"Pass through the kitchen, gentlemen," said Mrs. Sproul, eagerly. "I will set out a treat." They trudged that way with deep bows at the threshold to their newly drafted foreman, who still glared at them speechlessly.

When Mrs. Sproul returned at length, still fluttering in her excitement, he was reading the little pamphlet that had been left with him, a brick-red color slowly crawling up the back of his neck.

"Just think of it for an honor, Aaron," she stammered, "and you here in town only such a little while! Oh, I am so proud of you! Mr. Murray brought the things in his team and left them on the piazza. I'll run and get them."

She spread them on the sitting-room floor, kneeling before him like a priestess offering sacrifice. With his thumb in the pamphlet, he stared at the array.

There was a battered leather hat with a broad apron, or scoop, behind to protect the back. On a faded red shield above the visor was the word "Foreman." There were two equally battered leather buckets. There was a dented speaking-trumpet. These the Cap'n dismissed one by one with an impatient scowl. But he kicked at one object with his well foot.

"What's that infernal thing?" he demanded.

"A bed-wrench, Aaron. It's to take apart corded beds so as to get them out of houses that are on fire. There aren't hardly any corded beds now, of course, but it's a very old association that you're foreman of, and the members keep the old things. It's awfully nice to do so, I think. It's like keeping the furniture in old families. And that big bag there, with the puckerin'-string run around it, is the bag to put china and valuables into and lug away."

"And your idee of an honor, is it," he sneered, "is that I'm goin' to put that dingbusset with a leather back-fin onto my head and grab up them two leather swill-pails and stick that iron thing there under my arm and grab that puckering-string bag in my teeth and start tophet-te-larrup over this town a-chasin' fires? Say—" but his voice choked, and he began to read once more the pamphlet. The red on the back of his neck grew deeper.

At last the explosion occurred.

"Louada Murilla Sproul, do you mean to say that you've had this thing in your fam'ly once, and was knowin' what it meant, and then let them three Shanghaiers come in here and shove this bloodsucker bus'ness onto me, and git away all safe and sound? I had been thinkin' that your Todds and Wards was spreadin' some sail for villuns, but they're only moskeeters to Barb'ry pirates compared with this."

He cuffed his hand against the open pages of the pamphlet.

"It says here that the foreman has to set up a free dinner for 'em four times a year and ev'ry holiday. It says that the foreman is fined two dollars for ev'ry monthly meetin' that he misses, other members ten cents. He's fined ten dollars for ev'ry fire that he isn't at, other members a quarter of a dollar. He's fined one dollar for ev'ry time he's ketched without his hat, buckets, bag, and bed-wrench hung in his front hall where they belong, other members ten cents. And he's taxed a quarter of the whole expenses of gittin' to firemen's muster and back. Talk about lettin' blood with a gimlet! Why, they're after me with a pod-auger!"

All the afternoon he read the little book, cuffed it, and cursed. He snapped up Louada Murilla with scant courtesy when she tried to give him the history of Smyrna's most famous organization, and timorously represented to him the social eminence he had attained.

"It isn't as though you didn't have money, and plenty of it," she pleaded. "You can't get any more good out of it than by spending it that way. I tell you, Aaron, it isn't to be sneezed at, leading all the grand marches at the Ancients' dances and being boss of 'em all at the muster, with the band a-playin' and you leading 'em right up the middle of the street. It's worth it, Aaron—and I shall be so proud of you!"

He grumbled less angrily the next morning. But he still insisted that he didn't propose to let the consolidated Todds and Wards of Smyrna bunco him into taking the position, and said that he should attend the next meeting of the Ancients and resign.

But when, on the third evening after his election, the enthusiastic members of the Smyrna A. & H.F.A. came marching up from the village, the brass band tearing the air into ribbons with cornets and trombones, his stiff resolve wilted suddenly. He began to grin shamefacedly under his grizzled beard, and hobbled out onto the porch and made them a stammering speech, and turned scarlet with pride when they cheered him, and basked in the glory of their compliments, and thrilled when they respectfully called him "Chief." He even told Louada Murilla that she was a darling, when she, who had been forewarned, produced a "treat" from a hiding-place in the cellar.

"I knew you'd appreciate it all as soon as you got wonted to the honor, Aaron," she whispered, happy tears in her eyes. "It's the social prominence—that's all there is to it. There hasn't been a fire in the town for fifteen years, and you aren't going to be bothered one mite. Oh, isn't that band just lovely?"

The Cap'n went to bed late that night, his ears tingling with the adulation of the multitude, and in his excited insomnia understanding for the first time in his life the words: "Uneasy lies the head that wears a crown." He realized more fully now that his shipmaster days had given him a taste for command, and that he had come into his own again.

VI

The new chief of the Ancients devoted the first hours of the next morning to the arrangement of his fire-fighting gear in the front hall, and when all the items had been suspended, so that they would be ready to his hand as well as serve as ornament, he went out on the porch and sunned himself, revelling in a certain snug and contented sense of importance, such as he hadn't felt since he had stepped down from the quarter-deck of his own vessel. He even gazed at the protruding and poignant centre of that rose on his carpet slipper with milder eyes, and sniffed aromatic whiffs of liniment with appreciation of its invigorating odor.

It was a particularly peaceful day. From his porch he could view a wide expanse of rural scenery, and, once in a while, a flash of sun against steel marked the location of some distant farmer in his fields. There were no teams in sight on the highway, for the men of Smyrna were too busily engaged on their acres. He idly watched a trail of dun smoke that rose from behind a distant ridge and zigzagged across the blue sky. He admired it as a scenic attraction, without attaching any importance to it. Even when a woman appeared on the far-off ridge and flapped her apron and hopped up and down and appeared to be frantically signalling either the village in the valley or the men in the fields, he only squinted at her through the sunlight and wondered what ailed her. A sudden inspiring thought suggested that perhaps she had struck a hornets' nest. He chuckled.

A little later a ballooning cloud of dust came rolling down the road toward him and the toll-bridge that led to Smyrna village. He noted that the core of the cloud was a small boy, running so hard that his knees almost knocked under his chin. He spun to a halt in front of the Cap'n's gate and gasped:

"Fi-ah, fi-ah, fi-ah-h-h-h, Chief! Ben Ide's house is a-fi-ah. I'll holler it in the village and git 'em to ring the bell and start 'Hecla.'" Away he tore.

"Fire!" bawled Cap'n Aaron, starting for the front hall with a scuff, a hop, a skip, and jump, in order to favor his sprained toe. "Fire over to Ben Ide's!"

He had his foreman's hat on wrong side to when his wife came bursting out of the sitting-room into the hall. She, loyal though excited lady of the castle, shifted her knight's helmet to the right-about and stuffed his buckets, bag, and bed-wrench into his hands. The cord of his speaking-trumpet she slung over his neck.

"I helped get father ready once, twenty years ago," she stuttered, "and I haven't forgot! Oh, Aaron, I wish you hadn't got such a prejudice against owning a horse and against Marengo when he tried to sell you that one. Now you've got to wait till some one gives you a lift. You can't go on that foot to Ide's."

"Hoss!" he snorted. "Marengo! What he tried to sell me would be a nice thing to git to a fire with! Spavined wusser'n a carpenter's saw-hoss, and with heaves like a gasoline dory! I can hop there on one foot quicker'n he could trot that hoss there! But I'll git there. I'll git there!"

He went limping out of the door, loaded with his equipment.

The Methodist bell had not begun to ring, and it was evident that the messenger of ill tidings had not pattered into the village as yet.

But there was a team in sight. It was "Balm o' Joy" Brackett, his arms akimbo as he fished on the reins to hurry his horse. He was coming from the direction of the toll-bridge, and had evidently met the boy.

"I've got my lo'd—I've got my lo'd, but I'll leave behind me all o' the ro'd," he chirped, when the Cap'n went plunging toward him with the evident intention of getting on board.

"I'm foreman of the Ancients," roared the Cap'n, "and I have the right to press into service any craft I see passin'. Take me aboard, I say, dumblast ye!"

"This ain't no high seas," retorted Brackett, trying to lick past. "You can drive gents out of your dooryard, but you can't do no press-gang bus'ness on 'em."

It was apparent that even "Balm o' Joy's" bland nature could entertain resentment.

"'Tain't right to lay up grudges ag'inst a man that was fussed up like I was, Mister Brackett," pleaded the Cap'n, hopping along beside the van. "I've got to git to that fire, I tell you. I'm the foreman! I'll use you right, after this. I will, I tell you. Lemme on board."

"'Promus' flies high when it's hot and dry!" twittered the peddler, still cheerful but obstinate.

"I'll give ye five dollars to take me to Ben Ide's—ten!" he roared, when Brackett showed no sign of stopping.

"'Promus' on the ground can be better found. Whoa!" cried Brackett, promptly. "I'll take the fare before you climb up! You'll be so busy when you git to the fire that I wouldn't want to bother you then."

The Cap'n glowered but chewed his lips to prevent retort, pulled his wallet, and paid. Then he gathered his apparatus and grunted up to the high seat.

Far behind them the excited clang-clang of the Methodist bell was pealing its first alarm.

"By the time they git hosses up out of the fields and hitched onto 'Hecla,' and git their buckets and didoes and git started, I reckon things will be fried on both sides at Ben Ide's," chatted the peddler.

"Lick up! Lick up!" barked the Cap'n. "I'm payin' for a quick ride and not conversation."

Brackett clapped the reins along his nag's skinny flank, set his elbows on his knees, and began:

"There was old Hip Huff, who went by freight,
  To Newry Corner, in—"

"Luff, luff!" snorted the Cap'n, in disgust.

"Luff, luff?" queried the songster.

"Yes, luff! Avast! Belay! Heave to! I don't like caterwaulin'. You keep your mind right on drivin' that hoss."

"You must have been a pop'lar man all your life," remarked the peddler, with a baleful side-glance. "Does politeness come nat'ral to you, or did you learn it out of a book?"

The Cap'n made no reply. He only hitched himself forward as though trying to assist the momentum of the cart, and clutched his buckets, one in each hand.

A woman came flying out of the first house they passed and squalled:

"Where's the fire, Mr. Brackett, and is anybody burnt up, and hadn't you jest as liv' take my rags now? I've got 'em all sacked and ready to weigh, and I sha'n't be to home after to-day."

Brackett pulled up.

"Blast your infernal pelt," howled the Cap'n, "you drive on!"

"Bus'ness is bus'ness," muttered the peddler, "and you ain't bought me and my team with that little old ten dollars of yourn, and you can't do northin', anyway, till Hecla gits there with the boys, and when you're there I don't see what you're goin' to amount to with that sore toe."

He was clearly rebellious. Cap'n Sproul had touched the tenderest spot in T.W. Brackett's nature by that savage yelp at his vocal efforts. But the chief of the Ancients had been wounded as cruelly in his own pride. He stood up and swung a bucket over the crouching peddler.

"Drive on, you lubber," he howled, "or I'll peg you down through that seat like I'd drive a tack. Drive on!"

Brackett ducked his head and drove. And the Cap'n, summoning all the resources of a vocabulary enriched by a sea experience of thirty years, yelled at him and his horse without ceasing.

When they topped the ridge they were in full view of Ide's doomed buildings, and saw the red tongues of flame curling through the rolling smoke.

But a growing clamor behind made the Chief crane his neck and gaze over the top of the van.

"Hecla" was coming!

Four horses were dragging it, and two-score men were howling along with it, some riding, but the most of them clinging to the brake-beams and slamming along through the dust on foot. A man, perched beside the driver, was bellowing something through a trumpet that sounded like:

"Goff-off-errow, goff-off-errow, goff-off-errow!"

The peddler was driving sullenly, and without any particular enterprise. But this tumult behind made his horse prick up his ears and snort. When the nag mended his pace and began to lash out with straddling legs, the Cap'n yelled:

"Let him go! Let him go! They want us to get off the road!"

"Goff-off-errow!" the man still bellowed through the trumpet.

"I've got goods that will break and I'll be cuss-fired if I'll break 'em for you nor the whole Smyrna Fire Department!" screamed Brackett;

but when he tried to pull up his steed, the Cap'n, now wholly beside himself and intent only on unrestricted speed, banged a leather bucket down across the driver's hands.

Brackett dropped the reins, with a yell of pain, and they fell into the dust and dragged. The horse broke into a bunchy, jerky gallop, and lunged down the hill, the big van swaying wildly with an ominous rattling and crashing in its mysterious interior.

There were teams coming along a cross-road ahead of them and teams rattling from the opposite direction toward the fire, approaching along the highway they were travelling. Collisions seemed inevitable. But in a moment of inspiration the Cap'n grabbed the trumpet that hung from its red cord around his neck and began to bellow in his turn:

"Goff-off-errow, goff-off-errow!" It was as nearly as human voice could phrase "Get off the road" through the thing.

The terrifying bulk of the big van cleared the way ahead, even though people desperately risked tip-ups in the gutter. As it tore along, horses climbed fences with heads and tails up. There were men floundering in bushes and women squalling from the tops of rock-heaps.

The Chief of the Ancients did not halt to attend to his duties at the fire. He went howling past on the high seat of the van, over the next ridge and out of sight.

"We're goin' to tophet, and you done it, and you've got to pay for it," Brackett wailed over and over, bobbing about on the seat. But the Cap'n did not reply. Teams kept coming into sight ahead, and he had thought only for his monotonous bellow of "Goff-off-errow!"

Disaster—the certain disaster that they had despairingly accepted—met them at the foot of Rines' hill, two miles beyond Ide's. The road curved sharply there to avoid "the Pugwash," as a particularly mushy and malodorous bog was called in local terminology.

At the foot of the hill the van toppled over with a crash and anchored the steaming horse, already staggering in his exhaustion. Both men had scrambled to the top of the van, ready to jump into the Pugwash as they passed. The Cap'n still carried his equipment, both buckets slung upon one arm, and even in this imminent peril it never occurred to him to drop them. Lucky fate made their desperate leap for life a tame affair. When the van toppled they were tossed over the roadside into the bog, lighted on their hands and knees, and sank slowly into its mushiness like two Brobdingnagian frogs.

It was another queer play of fate that the next passer was Marengo Todd, whipping his way to the fire behind a horse that had a bit of wire pinched over his nose to stifle his "whistling."

Marengo Todd leaped out and presented the end of a fence-rail to Brackett first, and pulled him out.

When he stuck the end of the rail under the Cap'n's nose the Cap'n pushed it away with mud-smeared hands.

"I don't, myself, nuss grudges in times of distress, Cap Sproul," shouted Todd. "You kicked me. I know that. But you was in the wrong, and you got the wu'st of it. Proverdunce has allus settled my grudges for me in jest that way. I forgive and pass on, but Proverdunce don't. Take that fence-rail. It sha'n't ever be said by man that Marengo Todd nussed a grudge."

When the Cap'n was once more on solid ground, Todd, still iterating his forgiveness of past injuries, picked up a tin pie-plate that had been jarred out of the van among other litter, and began to scrape the black mud off the foreman of the Ancients in as matter-of-fact a way as though he were currycombing a horse.

The spirit of the doughty mariner seemed broken at last. He looked down at himself, at the mud-clogged buckets and his unspeakable bedragglement.

"I've only got one word to say to you right here and now, Cap'n," went on Todd, meekly, "and it's this, that no man ever gits jest where he wants to git, unless he has a ree-li'ble hoss. I've tried to tell you so before, but—but, well, you didn't listen to me the way you ought to." He continued to scrape, and the Cap'n stared mutely down at the foot that was encased in a muddy slipper.

"Now, there's a hoss standin' there—" pursued Todd.

"What will you take for that team jest as it stands?" blurted the mariner, desperately. The fire, the smoke of which was rolling up above the distant tree-tops, and his duty there made him reckless. As he looked down on Todd he hadn't the heart to demand of that meek and injured person that he should forget and forgive sufficiently to take him in and put him down at Ide's. It seemed like crowding the mourners. Furthermore, Cap'n Aaron Sproul was not a man who traded in humble apologies. His independence demanded a different footing with Todd, and the bitter need of the moment eclipsed economy. "Name your price!"

"A hundred and thutty, ev'rything throwed in, and I'll drive you there a mile a minit," gasped Todd, grasping the situation.

With muddy hands, trembling in haste, the Cap'n drew his long, fat wallet and counted out the bills. Brackett eyed him hungrily.

"You might jest as well settle with me now as later through the law," he cried.

But the Cap'n butted him aside, with an oath, and climbed into the wagon.

"You drive as though the devil had kicked ye," he yelled to Todd. "It's my hoss, and I don't care if you run the four legs off'm him."

Half-way to Ide's, a man leaped the roadside fence and jumped up and down before them in the highway. He had a shotgun in his hands.

"It's my brother—Voltaire," shouted Marengo, pulling up, though Cap'n Sproul swore tempestuously. "You've got to take him on. He b'longs to your fire comp'ny."

"I was out huntin' when I heard the bell," bellowed the new passenger, when he had scrambled to a place behind the wagon-seat, his back toward them and his legs hanging down. "I'm fu'st hoseman, and it's lucky you came along and giv' me a lift." He set his gun-butt down between his knees, the muzzle pointing up.

Cap'n Sproul had his teeth set hard upon a hank of his grizzled whiskers, and his eyes on the smoke ahead. Todd ran his wheezing horse up the ridge, and when they topped it they beheld the whole moving scene below them.

Men were running out of the burning house, throwing armfuls of goods right and left. The "Hecla" was a-straddle of the well, and rows of men were tossing at her brake-beams.

"Give her tar, give her tar!" yelled the man behind, craning his thin neck. Todd lashed at the horse and sent him running down the slope. At the foot of the declivity, just before they came to the lane leading into Ide's place, there was a culvert where the road crossed a brook.

The boarding in the culvert made a jog in the road, and when the wagon struck this at top speed its body flipped behind like the tongue of a catapult.

The man with the gun, having eyes and senses only for the fire and his toiling fellow-Ancients, was unprepared. He went up, out, and down in the dust, doggedly clinging to his gun. He struck the ground with it still between his knees. The impact of the butt discharged both barrels straight into the air.

Flanked by a roaring fire and howling crowd, and bombarded in the rear, even a horse with a bone spavin and the heaves will exhibit the spirit of Bucephalus. One of the rotten reins broke at Marengo's first terrified tug. In less time than it takes to tell, Cap'n Aaron Sproul, desperate and beholding only one resource—the tail flaunting over the dasher—seized it and gave a seaman's sturdy pull. The tail came away in his hands and left only a wildly brandishing stump. Even in that moment of horror, the Cap'n had eyes to see and wit to understand that this false tail was more of Marengo Todd's horse-jockey guile. The look that he turned on the enterprising doctor of caudal baldness was so perfectly diabolical that Marengo chose what seemed the lesser of two evils. He precipitated himself over the back of the seat, dropped to the ground as lightly as a cat, ran wildly until he lost his footing, and dove into some wayside alders. Cap'n Aaron Sproul was left alone with his newly acquired property!

When he hove in sight of his own house he saw Louada Murilla on the porch, gazing off at the smoke of the fire and evidently luxuriating in the consciousness that it was her husband who was that day leading the gallant forces of the Ancients.

As he stared wildly, home seemed his haven and the old house his rock of safety. He did not understand enough about the vagaries of horses and wagons to appreciate the risk. One rein still hung over the dasher.

"Only one jib down-haul left of all the riggin'," he groaned, and then grabbed it and surged on it.

The horse swung out of the road, the wagon careering wildly on two wheels. Sproul crossed the corner of some ploughed land, swept down a length of picket-fence, and came into his own lane, up which the horse staggered, near the end of his endurance. The wagon swung and came to grief against the stone hitching-post at the corner of the porch. Cap'n Sproul, encumbered still with buckets and bag and trumpet, floundered over the porch rail, through a tangled mass of woodbine vines, and into the arms of his distracted wife.

For five minutes after she had supported him to a chair she could do nothing but stare at him, with her hands clasped and her eyes goggling, and cry, "Aaron, Aaron, dear!" in crescendo. His sole replies to her were hollow sounds in his throat that sounded like "unk!"

"Where have you been?" she cried. "All gurry, and wet as sop? If you are hurt what made 'em let their Chief come home all alone with that wild hoss? Aaron, can't you speak?"

He only flapped a muddy hand at her, and seemed to be beyond speech. There was a dull, wondering look in his eyes, as though he were trying to figure out some abstruse problem. He did not brighten until a team came tearing up to the gate, and a man with a scoop fireman's hat on came running to the porch. The man saluted.

"Chief," he said, with the air of an aide reporting on the field of battle, "that house and barn got away from us, but we fit well for 'em—yas s'r, we fit well! It is thought queer in some quarters that you wasn't there to take charge, but I told the boys that you'd prob'ly got good reasons, and they'll git over their mad, all right. You needn't worry none about that!"

The Cap'n's sole reply was another of those hollow "unks!"

"But the boys is pretty well beat out, and so I've run over to ask if you'll let us use your ten-dollar fine for a treat? That will help their feelin's to'ards you a good deal, and—"

The Cap'n, without taking his eyes from the smug face of the man, swung one of the buckets and let drive at him. It missed. But he had got his range, and the next bucket knocked off the scoop hat. When the Cap'n scrambled to his feet, loaded with the bed-wrench for his next volley, the man turned and ran for his team. The bed-wrench caught him directly between the shoulders—a masterly shot. The trumpet flew wild, but by that time the emissary of the Ancients was in his wagon and away.

"Aaron!" his wife began, quaveringly, but the Cap'n leaped toward her, pulled the mouth of the puckering-bag over her head, and hopped into the house. When at last she ventured to peer in at the sitting-room window, he was tearing the book of "Rules of the Smyrna Ancient and Honorable Firemen's Association," using both his hands and his teeth, and worrying it as a dog worries a bone.

That was his unofficial resignation. The official one came as soon as he could control his language.

And for a certain, prolonged period in the history of the town of Smyrna it was well understood that Cap'n Aaron Sproul was definitely out of public affairs. But in public affairs it often happens that honors that are elusive when pursued are thrust upon him who does not seek them.

VII

The moderator of the Smyrna town meeting held his breath for just a moment so as to accentuate the hush in which the voters listened for his words, and then announced the result of the vote for first selectman of Smyrna:

"Whole number cast, one hundred thutty-two; necessary for a choice, sixty-seven; of which Colonel Gideon Ward has thutty-one."

A series of barking, derisive yells cut in upon his solemn announcement, and he rapped his cane on the marred table of the town hall and glared over his spectacles at the voters.

"And Cap'n Aaron Sproul has one hundred and —"

The howl that followed clipped his last words. Men hopped upon the knife-nicked settees of the town house and waved their hats while they hooted. A group of voters, off at one side, sat and glowered at this hilarity. Out of the group rose Colonel Gideon, his long frame unfolding with the angularity of a carpenter's two-foot rule. There were little dabs of purple on his knobby cheek-bones. His hair and his beard bristled. He put up his two fists as far as his arms would reach and vibrated them, like a furious Jeremiah calling down curses.

Such ferocious mien had its effect on the spectators after a time. Smyrna quailed before her ancient tyrant, even though he was dethroned.

"Almighty God has always wanted an excuse to destroy this town like Sodom and Gomorrah was destroyed," he shouted, his voice breaking into a squeal of rage; "now He's got it."

He drove his pointed cap onto his head, gave a parting shake of his fists that embraced moderator, voters, walls, floor, roof, and all appurtenances of the town house, and stalked down the aisle and out. The silence in town meeting was so profound that the voters heard him welting his horse as he drove away.

After a time the moderator drew a long breath, and stated that he did not see Cap'n Aaron Sproul in the meeting, and had been informed that he was not present.

"I come past his place this mornin'," whispered Old Man Jordan to his neighbor on the settee, "and he was out shovelin' snow off'm the front walk, and when I asked him if he wa'n't comin' to town meetin', he said that a run of the seven years' itch and the scurvy was pretty bad, but he reckoned that politics was wuss. I should hate to be the one that has to break this news to him."

"And seein' how it's necessary to have the first selectman here to be sworn in before the meetin' closes this afternoon," went on the moderator, "I'll appoint a committee of three to wait on Cap'n Aaron Sproul and notify him of the distinguished honor that has been done him this day by his feller townsmen."

He settled his spectacles more firmly upon his nose, and ran his gaze calculatingly over the assembled voters. No one of those patriotic citizens seemed to desire to be obtrusive at that moment.

"I'll appoint as chairman of that notifying committee," proceeded the moderator, "Entwistle Harvey, and as—"

"I shall have to decline the honor," interrupted Mr. Entwistle Harvey, rising promptly. The voters grinned. They thoroughly understood the reason for Mr. Harvey's reluctance.

"It ain't that I'm any less a reformer than the others that has to-day redeemed this town from ring rule and bossism," declared Mr. Harvey, amid applause; "it ain't that I don't admire the able man that has been selected to lead us up out of the vale of political sorrow—and I should be proud to stand before him and offer this distinguished honor from the voters of this town, but I decline because I—I—well, there ain't any need of goin' into personal reasons. I ain't the man for the place, that's all." He sat down.

"I don't blame him none for duckin'," murmured Old Man Jordan to his seat companion. "Any man that was in the crowd that coaxed Cap'n Sproul into takin' the foremanship of Heckly Fire Comp'ny has got a good excuse. I b'lieve the law says that ye can't put a man twice in peril of his life."

Cap'n Sproul's stormy relinquishment of the hateful honor that had been foisted upon him by the Smyrna fire-fighters was history recent enough to give piquant relish to the present situation. He had not withheld nor modified his threats as to what would happen to any other committee that came to him proffering public office.

The more prudent among Smyrna's voters had hesitated about making the irascible ex-mariner a candidate for selectman's berth.

But Smyrna, in its placid New England eddy, had felt its own little thrill from the great tidal wave of municipal reform sweeping the country. It immediately gazed askance at Colonel Gideon Ward, for twenty years first selectman of Smyrna, and growled under its breath about "bossism." But when the search was made for a candidate to run against him, Smyrna men were wary. Colonel Ward held too many mortgages and had advanced too many call loans not to be well fortified against rivals.

"The only one who has ever dared to twist his tail is his brother-in-law, the Cap'n," said Odbar Broadway, oracularly, to the leaders who had met in his store to canvass the political situation. "The Cap'n won't be as supple as some in town office, but he ain't no more hell 'n' repeat than what we've been used to for the last twenty years. He's wuth thutty thousand dollars, and Gid Ward can't foreclose no mo'gidge on him nor club him with no bill o' sale. He's the only prominunt man in town that can afford to take the office away from the Colonel. What ye've got to do is to go ahead and elect him, and then trust to the Lord to make him take it."

So that was what Smyrna had done on that slushy winter's day.

It did it with secret joy and with ballots hidden in its palms, where the snapping eyes of Colonel Ward could not spy.

And now, instead of invoking the higher power mentioned as a resource by Broadway, the moderator of the town meeting was struggling with human tools, and very rickety human tools they seemed to be.

Five different chairmen did he nominate, and with great alacrity the five refused to serve.

The moderator took off his glasses, and testily rapped the dented table.

"Feller citizens," he snapped, "this is gittin' to be boys' play. I realize puffickly that Cap'n Aaron Sproul, our first selectman-elect, has not been a seeker after public office since he retired as foreman of the Hecla Fire Company. I realize puffickly that he entertained some feelin' at the time that—that—he wasn't exactly cal'lated to be foreman of an engine company. But that ain't sayin' that he won't receive like gentlemen the committee that comes to tell him that he has been elected to the highest office in this town. I ain't got any more time to waste on cowards. There's one man here that ain't afraid of his own shadder. I call on Constable Zeburee Nute to head the committee, and take along with him Constables Wade and Swanton. And I want to say to the voters here that it's a nice report to go abroad from this town that we have to pick from the police force to get men with enough courage to tell a citizen that he's been elected first selectman. But the call has gone out for Cincinnatus, and he must be brought here."

The moderator's tone was decisive and his mien was stern. Otherwise, even the doughty Constable Nute might have refused to take orders, though they were given in the face and eyes of his admiring neighbors. He gnawed at his grizzled beard and fingered doubtfully the badge that, as chief constable of the town, he wore on the outside of his coat.

"Gents of the committee, please 'tend promptly to the duties assigned," commanded the moderator, "and we will pass on to the next article in the town warrant."

Mr. Nute rose slowly and marched out of the hall, the other two victims following without any especial signs of enthusiasm.

In the yard of the town house Mr. Nute faced them, and remarked:

"I have some ideas of my own as to a genteel way of gittin' him interested in this honor that we are about to bestow. Has any one else ideas?"

The other two constables shook their heads gloomily.

"Then I'll take the brunt of the talk on me and foller my ideas," announced Mr. Nute. "I've been studyin' reform, and, furthermore, I know who Cincinnatus was!"

The three men unhitched each his own team, and drove slowly, in single file, along the mushy highway.

It was one of Cap'n Aaron Sproul's mentally mild, mellow, and benign days, when his heart seemed to expand like a flower in the comforts of his latter-life domestic bliss. Never had home seemed so good—never the little flush on Louada Murilla's cheeks so attractive in his eyes as they dwelt fondly on her.

In the night he had heard the sleet clattering against the pane and the snow slishing across the clapboards, and he had turned on his pillow with a little grunt of thankfulness.

"There's things about dry land and the people on it that ain't so full of plums as a sailor's duff ought to be," he mused, "but—" And then he dozed off, listening to the wind.

In the morning, just for a taste of rough weather, he had put on his slicker and sea-boots and shovelled the slush off the front walk. Then he sat down with stockinged feet held in the radiance of an open Franklin stove, and mused over some old log-books that he liked to thumb occasionally for the sake of adding new comfort to a fit of shore contentment.

This day he was taking especial interest in the log-books, for he was again collaborating with Louada Murilla in that spasmodic literary effort that she had termed:

FROM SHORE TO SHORE

LINES FROM A MARINER'S ADVENTURES

The Life Story of the Gallant Captain Aaron Sproul

Written by His Affectionate Wife

"You can put down what's true," he said, continuing a topic that they had been pursuing, "that boxin' the compass and knowin' a jib down-haul from a pound of saleratus ain't all there is to a master mariner's business, not by a blamed sight. Them passuls of cat's meat that they call sailormen in these days has to be handled, —well, the superintendent of a Sunday-school wouldn't be fit for the job, unless he had a little special trainin'."

Louada Murilla, the point of her pencil at her lips, caught a vindictive gleam in his eyes.

"But it seems awful cruel, some of the things that you—you—I suppose you had to do 'em, Aaron! And yet when you stop and think that they've got immortal souls to save—"

"They don't carry any such duffle to sea in their dunnage-bags," snapped the skipper. "Moral suasion on them would be about like tryin' to whittle through a turkle's shell with a hummin'-bird's pin-feather. My rule most generally was to find one soft spot on 'em somewhere that a marlin-spike would hurt, and then hit that spot hard and often. That's the only way I ever got somewhere with a cargo and got back ag'in the same year."

"I suppose it has to be," sighed his wife, making a note. "It's like killing little calves for veal, and all such things that make the fond heart ache."

The Cap'n was "leaving" the grimy pages of a log-book. He paused over certain entries, and his face darkened. There was no more vindictiveness in his expression. It was regret and a sort of vague worry.

"What is it, Aaron?" asked his wife, with wistful apprehensiveness.

"Northin'," he growled.

"But I know it's something," she insisted, "and I'm always ready to share your burdens."

Cap'n Sproul looked around on the peace of his home, and some deep feeling seemed to surge in his soul.

"Louada Murilla," he said, sadly, "this isn't anything to be written in the book, and I didn't ever mean to speak of it to you. But there are times when a man jest has to talk about things, and he can't help it. There was one thing that I've been sorry for. I've said so to myself, and I'm goin' to say as much to you. Confession is good for the soul, so they say, and it may help me out some to tell you."

The horrified look on her face pricked him to speak further. 'Tis a titillating sensation, sometimes, to awe or shock those whom we love, when we know that forgiveness waits ready at hand.

"There was once—there was one man—I hit him dretful hard. He was a Portygee. But I hit him too hard. It was a case of mutiny. I reckon I could have proved it was mutiny, with the witnesses. But I hit him hard."

"Did he—?" gasped his wife.

"He did," replied the Cap'n, shortly, and was silent for a time.

"The thing for me to have done," he went on, despondently, "was to report it, and stood hearin'. But it was six weeks after we'd dropped him overboard—after the funeral, ye know—before we reached port. And there was a cargo ashore jest dancin' up and down to slip through the main hatch as soon as t' other one was over the rail— and freights 'way up and owners anxious for results, and me tryin' for a record, and all that, ye know. All is, there wa'n't nothin' said by the crew, for they wa'n't lookin' for trouble, and knowed the circumstances, and so I lo'ded and sailed. And that's all to date."

"But they say 'murder will out.'" Her face was white.

"It wa'n't murder. It was discipline. And I didn't mean to. But either his soft spot was too soft, or else I hit too hard. What I ought to have done was to report when my witnesses was right handy. Since I've settled and married and got property, I've woke up in the night, sometimes, and thought what would happen to me if that Portygee's relatives got track of me through one of the crew standin' in with 'em—blabbin' for what he could git out of it. I have to think about those things, now that I've got time to worry. Things looks different ashore from what they do aflo't, with your own ship under you and hustlin' to make money." He gazed round the room again, and seemed to luxuriate in his repentance.

"But if anything should be said, you could hunt up those men and— "

"Hunt what?" the Cap'n blurted. "Hunt tarheels once they've took their dunnage-bags over the rail? Hunt whiskers on a flea! What are you talkin' about? Why, Louada Murilla, I never even knowed what the Portygee's name was, except that I called him Joe. A skipper don't lo'd his mem'ry with that sculch any more'n he'd try to find names for the hens in the deck-coop.

"I made a mistake," he continued, after a time, "in not havin' it cleaned up, decks washed, and everything clewed snug at the time of it. But ev'ry man makes mistakes. I made mine then. It would be God-awful to have it come down on me when I couldn't prove nothin' except that I give him the best funeral I could. There ain't much of anything except grit in the gizzard of a United States court. They seem to think the Govumment wants every one hung. I remember a captain once who—"

He paused suddenly, for he caught sight of three muddy wagons trundling in procession into the yard. In the first one sat Constable Zeburee Nute, his obtrusive nickel badge on his overcoat.

Cap'n Sproul looked at Louada Murilla, and she stared at him, and in sudden panic both licked dry lips and were silent. The topic they had been pursuing left their hearts open to terror. There are moments when a healthy body suddenly absorbs germs of consumption that it has hitherto thrown off in hale disregard. There are moments when the mind and courage are overwhelmed by panic that reason does not pause to analyze.

VIII

Louada Murilla opened the front door when the chief constable knocked, after an exasperatingly elaborate hitching and blanketing of horses. She staggered to the door rather than walked. The Cap'n sat with rigid legs still extended toward the fire.

The three men filed into the room, and remained standing in solemn row. Mr. Nute, on behalf of the delegation, refused chairs that were offered by Mrs. Sproul. He had his own ideas as to how a committee of notification should conduct business. He stood silent and looked at Louada Murilla steadily and severely until she realized that her absence was desired.

She tottered out of the room, her terrified eyes held in lingering thrall by the woe-stricken orbs of the Cap'n.

Constable Nute eyed the door that she closed, waiting a satisfactory lapse of time, and then cleared his throat and announced:

"I want you to realize, Cap'n Sproul, that me and my feller constables here has been put in a sort of a hard position. I hope you'll consider that and govern yourself accordin'. First of all, we're obeyin' orders from them as has authority. I will say, however, that I have ideas as to how a thing ought to be handled, and my associates have agreed to leave the talkin' to me. I want to read you somethin' first," he said, fumbling at the buttons on his coat, "but that you may have some notion as to what it all points and be thinkin' it over, I'll give you a hint. To a man of your understandin', I don't s'pose I have to say more than 'Cincinnatus,' That one word explains itself and our errunt."

"I never knowed his last name," mumbled the Cap'n, enigmatically. "But I s'pose they've got it in the warrant, all right!" He was eying the hand that was seeking the constable's inside pocket. "I never was strong on Portygee names. I called him Joe."

Mr. Nute merely stared, without trying to catch the drift of this indistinct muttering.

While the Cap'n watched him in an agony of impatience and suspense, he slowly drew out a spectacle-case, settled his glasses upon his puffy nose, unfolded a sheet of paper on which a dirty newspaper clipping was pasted, and began to read:

"More than ever before in the history of the United States of America are loyal citizens called upon to throw themselves into the breach of municipal affairs, and wrest from the hands of the guilty—"

The ears of Cap'n Sproul, buzzing with his emotions, caught only a few words, nor grasped any part of the meaning. But the sonorous "United States of America" chilled his blood, and the word "guilty" made his teeth chatter.

He felt an imperious need of getting out of that room for a moment—of getting where he could think for a little while, out from under the starings of those three solemn men.

"I want to—I want to—" he floundered; "I would like to get on my shoes and my co't and—and—I'll be right back. I won't try to—I'll be right back, I say."

Mr. Nute suspended his reading, looked over his spectacles, and gave the required permission. Perhaps it occurred to his official sense that a bit more dignified attire would suit the occasion better. A flicker of gratification shone on his face at the thought that the Cap'n was so nobly and graciously rising to the spirit of the thing.

"It's come, Louada Murilla—it's come!" gulped Cap'n Sproul, as he staggered into the kitchen, where his wife cowered in a corner. "He's readin' a warrant. He's even got the Portygee's name. My Gawd, they'll hang me! I can't prove northin'."

"Oh, Aaron," sobbed his wife, and continued to moan. "Oh, Aaron—" with soft, heartbreaking cluckings.

"Once the law of land-piruts gets a bight 'round ye, ye never git away from it," groaned the Cap'n. "The law sharks is always waitin' for seafarin' men. There ain't no hope for me."

His wife had no encouragement to offer.

"Murder will out, Aaron," she quaked. "And they've sent three constables."

"Them other two—be they—?"

"They're constables."

"There ain't no hope. And it shows how desp'rit' they think I be. It shows they're bound to have me. It's life and death, Louada Murilla. If I don't git anything but State Prison, it's goin' to kill me, for I've lived too free and open to be penned up at my time o' life. It ain't fair—it ain't noways fair!" His voice broke. "It was all a matter of discipline. But you can't prove it to land-sharks. If they git me into their clutches I'm a goner."

His pistols hung on the wall where Louada Murilla had suspended them, draped with the ribbons of peace.

"There's only one thing to do," he whispered, huskily, pointing at the weapons with quivering finger. "I'll shoot 'em in the legs, jest to hold 'em up. I'll git to salt water. I know skippers that will take me aboard, even if they have to stand off the whole United States. I've got friends, Louada, as soon as I git to tide-water. It won't hurt 'em in there—a bullet in the leg. And it's life and death for me. There's foreign countries where they can't take me up. I know 'em, I've been there. And I'll send for you, Louada Murilla. It's the best I can think of now. It ain't what I should choose, but it's the best I can think of. I've had short notice. I can't let 'em take me."

As he talked he seemed to derive some comfort from action. He pulled on his boots. He wriggled into his coat. From a pewter pitcher high up on a dresser shelf he secured a fat wallet. But when he rushed to take down the pistols his wife threw herself into his arms.

"You sha'n't do that, Aaron," she cried. "I'll go to State Prison with you—I'll go to the ends of the world to meet you. But I couldn't have those old men shot in our own house. I realize you've got to get away. But blood will never wash out blood. Take one of their teams. Run the horse to the railroad-station. It's only four miles, and you've got a half-hour before the down-train. And I'll lock 'em into the setting-room, Aaron, and keep 'em as long as I can. And I'll come to you, Aaron, though I have to follow you clear around the world."

In the last, desperate straits of an emergency, many a woman's wits ring truer than a man's. When she had kissed him and departed on her errand to lock the front door he realized that her counsel was good.

He left the pistols on the wall. As he ran into the yard, he got a glimpse, through the sitting-room window, of the constables standing in solemn row. Never were innocent members of committee of notification more blissfully unconscious of what they had escaped. They were blandly gazing at the Cap'n's curios ranged on mantel and what-not.

It was a snort from Constable Swanton that gave the alarm. Mr. Nute's team was spinning away down the road, the wagon-wheels throwing slush with a sort of fireworks effect. Cap'n Sproul, like most sailors, was not a skilful driver, but he was an energetic one. The horse was galloping.

"He's bound for the town house before he's been notified officially," stammered Mr. Swanton.

"It ain't regular," said Constable Wade.

Mr. Nute made no remark. He looked puzzled, but he acted promptly. He found the front door locked and the kitchen door locked. But the window-catches were on the inside, and he slammed up the nearest sash and leaped out. The others followed. The pursuit was on as soon as they could get to their wagons, Mr. Wade riding with the chief constable.

The town house of Smyrna is on the main road leading to the railway-station. The constables, topping a hill an eighth of a mile behind the fugitive, expected to see him turn in at the town house. But he tore past, his horse still on the run, the wagon swaying wildly as he turned the corner beyond the Merrithew sugar orchard.

"Well, I swow," grunted Mr. Nute, and licked on.

The usual crowd of horse-swappers was gathered in the town-house yard, and beheld this tumultuous passage with professional interest. And, recognizing the first selectman-elect of Smyrna, their interest had an added flavor.

Next came the two teams containing the constables, lashing past on the run. They paid no attention to the amazed yells of inquiry from the horse-swappers, and disappeared behind the sugar orchard.

"You've got me!" said Uncle Silas Drake to the first out-rush of the curious from the town house. In his amazement, Uncle Silas was still holding to the patient nose of the horse whose teeth he had been examining. "They went past like soft-soap slidin' down the suller stairs, and that's as fur's I'm knowin'. But I want to remark, as my personal opinion, that a first seeleckman of this town ought to be 'tendin' to his duties made and pervided, instead of razooin' hosses up and down in front of this house when town meetin' is goin' on."

One by one, voters, mumbling their amazement, unhitched their horses and started along the highway in the direction the fugitives had taken. It seemed to all that this case required to be investigated. The procession whipped along briskly and noisily.

Colonel Gideon Ward, returning from the railroad-station, where he had been to order flat-cars for lumber, heard the distant clamor of voices, and stood up in his tall cart to listen. At that instant, around the bend of the road, twenty feet away, came a horse galloping wildly. Colonel Ward was halted squarely in the middle of the way. He caught an amazed glimpse of Cap'n Sproul trying to rein to one side with unskilled hands, and then the wagons met. Colonel Ward's wagon stood like a rock. The lighter vehicle, locking wheels, went down with a crash, and Cap'n Sproul shot head-on over the dasher into his brother-in-law's lap, as he crouched on his seat.

The advantage was with Cap'n Sproul, for the Colonel was underneath. Furthermore, Cap'n Sproul was thrice armed with the resolution of a desperate man. Without an instant's hesitation he drew back, hit Ward a few resounding buffets on either side of his head, and then tossed the dizzied man out of his wagon into the roadside slush. An instant later he had the reins, swung the frightened horse across the gutter and around into the road, and continued his flight in the direction of the railroad-station.

The constables, leading the pursuing voters by a few lengths, found Colonel Ward sitting up in the ditch and gaping in utter amazement and dire wrath at the turn of the road where Cap'n Sproul had swept out of sight.

The wreck of the wagon halted them.

"I s'pose you've jest seen our first selectman-elect pass this way, haven't ye?" inquired Mr. Nute, with official conservatism.

The Colonel had not yet regained his powers of speech. He jabbed with bony finger in the direction of the railroad, and moved his jaws voicelessly. Mr. Swanton descended from the wagon, helped him out of the ditch, and began to stroke the slush from his garments with mittened hand. As he still continued to gasp ineffectually, Mr. Nute drove on, leaving him standing by the roadside.

Cap'n Sproul was at bay on the station platform, feet braced defiantly apart, hat on the back of his head, and desperate resolve flaming from his eyes.

"Don't ye git out of your wagon, Nute," he rasped. "It's been touch and go once with the three of ye to-day. I could have killed ye like sheep. Don't git in my way ag'in. Take warnin'! It's life or death, and a few more don't make much difference to me now."

The chief constable stared at him with bulging eyes.

"I could have killed ye and I didn't," repeated the Cap'n. "Let that show ye that I'm square till I have to be otherwise. But I'm a desp'rit' man, Nute. I'm goin' to take that train." He brandished his fist at a trail of smoke up behind the spruces. "Gawd pity the man that gits in my way!"

"Somethin' has happened to his mind all of a sudden," whispered Mr. Wade. "He ought to be took care of till he gits over it. It would be a pity and a shame to let a prominent man like that git away and fall into the hands of strangers."

"All of ye take warnin'," bawled the Cap'n to his townsmen, who were crowding their wagons into the station square.

Constable Zeburee Nute drove his whip into the socket, threw down his reins, and stood up. The hollow hoot of the locomotive had sounded up the track.

"Feller citizens," he cried, "as chairman of the committee of notification, I desire to report that I have 'tended to my duties in so far as I could to date. But there has things happened that I can't figger out, and for which I ain't responsible. There ain't no time now for ifs, buts, or ands. That train is too near. A certain prominunt citizen that I don't need to name is thinkin' of takin' that train when he ain't fit to do so. There'll be time to talk it over afterward."

Cap'n Sproul was backing away to turn the corner of the station.

"I call on all of ye as a posse," bawled Mr. Nute. "Bring along your halters and don't use no vi'lence."

Samson himself, even though his weapon had been the jaw-bone of a megatherium, couldn't have resisted that onrush of the willing populace. In five minutes, the Cap'n, trussed hand and foot, and crowded in between Constables Nute and Wade, was riding back toward Smyrna town house, helpless as a veal calf bound for market.

"Now," resumed Mr. Nute, calmly, "now that you're with us, Cap'n, and seem to be quieted down a little, I'll perceed to execute the errunt put upon me as chairman of the notification committee."

With Mr. Wade driving slowly, he read the newspaper clipping that sounded the clarion call that summoned men of probity to public office, and at the close formally notified Cap'n Sproul that he had been elected first selectman of Smyrna. He did all this without enthusiasm, and sighed with official relief when it was over.

"And," he wound up, "it is the sentiment of this town that there ain't another man in it so well qualified to lead us up out of the valley of darkness where we've been wallerin'. We have called our Cincinnatus to his duty."

They had come around a bend of the road and now faced Colonel Ward, stumping along stolidly through the slush, following the trail of his team.

"That's the way he ought to be," roared the Colonel. "Rope him up! Put ox-chains on him. And I'll give a thousand dollars to build an iron cage for him. You're all crazy and he's your head lunatic."

Mr. Nute, inwardly, during all the time that he had been so calmly addressing his captive, was tortured with cruel doubts as to the Cap'n's sanity. But he believed in discharging his duty first. And he remembered that insane people were more easily prevailed upon by those who appeared to make no account of their whims.

During it all, Cap'n Sproul had been silent in utter amazement. The truth had come in a blinding flash that would have unsettled a man not so well trained to control emotion.

"Drive along," he curtly commanded Nute, paying no heed to the incensed Colonel's railings. "You look me in the eye," he continued, as soon as they were out of hearing. "Do you see any signs that I am out of my head, or that I need these ropes on me?"

"I can't say as I do," admitted the constable, after he had quailed a bit under the keen, straightforward stare of the ex-mariner's hard, gray eyes.

"Take 'em off, then," directed the Cap'n, in tones of authority. And when it was done, he straightened his hat, set back his shoulders, and said:

"Drive me to the town house where I was bound when that hoss of yours run away with me." Mr. Nute stared at him wildly, and drove on.

They were nearly to their destination before Constable Nute ventured upon what his twisted brow and working lips testified he had been pondering long.

"It ain't that I'm tryin' to pry into your business, Cap'n Sproul, nor anything of the kind, but, bein' a man that never intended to do any harm to any one, I can't figger out what grudge you've got against me. You said on the station platform that—"

"Nute," said the Cap'n, briskly, "as I understand it, you never went to sea, and you and the folks round here don't understand much about sailormen, hey?"

The constable shook his head.

"Then don't try to find out much about 'em. You wouldn't understand. The folks round here wouldn't understand. We have our ways. You have your ways. Some of the things you do and some of the things you say could be called names by me, providin' I wanted to be disagreeable and pick flaws. All men in this world are different—especially sailormen from them that have always lived inshore. We've got to take our feller man as we find him."

They were in the town-house yard—a long procession of teams following.

"And by-the-way, Nute," bawled the Cap'n, from the steps of the building as he was going in, using his best sea tones so that all might hear, "it was the fault of your horse that he run away, and you ought to be prosecuted for leavin' such an animile 'round where a sailorman that ain't used to hosses could get holt of him. But I'm always liberal about other folks' faults. Bring in your bill for the wagon."

Setting his teeth hard, he walked upon the platform of the town-hall, and faced the voters with such an air of authority and such self-possession that they cheered him lustily. And then, with an intrepidity that filled his secret heart with amazement as he talked, he made the first real speech of his life—a speech of acceptance.

"Yes, s'r, it was a speech, Louada Murilla," he declared that evening, as he sat again in their sitting-room with his stockinged feet to the blaze of the Franklin. "I walked that platform like it was a quarter-deck, and my line of talk run jest as free as a britches-buoy coil. And when I got done, they was up on the settees howlin' for me. If any man came back into that town-house thinkin' I was a lunatic on account of what happened to-day, they got a diff'runt notion before I got done. Why, they all come 'round and shook my hand, and said they must have been crazy to tackle a prominunt citizen that way on the word of old Nute. It must have been a great speech I made. They all said so."

He relighted his pipe.

"What did you say, Aaron?" eagerly asked his wife. "Repeat it over."

He smoked awhile.

"Louada Murilla," he said, "when I walked onto that platform my heart was goin' like a donkey-engine workin' a winch, there was a sixty-mile gale blowin' past my ears, and a fog-bank was front of my eyes. And when the sun came out ag'in and it cleared off, the moderator was standin' there shaking my hand and tellin' me what a speech it was. It was a speech that had to be made. They had to be bluffed. But as to knowin' a word of what I said, why, I might jest as well try to tell you what the mermaid said when the feller brought her stockin's for her birthday present.

"The only thing that I can remember about that speech," he resumed, after a pause, and she gazed on him hopefully, "is that your brother Gideon busted into the town house and tried to break up my speech by tellin' 'em I was a lunatic. I ordered the constables to put him out."

"Did they?" she asked, with solicitude.

"No," he replied, rubbing his nose, reflectively. "'Fore the constables got to him, the boys took holt and throwed him out of the window. I reckon he's come to a realizin' sense by this time that the town don't want him for selectman."

He rapped out the ashes and put the pipe on the hearth of the Franklin.

"I'm fair about an enemy, Louada Murilla, and I kind of hate to rub it into Gideon. But now that I'm on this bluff about what happened to-day, I've got to work it to a finish. I'm goin' to sue Gid for obstructin' the ro'd and smashin' Nute's wagon, and then jumpin' out and leavin' me to be run away with. The idea is, there are some fine touches needed in lyin' out of that part of the scrape, and, as the first selectman of Smyrna, I can't afford to take chances and depend on myself, and be showed up. I don't hold any A.B. certificate when it comes to lyin'. So for them fancy touches, I reckon I'll have to break my usual rule and hire a lawyer."

He rose and yawned.

The Skipper and the Skipped

"Is the cat put out, Louada?"

And when she had replied in the affirmative, he said:

"Seein' it has been quite a busy day, let's go to bed."

IX

Mrs. Hiram Look, lately "Widder Snell," appearing as plump, radiant, and roseate as a bride in her honeymoon should appear—her color assisted by the caloric of a cook-stove in June—put her head out of the buttery window and informed the inquiring Cap'n Aaron Sproul that Hiram was out behind the barn.

"Married life seems still to be agreein' with all concerned," suggested Cap'n Sproul, quizzically. "Even that flour on your nose is becomin'."

"Go 'long, you old rat!" tittered Mrs. Look. "Better save all your compliments for your own wife!"

"Oh, I tell her sweeter things than that," replied the Cap'n, serenely. With a grin under his beard, he went on toward the barn.

Smyrna gossips were beginning to comment, with more or less spite, on the sudden friendship between their first selectman and Hiram Look, since Look—once owner of a road circus—had retired from the road, had married his old love, and had settled down on the Snell farm. Considering the fact that the selectman and showman had bristled at each other like game-cocks the first time they met, Smyrna wondered at the sudden effusion of affection that now kept them trotting back and forth on almost daily visits to each other.

Batson Reeves, second selectman of Smyrna, understood better than most of the others. It was on him as a common anvil that the two of them had pounded their mutual spite cool. Hiram, suddenly reappearing with a plug hat and a pet elephant, after twenty years of wandering, had won promptly the hand of Widow Snell, *nee* Amanda Purkis, whose self and whose acres Widower Reeves was just ready to annex. And Hiram had thereby partially satisfied the old boyhood grudge planted deep in his stormy temper when Batson Reeves had broken up the early attachment between Hiram Look and Amanda Purkis. As for First Selectman Sproul, hot in his fight with Reeves for official supremacy, his league with Hiram, after an initial combat to try spurs, was instant and cordial as soon as he had understood a few things about the showman's character and purpose.

"Birds of a feather!" gritted Reeves, in his confidences with his intimates. "An' old turkle-back of a sea-capt'in runnin' things in this town 'fore he's been here two years, jest 'cause he's got cheek enough and thutty thousand dollars —and now comes that old gas-bag with a plug hat on it, braggin' of his own thutty thousand dollars, and they hitch up! Gawd help Smyrna, that's all I say!"

And yet, had all the spiteful eyes in Smyrna peered around the corner of the barn on that serene June forenoon, they must have softened just a bit at sight of the placid peace of it all.

The big doors were rolled back, and "Imogene," the ancient elephant whose fond attachment to Hiram had preserved her from the auction-block, bent her wrinkled front to the soothing sunshine and "weaved" contentedly on her slouchy legs. She was watching her master with the thorough appreciation of one who has understood and loved the "sportin' life."

Hiram was in shirt-sleeves and bareheaded, his stringy hair combed over his bald spot. His long-tailed coat and plug hat hung from a wooden peg on the side of the barn. In front of him was a loose square of burlap, pegged to the ground at one edge, its opposite edge nailed to the barn, and sloping at an angle of forty-five degrees.

As Cap'n Sproul rounded the corner Hiram had just tossed a rooster in the air over the burlap. The bird came down flapping its wings; its legs stuck out stiffly. When it struck the rude net it bounded high, and came down again, and continued its grotesque hornpipe until it finally lost its spring.

"I'm only givin' P.T. Barnum his leg-exercise," said Hiram, recovering the rooster and sticking him under one arm while he shook hands with his caller. "I don't expect to ever match him again in this God-forsaken country, but there's some comfort in keepin' him in trainin'. Pinch them thighs, Cap'n! Ain't they the wickin'?"

"I sh'd hate to try to eat 'em," said the Cap'n, gingerly poking his stubby finger against the rooster's leg.

"Eat 'em!" snapped the showman, raking the horns of his long mustache irritably away from his mouth. "You talk like the rest of these farmers round here that never heard of a hen bein' good for anything except to lay eggs and be et for a Thanksgivin' dinner." He held the rooster a-straddle his arm, his broad hand on its back, and shook him under the Cap'n's nose. "I've earnt more'n a thousand dollars with P.T. — and that's a profit in the hen business that all the condition powders this side of Tophet couldn't fetch."

"A thousand dollars!" echoed Cap'n Sproul, stuffing his pipe. He gazed at P.T. with new interest. "He must have done some fightin' in his day."

"Fight!" cried the showman. He tossed the rooster upon the burlap once more. "Fight! Look at that leg action! That's the best yaller-legged, high-station game-cock that ever pecked his way out of a shell. I've taken all comers 'twixt Hoorah and Hackenny, and he ain't let me down yet. Look at them brad-awls of his!"

"Mebbe all so, but I don't like hens, not for a minit," growled the first selectman, squinting sourly through his tobacco-smoke at the dancing fowl.

Hiram got a saucer from a shelf inside the barn and set it on the ground.

"Eat your chopped liver, P.T.," he commanded; "trainin' is over."

He relighted his stub of cigar and bent proud gaze on the bird.

"No, sir," pursued the Cap'n, "I ain't got no use for a hen unless it's settin', legs up, on a platter, and me with a carvin'-knife."

"Always felt that way?" inquired Hiram.

"Not so much as I have sence I've been tryin' to start my garden this spring. As fur back as the time I was gittin' the seed in, them hens of Widder Sidene Pike, that lives next farm to mine, began their hellishness, with that old wart-legged ostrich of a rooster of her'n to lead 'em. They'd almost peck the seeds out of my hand, and the minit I'd turn my back they was over into that patch, right foot, left foot, kick heel and toe, and swing to pardners—and you couldn't see the sun for dirt. And at every rake that rooster lifts soil enough to fill a stevedore's coal-bucket."

"Why don't you shoot 'em?" advised Hiram, calmly.

"Me—the first s'lectman of this town out poppin' off a widder's hens? That would be a nice soundin' case when it got into court, wouldn't it?"

"Get into court first and sue her," advised the militant Hiram.

"I donno as I've ever said it to you, but I've al'ays said it to close friends," stated the Cap'n, earnestly, "that there are only three things on earth I'm afraid of, and them are: pneumony, bein' struck by lightnin', and havin' a land-shark git the law on me. There ain't us'ly no help for ye."

He sighed and smoked reflectively. Then his face hardened.

"There's grown to be more to it lately than the hen end. Have you heard that sence Bat Reeves got let down by she that was Widder Snell"—he nodded toward the house—"he has been sort of caught on the bounce, as ye might say, by the Widder Pike? Well, bein' her close neighbor, I know it's so. And, furdermore, the widder's told my wife, bein' so tickled over ketchin' him that she couldn't hold it to herself. Now, for the last week, every time that old red-gilled dirt-walloper has led them hens into my garden, I've caught Bat Reeves peekin' around the corner of the widder's house watchin' 'em. If there's any such thing as a man bein' able to talk human language to

89

a rooster, and put sin and Satan into him, Reeves is doin' it. But what's the good of my goin' and lickin' him? It'll mean law. That's what he's lookin' for—and him with that old gandershanked lawyer for a brother! See what they done to you!"

Hiram's eyes grew hard, and he muttered irefully. For cuffing Batson Reeves off the Widow Snell's door-step he had paid a fat fine, assessed for the benefit of the assaulted, along with liberal costs allowed to Squire Alcander Reeves.

"They can't get any of my money that way," pursued the Cap'n. "I'd pay suthin' for the privilege of drawin' and quarterin' him, but a plain lickin' ain't much object. A lickin' does him good."

"And it's so much ready money for that skunk," added the showman. He cocked his head to one side to avoid his cigar smoke, and stared down on P.T. pecking the last scraps of raw liver from the saucer.

"I understand you to say, do I," resumed Hiram, "that he is shooing them hens—or, at least, condonin' their comin' down into your garden ev'ry day?"

"I run full half a mile jest before I came acrost to see you, chasin' 'em out," said the Cap'n, gloomily, "and I'll bet they was back in there before I got to the first bars on my way over here."

P.T., feeling the stimulus of the liver, crooked his neck and crowed spiritedly. Then he scratched the side of his head with one toe, shook himself, and squatted down contentedly in the sun.

"In the show business," said Hiram, "when I found a feller with a game that I could play better 'n him, I was always willin' to play his game." He stuck up his hand with the fingers spread like a fan, and began to check items. "A gun won't do, because it's a widder's hens; a fight won't do, because it's Bat Reeves; law won't do, because he's got old heron-legged Alcander right in his family. Now this thing is gittin' onto your sperits, and I can see it!"

"It is heiferin' me bad," admitted the Cap'n. "It ain't so much the hens—though Gawd knows I hate a hen bad enough—but it's Bat Reeves standin' up there grinnin' and watchin' me play tag-you're-it with Old Scuff-and-kick and them female friends of his. For a man that's dreamed of garden-truck jest as he wants it, and never had veg'tables enough in twenty years of sloshin' round the world on shipboard, it's about the most cussed, aggravatin' thing I ever got against. And there I am! Swear and chase—and northin' comin' of it!"

Hiram clenched his cigar more firmly in his teeth, leaned over carefully, and picked up the recumbent P.T.

He tucked the rooster under his arm and started off.

"Let's go 'crost back lots," he advised. "What people don't see and don't know about won't hurt 'em, and that includes your wife and mine.

"It won't be no kind of a hen-fight, you understand," Hiram chatted as they walked, "'cause that compost-heap scratcher won't last so long as old Brown stayed in heaven. For P.T., here, it will be jest bristle, shuffle, one, two—brad through each eye, and—'Cock-a-doodle-doo!' All over! But it will give you a chance to see some of his leg-work, and a touch or two of his fancy spurrin'—and then you can take old Sculch-scratcher by the legs and hold him up and inform Bat Reeves that he can come and claim property. It's his own game—and we're playin' it! There ain't any chance for law where one rooster comes over into another rooster's yard and gets done up. Moral: Keep roosters in where the lightnin' won't strike 'em."

When they topped Hickory Hill they had a survey of Cap'n Sproul's acres. Here and there on the brown mould of his garden behind the big barn were scattered yellow and gray specks.

"There they be, blast 'em to fury!" growled the Cap'n.

His eyes then wandered farther, as though seeking something familiar, and he clutched the showman's arm as they walked along.

"And there's Bat Reeves's gray hoss hitched in the widder's dooryard."

"Mebbe he'll wait and have fricasseed rooster for dinner," suggested Hiram, grimly. "That's all his rooster'll be good for in fifteen minutes."

"It would be the devil and repeat for us if the widder's rooster should lick—and Bat Reeves standin' and lookin' on," suggested the Cap'n, bodingly.

Hiram stopped short, looked this faltering faint-heart all over from head to heel with withering scorn, and demanded: "Ain't you got sportin' blood enough to know the difference between a high-station game-cock and that old bow-legged Mormon down there scratchin' your garden-seeds?"

"Well," replied the Cap'n, rather surlily, "I ain't to blame for what I don't know about, and I don't know about hens, and I don't want to know. But I do know that he's more'n twice as big as your rooster, and he's had exercise enough in my garden this spring to be more'n twice as strong. All is, don't lay it to me not warnin' you, if you lose your thousand-dollar hen!"

"Don't you wear your voice out tryin' to tell me about my business in the hen-fightin' line," snapped the showman, fondly "huggling" P.T. more closely under his arm. "This is where size don't count. It's skill. There won't be enough to call it a scrap."

They made a detour through the Sproul orchard to avoid possible observation by Louada Murilla, the Cap'n's wife, and by so doing showed themselves plainly to any one who might be looking that way from the widow's premises. This was a part of the showman's plan. He hoped to attract Reeves's attention. He did. They saw him peering under his palm from the shed door, evidently suspecting that this combination of his two chief foes meant something sinister. He came out of the shed and walked down toward the fence when he saw them headed for the garden.

"Watchin' out for evidence in a law case, probably," growled Cap'n Sproul, the fear of onshore artfulness ever with him. "He'd ruther law it any time than have a fair fight, man to man, and that's the kind of a critter I hate."

"The widder's lookin' out of the kitchen winder," Hiram announced, "and I'm encouraged to think that mebbe he'll want to shine a little as her protector, and will come over into the garden to save her hen. Then will be your time. He'll be trespassin', and I'll be your witness. Go ahead and baste the stuffin' out of him."

He squatted down at the edge of the garden-patch, holding the impatient P.T. between his hands.

"Usually in a reg'lar match I scruffle his feathers and blow in his eye, Cap'n, but I won't have to do it this time. It's too easy a proposition. I'm jest tellin' you about it so that if you ever git interested in fightin' hens after this, you'll be thankful to me for a pointer or two."

"I won't begin to take lessons yet a while," the Cap'n grunted. "It ain't in my line."

Hiram tossed his feathered gladiator out upon the garden mould.

"S-s-s-s-! Eat him up, boy!" he commanded.

P.T. had his eye on the foe, but, with the true instinct of sporting blood, he would take no unfair advantage by stealthy advance on the preoccupied scratcher. He straddled, shook out his glossy ruff, and crowed shrilly.

The other rooster straightened up from his agricultural labors, and stared at this lone intruder on his family privacy. He was a tall, rakish-looking fowl, whose erect carriage and lack of tail-feathers made him look like a spindle-shanked urchin as he towered there among the busy hens.

In order that there might be no mistake as to his belligerent intentions, P.T. crowed again.

The other replied with a sort of croupy hoarseness.

"Sounds like he was full to the neck with your garden-seeds," commented Hiram. "Well, he won't ever eat no more, and that's something to be thankful for."

The game-cock, apparently having understood the word to come on, tiptoed briskly across the garden. The other waited his approach, craning his long neck and twisting his head from side to side.

Reeves was now at the fence.

"I'll bet ye ten dollars," shouted Hiram, "that down goes your hen the first shuffle."

"You will, hey?" bawled Reeves, sarcastically. "Say, you didn't bring them three shells and rubber pea that you used to make your livin' with, did ye?"

The old showman gasped, and his face grew purple. "I licked him twenty years ago for startin' that lie about me," he said, bending blazing glance on the Cap'n. "Damn the expense! I'm goin' over there and kill him!"

"Wait till your rooster kills his, and then take the remains and bat his brains out with 'em," advised the Cap'n, swelling with equal wrath. "Look! He's gettin' at him!"

P.T. put his head close to the ground, his ring of neck-feathers glistening in the sun, then darted forward, rising in air as he did so. The other rooster, who had been awaiting his approach, stiffly erect, ducked to one side, and the game-cock went hurtling past.

"Like rooster, like master!" Hiram yelled, savagely. "He's a coward. Why don't he run and git your brother, Alcander, to put P.T. under bonds to keep the peace? Yah-h-h-h! You're all cowards."

The game-cock, accustomed to meet the bravery of true champions of the pit, stood for a little while and stared at this shifty foe. He must have decided that he was dealing with a poltroon with whom science and prudence were not needed. He stuck out his neck and ran at Long-legs, evidently expecting that Long-legs would turn and flee in a panic. Long-legs jumped to let him pass under, and came down on the unwary P.T. with the crushing force of his double bulk. The splay feet flattened the game-cock to the ground, and, while he lay there helpless, this victor-by-a-fluke began to peck and tear at his head and comb in a most brutal and unsportsmanlike manner.

With a hoarse howl of rage and concern, Hiram rushed across the garden, the dirt flying behind him. The hens squawked and fled, and the conqueror, giving one startled look at the approaching vengeance, abandoned his victim, and closed the line of retreat over the fence.

"He didn't git at his eyes," shouted Hiram, grabbing up his champion from the dirt, "but"—making hasty survey of the bleeding head—"but the jeebingoed cannibal has et one gill and pretty near pecked his comb off. It wa'n't square! It wa'n't square!" he bellowed, advancing toward the fence where Reeves was leaning. "Ye tried to kill a thousand-dollar bird by a skin-game, and I'll have it out of your hide."

Reeves pulled a pole out of the fence.

"Don't ye come across here," he gritted. "I'll brain ye! It was your own rooster-fight. You put it up. You got licked. What's the matter with you?" A grin of pure satisfaction curled under his beard.

"You never heard of true sport. You don't know what it means. He stood on him and started to eat him. All he thinks of is eatin' up something. It wa'n't fair." Hiram caressed the bleeding head of P.T. with quivering hand.

"Fair!" sneered Reeves. "You're talkin' as though this was a prize-fight for the championship of the world! My—I mean, Mis' Pike's rooster licked, didn't he? Well, when a rooster's licked, he's licked, and there ain't nothin' more to it."

"That's your idee of sport, is it?" demanded Hiram, stooping to wipe his bloody hand on the grass.

"It's my idee of a rooster-fight," retorted Reeves. In his triumph he was not unwilling to banter repartee with the hateful Hiram. "You fellers with what you call sportin' blood"—he sneered the words—"come along and think nobody else can't do anything right but you. You fetch along cat-meat with feathers on it"—he pointed at the vanquished P.T.—"and expect it to stand any show with a real fighter." Now he pointed to the Widow Pike's rooster sauntering away with his harem about him. "He ain't rid' around with a circus nor followed the sportin' life, and he's al'ays lived in the country and minded his own business, but he's good for a whole crateful of your sportin' blooders—and so long as he licks, it don't make no difference how he does it."

The personal reference in this little speech was too plain for Hiram to disregard.

His hard eyes narrowed, and hatred of this insolent countryman blazed there. The countryman glared back with just as fierce bitterness.

"Mebbe you've got money to back your opinion of Widder Pike's hen there?" suggested the showman. "Money's the only thing that seems to interest you, and you don't seem to care how you make it."

Reeves glanced from the maimed P.T., gasping on Hiram's arm, to the victorious champion who had defeated this redoubtable bird so easily. His Yankee shrewdness told him that the showman had undoubtedly produced his best for this conflict; his Yankee cupidity hinted that by taking advantage of Hiram's present flustered state of mind he might turn a dollar. He glanced from Hiram to Cap'n Sproul, standing at one side, and said with careless superiority:

"Make your talk!"

"I've got five hundred that says I've got the best hen."

"There ain't goin' to be no foolishness about rules and sport, and hitchin' and hawin', is there? It's jest hen that counts!"

"Jest hen!" Hiram set his teeth hard.

"Five hundred it is," agreed Reeves. "But I need a fortni't to collect in some that's due me. Farmin' ain't such ready-money as the circus bus'ness."

"Take your fortni't! And we'll settle place later. And that's all, 'cause it makes me sick to stand anywhere within ten feet of you."

Hiram strode away across the fields, his wounded gladiator on his arm.

And, as it was near dinner-time, Cap'n Sproul trudged into his own house, his mien thoughtful and his air subdued.

On his next visit to Hiram, the Cap'n didn't know which was the most preoccupied—the showman sitting in the barn door at Imogene's feet, or the battered P.T. propped disconsolately on one leg. Both were gazing at the ground with far-away stare, and Hiram was not much more conversational than the rooster.

The next day Hiram drove into the Sproul dooryard and called out the Cap'n, refusing to get out of his wagon.

"I shall be away a few days—mebbe more, mebbe less. I leave time and place to you." And he slashed at his horse and drove away.

X

It was certainly a queer place that Cap'n Sproul decided upon after several days of rumination. His own abstraction during that time, and the unexplained absence of Hiram, the bridegroom of a month, an absence that was prolonged into a week, caused secret tears and apprehensive imaginings in both households.

Hiram came back, mysterious as the Sphinx.

Cap'n Sproul arranged for a secret meeting of the principals behind his barn, and announced his decision as to place.

"The poor-farm!" both snorted in unison. "What—"

"Hold right on!" interrupted the Cap'n, holding up his broad palms; "it can't be in *his* barn on account of his wife; it can't be in *my* barn on account of my wife. Both of 'em are all wrought up and suspectin' somethin'. Some old pick-ed nose in this place is bound to see us if we try to sneak away into the woods. Jim Wixon, the poor-farm keeper, holds his job through me. He's square, straight, and minds his own business. I can depend on him. He'll hold the stakes. There ain't another man in town we can trust. There ain't a place as safe as the poor-farm barn. Folks don't go hangin' round a poor-farm unless they have to. It's for there the ev'nin' before the Fourth. Agree, or count me out. The first selectman of this town can't afford to take too many chances, aidin' and abettin' a hen-fight."

Therefore there was nothing else for it. The principals accepted sullenly, and went their ways.

The taciturnity of Hiram Look was such during the few days before the meeting that Cap'n Sproul regretfully concluded to keep to his own hearthstone. Hiram seemed to be nursing a secret. The Cap'n felt hurt, and admitted as much to himself in his musings.

He went alone to the rendezvous at early dusk. Keeper Wixon, of the poor-farm, had the big floor of the barn nicely swept, had hung lanterns about on the wooden harness-pegs, and was in a state of great excitement and impatience.

Second Selectman Reeves came first, lugging his crate from his beach-wagon. The crate held the Widow Pike's rooster. His nomination had his head up between the slats, and was crowing regularly and raucously.

"Choke that dam fog-horn off!" commanded the Cap'n. "What are ye tryin' to do, advertise this sociable?"

"You talk like I was doin' that crowin' myself," returned Reeves, sulkily. "And nobody ain't goin' to squat his wizen and git him out of breath. Hands off, and a fair show!"

Hiram Look was no laggard at the meeting. He rumbled into the yard on the box of one of his animal cages, pulled out a huge bag containing something that kicked and wriggled, and deposited his burden on the barn floor.

"Now," said he, brusquely, "business before pleasure! You've got the stakes, eh, Wixon?"

"In my wallet here—a thousand dollars," replied the keeper, a little catch in his voice at thought of the fortune next his anxious heart.

"And the best hen takes the money; no flummery, no filigree!" put in Reeves.

Hiram was kneeling beside his agitated bag, and was picking at the knots in its fastening. "This will be a hen-fight served up Smyrna style," he said, grimly. "And, as near as I can find out, that style is mostly—scrambled!"

"I've got a favor to ask," stammered Wixon, hesitatingly. "It don't mean much to you, but it means a good deal to others. Bein' penned up on a poor-farm, with nothin' except three meals a day to take up your mind, is pretty tough on them as have seen better days. I'll leave it to Cap'n Sproul, here, if I ain't tried to put a little kindness and human feelin' into runnin' this place, and—"

Hiram was untying the last knot. "Spit out what you're drivin' at," he cried bluntly; "this ain't no time for sideshow barkin'. The big show is about to begin."

"I want to invite in the boys," blurted Wixon. And when they blinked at him amazedly, he said:

"The five old fellers that's here, I mean. They're safe and mum, and they're jest dyin' for a little entertainment, and it's only kindness to them that's unfortunate, if you—"

"What do you think this is, a livin'-picture show got up to amuse a set of droolin' old paupers?" demanded Hiram, with heat.

"Well, as it is, they suspect suthin'," persisted Wixon. "All they have to do to pass time is to suspect and projick on what's goin' on and what's goin' to happen. If you'll let me bring 'em, I can shet their mouths. If they don't come in, they're goin' to suspect suthin' worse than what it is—and that's only human natur'—and not to blame for it."

The two selectmen protested, official alarm in their faces, but Hiram suddenly took the keeper's side, after the manner of his impetuous nature, and after he had shrewdly noted that Reeves seemed to be most alarmed.

"I'm the challenger," he roared. "I've got something to say. Bring 'em, Wixon. Let 'em have a taste of fun. I may wind up on the poor-farm myself. Bring 'em in. There's prob'ly more sportin' blood in the paupers of this town than in the citizens. Bring 'em in, and let's have talkin' done with."

In a suspiciously short time Wixon led in his charges—five hobbling old men, all chewing tobacco and looking wondrously interested.

"There!" said Hiram, an appreciative glint in his eyes. "Nothin' like havin' an audience, even if they did come in on passes. I've never given a show before empty benches yet. And now, gents"—the old spirit of the "barker" entered into him—"you are about to behold a moral and elevatin' exhibition of the wonders of natur'. I have explored the jungles of Palermo, the hills of Peru Corners, the valleys of North Belgrade, never mindin' time and expense, and I've got something that beats the wild boy Tom and his little sister Mary. Without takin' more of your valuable time, I will now present to your attention"—he tore open the bag—"Cap'n Kidd, the Terror of the Mountains."

The wagging jaws of the old paupers stopped as if petrified. Keeper Wixon peered under his hand and retreated a few paces. Even doughty Cap'n Sproul, accustomed to the marvels of land and sea, snapped his eyes. As for Reeves, he gasped "Great gorlemity!" under his breath, and sat down on the edge of his crate, as though his legs had given out.

The creature that rose solemnly up from the billowing folds of the bagging had a head as smooth and round as a door-knob, dangling, purple wattles under its bill, and breast of a sanguinary red, picked clean of feathers. There were not many feathers on the fowl, anyway. Its tail was merely a spreading of quills like spikes. It was propped on legs like stilts, and when it stretched to crow it stood up as tall as a yard-stick.

"Let out your old doostrabulus, there!" Hiram commanded.

"That ain't no hen," wailed his adversary.

"It's got two legs, a bill, and a place for tail-feathers, and that's near enough to a hen for fightin' purposes in this town—accordin' to what I've seen of the sport here," insisted the showman. "The principal hen-fightin' science in Smyrna seems to be to stand on t' other hen and peck him to pieces! Well, Reeves, Cap'n Kidd there ain't got so much pedigree as some I've owned, but as a stander and pecker I'm thinkin' he'll give a good, fair account of himself."

"It's a gum-game," protested Reeves, agitatedly, "and I ain't goin' to fight no ostrich nor hen-hawk."

"Then I'll take the stakes without further wear or tear," said Hiram. "Am I right, boys?" A unanimous chorus indorsed him. "And this here is something that I reckon ye won't go to law about," the showman went on, ominously, "even if you have got a lawyer in the family. You ketch, don't you?"

The unhappy second selectman realized his situation, sighed, and pried a slat off the crate. His nomination was more sanguine than he. The rooster hopped upon the crate, crowed, and stalked out onto the barn floor with a confidence that made Reeves perk up courage a bit.

Cap'n Kidd showed abstraction rather than zeal. He was busily engaged in squinting along his warty legs, and at last detected two or three objects that were annoying him. He picked them off leisurely. Then he ran his stiff and scratchy wing down his leg, yawned, and seemed bored.

When the other rooster ran across and pecked him viciously on his red expanse of breast, he cocked his head sideways and looked down wonderingly on this rude assailant. Blood trickled from the wound, and Reeves giggled nervously. Cap'n Sproul muttered something and looked apprehensive, but Hiram, his eyes hard and his lips set, crouched at the side of the floor, and seemed to be waiting confidently.

Widow Pike's favorite stepped back, rapped his bill on the floor several times, and then ran at his foe once more. A second trail of blood followed his blow. This time the unknown ducked his knobby head at the attacker. It looked like a blow with a slung-shot. But it missed, and Reeves tittered again.

"Fly up and peck his eye out, Pete!" he called, cheerily.

It is not likely that Peter understood this adjuration, notwithstanding Cap'n Sproul's gloomy convictions on that score in the past. But, apparently having tested the courage of this enemy, he changed his tactics, leaped, and flew at Cap'n Kidd with spurring feet.

Then it happened!

It happened almost before the little group of spectators could gasp.

Cap'n Kidd threw himself back on the bristling spines of his tail, both claws off the floor. Peter's spurring feet met only empty air, and he fell on the foe.

Foe's splay claws grabbed him around the neck and clutched him like a vise, shutting off his last, startled squawk. Then Cap'n Kidd darted forward that knobby head with its ugly beak, and tore off Peter's caput with one mighty wrench.

"'Tain't fair! It's jest as I said it was! 'Tain't square!" screamed Reeves.

But Hiram strode forward, snapping authoritative fingers under Wixon's nose. "Hand me that money!" he gritted, and Wixon, his eyes on the unhappy bird writhing in Cap'n Kidd's wicked grasp, made no demur. The showman took it, even as the maddened Reeves was clutching for the packet, tucked it into his breast pocket, and drove the second selectman back with a mighty thrust of his arm. The selectman stumbled over the combatants and sat down with a shock that clicked his teeth. Cap'n Kidd fled from under, and flew to a high beam.

"He ain't a hen!" squalled Reeves.

At that moment the barn door was opened from the outside, and through this exit Cap'n Kidd flapped with hoarse cries, whether of triumph or fright no one could say.

The lanterns' light shone on Widow Sidenia Pike, her face white from the scare "Cap'n Kidd's" rush past her head had given her, but with determination written large in her features.

She gazed long at Reeves, sitting on the floor beside the defunct rooster. She pointed an accusatory finger at it.

"Mr. Reeves," she said, "you've been lyin' to me two weeks, tryin' to buy that rooster that I wouldn't sell no more'n I'd sell my first husband's gravestun'. And when you couldn't git it by lyin', you stole it off'm the roost to-night. And to make sure there won't be any more lies, I've followed you right here to find out the truth. Now what does this mean?"

There was a soulful pause.

"Lie in small things, lie in big!" she snapped. "I reckon I've found ye out for a missabul thing!"

Hiram, standing back in the shadows, nudged Cap'n Sproul beside him, and wagged his head toward the open door. They went out on tiptoe.

"If he wants to lie some more, our bein' round might embarrass him," whispered Hiram. "I never like to embarrass a man when he's down—and—and her eyes was so much on Reeves and the rooster I don't believe she noticed us. And what she don't know won't hurt her none. But"—he yawned—"I shouldn't be a mite surprised if another one of Bat Reeves's engagements was busted in this town. He don't seem to have no luck at all in marryin' farms with the wimmen throwed in." The Cap'n didn't appear interested in Reeves's troubles. His eyes were searching the dim heavens.

"What do you call that thing you brought in the bag?" he demanded.

"Blamed if I know!" confessed Hiram, climbing upon his chariot. "And I'm pretty well up on freaks, too, as a circus man ought to be. I jest went out huntin' for suthin' to fit in with the sportin' blood as I found it in this place—and I reckon I got it! Mebbe 'twas a cassowary, mebbe 'twas a dodo—the man himself didn't know—said even the hen that hatched it didn't seem to know. 'Pologized to me for asking me two dollars for it, and I gave him five. I hope it will go back where it come from. It hurt my eyes to look at it. But it was a good bargain!" He patted his breast pocket.

"Come over to-morrow," he called to the Cap'n as he drove away. "I sha'n't have so much on my mind, and I'll be a little more sociable! Listen to that bagpipe selection!"

Behind them they heard the whining drone of a man's pleading voice and a woman's shrill, insistent tones, a monotony of sound flowing on—and on—and on!

XI

The president of the "Smyrna Agricultural Fair and Gents' Driving Association" had been carrying something on his mind throughout the meeting of the trustees of the society—the last meeting before the date advertised for the fair. And now, not without a bit of apprehensiveness, he let it out.

"I've invited the Honer'ble J. Percival Bickford to act as the starter and one of the judges of the races," he announced.

Trustee Silas Wallace, superintendent of horses, had put on his hat. Now he took it off again.

"What!" he almost squalled.

"You see," explained the president, with eager conciliatoriness, "we've only got to scratch his back just a little to have him—"

"Why, 'Kittle-belly' Bickford don't know no more about hoss-trottin' than a goose knows about the hard-shell Baptist doctrine," raved Wallace, his little eyes popping like marbles.

"I don't like to hear a man that's done so much for his native town called by any such names," retorted the president, ready to show temper himself, to hide his embarrassment. "He's come back here and—"

Trustee Wallace now stood up and cracked his bony knuckles on the table, his weazened face puckered with angry ridges.

"I don't need to have a printed catalogue of what Jabe Bickford has done for this town. And I don't need to be told what he's done it for. He's come back from out West, where he stole more money than he knew what to do with, and—"

"I protest!" cried President Thurlow Kitchen. "When you say that the Honer'ble J. Percival Bickford has stolen—"

"Well, promoted gold-mines, then! It's only more words to say the same thing. And he's back here spendin' his loose change for daily doses of hair-oil talk fetched to him by the beggin' old suckers of this place."

"I may be a beggin' old sucker," flared the president, "but I've had enterprise enough and interest in this fair enough to get Mr. Bickford to promise us a present of a new exhibition hall, and it's only right to extend some courtesy to him in return."

"It was all right to make him president of the lib'ry association when he built the lib'ry, make him a deacon when he gave the organ for the meetin'-house, give him a banquet and nineteen speeches tellin' him he was the biggest man on earth when he put the stone watering-trough in—all that was all right for them that thought it was all right. But when you let 'Kittle-belly' Bickford—"

"Don't you call him that," roared President Kitchen, thumping the table.

"Duke, then! Dammit, crown him lord of all! But when you let him hang that pod of his out over the rail of that judges' stand and bust up a hoss-trot programmy that I've been three months gettin' entries for—and all jest so he can show off a white vest and a plug hat and a new gold stop-watch and have the band play 'Hail to the Chief'—I don't stand for it—no, sir!"

"The trouble is with you," retorted the president with spirit, "you've razoo-ed and hoss-jockeyed so long you've got the idea that all there is to a fair is a plug of chaw-tobacco, a bag of peanuts, and a posse of nose-whistlin' old pelters skatin' round a half-mile track."

"And you and 'Kit'—you and Duke Jabe, leave you alone to run a fair—wouldn't have nothin' but his new exhibition hall filled with croshayed tidies and hooked rugs."

"Well, I move," broke in Trustee Dunham, "that we git som'ers. I'm personally in favor of pleasin' Honer'ble Bickford and takin' the exhibition hall."

"That's right! That's business!" came decisive chorus from the other three trustees. "Let's take the hall."

Wallace doubled his gaunt form, propped himself on the table by his skinny arms, and stared from face to face in disgust unutterable.

"Take it?" he sneered. "Why, you'll take anything! You're takin' up the air in this room, like pumpin' up a sulky tire, and ain't lettin' it out again! Good-day! I'm goin' out where I can get a full breath."

He whirled on them at the door.

"But you hark to what I'm predictin' to you! If you don't wish the devil had ye before you're done with that old balloon with a plug hat on it in your judges' stand, then I'll trot an exhibition half mile on my hands and knees against Star Pointer for a bag of oats. And I'm speakin' for all the hossmen in this county."

When this uncomfortable Jeremiah had departed, leaving in his wake a trailing of oaths and a bouquet of stable aroma, the trustees showed relief, even if enthusiasm was notably absent.

"It's going to raise the tone of the fair, having him in the stand—there ain't any getting round that," said the president. "The notion seemed to strike him mighty favorable. 'It's an idea!' said he to me. 'Yes, a real idea. I will have other prominent gentlemen to serve with me, and we will be announced as paytrons of the races. That will sound well, I think.' And he asked me what two men in town was best fixed financially, and, of course, I told him Cap'n Aaron Sproul, our first selectman, and Hiram Look. He said he hadn't been in town long enough to get real well acquainted with either of them yet, but hoped they were gentlemen. I told him they were. I reckon that being skipper of a ship and ownin' a circus stands as high as the gold-mine business."

"Well," said one of the trustees, with some venom, "Jabe Bickford is doin' a good deal for this town, one way and another, but he wants to remember that his gran'ther had to call on us for town aid, and that there wa'n't nary ever another Bickford that lived in this town or went out of it, except Jabe, that could get trusted for a barrel of flour. Puttin' on his airs out West is all right, but puttin' 'em on here to home, among us that knows him and all his breed, is makin' some of the old residents kind of sick. Si Wallace hadn't ought to call him by that name he did, but Si is talkin' the way a good many feel."

"If an angel from heaven should descend on this town with the gift of abidin' grace," said President Kitchen, sarcastically, "a lot of folks here would get behind his back and make faces at him."

"Prob'ly would," returned the trustee, imperturbably, "if said angel wore a plug hat and kid gloves from mornin' till night, said 'Me good man' to old codgers who knowed him when he had stone-bruises on his heels as big as pigeon's aigs, and otherwise acted as though he was cream and every one else was buttermilk."

"Well, when some of the rest of you have done as much for this town as Honer'ble Bickford," broke in the president, testily, "you can have the right to criticise. As it is, I can't see anything but jealousy in it. And I've heard enough of it. Now, to make this thing all pleasant and agreeable to the Honer'ble Bickford, we've got to have Cap'n Sproul and Hiram Look act as judges with him. 'Tis a vote! Now, who will see Cap'n Sproul and—"

"Considerin' what has happened to those who have in times past tried to notify Cap'n Sproul of honors tendered to him in this town, you'd better pick out some one who knows how to use the wireless telegraph," suggested one of the trustees.

"There won't be any trouble in gettin' Hiram Look to act," said the president. "He's just enough of a circus feller to like to stand up before the crowd and show authority. Well, then"—the president's wits were sharpened by his anxiety over the proposed exhibition hall—"let Mr. Look arrange it with Cap'n Sproul. They're suckin' cider through the same straw these days."

And this suggestion was so eminently good that the meeting adjourned in excellent humor that made light of all the gloomy prognostications of Trustee Wallace.

As though good-fortune were in sooth ruling the affairs of the Smyrna A.F. & G.D.A., Hiram Look came driving past as the trustees came out of the tavern, their meeting-place.

He stroked his long mustache and listened. At first his silk hat stuck up rigidly, but soon it began to nod gratified assent.

"I don't know much about hoss-trottin' rules, but a man that's been in the show business for thirty years has got enough sportin' blood in him for the job, I reckon. Bickford and Sproul, hey? Why, yes! I'll hunt up the Cap, and take him over to Bickford's, and we'll settle preliminaries, or whatever the hoss-talk is for gettin' together. I'd rather referee a prize-fight, but you're too dead up this way for real sport to take well. Nothing been said to Sproul? All right! I'll fix him."

Cap'n Sproul was in his garden, surveying the growing "sass" with much content of spirit. He cheerfully accepted Hiram's invitation to take a ride, destination not mentioned, and they jogged away toward "Bickburn Towers," as the Honorable J. Percival had named the remodelled farm-house of his ancestors.

Hiram, whose gift was language, impetuous in flow and convincing in argument, whether as barker or friend, conveyed the message of the trustees to Cap'n Sproul. But the first selectman of Smyrna did not display enthusiasm. He scowled at the buggy dasher and was silent.

"Men that have been out and about, like you and I have been, need something once in a while to break the monotony of country life," concluded Hiram, slashing his whip at the wayside alders.

"You and me and him," observed the Cap'n, with sullen prod of his thumb in direction of the "gingerbready" tower of the Bickford place rising over the ridge, "marooned in that judges' stand like penguins on a ledge—we'll be li'ble to break the monotony. Oh yes! There ain't no doubt about that."

"Why, there'll be northin' to it!" blustered Hiram, encouragingly. "I'll swear 'em into line, you holler 'Go!' and the Honer'ble Bickford will finger that new gold stop-watch of his and see how fast they do it. Northin' to it, I say!"

"This is the blastedest town a man ever settled down in to spend his last days in peace and quietness," growled the Cap'n. "There's a set of men here that seem to be perfickly happy so long as they're rollin' up a gob of trouble, sloppin' a little sweet-oil and molasses on the outside and foolin' some one into swallerin' it. I tell ye, Look, I've lived here a little longer than you have, and when you see a man comin' to offer you what they call an honor, kick him on general principles, and kick him hard."

"Doctors ought to be willin' to take their own medicine," retorted Hiram, grimly. "Here you be, first selec'man and—"

"They caught me when I wa'n't lookin'—not bein' used to the ways of land-piruts," replied the Cap'n, gloomily. "I was tryin' to warn you as one that's been ahead and knows."

"Why, that's just what I like about this town," blurted Hiram, undismayed. "When I came home to Palermo a year ago or so, after all my wanderin's, they wouldn't elect me so much as hog-reeve—seemed to be down on me all 'round. But here—heard what they did last night?" There was pride in his tones. "They elected me foreman of the Smyrna Ancient and Honer'ble Firemen's Association."

"And you let 'em hornswoggle you into takin' it?" demanded the Cap'n.

"Leather buckets, piazzy hat, speakin'-trumpet, bed-wrench, and puckerin'-string bag are in my front hall this minit," said Hiram, cheerily, "and the wife is gittin' the stuff together for the feed and blow-out next week. I'm goin' to do it up brown!"

The Cap'n opened his mouth as though to enter upon revelations. But he shut it without a word.

"It ain't no use," he reflected, his mind bitter with the memories of his own occupancy of that office. "It's like the smallpox and the measles; you've got to have a run of 'em yourself before you're safe from ketchin' 'em."

The Honorable J. Percival Bickford, rotund and suave with the mushiness of the near-gentleman, met them graciously in the hall, having waited for the servant to announce them.

Hiram did most of the talking, puffing at one of the host's long cigars. Cap'n Sproul sat on the edge of a spider-legged chair, great unhappiness on his countenance. Mr. Bickford was both charmed and delighted, so he said, by their acceptance, and made it known that he had suggested them, in his anxiety to have only gentlemen of standing associated with him.

"As the landed proprietors of the town, as you might say," he observed, "it becomes us as due our position to remove ourselves a little from the herd. In the judges' stand we can, as you might say, be patrons of the sports of the day, without loss of dignity. I believe — and this is also my suggestion — that the trustees are to provide an open barouche, and we will be escorted from the gate to the stand by a band of music. That will be nice. And when it is over we will award the prizes, as I believe they call it — "

"Announce winners of heats and division of purses," corrected Hiram, out of his greater knowledge of sporting affairs. "I'll do that through a megaphone. When I barked in front of my show you could hear me a mile."

"It will all be very nice," said Mr. Bickford, daintily flecking cigar ash from his glorious white waistcoat. "Er—by the way—I see that you customarily wear a silk hat, Mr. Look."

"It needs a plug hat, a lemon, and a hunk of glass to run a circus," said the ex-showman.

"Yes, men may say what they like, Mr. Look, the people expect certain things in the way of garb from those whom they honor with position. Er—do you wear a silk hat officially, Captain Sproul, as selectman?"

"Not by a—never had one of the things on!" replied the Cap'n, moderating his first indignant outburst.

"I'm going to do you a bit of neighborly kindness," said Mr. Bickford, blandly. "James," he called to the servant, "bring the brown bandbox in the hall closet. It's one of my hats," he explained. "I have several. You may wear it in the stand, with my compliments, Captain Sproul. Then we'll be three of a kind, eh? Ha, ha!"

The Cap'n licked his lips as though fever burned there, and worked his Adam's apple vigorously. Probably if he had been in the accustomed freedom of outdoors he would have sworn soulfully and smashed the bandbox over the Honorable J. Percival's bald head. Now, in the stilted confines of that ornate parlor, he nursed the bandbox on his knees, as part of the rest of the spider-legged and frail surroundings. When they retired to their team he carried the bandbox held gingerly out in front of him, tiptoeing across the polished floor.

"What? Me wear that bird-cage?" he roared, when they were out of hearing. "Not by the great jeehookibus!"

"Yes, you will," returned Hiram, with the calm insistence of a friend. "You ain't tryin' to make out that what I do ain't all right and proper, are you?"

Cap'n Sproul checked an apparent impulse to toss the bandbox into the roadside bushes, and after a moment tucked the thing under the seat to have it out of the way of his tempted hands. Then he wrenched off a huge chew of tobacco whose rumination might check his impulse toward tempestuous language.

He tried the hat on that night in the presence of his admiring wife, gritting curses under his breath, his skin prickling with resentment. He swore then that he would never wear it. But on the day of the race he carried it in its box to the selectman's office, at which common meeting-place the three judges were to be taken up by the official barouche of the Smyrna Fair Association.

Under the commanding eye of Hiram Look he put on the head-gear when the barouche was announced at the door, and went forth into the glare of publicity with a furtive sense of shame that flushed his cheek. By splitting the top of his hack, Ferd Parrott, landlord of Smyrna tavern, had produced a vehicle that somewhat resembled half a watermelon. Ferd drove, adorned also with a plug hat from the stock of the Honorable Percival.

Just inside the gate of the fair-grounds waited the Smyrna "Silver Cornet Band." It struck up "Hail to the Chief," to the violent alarm of the hack-horses.

"We're goin' to get run away with sure's you're above hatches!" bellowed Cap'n Sproul, standing up and making ready to leap over the edge of the watermelon. But Hiram Look restrained him, and the band, its trombones splitting the atmosphere, led away with a merry march.

When they had circled the track, from the three-quarters pole to the stand, and the crowd broke into plaudits, Cap'n Sproul felt a bit more comfortable, and dared to straighten his neck and lift his head-gear further into the sunshine.

He even forgot the hateful presence of his seat-mate, a huge dog that Mr. Bickford had invited into the fourth place in the carriage.

"A very valuable animal, gentlemen," he said. "Intelligent as a man, and my constant companion. To-day is the day of two of man's best friends—the horse and the dog—and Hector will be in his element."

But Hector, wagging and slavering amiably about in the narrow confines of the little stand to which they climbed, snapped the Cap'n's leash of self-control ere five minutes passed.

"Say, Mr. Bickford," he growled, after one or two efforts to crowd past the ubiquitous canine and get to the rail, "either me or your dog is in the way here."

"Charge, Hector!" commanded Mr. Bickford, taking one eye from the cheering multitude. The dog "clumped" down reluctantly.

"We might just as well get to an understandin'," said the Cap'n, not yet placated. "I ain't used to a dog underfoot, I don't like a dog, and I won't associate with a dog. Next thing I know I'll be makin' a misstep onto him, and he'll have a hunk out of me."

"Why, my dear captain," oozed Hector's proprietor, "that dog is as intelligent as a man, as mild as a kitten, and a very—"

"Don't care if he's writ a dictionary and nussed infants," cried the Cap'n, slatting out his arm defiantly; "it's him or me, here; take your choice!"

"I—I think your dog would be all right if you let him stay down-stairs under the stand," ventured President Kitchen, diplomatically.

"He's a valuable animal," demurred Mr. Bickford, "and—" He caught the flaming eye of the Cap'n, and added: "But if you'll have a man sit with him he may go.

"Now we'll settle down for a real nice afternoon," he went on, conciliatingly. "Let's see: This here is the cord that I pull to signal the horses to start, is it?"

"No, no!" expostulated President Kitchen, "you pull that bell-cord to call them back if the field isn't bunched all right at the wire when they score down for the word. If all the horses are in position and are all leveled, you shout 'Go!' and start your watch."

"Precisely," said Mr. Bickford.

"It's the custom," went on the president, solicitous for the success of his strange assortment of judges, yet with heart almost failing him, "for each judge to have certain horses that he watches during the mile for breaks or fouls. Then he places them as they come under the wire. That is so one man won't have too much on his mind."

"Very, very nice!" murmured the Honorable J. Percival. "We are here to enjoy the beautiful day and the music and the happy throngs, and we don't want to be too much taken up with our duties." He pushed himself well out into view over the rail, held his new gold watch in one gloved hand, and tapped time to the band with the other.

XII

A narrow flight of rickety, dusty stairs conducted one from the dim, lower region of the little stand through an opening in the floor of the judge's aerie. There was a drop-door over the opening, held up by a hasp.

Now came a thumping of resolute feet on the stairs; a head projected just above the edge of the opening, and stopped there.

"President, trustees, and judges!" hailed a squeaky voice.

Cap'n Sproul recognized the speaker with an uncontrollable snort of disgust.

It was Marengo Todd, most obnoxious of all that hateful crowd of the Cap'n's "wife's relations"—the man who had misused the Cap'n's honeymoon guilelessness in order to borrow money and sell him spavined horses.

Marengo surveyed them gloomily from under a driving-cap visor huge as a sugar-scoop. He flourished at them a grimy sheet of paper.

"Mister President, trustees, and judges, I've got here a dockyment signed by seventeen—"

President Kitchen knew that Marengo Todd had been running his bow-legs off all the forenoon securing signatures to a petition of protest that had been inspired by Trustee Silas Wallace. The president pushed away the hand that brandished the paper.

"What do you take this for—an afternoon readin'-circle?" he demanded. "If you're goin' to start your hoss in this thirty-four class you want to get harnessed. We're here to trot hosses, not to peruse dockyments."

"This 'ere ain't no pome on spring," yelled Marengo, banging the dust out of the floor with his whip-butt and courageously coming up one step on the stairs. "It's a protest, signed by seventeen drivers, and says if you start these events with them three old sofy pillers, there, stuffed into plug hats, for judges, we'll take this thing clear up to the Nayshunal 'Sociation and show up this fair management. There, chaw on that!"

"Why, bless my soul!" chirruped the Honorable Bickford, "this man seems very much excited. You'll have to run away, my good man! We're very busy up here, and have no time to subscribe to any papers."

Mr. Bickford evidently believed that this was one of the daily "touches" to which he had become accustomed.

"Don't ye talk to me like I was one of your salaried spittoon-cleaners," squealed Marengo, emboldened by the hoarse and encouraging whispers of Trustee Wallace in the dim depths below. The name that much repetition by Wallace had made familiar slipped out before he had time for second thought. "I knowed ye, Kittle-belly Bickford, when ye wore patches on your pants bigger'n dinner-plates and — "

President Kitchen let loose the hasp that held up the drop-door and fairly "pegged" Mr. Todd out of sight. He grinned apologetically at a furious Mr. Bickford.

"Order the marshal to call the hosses for the thirty-four trot, Honer'ble," he directed, anxious to give the starter something to do to take his mind off present matters.

Mr. Bickford obeyed, finding this exercise of authority a partial sop to his wounded feelings.

Cap'n Sproul pendulumed dispiritedly to and fro in the little enclosure, gloomily and obstinately waiting for the disaster that his seaman's sense of impending trouble scented. Hiram Look was frankly and joyously enjoying a scene that revived his old circus memories.

Eleven starters finally appeared, mostly green horses. The drivers were sullen and resentful. Marengo Todd was up behind a Gothic ruin that he called "Maria M." When he jogged past the judges' stand to get position, elbows on his knees and shoulders hunched up, the glare that he levelled on Bickford from under his scoop visor was absolutely demoniac. The mutter of his denunciation could be heard above the yells of the fakers and the squawk of penny whistles.

Occasionally he scruffed his forearm over his head as though fondling something that hurt him.

To start those eleven rank brutes on that cow-lane of a track would have tested the resources and language of a professional. When they swung at the foot of the stretch and came scoring for the first time it was a mix-up that excited the vociferous derision of the crowd. Nearly every horse was off his stride, the drivers sawing at the bits.

Marengo Todd had drawn the pole, but by delaying, in order to blast the Honorable J. Percival with his glances, he was not down to turn with the others, and now came pelting a dozen lengths behind, howling like a Modoc.

Some railbird satirist near the wire bawled "Go!" as the unspeakable riot swept past in dust-clouds. The Honorable Bickford had early possessed himself of the bell-cord as his inalienable privilege. He did not ring the bell to call the field back. He merely leaned far out, clutching the cord, endeavoring to get his eye on the man who had shouted "Go!" He declaimed above the uproar that the man who would do such a thing as that was no gentleman, and declared that he should certainly have a constable arrest the next man who interfered with his duties.

In the mean time President Kitchen was frantically calling to him to ring the gong. The horses kept going, for a driver takes no chances of

119

losing a heat by coming back to ask questions. It was different in the case of Marengo Todd, driver of the pole-horse, and entitled to "protection." He pulled "Maria M." to a snorting halt under the wire and poured forth the vials of his artistic profanity in a way that piqued Cap'n Sproul's professional interest, he having heard more or less eminent efforts in his days of seafaring.

Lashed in this manner, the Honorable J. Percival Bickford began retort of a nature that reminded his fellow-townsmen that he was "Jabe" Bickford, of Smyrna, before he was donor of public benefits and libraries.

The grimness of Cap'n Sproul's face relaxed a little. He forgot even the incubus of the plug hat. He nudged Hiram.

"I didn't know he had it in him," he whispered. "I was afraid he was jest a dude and northin' else."

In this instance the dog Hector seemed to know his master's voice, and realized that something untoward was occurring. He came bounding out from under the stand and frisked backward toward the centre of the track in order to get a square look at his lord. In this blind progress he bumped against the nervous legs of "Maria M." She promptly expressed her opinion of the Bickford family and its attaches by rattling the ribs of Hector by a swift poke with her hoof.

The dog barked one astonished yap of indignation and came back with a snap that started the crimson on "Maria's" fetlock. She kicked him between the eyes this time—a blow that floored him. The next instant "Maria M." was away, Todd vainly struggling with the reins and trailing the last of his remarks over his shoulder. The dog was no quitter. He appeared to have the noble blood of which his master had boasted. After a dizzy stagger, he shot away after his assailant— a cloud of dust with a core of dog.

The other drivers, their chins apprehensively over their shoulders, took to the inner oval of the course or to the side lines. Todd, "Maria

M.," and Hector were, by general impulse, allowed to become the whole show.

When the mare came under the wire the first time two swipes attempted to stop her by the usual method of suddenly stretching a blanket before her. She spread her legs and squatted. Todd shot forward. The mare had a long, stiff neck. Her driver went astraddle of it and stuck there like a clothes-pin on a line. Hector, in his cloud of dust, dove under the sulky and once more snapped the mare's leg, this time with a vigor that brought a squeal of fright and pain out of her. She went over the blanket and away again. The dog, having received another kick, and evidently realizing that he was still "it" in this grotesque game of tag, kept up the chase.

No one who was at Smyrna fair that day ever remembered just how many times the antagonists circled the track. But when the mare at last began to labor under the weight of her rider, a half-dozen men rushed out and anchored her. The dog growled, dodged the men's kicking feet, and went back under the stand.

"What is this, jedges, a dog-fight or a hoss-trot?" raved Todd, staggering in front of the stand and quivering his thin arms above his head. "Whose is that dog? I've got a right to kill him, and I'm going to. Show yourself over that rail, you old sausage, with a plug hat on it, and tell me what you mean by a send-off like that! What did I tell ye, trustees? It's happened. I'll kill that dog."

"I want you to understand," bellowed the Honorable Bickford, using the megaphone, "you are talking about my dog—a dog that is worth more dollars than that old knock-kneed plug of yours has got hairs in her mane. Put your hand on that dog, and you'll go to State Prison."

"Then I'll bet a thousand dollars to a doughnut ye set that dog on me," howled Marengo. "I heard ye siss him!"

The Honorable J. Percival seemed to be getting more into the spirit of the occasion.

"You're a cross-eyed, wart-nosed liar!" he retorted, with great alacrity.

"I'll stump ye down here," screamed Todd. "I can lick you and your dog, both together."

"If I was in your place," said "Judge" Hiram Look, his interest in horse-trotting paling beside this more familiar phase of sport, "I'd go down and cuff his old chops. You'll have the crowd with you if you do."

But Mr. Bickford, though trembling with rage, could not bring himself to correlate fisticuffs and dignity.

"He is a miserable, cheap horse-jockey, and I shall treat him with the contempt he deserves," he blustered. "If it hadn't been for my dog his old boneyard could never have gone twice around the track, anyway."

The crowds on the grand stand were bellowing: "Trot hosses! Shut up! Trot hosses!"

"Er—what other races have we?" inquired the Honorable J. Percival, as blandly as his violated feelings would allow.

"We haven't had any yet," cried a new voice in the stand—the wrathful voice of Trustee Silas Wallace, of the horse department. After quite a struggle he had managed to tip President Kitchen off the trap-door and had ascended. "We never will have any, either," he shouted, shaking his finger under the president's nose. "What did I tell you would happen? We'll be reported to the National Association."

The crowd across the way roared and barked like beasts of prey, and the insistent and shrill staccato of Marengo Todd sounded over all.

Cap'n Sproul deliberately and with much decision took off his silk hat and held it toward the Honorable Bickford.

"I resign!" he said. "I was shanghaied into this thing against my good judgment, and it's come out just as I expected it would. It ain't no place for me, and I resign!"

"It isn't any place for gentlemen," agreed Mr. Bickford, ignoring the proffered hat. "We seem to be thrown in among some very vulgar people," he went on, his ear out for Marengo's taunts, his eyes boring Trustee Wallace. "It is not at all as I supposed it would be. You cannot expect us to be patrons of the races under these circumstances, Mr. Kitchen. You will please call our barouche. We leave in great displeasure."

"I don't give a red hoorah how you leave, so long as you leave before you've busted up this fair—trot programmy and all," retorted Mr. Wallace, bridling. "I've got three men waitin' ready to come into this stand. They don't wear plug hats, but they know the diff'runce between a dog-fight and a hoss-trot."

"Take this! I don't want it no more," insisted the Cap'n, stung by this repeated reference to plug hats. He poked the head-gear at Mr. Bickford. But that gentleman brushed past him, stumped down the stairs, and strode into the stretch before the stand, loudly calling for the carriage.

Marengo Todd, accepting his sudden and defiant appearance as gage of battle, precipitately withdrew, leaping the fence and disappearing under the grand-stand.

It was five minutes or more ere the barouche appeared, Mr. Parrott requiring to be coaxed by President Kitchen to haul the three disgraced dignitaries away. He seemed to sniff a mob sentiment that might damage his vehicle.

Mr. Bickford's two associates followed him from the stand, the Cap'n abashed and carrying the tall hat behind his back, Hiram Look muttering disgusted profanity under his long mustache.

"I want to say, gentlemen," cried Mr. Bickford, utilizing the interval of waiting to address the throng about him, "that you have no right to blame my dog. He is a valuable animal and a great family pet, and he only did what it is his nature to do."

Marengo Todd was edging back into the crowd, his coat off and something wrapped in the garment.

"Blame no creature for that which it is his nature to do," said Mr. Bickford. "He was attacked first, and he used the weapons nature provided."

"Fam'ly pets, then, has a right to do as it is their nature for to do?" squealed Todd, working nearer.

Mr. Bickford scornfully turned his back on this vulgar railer. The carriage was at hand.

"How about pets known as medder hummin'-birds?" demanded Todd.

The Cap'n was the first in. Hiram came next, kicking out at the amiable Hector, who would have preceded him. When the Honorable J. Percival stepped in, some one slammed the carriage-door so quickly on his heels that his long-tailed coat was caught in the crack.

Todd forced his way close to the carriage as it was about to start. His weak nature was in a state of anger bordering on the maniacal.

"Here's some more family pets for you that ain't any dangerouser than them you're cultivatin'. Take 'em home and study 'em."

He climbed on the wheel and shook out of the folds of his coat a hornets' nest that he had discovered during his temporary exile under the grand-stand. It dropped into Mr. Bickford's lap, and with a swat of his coat Todd crushed it where it lay. It was a coward's revenge, but it was an effective one.

Mr. Bickford leaped, either in pain or in order to pursue the fleeing Marengo, and fell over the side of the carriage. His coat-tail held fast in the door, and suspended him, his toes and fingers just touching the ground. When he jumped he threw the nest as far as he could, and it fell under the horses. Hiram endeavored to open the hack-door as the animals started—but who ever yet opened a hack-door in a hurry?

Cap'n Aaron Sproul's first impulse was the impulse of the sailor who beholds dangerous top-hamper dragging at a craft's side in a squall. He out with his big knife and cut off the Honorable Bickford's coat-tails with one mighty slash, and that gentleman rolled in the dust over the hornets' nest, just outside the wheels, as the carriage roared away down the stretch.

Landlord Parrott was obliged to make one circuit of the track before he could control his steeds, but the triumphal rush down the length of the yelling grand-stand was an ovation that Cap'n Sproul did not relish. He concealed the hateful plug hat between his knees, and scowled straight ahead.

Parrott did not go back after the Honorable Bickford.

The loyal and apologetic Kitchen assisted that gentleman to rise, brushed off his clothes—what were left of them—and carried him to "Bickburn Towers" in his buggy, with Hector wagging sociably in the dust behind.

Mr. Bickford fingered the ragged edge of his severed coat-tails, and kept his thoughts to himself during his ride.

When the old lady Sampson called at the Towers next day with a subscription paper to buy a carpet for the Baptist vestry, James informed her that Mr. Bickford had gone out West to look after his business interests.

When Hiram Look set Cap'n Aaron Sproul down at his door that afternoon he emphasized the embarrassed silence that had continued during the ride by driving away without a word. Equally as saturnine, Cap'n Sproul walked through his dooryard, the battered plug hat in his hand, paying no heed to the somewhat agitated questions of his wife. She watched his march into the corn-field with concern.

She saw him set the hat on the head of a scarecrow whose construction had occupied his spare hours, and in which he felt some little pride. But after surveying the result a moment he seemed to feel that he had insulted a helpless object, for he took the hat off, spat into it, and kicked it into shapeless pulp. Then he came back to the house and grimly asked his wife if she had anything handy to take the poison out of hornet stings.

XIII

In Newry, on the glorious Fourth of July, the Proud Bird of Freedom wears a red shirt, a shield hat, and carries a speaking-trumpet clutched under one wing. From the court-house—Newry is the county's shire town—across to the post-office is stretched the well-worn banner:

WELCOME TO THE COUNTY'S
BRAVE FIRE-LADDIES

That banner pitches the key for Independence Day in Newry. The shire patriotically jangles her half-dozen bells in the steeples at daylight in honor of Liberty, and then gives Liberty a stick of candy and a bag of peanuts, and tells her to sit in the shade and keep her eye out sharp for the crowding events of the annual firemen's muster. This may be a cavalier way of treating Liberty, but perhaps Liberty enjoys it better than being kept on her feet all day, listening to speeches and having her ear-drums split by cannon. Who knows? At all events, Newry's programme certainly suits the firemen of the county, from Smyrna in the north to Carthage in the south. And the firemen of the county and their women are the ones who do their shopping in Newry! Liberty was never known to buy as much as a ribbon for her kimono there.

So it's the annual firemen's muster for Newry's Fourth! Red shirts in the forenoon parade, red language at the afternoon tub-trials, red fire in the evening till the last cheer is yawped.

So it was on the day of which this truthful chronicle treats.

Court Street, at ten, ante-meridian, was banked with eager faces. Band music, muffled and mellow, away off somewhere where the parade was forming! Small boys whiling away the tedium of waiting with snap-crackers. Country teams loaded to the edges, and with little Johnny scooched on a cricket in front, hustling down the line of parade to find a nook. Anxious parents scuttling from side to side of the street, dragging red-faced offspring with the same haste and uncertainty hens display to get on the other side of the road —having no especial object in changing, except to change. Chatter of voices, hailings of old friends who signified delighted surprise by profanity and affectionate abuse. Everlasting wailings of penny squawkers!

Behold Newry ready for its annual: "See the Conquering Heroes Come!"

Uncle Brad Trufant stood on the post-office steps, dim and discontented eyes on the vista of Court Street, framed in the drooping elms.

"They don't get the pepper sass into it these days they used to," he said. "These last two years, if it wa'n't for the red shirts and some one forgettin' and cussin' once in a while, you'd think they was classes from a theological seminary marchin' to get their degrees. I can remember when we came down from Vienny twenty years ago with old Niag'ry, and ev'ry man was over six feet tall, and most of 'em had double teeth, upper and lower, all the way 'round. And all wore red shirts. And ev'ry man had one horn, and most of 'em tew. We broke glass when we hollered. We tore up ground when we jumped. We cracked the earth when we lit. Them was real days for firemen!"

"Ain't seen the Smyrna Ancient and Honorable Firemen's Association, Hiram Look foreman, and his new fife-and-drum corps, and the rest of the trimmin's, have you, Uncle Brad?" drawled a man near him. "Well, don't commit yourself too far on old Vienny till the Smyrna part of the parade gets past. I see 'em this mornin' when they unloaded Hecly One and the trimmin's 'foresaid, and I'd advise you to wait a spell before you go to callin' this muster names."

It became apparent a little later that hints of this sort were having their effect on the multitude. Even the head of the great parade, with old John Burt, chief marshal, titupping to the grunt of brass horns, stirred only perfunctory applause. The shouts for Avon's stalwart fifty, with their mascot gander waddling on the right flank, were evidently confined to the Avon excursionists. Starks, Carthage, Salem, Vienna strode past with various evolutions—open order, fours by the right, double-quick, and all the rest, but still the heads turned toward the elm-framed vista of the street. The people were expecting something. It came.

Away down the street there sounded—raggity-tag! raggity-tag!—the tuck of a single drum. Then—pur-r-r-r!

"There's old Smyrna talkin' up!" shrilled a voice in the crowd.

And the jubilant plangor of a fife-and-drum corps burst on the listening ears.

"And there's his pet elephant for a mascot! How's that for Foreman Hiram Look and the Smyrna Ancients and Honer'bles?" squealed the voice once more.

The drum corps came first, twenty strong, snares and basses rattling and booming, the fifers with arms akimbo and cheeks like bladders.

Hiram Look, ex-showman and once proprietor of "Look's Leviathan Circus and Menagerie," came next, lonely in his grandeur. He wore his leather hat, with the huge shield-fin hanging down his back, the word "Foreman" newly lettered on its curved front. He carried two leather buckets on his left arm, and in his right hand flourished his speaking-trumpet. The bed-wrench, chief token of the antiquity of the Ancients, hung from a cord about his neck, and the huge bag, with a puckering-string run about its mouth, dangled from his waist.

At his heels shambled the elephant, companion of his circus wanderings, and whose old age he had sworn to protect and make peaceful. A banner was hung from each ear, and she slouched along at a brisk pace, in order to keep the person of her lord and master within reach of her moist and wistful trunk. She wore a blanket on which was printed: "Imogene, Mascot of the Smyrna Ancients." Imogene was making herself useful as well as ornamental, for she was harnessed to the pole of "Hecla Number One," and the old tub "ruckle-chuckled" along at her heels on its little red trucks. From its brake-bars hung the banners won in the past-and-gone victories of twenty years of musters. Among these was one inscribed "Champions."

And behind Hecla marched, seventy-five strong, the Ancients of Smyrna, augmented, by Hiram Look's enterprise, until they comprised nearly every able-bodied man in the old town.

To beat and pulse of riotous drums and shrilling fifes they were roaring choruses. It was the old war song of the organization, product of a quarter-century of rip-roaring defiance, crystallized from the lyrics of the hard-fisted.

They let the bass drums accent for them.

> "Here wec-come from old Sy-myrná
>   Here wec-come with Hecly One;
> She's the prunes for a squirt, gol durn her —
>   We've come down for fight or fun.
> Shang, de-rango! We're the bo-kay,
> Don't giveadam for no one no way.

> "Here wec-come — sing old A'nt Rhody!
>   See old Hecly paw up dirt.
> Stuff her pod with rocks and sody,
>   Jee-ro C'ris'mus, how she'll squirt!
> Rip-te-hoo! And a hip, hip, holler,
> We'll lick hell for a half a dollar!"

The post-office windows rattled and shivered in the sunshine. Horses along the line of march crouched, ducked sideways, and snorted in panic. Women put their fingers in their ears as the drums passed. And when at the end of each verse the Ancients swelled their red-shirted bosoms and screamed, Uncle Trufant hissed in the ear of his nearest neighbor on the post-office steps: "The only thing we need is the old Vienny company here to give 'em the stump! Old Vienny, as it used to be, could lick 'em, el'funt and all."

The Smyrna Ancients were file-closers of the parade; Hiram Look had chosen his position with an eye to effect that made all the other companies seem to do mere escort duty. The orderly lines of spectators poured together into the street behind, and went elbowing in noisy rout to the village square, the grand rallying-point and arena of the day's contests. There, taking their warriors' ease before the battle, the Ancients, as disposed by their assiduous foreman, continued the centre of observation.

Uncle Brad Trufant, nursing ancient memories of the prowess of Niagara and the Viennese, voiced some of the sentiment of the envious when he muttered: "Eatin', allus eatin'! The only fire they can handle is a fire in a cook-stove."

On this occasion Foreman Look had responded nobly to the well-known gastronomic call of his Ancients. No one understood better than he the importance of the commissary in a campaign. The dinner he had given the Ancients to celebrate his election as foreman had shown him the way to their hearts.

Bringing up the rear had rumbled one of his circus-vans. Now, with the eyes of the hungry multitude on him, he unlocked the doors and disclosed an interior packed full of individual lunch-baskets. His men cheered lustily and formed in line.

Foreman Look gazed on his cohorts with pride and fondness.

"Gents," he said, in a clarion voice that took all the bystanders into his confidence, "you're never goin' to make any mistake in followin' me. Follow me when duty calls—follow me when pleasure speaks, and you'll always find me with the goods."

He waved his hand at the open door of the van.

Two ladies had been awaiting the arrival of the Ancients in the square, squired by a stout man in blue, who scruffed his fingers through his stubbly gray beard from time to time with no great ease of manner. Most of the spectators knew him. He was the first selectman of Smyrna, Cap'n Aaron Sproul. And when the ladies, at a signal from Foreman Look, took stations at the van door and began to distribute the baskets, whisperings announced that they were respectively the wives of Cap'n Sproul and the foreman of Hecla One. The ladies wore red, white, and blue aprons, and rosettes of patriotic hues, and their smiling faces indicated their zest in their duties.

Uncle Trufant, as a hound scents game, sniffed Cap'n Sproul's uneasy rebelliousness, and seemed to know with a sixth sense that only Hiram's most insistent appeals to his friendship, coupled with the coaxings of the women-folk, had dragged him down from Smyrna. Uncle Trufant edged up to him and pointed wavering cane at the festive scene of distribution.

"Seems to be spendin' his money on 'em, all free and easy, Cap'n."

The Cap'n scowled and grunted.

"It's good to have a lot of money like he's got. That's the kind of a foreman them caterpillars is lookin' for. But if greenbacks growed all over him, like leaves on a tree, they'd keep at him till they'd gnawed 'em all off."

He glowered at the briskly wagging jaws and stuffed cheeks of the feeding protégés of Foreman Look.

"I reckon he'll wake up some day, same's you did, and reelize what they're tryin' to do to him. What you ought to done was settle in Vienny. We've heard out our way how them Smyrna bloodsuckers have—"

Cap'n Sproul whirled on the ancient detractor, whiskers bristling angrily. He had never been backward in pointing out Smyrna's faults. But to have an outsider do it in the open forum of a firemen's muster was a different matter.

"Before I started in to criticise other towns or brag about my own, Trufant," he snorted, "I'd move over into some place where citizens like you, that's been dead ten years and ought to be buried, ain't walkin' round because there ain't soil enough left in town to bury 'em in." This was biting reference to Vienna's ledgy surface.

"I'd ruther walk on granite than have web feet and paddle in muck," retorted Uncle Trufant, ready with the ancient taunt as to the big bog that occupied Smyrna's interior.

"Ducks are good property," rejoined the Cap'n, serenely, "but I never heard of any one keepin' crows for pets nor raisin' 'em for market. There ain't anything but a crow will light on your town, and they only do it because the sight of it makes 'em faint."

Stimulated because bystanders were listening to the colloquy, Uncle Trufant shook his cane under Cap'n Sproul's nose.

"That's what ye be in Smyrna—ducks!" he squealed. "You yourself come to your own when ye waddled off'm the deck of a ship and settled there. Down here to-day with an el'funt and what's left of a busted circus, and singin' brag songs, when there ain't a man in this county but what knows Smyrna never had the gristle to put up a fight man-fashion at a firemen's muster. Vienny can shake one fist at ye and run ye up a tree. Vienny has allus done it. Vienny allus will do it. Ye can't fight!"

Hiram had cocked his ear at sound of Uncle Trufant's petulant squeal. He thrust close to them, elbowing the crowd.

"Fight! Why, you old black and tan, what has fightin' got to do with the makin' of a fire department? There's been too much fightin' in years past. It's a lot of old terriers like you that had made firemen looked down on. Your idee of fire equipment was a kag of new rum and plenty of brass knuckles. I can show ye that times has changed!

Look at that picture there!" He waved his hairy hand at the ladies who were distributing the last of the lunch-baskets. "That's the way to come to muster—come like gents, act like gents, eat like gents, and when it's all over march with your lady on your arm."

"Three cheers for the ladies!" yelled an enthusiastic member of the Smyrna company. The cheers coming up had to crowd past food going down, but the effect was good, nevertheless.

"That's the idea!" shouted Hiram. "Peace and politeness, and everybody happy. If that kind of a firemen's muster don't suit Vienny, then her company better take the next train back home and put in the rest of the day firin' rocks at each other. If Vienny stays here she's got to be genteel, like the rest of us—and the Smyrna Ancients will set the pace. Ain't that so, boys?"

His men yelled jubilant assent.

Uncle Trufant's little eyes shuttled balefully.

"Oh, that's it, is it?" he jeered. "I didn't know I'd got into the ladies' sewin'-circle. But if you've got fancy-work in them shoppin'-bags of your'n, and propose to set under the trees this afternoon and do tattin', I wouldn't advise ye to keep singin' that song you marched in here with. It ain't ladylike. Better sing, 'Oh, how we love our teacher dear!'"

"Don't you fuss your mind about us in any way, shape, or manner," retorted the foreman. "When we march we march, when we eat we eat, when we sing we sing, when we squirt"—he raised his voice and glared at the crowd surrounding—"we'll give ye a stream that the whole Vienny fire company can straddle and ride home on like it was a hobby-horse." And, concluding thus, he fondled his long mustaches away from his mouth and gazed on the populace with calm pride. Cæsar on the plains of Pharsalia, Pompey triumphant on the shores of Africa, Alexander at the head of his conquering Macedonians had not more serenity of countenance to display to the multitude.

XIV

Up came trotting a brisk little man with a notebook in one hand, a stubby lead-pencil in the other, a look of importance spread over his flushed features, and on his breast a broad, blue ribbon, inscribed: "Chief Marshal."

"Smyrna has drawed number five for the squirt," he announced, "fallerin' Vienny. Committee on tub contests has selected Colonel Gideon Ward as referee."

Hiram's eyes began to blaze, and Cap'n Sproul growled oaths under his breath. During the weeks of their growing intimacy the Cap'n had detailed to his friend the various phases of Colonel Gideon's iniquity as displayed toward him. Though the affairs of Hiram Look had not yet brought him into conflict with the ancient tyrant of Smyrna, Hiram had warmly espoused the cause and the grudge of the Cap'n.

"I'll bet a thousand dollars against a jelly-fish's hind leg that he begged the job so as to do you," whispered Sproul. "I ain't been a brother-in-law of his goin' on two years not to know his shenanigan. It's a plot."

"Who picked out that old cross between a split-saw and a bull-thistle to umpire this muster?" shouted the foreman of the Ancients, to the amazement of the brisk little man.

"Why, he's the leadin' man in this section, and a Smyrna man at that," explained the marshal. "I don't see how your company has got any kick comin'. He's one of your own townsmen."

"And that's why we know him better than you do," protested Hiram, taking further cue from the glowering gaze of Cap'n Sproul. "You put him out there with the tape, and you'll see—"

"'Peace and politeness, and everybody happy,'" quoted Uncle Trufant, maliciously. The serenity had departed from Foreman Look's face.

"You don't pretend to tell me, do ye, that the Smyrna Ancients are afraid to have one of their own citizens as a referee?" demanded the brisk little man suspiciously. "If that's so, then there must be something decayed about your organization."

"I don't think they're down here to squirt accordin' to the rules made and pervided," went on the ancient Vienna satirist. "They've brought Bostin bags and a couple of wimmen, and are goin' to have a quiltin'-bee. P'raps they think that Kunnel Gid Ward don't know a fish-bone stitch from an over-and-over. P'raps they think Kunnel Ward ain't ladylike enough for 'em."

Not only had the serenity departed from the face of Foreman Look, the furious anger of his notoriously short temper had taken its place.

"By the jumped-up jedux," he shouted, "you pass me any more of that talk, you old hook-nosed cockatoo, and I'll slap your chops!"

The unterrified veteran of the Viennese brandished his cane to embrace the throng of his red-shirted townsmen, who had been crowding close to hear. At last his flint had struck the spark that flashed with something of the good old times about it.

"And what do you suppose the town of Vienny would be doin' whilst you was insultin' the man who was the chief of old Niag'ry Company for twenty years?" he screamed.

"There's one elephant that I know about that would be an orphin in about fifteen seconds," growled one of the loyal members of the Vienna company, the lust of old days of rivalry beginning to stir in his blood.

"Would, hey?" shouted an Ancient, with the alacrity of one who has old-time grudges still unsettled. He put a sandwich back into his basket untasted, an ominous sign of how belligerency was overcoming appetite. "Well, make b'lieve I'm the front door of the orphin asylum, and come up and rap on me!"

With a promptitude that was absolutely terrifying the two lines of red shirts began to draw together, voices growling bodingly, fists clinching, eyes narrowing with the reviving hatred of old contests. The triumphal entry of the Smyrna Ancients, their display of prosperity, their monopoly of the plaudits and attention of the throngs, the assumption of superior caste and manners, had stirred resentment under every red shirt in the parade. But Vienna, hereditary foe, seemed to be the one tacitly selected for the brunt of the conflict.

"Hiram!" pleaded his wife, running to him and patting his convulsed features with trembling fingers. "You said this was all goin' to be genteel. You said you were goin' to show 'em how good manners and politeness ought to run a firemen's muster. You said you were!"

By as mighty an effort of self-control as he ever exercised in his life, Hiram managed to gulp back the sulphurous vilification he had ready at his tongue's end, and paused a moment.

"That's right! I did say it!" he bellowed, his eyes sweeping the crowd over his wife's shoulder. "And I mean it. It sha'n't be said that the Smyrna Ancients were anything but gents. Let them that think a bunged eye and a bloody nose is the right kind of badges to wear away from a firemen's muster keep right on in their hellish career. As for us"—he tucked his wife's arm under his own—"we remember there's ladies present."

"Includin' the elephant," suggested the irrepressible Uncle Trufant, indicating with his cane Imogene "weaving" amiably in the sunshine.

Cap'n Sproul crowded close and growled into the ear of the venerable mischief-maker: "I don't know who set you on to thorn this crowd of men into a fight, and I don't care. But there ain't goin' to be no trouble here, and, if you keep on tryin' to make it, I'll give you one figger of the Portygee fandle-dingo."

"What's that?" inquired Uncle Trufant, with interest.

"An almighty good lickin'," quoth the peacemaker. "I ain't a member of a fire company, and I ain't under no word of honor not to fight."

The two men snapped their angry eyes at each other, and Uncle Trufant turned away, intimidated for the moment. He confessed to himself that he didn't exactly understand how far a seafaring man could be trifled with.

Vienna gazed truculently on Smyrna for a time, but Smyrna, obeying their foreman's adjurations, mellowed into amiable grins and went on with their lunches.

"Where's that Spitz poodle with the blue ribbon?" inquired the Cap'n of Hiram, having reference to the brisk little man and his side whiskers. "It don't appear to me that you pounded it into his head solid enough about our not standin' for Gid Ward."

In the stress of other difficulties Hiram had forgotten the dispute that started the quarrel.

"Don't let's have any more argument, Hiram," pleaded his wife.

"She's right, Cap'n," said the foreman. "Standin' up for your rights is good and proper business, but it's a darn slippery place we're tryin' to stand on. Let the old pirate referee. We can outsquirt 'em. He won't dast to cheat us. I'm goin' to appoint you to represent Smyrna up there at the head of the stream. Keep your eye out for a square deal."

"I don't know a thing about squirtin', and I won't get mixed in," protested the Cap'n. But the members of the Smyrna company crowded around him with appeals.

"There's only this to know," urged Hiram. "The judges lay down sheets of brown paper and measure to the farthest drop. All you've got to do is keep your eye out and see that we get our rights. You'll only be actin' as a citizen of our town—and as first selectman you can insist on our rights. And you can do it in a gentlemanly way, accordin' to the programme we've mapped out. Peace and politeness—that's the motto for Smyrna."

And in the end Cap'n Sproul allowed himself to be persuaded.

But it was scarcely persuasion that did it.

It was this plaintive remark of the foreman: "Are you goin' to stand by and see Gideon Ward do us, and then give you the laugh?"

Therefore the Cap'n buttoned his blue coat tightly and trudged up to where the committee was busy with the sheets of brown paper, weighting them with stones so that the July breeze could not flutter them away.

Starks, Carthage, and Salem made but passable showing. They seemed to feel that the crowd took but little interest in them. The listless applause that had greeted them in the parade showed that.

Then, with a howl, half-sullen, half-ferocious, Vienna trundled old Niagara to the reservoir, stuck her intake pipe deep in the water, and manned her brake-beams. To the surprise of the onlookers her regular foreman took his station with the rest of the crew. Uncle Brad Trufant, foreman emeritus, took command. He climbed slowly upon her tank, braced himself against the bell-hanger, and shook his cane in the air.

"Look at me!" he yelled, his voice cracking into a squall. "Look at me and remember them that's dead and gone, your fathers and your grands'rs, whose old fists used to grip them bars right where you've got your hands. Think of 'em, and then set your teeth and yank the 'tarnal daylights out of her. Are ye goin' to let me stand here—me that has seen your grands'rs pump—and have it said that old Niag'ry was licked by a passul of knittin'-work old-maids, led by an elephant and a peep-show man? Be ye goin' to let 'em outsquirt ye? Why, the wimmen-folks of Vienny will put p'isen in your biscuits if you go home beat by anything that Smyrna can turn out. Git a-holt them bars! Clench your chaws! Now, damye, ye toggle-j'inted, dough-fingered, wall-eyed sons of sea-cooks, give her tar—*give—her—tar!*"

It was the old-fashioned style of exordium by an old-fashioned foreman, who believed that the best results could be obtained by the most scurrilous abuse of his men—and the immediate efforts of Vienna seemed to endorse his opinion.

With the foreman marking time with "Hoomp!—hoomp!" they began to surge at the bars, arms interlaced, hands, brown and gristly, covering the leather from end to end. The long, snaking hose filled and plumped out with snappings.

Uncle Trufant flung his hat afar, doubled forward, and with white hair bristling on his head began to curse horribly. Occasionally he rapped at a laggard with his cane. Then, like an insane orchestra-leader, he sliced the air about his head and launched fresh volleys of picturesque profanity.

Old Niagara rocked and danced. The four hosemen staggered as the stream ripped from the nozzle, crackling like pistol discharges. There was no question as to Uncle Trufant's ability to get the most out of the ancient pride of Vienna. He knew Niagara's resources.

"Ease her!" he screamed, after the first dizzy staccato of the beams. "Ease her! Steady! Get your motion! Up—down! Up—down! Get your motion! Take holt of her! Lift her! Now—now—*now!* For the last ounce of wickin' that's in ye! Give her—*hell!*"

It was the crucial effort. Men flung themselves at the beams. Legs flapped like garments on a clothes-line in a crazy gale. And when Uncle Trufant clashed the bell they staggered away, one by one, and fell upon the grass of the square.

"A hundred and seventeen feet, eight inches and one-half!" came the yell down the line, and at the word Vienna rose on her elbows and bawled hoarse cheers.

The cheer was echoed tumultuously, for every man in the crowd of spectators knew that this was full twenty feet better than the record score of all musters—made by Smyrna two years before, with wind and all conditions favoring.

"That's what old times and old-fashioned cussin' can do for ye," declared Uncle Trufant.

A man—a short, squat man in a blue coat—came pelting down the street from the direction of the judges. It was Cap'n Aaron Sproul. People got out of his way when they got a glimpse of the fury on his face. He tore into the press of Smyrna fire-fighters, who were massed about Hecla, their faces downcast at announcement of this astonishing squirt.

"A hunderd and seventeen northin'! A hunderd and seventeen northin'!" Cap'n Sproul gasped over and over. "I knowed he was in to do us! I see him do it! It wa'n't no hunderd and seventeen! It's a fraud!"

"You're a liar!" cried Uncle Trufant, promptly. But the Cap'n refused to be diverted into argument.

"I went up there to watch Gid Ward, and I watched him," he informed the Ancients. "The rest of 'em was watchin' the squirt, but I was watchin' that land-pirut. I see him spit on that paper twenty feet further'n the furthest drop of water, and then he measured from that spit. That's the kind of a man that's refereein' this thing. He's here to do us! He's paying off his old town-meetin' grudge!"

"Oh, I can't think that of my brother!" cried the Cap'n's wife.

"Remember, Hiram, that you've agreed—" began the cautious spouse of the foreman, noting with alarm the rigid lines beginning to crease her husband's face.

"There ain't no mistake about his measurin' to that spit?" demanded Hiram of the Cap'n, in the level tones of one already convinced but willing to give the accused one a last chance.

"He done it—I swear he done it."

"I'd thought," pursued the foreman of the Ancients, "that a firemen's muster could be made genteel, and would make a pleasant little trip for the ladies. I was mistaken." At the look in his eyes his wife began eager appeal, but he simply picked her up and placed her in the van from which the lunch-baskets had been taken. "There's Mis' Look," he said to the Cap'n. "She'll be glad to have the company of Mis' Sproul."

Without a word the Cap'n picked up Louada Murilla and placed her beside the half-fainting Mrs. Look. Hiram closed the doors of the van.

"Drive out about two miles," he ordered the man on the box, "and then let the ladies git out and pick bokays and enjoy nature for the rest of the afternoon. It's—it's—apt to be kind of stuffy here in the village."

And the van rumbled away down the street toward the vista framed in the drooping elms.

"Now, gents," said Hiram to his men, "if this is a spittin'-at-a-crack contest instead of a tub-squirt, I reckon we'd better go to headquarters and find out about it."

But at Smyrna's announced determination to raid the referee, Vienna massed itself in the way. It began to look like the good old times, and the spectators started a hasty rush to withdraw from the scene.

But Vienna was too openly eager for pitched battle.

To stop then and give them what they had been soliciting all day seemed too much like gracious accommodation in the view of Foreman Look. His business just at that moment was with Colonel Gideon Ward, and he promptly thought of a way to get to him.

At a signal the intelligent Imogene hooped her trunk about him and hoisted him to her neck. Then she started up the street, brandishing the trunk before her like a policeman's billy and "roomping" in hoarse warning to those who encumbered her path.

A charge led by an elephant was not in the martial calculations of the Viennese. They broke and fled incontinently.

Perhaps Colonel Gideon Ward would have fled also, but the crowd that had gathered to watch the results of the hose-play was banked closely in the street.

"Make way!" bellowed Foreman Look. "There's only one man I want, and I'm goin' to have him. Keep out of my road and you won't get hurt. Now, Colonel Gideon Ward," he shouted, from his grotesque mount, as that gentleman, held at bay partly by his pride and partly by the populace, came face to face with him, "I've been in the circus business long enough to know a fake when I see one. You've been caught at it. Own up!"

The Colonel snorted indignantly and scornfully.

"You don't own up, then?" queried Hiram.

"I'll give you five minutes to stop circusin' and get your tub astraddle that reservoir," snapped the referee.

"It occurs to me," went on Hiram, "that you can spit farther if you're up a tree. We want you to do your best when you spit for us."

Colonel Ward blinked without appearing to understand.

But the foreman of the Smyrna Ancients immediately made it evident that he had evolved a peculiar method of dealing with the case in hand. He drove Imogene straight at the goggling referee.

"Up that tree!" roared Hiram. "She'll kill you if you don't."

Indeed, the elephant was brandishing her trunk in a ferocious manner. A ladder was leaning against a near-by elm, and Colonel Ward, almost under the trudging feet of the huge beast, tossed dignity to the winds. He ran up the ladder, and Imogene, responding to a cuff on her head, promptly dragged it away from the tree.

"Only three minutes left to get Hecla into position," Hiram shouted. "Referee says so. Lively with her!"

Around and around in a circle he kept Imogene shambling, driving the crowd back from the tree. The unhappy Colonel was marooned there in solitary state.

At first the Vienna company showed a hesitating inclination to interfere with the placing of Hecla, suspecting something untoward in the astonishing elevation of the referee. But even Uncle Trufant was slow to assume the responsibility of interfering with a company's right of contest.

The Ancients located their engine, coupled the hose, and ran it out with alacrity.

"Colonel Ward," shouted Hiram, "you've tried to do it, but you can't. If it's got to be dog eat dog, and no gents need apply at a firemen's muster, then here's where we have our part of the lunch. Did you measure in twenty extry feet up to your spit mark? Speak up! A quick answer turneth away the hose!"

By this time the crew was gently working the brakes of old Hecla. The hose quivered, and the four men at the nozzle felt it twitching as the water pressed at the closed valve. They were grinning, for now they realized the nature of their foreman's mode of persuasion.

Vienna realized it, too, for with a howl of protest her men came swarming into the square.

"Souse the hide off'm the red-bellied sons of Gehenna!" Hiram yelled, and the hosemen, obedient to the word, swept the hissing stream on the enemy.

Men who will face bullets will run from hornets.

Men who will charge cannon can be routed by water.

The men at the brakes of old Hecla pumped till the tub jigged on her trucks like a fantastic dancer. To right, to left, in whooshing circles, or dwelling for an instant on some particularly obstreperous Vienna man, the great stream played. Some were knocked flat, some fell and were rolled bodily out of the square by the stream, others ran wildly with their arms over their heads. The air was full of leather hats, spinning as the water struck them. Every now and then the hosemen elevated the nozzle and gave Colonel Gideon Ward his share. A half-dozen times he nearly fell off his perch and flapped out like a rag on a bush.

"It certainly ain't no place for ladies!" communed Hiram with himself, gazing abroad from his elevated position on Imogene's neck. "I thought it was once, but it ain't."

"Colonel Gideon Ward," he shouted to the limp and dripping figure in the tree, "do you own up?"

The Colonel withdrew one arm to shake his fist at the speaker, and narrowly saved himself by instantly clutching again, for the crackling stream tore at him viciously.

"We'll drownd ye where ye hang," roared the foreman of the Ancients, "before we'll let you or any other pirate rinky-dink us out of what belongs to us."

Like some Hindu magician transplanted to Yankeedom he bestrode the neck of his elephant, and with his hand summoned the waving stream to do his will. Now he directed its spitting force on the infuriated Colonel; now he put to flight some Vienna man who plucked up a little fleeting courage.

And at last Colonel Ward knuckled. There was nothing else to do.

"I made a mistake," he said, in a moment of respite from the stream.

"You spit on the paper and measured in twenty extry feet jest as Cap'n Aaron Sproul said you did," insisted Hiram. "Say that, and say it loud, or we'll give old Hecly the wickin' and blow you out of that tree."

And after ineffectual oaths the Colonel said it—said it twice, and the second time much the louder.

"Then," bellowed the triumphant Hiram, "the record of old Hecly Number One still stands, and the championship banner travels back to Smyrna with us to-night, jest as it travelled down this mornin'."

"Hain't you goin' to squirt?" asked some one posted safely behind a distant tree.

"If you'd been payin' 'tention as you ought to be you'd have jest seen us squirtin'," replied the foreman of the Ancients with quiet satire. "And when we squirt, we squirt to win."

Cap'n Aaron Sproul turned away from a rapt and lengthy survey of Colonel Ward in the tree.

"Did you ever ride on an elephant, Cap'n Sproul?" inquired Hiram.

"Never tried it," said the seaman.

"Well, I want you to come up here with me. Imogene will h'ist you. I was thinkin', as it's gettin' rather dull here in the village just now"— Hiram yawned obtrusively—"we'd go out and join the ladies. I reckon the company'd like to go along and set on the grass, and pee-ruse nature for a little while, and eat up what's left in them lunch-baskets."

Ten minutes later the Smyrna Ancients and Honorables took their departure down the street bordered by the elms. Hiram Look and Cap'n Aaron Sproul swayed comfortably on Imogene's broad back. The fife-and-drum corps followed, and behind marched the champions, dragging Hecla Number One on its ruckling trucks.

Then, with the bass drums punctuating and accenting, they sang:

"Rip-te-hoo! And a hip, hip, holler!
We'll lick hell for a half a dollar!"

And it wasn't till then that some bystander tore his attention away long enough to stick a ladder up the elm-tree and let Colonel Gideon Ward scrape his way despondently down.

XV

Probably Constable Zeburee Nute could not have picked out a moment more inauspicious for tackling First Selectman Aaron Sproul on business not immediately connected with the matter then in hand.

First Selectman Sproul was standing beside a granite post, pounding his fist on it with little regard to barked knuckles and uttering some perfectly awful profanity.

A man stood on the other side of the post, swearing with just as much gusto; the burden of his remarks being that he wasn't afraid of any by-joosly old split codfish that ever came ashore—insulting reference to Cap'n Sproul's seafaring life.

Behind Cap'n Sproul were men with pickaxes, shovels, and hoes—listening.

Behind the decrier of mariners were men with other shovels, hoes, and pickaxes—listening.

The granite post marked the town line between Smyrna and Vienna.

The post was four miles or so from Smyrna village, and Constable Nute had driven out to interview the first selectman, bringing as a passenger a slim, pale young man, who was smoking cigarettes, one after the other.

They arrived right at the climax of trouble that had been brooding sullenly for a week. In annual town-meeting Smyrna and Vienna had voted to change over the inter-urban highway so that it would skirt Rattledown Hill instead of climbing straight over it, as the fathers had laid it out in the old days for the sake of directness; forgetting that a pail bail upright is just as long as a pail bail lying horizontal.

First Selectman Sproul had ordered his men to take a certain direction with the new road in order to avoid some obstructions that would entail extra expense on the town of Smyrna.

Selectman Trufant, of Vienna, was equally as solicitous about saving expense on behalf of his own town, and refused to swing his road to meet Smyrna's highway. Result: the two pieces of highway came to the town line and there stopped doggedly. There were at least a dozen rods between the two ends. To judge from the language that the two town officers were now exchanging across the granite post, it seemed likely that the roads would stay separated.

"Our s'leckman can outtalk him three to one," confided one of the Smyrna supporters to Constable Nute. "I never heard deep-water cussin' before, with all the trimmin's. Old Trufant ain't got northin' but side-hill conversation, and I reckon he's about run down."

Constable Nute should have awaited more fitting opportunity, but Constable Nute was a rather direct and one-ideaed person. As manager of the town hall he had business to transact with the first selectman, and he proceeded to transact it.

"Mister S'leckman," he shouted, "I want to introduce you to Perfessor—Perfessor—I ain't got your name yit so I can speak it," he said, turning to his passenger.

"Professor Derolli," prompted the passenger, flicking his cigarette ash.

Cap'n Sproul merely shot one red glance over his shoulder, and then proceeded with his arraignment of Vienna in general—mentally, morally, socially, politically, and commercially.

"The perfessor," bawled Constable Nute, unable to get his team very near the selectman on account of the upheaved condition of the road, "has jest arranged with me to hire the town hall for a week, and he wants to arrange with the selectmen to borrow the use of the graveyard for a day or so."

The constable's vociferousness put the Cap'n out of voice, and he whirled to find that his auditors had lost all interest in the road dispute, and naturally, too.

"To borrow the use of the graveyard, said privilege bein' throwed in, considerin' that he hires the town hall for a week," repeated the constable.

Cap'n Sproul hated cigarettes; and he hated slim, pale young men who dressed foppishly, classing all such under the general term "dude." The combination of the two, attending the interruption of his absorbing business of the moment, put a wire edge on his temper.

"Graveyard! Yes!" he roared. "I'll appoint his funeral for two o'clock this afternoon, and I'll guarantee to have the corpse ready."

"In transactin' business it ain't no time for jokin'," protested the direct Mr. Nute.

"There's no joke to it," returned the Cap'n, viciously, seizing a pickaxe.

"It ain't much of a way for a first selectman of a town to act in public," persisted Constable Nute, "when town business is put before him."

That remark and a supercilious glance from the professor through his cigarette smoke brought the Cap'n on the trot to the side of the wagon.

"I'm 'tendin' to town business—don't you forget that! And I'm 'tendin' to it so close that I ain't got time to waste on any cheap peep-show critters. Don't want 'em in town. Clear out!"

"I'll make you sorry for insulting a gentleman," the professor threatened.

"Clear out!" insisted the Cap'n. "You ain't got any right drivin' onto this road. It ain't been opened to travel — "

"And it looks as though it never would be," remarked Constable Nute, sarcastically; but, daunted by the glare in the Cap'n's eyes, he began to turn his horse. "I want you to understand, S'leckman Sproul, that there are two other s'leckmen in this town, and you can't run everything, even if you've started in to do it."

It was pointed reference to the differences that existed in the board of selectmen, on account of Cap'n Sproul's determination to command.

Two very indignant men rode away, leaving a perfectly furious one standing in the road shaking his fists after them. And he was the more angry because he felt that he had been hastier with the constable than even his overwrought state of mind warranted. Then, as he reflected on the graveyard matter, his curiosity began to get the better of his wrath, and to the surprise of his Vienna antagonist he abandoned the field without another word and started for Smyrna village with his men and dump-carts.

But dump-carts move slowly, and when the Cap'n arrived at the town house Constable Zeburee Nute was nailing up a hand-bill that announced that Professor Derolli, the celebrated hypnotist, would occupy the town hall for a week, and that he would perform the remarkable feat of burying a subject in the local graveyard for forty-eight hours, and that he would "raise this subject from the dead," alive and well. The ink was just dry on a permit to use the graveyard, signed by Selectmen Batson Reeves and Philias Blodgett. The grim experiment was to wind up the professor's engagement. In the mean time he was to give a nightly entertainment at the hall, consisting of hypnotism and psychic readings, the latter by "that astounding occult seer and prophetess, Madame Dawn."

Cap'n Sproul went home growling strong language, but confessing to himself that he was a little ashamed to enter into any further contest with the cigarette-smoking showman and the two men who were the Cap'n's hated associates on the board of selectmen.

That evening neighbor Hiram Look called with Mrs. Look on their way to the village to attend the show, but Cap'n Sproul doggedly resisted their appeals that he take his wife and go along, too. He opposed no objection, however, when Louada Murilla decided that she would accept neighbor Look's offer of escort.

But when she came back and looked at him, and sighed, and sighed, and looked at him till bedtime, shaking her head sadly when he demanded the reason for her pensiveness, he wished he had made her stay at home. He decided that Zeburee Nute had probably been busy with his tongue as to that boyish display of temper on the Rattledown Hill road.

Hiram Look came over early the next morning and found the Cap'n thinning beets in his garden. The expression on the visitor's face did not harmonize with the brightness of the sunshine.

"I don't blame you for not goin'," he growled. "But if you had an idea of what they was goin' to do to get even, I should 'a' most thought you'd 'a' tipped me off. It would have been the part of a friend, anyway."

The Cap'n blinked up at him in mute query.

"It ain't ever safe to sass people that's got the ear of the public, like reporters and show people," proceeded Hiram, rebukingly. "I've been in the show business, and I know. They can do you, and do you plenty, and you don't stand the show of an isuckle in a hot spider."

"What are ye tryin' to get through you, anyway?" demanded the first selectman.

"Hain't your wife said northin' about it?"

"She's set and looked at me like I was a cake that she'd forgot in the oven," confided the Cap'n, sullenly; "but that's all I know about it."

"Well, that's about what I've had to stand in my fam'ly, too. I tell ye, ye hadn't ought to have sassed that mesmerist feller. Oh, I heard all about it," he cried, flapping hand of protest as the Cap'n tried to speak. "I don't know why you done it. What I say is, you ought to have consulted me. I know show people better'n you do. Then you ain't heard nothin' of what she said?"

"If you've got anything to tell me, why in the name of the three-toed Cicero don't you tell it?" blurted the Cap'n, indignantly.

He got up and brushed the dirt off his knees. "If there's anything that stirs my temper, it's this mumble-grumble, whiffle-and-hint business. Out and open, that's my style." He was reflecting testily on the peculiar reticence of his wife.

"I agree with you," replied Hiram, calmly. But his mind was on another phase of the question. "If she had been out and open it wouldn't have been so bad. It's this hintin' that does the most mischief. Give folks a hint, and a nasty imagination will do the rest. That's the way she's workin' it."

"She? Who?"

"Your mesmerist fellow's runnin' mate—that woman that calls herself Madame Dawn, and reads the past and tells the future."

"There ain't nobody can do no such thing," snapped Cap'n Sproul. "They're both frauds, and I didn't want 'em in town, and I was right about it."

"Bein' as how I was in the show business thirty years, you needn't feel called on to post me on fakes," said Hiram, tartly. "But the bigger the fake is the better it catches the crowd. If she'd simply been an old scandal-monger at a quiltin'-bee and started a story about us, we could run down the story and run old scandal-grabber up a tree.

But when a woman goes into a trance and a sperit comes teeterin' out from the dark behind the stage and drops a white robe over her, and she begins to occult, or whatever they call it, and speaks of them in high places, and them with fat moneybags, and that ain't been long in our midst, and has come from no one jest knows where, and that she sees black shadders followin' 'em, along with wimmen weepin' and wringin' of their hands—well, when a woman sets on the town-hall stage and goes on in that strain for a half-hour, it ain't the kind of a show that I want to be at—not with my wife and yourn on the same settee with me."

He scowled on the Cap'n's increasing perturbation.

"A man is a darned fool to fight a polecat, Cap'n Sproul, and you ought to have known better than to let drive at him as you did."

"She didn't call names, did she?" asked the Cap'n.

"Call names! Of course she didn't call names. Didn't have to. There's the difference between scandal and occultin'. We can't get no bind on her for what she said. Now here are you and me, back here to settle down after roamin' the wide world over; jest got our feet placed, as you might say, and new married to good wimmen—and because we're a little forehanded and independent, and seem to be enjoyin' life, every one is all ready to believe the worst about us on general principles. Mossbacks are always ready to believe that a man that's travelled any has been raising seventeen kinds of tophet all his life. All she had to do was go into a trance, talk a little Injun, and then hint enough to set their imaginations to workin' about us. Up to now, judgin' by the way she's been lookin' at me, my wife believes I've got seven wives strewed around the country somewhere, either alive or buried in cellars. As to your wife, you bein' a seafarin' character, she's prob'ly got it figgered that a round-up of your fam'ly circle, admittin' all that's got a claim on you, would range all the way from a Hindu to a Hottentot, and would look like a congress of nations. In about two days more—imagination still workin', and a few old she devils in this place startin' stories to help it along—our wives will be hoppin' up every ten minutes to look down the road and see if any of the victims have hove in sight. And what can we do?"

Hiram lunged a vigorous kick straight before him.

"Find me that hole I just made in the air and I'll tell you, Cap'n," he added, with bitter irony.

"It's—it's worse than what I figgered on," remarked the Cap'n, despondently, after a thoughtful pause. "If a woman like Louada Murilla will let herself get fooled and stirred up in that kind of a way by a fly-by-night critter, there ain't much hope of the rest of the neighborhood."

"It's a kind of lyin' that there ain't no fightin'," Hiram asserted. "And there are certain ones in this place that will keep it in the air. Now I didn't sass that mesmerist. But I got it about as tough as you did. I'll bet a thousand to one that Bat Reeves is gettin' back at me for cuttin' him out with the widder. It's reasonable," he declared, warming to the topic and checking items off on his stubby fingers. "Here's your mesmerist rushin' hot to Reeves complainin' about you and gettin' a permit from Reeves, along with a few pointers about you for occult use. Reeves hates you bad enough, but he hates me worse. And he sees to it that I get occulted, too. He ain't lettin' a chance like that slip past as soon as that perfessor lets him see what occultin' will do to a man. Why, condemn his hide and haslet, I believe he swapped that permit for a dose of so much occultin'—and I've got the dose."

"I should hate at my age to have to start in and go to sea again," mourned the Cap'n, after long meditation; "but I reckon I'll either have to do that or go up in a balloon and stay there. There's too many tricks for me on land. They ring in all they can think of themselves, and then they go to work and get a ghost to help. I can't whale the daylights out of the ghost, and I don't suppose it would be proper for a first selectman to cuff the ears of the woman that said females was followin' me, wailin' and gnashin' their teeth, but I can lick that yaller-fingered, cigarette-suckin' dude, and pay the fine for so doin'—and reckon I've got my money's worth."

"You need a guardeen," snorted Hiram. "She will put on her robe and accuse you of havin' the ghost of a murdered man a-chasin' you."

The Cap'n grew white under his tan at this remark, made by Hiram in all guilelessness, and the memory of a certain Portuguese sailor, slipped overboard after a brief but busy mutiny, went shuddering through his thoughts.

"Ain't got anything like that on your conscience, have you?" demanded the old showman, bluntly.

"She didn't say anything only about women, did she?" evaded the Cap'n.

"Didn't notice anything last night. She may be savin' something else for this evenin'," was Hiram's consoling answer. His air and the baleful glance he bent on his neighbor indicated that he still held that irascible gentleman responsible for their joint misfortune. And, to show further displeasure, he whirled and stumped away across the fields toward his home.

Cap'n Aaron Sproul attended the show at the town hall that evening.

He went alone, after his wife had plaintively sighed her refusal to accompany him. He hadn't intended to go. But he was drawn by a certain fatal fascination. He had a sailor's superstitious half-belief in the supernatural. He had caught word during the day of some astonishing revelations made by the seeress as to other persons in town, either by lucky guess or through secret pre-information, as his common sense told him. And yet his sneaking superstition whispered that there was "something in it, after all." If that mesmerist's spirit of retaliation should carry him to the extent of hinting about that Portuguese sailor, Cap'n Sproul resolved to be in that hall, ready to stand up and beard his defamers.

Evidently Professor Derolli spotted his enemy; for Madame Dawn, in order that vengeance should be certain of its mark, repeated the vague yet perfectly obvious hints of the preceding evening; and Cap'n Sproul was thankful for the mystic gloom of the hall that hid his fury and his shame. He stole out of the place while the lights were still low. He feared for his self-restraint if he were to remain, and he realized what a poor figure he would make standing up there and replying to the malicious farrago of the woman under the veil.

XVI

For the rest of the professor's engagement Cap'n Aaron Sproul and Hiram Look kept sullenly to their castles, nursing indignant sense of their wrongs. They got an occasional whiff of the scandal that was pursuing their names. Though their respective wives strove with pathetic loyalty to disbelieve all that the seeress had hinted at, and moved in sad silence about their duties, it was plain that the seed of evil had been planted deep in their imaginations. Poor human nature is only what it is, after all!

"Two better women never lived than them of ourn, and two that would be harder to turn," said Hiram to the Cap'n, "but it wouldn't be human nature if they didn't wonder sometimes what we'd been up to all them years before we showed up here, and what that cussed occulter said has torched 'em on to thinkin' mighty hard. The only thing to do is to keep a stiff upper lip and wait till the clouds roll by. They'll come to their senses and be ashamed of themselves, give 'em time and rope enough."

Second Selectman Batson Reeves busied himself as a sort of master of ceremonies for Professor Derolli, acted as committee of investigation when the professor's "stock subject" remained for a day and night in a shallow trench in the village cemetery, and even gave them the best that his widower's house could afford at a Sunday dinner.

In the early flush of an August morning about a week after the departure of the hypnotic marvel and his companions, a mutual impulse seemed to actuate Selectman Sproul and Hiram Look at a moment surprisingly simultaneous. They started out their back doors, took the path leading over the hill between their farms, and met under the poplars at a point almost exactly half-way. It would be difficult to state which face expressed the most of embarrassed concern as they stood silently gazing at each other.

"I was comin' over to your house," said Hiram.

"I was startin' for yourn," said the Cap'n.

Then both, like automatons pulled by the same string, dove hand into breast-pocket and pulled out a crumpled letter.

"Well, I'll be dummed!" quoth the two in one voice.

"I don't understand northin' about it," said Hiram, plaintively. "But whatever it is, it has put me in a devil of a fix."

"If you're havin' any more trouble to your house than I'm havin' over to mine, then you've somethin' that I don't begrudge you none," added the Cap'n, gloomily.

"Woman left it," related Hiram. "It was in the edge of the evenin', and I hadn't come in from the barn. Woman throwed it onto the piazza and run. Reckon she waited her chance so't my wife would get holt of it. She did. She read it. And it's hell 'n' repeat on the Look premises."

"Ditto and the same, word for word," said the Cap'n.

"The handwritin' ain't much different," said the ex-showman, clutching Sproul's letter and comparing the two sheets. "But it's wimmen's work with a pen—there ain't no gettin' round that."

Then his voice broke into quavering rage as he went on.

"You jest think of a lovin', trustin', and confidin' woman gettin' holt of a gob of p'isen like that!" He shook the crackling sheet over his head. "'Darlin' Hiram, how could you leave me, but if you will come away with me now all will be forgiven and forgotten, from one who loves you truly and well, and has followed you to remind you of your promise.' My Gawd, Cap'n, ain't that something to raise a blister on the motto, 'God Bless Our Home'?"

"It's done it over to my house," said the Cap'n, lugubriously.

"There never was any such woman—there never could have been any such woman," Hiram went on in fervid protest. "There ain't nobody with a license to chase me up."

"Ditto and the same," chimed in Cap'n Sproul.

"No one!"

"No one!" echoed the Cap'n.

They stood and looked at each other a little while, and then their eyes shifted in some embarrassment.

"Of course," said Hiram, at last, moderating his tone of indignation, "when a man ain't had no anchor he might have showed attentions such as ladies expect from gents, and sometimes rash promises is made. Now, perhaps—you understand I'm only supposin'—perhaps you've got some one in mind that might have misjudged what you said to her—some one that's got a little touched in her head, perhaps, and she's come here. In that case it might give us a clue if you're a mind to own up."

The Cap'n flushed at this clumsy attempt of Hiram to secure a confidence.

"Seein' that you've thought how it might be done all so quick and handy, showin' what's on your mind, I reckon you'd better lay down cards first," he said, significantly.

"I think it's jest a piece of snigdom by some one tryin' to hurt us," proceeded Hiram, boring the Cap'n with inquisitive gaze. "But you never can tell what's what in this world, and so long as we're looking for clues we might as well have an understandin', so's to see if there's any such thing as two wimmen meetin' accidental and comparin' notes and gettin' their heads together."

"None for me," said the Cap'n, but he said it falteringly.

"Well, there's none for me, either, but there's such a thing as havin' what you've said misjudged by wimmen. Where the wimmen ain't strong-headed, you know." He hesitated for a time, fiddling his forefinger under his nose. "There was just one woman I made talk to in my life such as a gent shouldn't have made without backin' it up. If she'd been stronger in her head I reckon she'd have realized that bein' sick, like I was, and not used to wimmen, and bein' so grateful for all her care and attention and kindness and head-rubbin', I was sort of took unawares, as you might say. A stronger-headed woman would have said to herself that it wasn't to be laid up against me. But as soon as I got to settin' up and eatin' solid food I could see that she was sappy, and prob'ly wanted to get out of nussin' and get married, and so she had it all written down on her nuss-diary what I said, mixed in with temperature, pulse, and things. I—"

Cap'n Sproul's eyes had been widening, and his tongue was nervously licking wisps of whisker between his lips.

"Was that in a Bost'n horsepittle?" he asked, with eager interest.

"That's where. In the fall three years ago. Pneumony."

"Mine was rheumatic fever two years ago," said the Cap'n. "It's what drove me off'm deep water. She was fat, wasn't she, and had light hair and freckles across the bridge of her nose, and used to set side of the bed and hum: 'I'm a pilgrim, faint and weary'?"

"Damme if you didn't ring the bell with that shot!" cried the old showman in astonishment.

"Well, it's just ditto and the same with me," said the Cap'n, rapping his knuckles on his breast. "Same horsepittle, same nuss, same thing generally—only when I was sickest I told her I had property wuth about thutty thousand dollars."

"So did I," announced Hiram. "It's funny that when a man's drunk or sick he's got to tell first comers all he knows, and a good deal more!" He ran his eyes up and down over Cap'n Sproul with fresh

161

interest. "If that don't beat tophet! You and me both at that horsepittle and gettin' mixed up with the same woman!"

"This world ain't got no special bigness," said the Cap'n. "I've sailed round it a dozen times, and I know."

The showman grasped the selectman by the coat-lapel and demanded earnestly: "Didn't you figger it as I did, when you got so you could set up and take notice, that she wasn't all right in her head?"

"Softer'n a jelly-fish!" declared the Cap'n, with unction.

"Then she's got crazier, and up all of a sudden and followed us — and don't care which one she gets!"

"Or else got sensibler and remembered our property and come around to let blood."

"Bound to make trouble, anyway."

"She's made it!" The Cap'n turned doleful gaze over his shoulder at the chimney of his house.

"Bein' crazy she can make a lot more of it. I tell you, Cap'n, there's only this to do, and it ought to work with wimmen-folks as sensible as our'n are. We'll swap letters, and go back home and tell the whole story and set ourselves straight. They're bound to see the right side of it."

"There ain't any reckonin' on what a woman will do," observed the Cap'n, gloomily. "The theory of tellin' the truth sounds all right, and *is* all right, of course. But I read somewhere, once, that a woman thrives best on truth diluted with a little careful and judicious lyin'. And the feller seemed to know what he was talkin' about."

"It's the truth for me this time," cried Hiram, stoutly.

"Well, then, ditto and the same for me. But if it's comin' on to blow, we might as well get another anchor out. I'll start Constable Denslow 'round town to see what he can see. If he's sly enough and she's still here he prob'ly can locate her. And if he can scare her off, so much the better."

Constable Denslow, intrusted with only scant and vague information, began his search for a supposed escaped lunatic that day. Before nightfall he reported to the Cap'n that there were no strangers in town. However, right on the heels of that consoling information came again that terror who travelled by night! In the dusk of early evening another letter was left for Aaron Sproul, nor was the domicile of Hiram Look slighted by the mysterious correspondent.

Moved by common impulse the victims met in the path across the fields next morning.

"Another one of them bumbs dropped at my house last night!" stated Hiram, though the expression on his countenance had rendered that information superfluous.

"Ditto and the same," admitted the Cap'n. "Haven't brought yourn, have you?"

"Wife's holdin' onto it for evidence when she gets her bill of divorce," said Hiram.

"Ditto with me," affirmed Cap'n Sproul. "Tellin' mine the truth was what really started her mad up. It was just plain mystery up to that time, and she only felt sorry. When I told her the truth she said if it was that bad it would prob'ly turn out to be worse, and so long's I'd owned up to a part of it I'd better go ahead and tell the rest, and so on! And now she won't believe anything I try to tell her."

"Same over to my place," announced his despondent friend.

"It's your own cussed fault," blazed the Cap'n. "My notion was to lie to 'em. You can make a lie smooth and convincin'. The truth of this thing sounds fishy. It would sound fishy to me if I didn't know it was so."

"Since I got out of the circus business I've been tryin' to do business with less lyin', but it doesn't seem to work," mourned Hiram. "Maybe what's good for the circus business is good for all kinds. Seems to be that way! Well, when you'd told her the straight truth and had been as square as you could, what did you say to her when she flared up?"

"Northin'," answered the Cap'n. "Didn't seem to be northin' to say to fit the case."

"Not after the way they took the truth when it was offered to 'em," agreed Hiram. "I didn't say anything out loud. I said it to myself, and it would have broke up the party if a little bird had twittered it overhead at a Sunday-school picnic."

That day Jackson Denslow, pricked by a fee of ten dollars, made more searching investigation. It was almost a census. Absolutely no trace of such a stranger! Denslow sullenly said that such a domiciliary visit was stirring up a lot of talk, distrust, and suspicion, and, as he couldn't answer any questions as to who she was, where she came from, and what was wanted of her, nor hint as to who his employers were, it was currently stated that he had gone daffy over the detective business. His tone of voice indicated that he thought others were similarly afflicted. He allowed that no detective could detect until he had all the facts.

He demanded information and sneered when it was not given.

It was an unfortunate attitude to take toward men, the triggers of whose tempers had been cocked by such events as had beset Hiram Look and Aaron Sproul. Taking it that the constable was trying to pry into their business in order to regale the public on their misfortunes, Hiram threw a town-ledger at him, and the Cap'n kicked at him as he fled through the door of the office.

That night each was met at the front door by hysterics, and a third letter. The mystery was becoming eerie.

"Dang rabbit her miserable pelt!" growled Hiram at the despairing morning conference under the poplars. "She must be livin' in a hole round here, or else come in a balloon. I tell you, Cap'n Sproul, it's got to be stopped some way or the two families will be in the lunatic asylum inside of a week."

"Or more prob'ly in the divorce court. Louada Murilla vows and declares she'll get a bill if I don't tell her the truth, and when you've told the truth once and sworn to it, and it don't stick, what kind of a show is a lie goin' to stand, when a man ain't much of a liar?"

"If she's goin' to be caught we've got to catch her," insisted Hiram. "She's crazy, or else she wouldn't be watchin' for us to leave the house so as to grab in and toss one of them letters. Looks to me it's just revenge, and to make trouble. The darned fool can't marry both of us. I didn't sleep last night—not with that woman of mine settin' and boohooin'. I just set and thought. And the result of the thinkin' is that we'll take our valises to-day and march to the railroad-station in the face and eyes of everybody so that it will get spread round that we've gone. And we'll come back by team from some place down the line, and lay low either round your premises or mine and ketch that infernal, frowzle-headed sister of Jim the Penman by the hind leg and snap her blasted head off."

"What be you goin' to tell the wimmen?"

"Tell 'em northin'."

"There'll be the devil to pay. They'll think we're elopin'."

"Well, let 'em think," said Hiram, stubbornly. "They can't do any harder thinkin' than I've been thinkin', and they can't get a divorce in one night. When we ketch that woman we can preach a sermon to 'em with a text, and she'll be the text."

Cap'n Sproul sighed and went for his valise.

"What she said to me as I come away curled the leaves in the front yard," confided Hiram, as they walked together down the road.

"Ditto and the same," mourned the Cap'n.

At dusk that evening they dismounted from a Vienna livery-hitch on a back road in Smyrna, paid the driver and dismissed the team, and started briskly through the pastures across lots toward Hiram Look's farm.

An hour later, moving with the stealth of red Indians, they posted themselves behind the stone wall opposite the lane leading into the Look dooryard. They squatted there breathing stertorously, their eyes goggling into the night.

The Cap'n, with vision trained by vigils at sea, was the first to see the dim shape approaching. When she had come nearer they saw a tall feather nodding against the dim sky.

"Let's get her before she throws the letter—get her with the goods on her!" breathed Hiram, huskily. And when she was opposite they leaped the stone wall.

She had seasonable alarm, for several big stones rolled off the wall's top. And she turned and ran down the road with the two men pounding along fiercely in pursuit.

"My Gawd!" gasped Aaron, after a dozen rods; "talk about— gayzelles—she's—she's—"

He didn't finish the sentence, preferring to save his breath.

But skirts are an awkward encumbrance in a sprinting match. Hiram, with longer legs than the pudgy Cap'n, drew ahead and overhauled the fugitive foot by foot. And at sound of his footsteps behind her, and his hoarse grunt, "I've got ye!" she whirled and, before the amazed showman could protect himself, she struck out and knocked him flat on his back. But when she turned again to run she stepped on her skirt, staggered forward dizzily, and fell in a heap. The next instant the Cap'n tripped over Hiram, tumbled heavily, rolled over twice, and brought up against the prostrate fugitive, whom he clutched in a grasp there was no breaking.

"Don't let her hit ye," howled Hiram, struggling up. "She's got an arm like a mule's hind leg."

"And whiskers like a goat!" bawled the Cap'n, choking in utter astonishment. "Strike a match and let's see what kind of a blamenation catfish this is, anyhow."

And a moment later, the Cap'n's knees still on the writhing figure, they beheld, under the torn veil, by the glimmer of the match, the convulsed features of Batson Reeves, second selectman of the town of Smyrna.

"Well, marm," remarked Hiram, after a full thirty seconds of amazed survey, "you've sartinly picked out a starry night for a ramble."

Mr. Reeves seemed to have no language for reply except some shocking oaths.

"That ain't very lady-like talk," protested Look, lighting another match that he might gloat still further. "You ought to remember that you're in the presence of your two 'darlin's.' We can't love any one that cusses. You'll be smokin' a pipe or chawin' tobacker next." He chuckled, and then his voice grew hard. "Stop your wigglin', you blasted, livin' scarecrow, or I'll split your head with a rock, and this town will call it good reddance. Roll him over onto his face, Cap'n Sproul."

A generous strip of skirt, torn off by Reeves's boot, lay on the ground. Hiram seized it and bound the captive's arms behind his back. "Now let him up, Cap," he commanded, and the two men helped the unhappy selectman to his feet.

"So it's you, hey?" growled Hiram, facing him. "Because I've come here to this town and found a good woman and married her, and saved her from bein' fooled into marryin' a skunk like you, you've put up this job, hey? Because Cap'n Sproul has put you where you belong in town business, you're tryin' to do him, too, hey? What do you reckon we're goin' to do with you?"

It was evident that Mr. Reeves was not prepared to state. He maintained a stubborn silence.

Cap'n Sproul had picked up the hat with the tall feather and was gingerly revolving it in his hands.

"You're a nice widderer, you are!" snorted Hiram. "A man that will wear a deceased's clothes in order to help him break up families and spread sorrow and misery round a neighborhood, would be a second husband to make a woman both proud and pleased. Cap'n, put that hat and veil back onto him. I'll hold him."

Mr. Reeves consented to stand still only after he had received a half-dozen open-handed buffets that made his head ring.

"There!" ejaculated Hiram, after the Cap'n's unaccustomed fingers had arranged the head-gear. "Bein' that you're dressed for company, we'll make a few calls. Grab a-holt, Cap'n."

"I'll die in my tracks right here, first," squalled Reeves, guessing their purpose. But he was helpless in their united clutch. They rushed him up the lane, tramped along the piazza noisily, jostled through the front door, and presented him before Hiram's astounded wife.

"Mis' Look," said her husband, "here's the lady that's in love with me, and that has been leavin' me letters. It bein' the same lady that was once in love with you, I reckon you'll appreciate my feelin's in the matter. There's just one more clue that we need to clinch this thing—and that's another one of those letters. The Cap'n and I don't know how to find a pocket in a woman's dress. We're holdin' this lady. You hunt for the pocket, Mis' Look."

The amazement on her comely face changed to sudden and indignant enlightenment.

"The miserable scalawag!" she cried. The next instant, with one thrust of her hand, she had the damning evidence. There were two letters.

"She ain't delivered the one to darlin' Cap'n Sproul this evenin'," Hiram remarked, persisting still in his satiric use of the feminine pronoun. "If you'll put on your bonnet, Mis' Look, we'll all sa'nter acrost to the Cap'n's and see that Louada Murilla gets hers. Near's I can find out, the rules of this special post-office is that all love-letters to us pass through our wives' hands."

In the presence of Mrs. Sproul, after the excitement of the dramatic entrance had subsided, the unhappy captive attempted excuses, cringing pitifully.

"I didn't think of it all by myself," he bleated. "It was what the Dawn woman said, and then when I mentioned that I had some grudges agin' the same parties she wrote the notes, and the perfessor planned the rest, so't we could both get even. But it wasn't my notion. I reckon he mesmerized me into it. I ain't to blame. Them mesmerists has awful powers."

"Ya-a-a-as, that's probably just the way of it!" sneered Hiram, with blistering sarcasm. "But you'll be unmesmerized before we get done with you. There's nothin' like makin' a good job of your cure, seein' that you was unfort'nit' enough to get such a dose of it that it's lasted you a week. Grab him, Cap'n."

"What be ye goin' to do now?" quavered Reeves.

"Take you down into the village square, and, as foreman of the Ancient and Honer'ble Firemen's Association, I'll ring the bell and call out the department, stand you up in front of them all in your flounces fine, and tell 'em what you've been doin' to their chief. I guess all the heavy work of gettin' even with you will be taken off'm my hands after that."

Reeves groaned.

"As first selectman," broke in the Cap'n, "and interested in keepin' bad characters out of town, I shall suggest that they take and ride you into Vienny on a rail."

"With my fife and drum corps ahead," shouted Hiram, warming to the possibilities.

"I'll die here in my tracks first!" roared the captive.

"It's kind of apparent that Madame Dawn didn't give you lessons in prophesyin', along with the rest of her instruction," remarked Hiram. "That makes twice this evenin' that you've said you were goin' to die, and you're still lookin' healthy. Come along! Look happy, for you're goin' to be queen of the May, mother!"

But when they started to drag him from the room both women interposed.

"Hiram, dear," pleaded his wife, "please let the man go. Louada Murilla and I know now what a scalawag he is, and we know how we've misjudged both you and Cap'n Sproul, and we'll spend the rest of our lives showin' you that we're sorry. But let him go! If you make any such uproar as you're talkin' of it will all come out that he made your wives believe that you were bad men. It will shame us to death, Hiram. Please let him go."

"Please let him go, Aaron," urged Mrs. Sproul, with all the fervor of her feelings. "It will punish him worst if you drop him here and now, like a snake that you've picked up by mistake."

Cap'n Sproul and Hiram Look stared at each other a long time, meditating. They went apart and mumbled in colloquy. Then the Cap'n trudged to his front door, opened it, and held it open. Hiram cut the strip that bound their captive's wrists.

The second selectman had not the courage to raise his eyes to meet the stares directed on him. With head bowed and the tall feather nodding over his face he slunk out into the night. And Hiram and the Cap'n called after him in jovial chorus:

"Good-night, marm!"

"This settling down in life seems to be more or less of a complicated performance," observed Cap'n Sproul when the four of them were alone, "but just at this minute I feel pretty well settled. I reckon I've impressed it on a few disturbers in this town that I'm the sort of a man that's better left alone. It looks to me like a long, calm spell of weather ahead."

XVII

Mr. Gammon's entrance into the office of the first selectman of Smyrna was unobtrusive. In fact, to employ a paradox, it was so unobtrusive as to be almost spectacular.

The door opened just about wide enough to admit a cat, were that cat sufficiently slab-sided, and Mr. Gammon slid his lath-like form in edgewise. He stood beside the door after he had shut it softly behind him. He gazed forlornly at Cap'n Aaron Sproul, first selectman. Outside sounded a plaintive *"Squawnk!"*

Cap'n Sproul at that moment had his fist up ready to spack it down into his palm to add emphasis to some particularly violent observation he was just then making to Mr. Tate, highway "surveyor" in Tumble-dick District. Cap'n Sproul jerked his chin around over his shoulder so as to stare at Mr. Gammon, and held his fist poised in air.

"Squawnk!" repeated the plaintive voice outside.

Mr. Gammon had a head narrowed in the shape of an old-fashioned coffin, and the impression it produced was fully as doleful. His neighbors in that remote section of Smyrna known as "Purgatory," having the saving grace of humor, called him "Cheerful Charles."

The glare in the Cap'n's eyes failed to dislodge him, and the Cap'n's mind was just then too intent on a certain topic to admit even the digression of ordering Mr. Gammon out.

"What in the name of Josephus Priest do I care what the public demands?" he continued, shoving his face toward the lowering countenance of Mr. Tate. "I've built our end of the road to the town-line accordin' to the line of survey that's best for this town, and now if Vienny ain't got a mind to finish their road to strike the end of our'n, then let the both of 'em yaw apart and end in the sheep-pastur'. The public ain't runnin' this. It's *me*—the first selectman.

You are takin' orders from *me*—and you want to understand it. Don't you nor any one else move a shovelful of dirt till I tell you to."

Hiram Look, retired showman and steady loafer in the selectman's office, rolled his long cigar across his lips and grunted indorsement.

"*Squawnk!*" The appeal outside was a bit more insistent.

Mr. Gammon sighed. Hiram glanced his way and noted that he had a noose of clothes-line tied so tightly about his neck that his flabby dewlap was pinched. He carried the rest of the line in a coil on his arm.

"Public says—" Mr. Tate began to growl.

"Well, what does public say?"

"Public that has to go around six miles by crossro'ds to git into Vienny says that you wa'n't elected to be no crowned head nor no Seizer of Rooshy!" Mr. Tate, stung by memories of the taunts flung at him as surveyor, grew angry in his turn. "I live out there, and I have to take the brunt of it. They think you and that old fool of a Vienny selectman that's lettin' a personal row ball up the bus'ness of two towns are both bedeviled."

"She's prob'ly got it over them, too," enigmatically observed Mr. Gammon, in a voice as hollow as wind in a knot-hole.

This time the outside "*Squawnk*" was so imperious that Mr. Gammon opened the door. In waddled the one who had been demanding admittance.

"It's my tame garnder," said Mr. Gammon, apologetically. "He was lonesome to be left outside."

A fuzzy little cur that had been sitting between Mr. Tate's earth-stained boots ran at the gander and yapped shrilly. The big bird curved his neck, bristled his feathers, and hissed.

"Kick 'em out of here!" snapped the Cap'n, indignantly.

"Any man that's soft-headed enough to have a gander followin' him round everywhere he goes ought to have a guardeen appointed," suggested Mr. Tate, acidulously, after he had recovered his dog and had cuffed his ears.

"My garnder is a gent side of any low-lived dog that ever gnawed carrion," retorted Mr. Gammon, his funereal gloom lifting to show one flash of resentment.

"Look here!" sputtered the Cap'n, "this ain't any Nat'ral History Convention. Shut up, I tell ye, the two of you! Now, Tate, you can up killick and set sail for home. I've given you your course, and don't you let her off one point. You tell the public of this town, and you can stand on the town-line and holler it acrost into Vienny, that the end of that road stays right there."

Mr. Tate, his dog under his arm, paused at the door to fling over his shoulder another muttered taunt about "bedevilment," and disappeared.

"Now, old button on a graveyard gate, what do you want?" demanded Cap'n Sproul, running eye of great disfavor over Mr. Gammon and his faithful attendant. He had heard various reports concerning this widower recluse of Purgatory, and was prepared to dislike him.

"I reckoned she'd prob'ly have it over you, too," said Mr. Gammon, drearily. "It's like her to aim for shinin' marks."

Cap'n Sproul blinked at him, and then turned dubious gaze on Hiram, who leaned back against the whitewashed wall, nesting his head comfortably in his locked fingers.

"If she's bedeviled me and bedeviled you, there ain't no tellin' where she'll stop," Mr. Gammon went on. "And you bein' more of a shinin' mark, it will be worse for you."

"Look here," said the first selectman, squaring his elbows on the table and scowling on "Cheerful Charles," "if you've come to me to get papers to commit you to the insane horsepittle, you've proved your case. You needn't say another word. If it's any other business, get it out of you, and then go off and take a swim with your old web-foot — *there!*"

Mr. Gammon concealed any emotion that the slur provoked. He came along to the table and tucked a paper under the Cap'n's nose.

"There's what Squire Alcander Reeves wrote off for me, and told me to hand it to you. He said it would show you your duty."

The selectman stared up at Mr. Gammon when he uttered the hateful name of Reeves. Mr. Gammon twisted the noose on his neck so that the knot would come under his ear, and endured the stare with equanimity.

With spectacles settled on a nose that wrinkled irefully, the Cap'n perused the paper, his eyes growing bigger. Then he looked at the blank back of the sheet, stared wildly at Mr. Gammon, and whirled to face his friend Look.

"Hiram," he blurted, "you listen to this: 'Pers'nally appeared before me this fifteenth day of September Charles Gammon, of Smyrna, and deposes and declares that by divers arts, charms, spells, and magic, incantations, and evil hocus-pocus, one — one —'"

"Arizima," prompted Mr. Gammon, mournfully. The Cap'n gazed on him balefully, and resumed:

"'One Arizima Orff has bewitched and bedeviled him, his cattle, his chattels, his belongings, including one calf, one churn, and various ox-chains. It is therefore the opinion of the court that the first selectman of Smyrna, as chief municipal officer, should investigate this case under the law made and provided for the detection of witches, and for that purpose I have put this writing in the hands of

Mr. Gammon that he may summon the proper authority, same being first selectman aforesaid.'"

"That is just how he said it to me," confirmed "Cheerful Charles." "He said that it was a thing for the selectman to take hold of without a minute's delay. I wish you'd get your hat and start for my place now and forthwith."

Cap'n Sproul paid no attention to the request. He was searching the face of Hiram with eyes in which the light was growing lurid.

"I'm goin' over to his office and hosswhip him, and I want you to come along and see me do it." He crumpled the paper into a ball, threw it into a corner, and stumped to the window.

"It's just as I reckoned," he raged. "He was lookin' out to see how the joke worked. I see him dodge back. He's behind the curtain in his office." Again he whirled on Hiram. "After what the Reeves family has tried to do to us," he declared, with a flourish of his arm designed to call up in Mr. Look's soul all the sour memories of things past, "he's takin' his life in his hands when he starts in to make fun of me with a lunatic and a witch-story."

Mr. Gammon had recovered the dishonored document, and was smoothing it on the table.

"That's twice you've called me a lunatic," he remonstrated. "You call me that again, and you'll settle for slander! Now, I've come here with an order from the court, and your duty is laid before you. When a town officer has sworn to do his duty and don't do it, a citizen can make it hot for him." Mr. Gammon, his bony hands caressing his legal document, was no longer apologetic. "Be you goin' to do your duty—yes or no?"

"If—if—you ain't a—say, what have you got that rope around your neck for?" demanded the first selectman.

"To show to the people that if I ain't protected from persecution and relieved of my misery by them that's in duty bound to do the same, I'll go out and hang myself—and the blame will then be placed where it ought to be placed," declared Mr. Gammon, shaking a gaunt finger at the Cap'n.

As a man of hard common sense the Cap'n wanted to pounce on the paper, tear it up, announce his practical ideas on the witchcraft question, and then kick Mr. Gammon and his gander into the middle of the street. But as town officer he gazed at the end of that monitory finger and took second thought.

And as he pondered, Hiram Look broke in with a word.

"I know it looks suspicious, comin' from a Reeves," said he, "but I hardly see anything about it to start your temper so, Cap."

"Why, he might just as well have sent me a writin' to go out and take a census of the hossflies between here and the Vienny town-line," sputtered the first selectman; "or catch the moskeeters in Snell's bog and paint 'em red, white, and blue. I tell you, it's a dirty, sneakin', underhand way of gettin' me laughed at."

"I ain't a humorous man myself, and there ain't no—" began Mr. Gammon.

"Shut up!" bellowed the Cap'n. "It was only last week, Hiram, that that old gob of cat-meat over there that calls himself a lawyer said I'd taken this job of selectman as a license to stick my nose into everybody's business in town. Now, here he is, rigging me out with a balloon-jib and stays'ls"—he pointed a quivering finger at the paper that Mr. Gammon was nursing—"and sendin' me off on a tack that will pile me up on Fool Rocks. Everybody can say it of me, then—that I'm stickin' my nose in. Because there ain't any witches, and never was any witches."

"Ain't witches?" squealed Mr. Gammon. "Why, you—"

But Hiram checked the outburst with flapping palm.

"Here!" he cried. "The two of you wait just a minute. Keep right still until I come back. Don't say a word to each other. It will only be wasting breath."

He went out, and they heard him clumping up the stairs into the upper part of the town house.

He came back with several books in the hook of his arm and found the two mute and not amiable. He surveyed them patronizingly, after he had placed the books on the table.

"Gents, once when I was considerably younger and consequently reckoned that I knew about all there was to know, not only all the main points, but all the foot-notes, I didn't allow anybody else to know anything. And I used to lose more or less money betting that this and that wasn't so. Then up would come the fellow with the cyclopedy and his facts and his figgers. At last I was so sure of one thing that I bet a thousand on it, and a fellow hit me over the head with every cyclopedy printed since the time Noah waited for the mud to dry. I got my lesson! After that I took my tip from the men that have spent time findin' out. I'm more or less of a fool now, but before that I was such a fool that I didn't know that I didn't know enough to know that I didn't know."

"What did you bet on?" inquired the Cap'n, with a gleam of interest.

"None of your business!" snapped Hiram, a red flush on his cheek. "But if I'd paid more attention to geography in my school than I did to tamin' toads and playin' circus I wouldn't have bet."

He opened one of the books that he had secured in his trip to the town library.

"Now, you say offhand, Cap, that there never was such a thing as a witch. Well, right here are the figgers to show that between 1482 and 1784 more than three hundred thousand wimmen were put to death in Europe for bein' witches. There's the facts under 'Witches' in your own town cyclopedy."

Cap'n Sproul did not appear to be convinced.

"There it is, down in black and white," persisted Hiram. "Now, how about there never bein' any witches?" He tapped his finger on the open page.

"If the book says that, witches must be extinker than dodos. Your cyclopedy don't say anything about any of 'em gettin' away and comin' over to this country, does it?"

"Of *course* we've had 'em in this country," said Hiram, opening another book. "Caught 'em by the dozen in Salem! Cotton Mather made a business of it. You don't think a man like Cotton Mather is lettin' himself be fooled on the witch question, do you? Here's the book he wrote. A man that's as pious as Cotton Mather ain't makin' up lies and writin' 'em down, and puttin' himself on record."

"There's just as many witches to-day as there ever was," cried the corroborative Mr. Gammon. "The trouble is they ain't hunted out and brought to book for their infernal actions. There's hundreds and hundreds of folks goin' through this life pestered all the time with trouble that's made for 'em by a witch, and they don't know what's the matter with 'em. But they can't fool me. I know witches when I see 'em. And when she turns herself into a cat and —"

"Does *what*?" demanded the Cap'n, testily.

"Why, it wa'n't more'n three nights ago that I heard her yowlin' away in my barn chamber, and there she was, turned into a cat most as big as a ca'f, and I throwed an iron kittle at her and she come right through the bottom of it like it was a paper hoop. There, now! What have you got to say to that?"

"That you are about as handy a liar as I ever had stand up in front of me," returned the Cap'n, with animation. He whirled on Hiram and gesticulated at the books. "Do you mean to tell me that you're standin' in with him on any such jing-bedoozled, blame' foolishness as this? I took you to be man-grown."

"It's always easy enough to r'ar up in this world and blart that things ain't so," snapped Hiram, with some heat. "Fools do that thing right along. I don't want you to be that kind. Live and learn."

"Witches or no witches, cyclopedy or no cyclopedy, what I want to know is, do you want to have it passed round this community that the two of us set here—men that have been round this world as much as we have—and heard a man tell a cat-and-kittle story like that, and lapped it down? They'll be here sellin' us counterfeit money and gold bricks next."

Hiram blinked a little doubtfully at Mr. Gammon, and his rope and gander, and probably, under ordinary circumstances, would have flouted that gentleman. But the authority of the encyclopedia gave his naturally disputatious nature a stimulus not to be resisted. Beating the page with the back of his hand, he assembled his proof that there had been witches, that there are witches, and that there will be more witches in the future. And he wound up by declaring that Mr. Gammon probably knew what he was talking about—a statement that Mr. Gammon indorsed with a spirited tale of how his ox-chains had been turned into mighty serpents in his dooryard, and had thrashed around there all night to his unutterable distress and alarm. Again he demanded investigation of his case, and protection by the authorities.

In this appeal he was backed by Hiram, who volunteered his assistance in making the investigation. And in the end, Cap'n Sproul, as first selectman of Smyrna, consented to visit the scene of alleged enchantment in "Purgatory," though as private citizen he criticised profanely the state of mind that allowed him to go on such an errand. He gnawed his beard, and a flush of something like shame settled on his cheek. It seemed to him that he was allowing himself to be cajoled into a mild spree of lunacy.

"And there bein' no time like the present, and my horse bein' hitched out there in the shed," advised Hiram, briskly, "why not go now? Did you ride out from your place or walk?" he inquired of "Cheerful Charles."

"Walked," replied Mr. Gammon, dejectedly. "My hoss is bewitched, too. Can't get him out of the stable."

"We'll take you along with us," was Hiram's kindly proffer.

"Him and that gander?" protested the Cap'n.

"I can set in behind with the garnder under my arm," urged Mr. Gammon, meekly.

The Cap'n came around the table and angrily twitched the rope off Mr. Gammon's neck. That much concession to the convenances he demanded with a vigor that his doleful constituent did not gainsay.

When they drove away the baleful eye of the first selectman spied Squire Alcander Reeves furtively regarding them through the dingy glass of his office window.

"Me off witch-chasin' and him standin' there grinnin' at it like a jezeboo!" he gritted. And he surveyed, with no very gracious regard, his companions in this unspeakable quest.

When they were well out of the village Mr. Gammon twisted his neck and sought to impart more information over the back of the seat.

"I tell you, she's a cooler when it comes to bedevilin'. She had an old Leghorn hen that a mink killed just after the hen had brought out a brood of chickens. And what do you s'pose she done? Why, she went right to work and put a cluck onto the cat, and the cat has brooded 'em ever since."

The Cap'n emitted a snort of disgust.

"And here we are, two sensible men, ridin' around over this town an' tryin' to make head and tail out of such guff as that! Do you pretend to tell me for one minute, Hiram Look, that you take any kind of stock in this sort of thing? Now, just forget that cyclopedy business and your ancient history for a few minutes and be honest. Own up that you were arguin' to hear yourself talk, and that you're dragging me out here to pass away the time."

Hiram scratched his nose and admitted that now the Cap'n had asked for friendly candor, he really didn't take much stock in witches.

"There! I knew it!" cried the selectman, with unction and relief. "And now that you've had your joke and done with it, let's dump out old coffin-mug and his gander and turn round and go back about our business."

But Hiram promptly whipped along.

"Oh, thunder!" he ejaculated. "While we're about it, we might as well see it through. My curiosity is sort of stirred up."

The Cap'n was angry in good earnest again.

"Curiosity!" he snarled. "Now you've named it. I wouldn't own up to bein' such a pickid-nosed old maid as that, not for a thousand dollars!"

Hiram was wholly unruffled.

"How do you suppose any one ever knew enough to write a cyclopedy," said he, "if they didn't go investigate and find out? They went official, just as we are goin' now."

Hiram seemed to take much content in that phase of the situation, feeling that mere personal inquisitiveness was dignified in this case under the aegis of law and authority. It was exactly this view of the matter that most disturbed Cap'n Aaron Sproul, for that hateful

Pharisee, Squire Reeves, had supplied the law to compel his own authority as selectman.

He sat with elbows on his knees, gloomily surveying a dim reflection of himself in the dasher of Hiram's wagon. In pondering on the trammels of responsibility the sour thought occurred to him, as it had many times in the past year, that commanding a town was a different proposition from being ruler of the *Jefferson P. Benn* on the high seas—with the odds in favor of the *Benn*.

XVIII

The Cap'n had never visited that retired part of the town called "Purgatory." He found Mr. Gammon's homestead to be a gray and unkempt farm-house from which the weather had scrubbed the paint. The front yard was bare of every vestige of grass and contained a clutter that seemed to embrace everything namable, including a gravestone.

"What be ye gettin' ready for—an auction?" growled the Cap'n, groutily, his seaman's sense of tidiness offended. "Who do you expect will bid in a second-hand gravestone?"

"It ain't second-hand," replied the owner, reprovingly, as he eased himself out of the wagon. "Mis' Gammon, my first wife, is buried there. 'Twas by her request. She made her own layin'-out clothes, picked her bearers and music, and selected the casket. She was a capable woman."

"It's most a wonder to me that he ever took the crape off'm the door-knob," remarked Hiram, in a husky aside to the Cap'n, not intending to be overheard and somewhat crestfallen to find that he had been.

"I didn't for some time, till it got faded," explained Mr. Gammon, without display of resentment. "I had the casket-plate mounted on black velvet and framed. It's in the settin'-room. I'll show it to you before you leave."

Hiram pulled his mouth to one side and hissed under shelter of his big mustache: "Well, just what a witch would want of *that* feller, unless 'twas to make cracked ice of him, blame me if I know!"

Mr. Gammon began apprehensive survey of his domains.

"Let's go home," muttered the Cap'n, his one idea of retreat still with him. "What do you and I know about witches, anyway, even if there are such things? We've done our duty! We've been here. If he gets us to investigatin' it will be just like him to want us to dig that woman up."

His appeal was suddenly interrupted. Mr. Gammon, peering about his premises for fresh evidences of witchcraft accomplished during his absence, bellowed frantic request to "Come, see!" He was behind the barn, and they hastened thither.

"My Gawd, gents, they've witched the ca'f!" Their eyes followed the direction of his quivering finger.

A calf was placidly surveying them from among the branches of a "Sopsy-vine" apple-tree, munching an apple that he had been able to reach. Whatever agency had boosted him there had left him wedged into the crotch of the limbs so that he could not move, though he appeared to be comfortable.

"It jest takes all the buckram out of me—them sights do," wailed Mr. Gammon. "I can't climb up there and do it. One of you will have to." He pulled out a big jackknife, opened it with his yellow teeth, and extended it.

"Have to do what?" demanded Hiram.

"Cut off his ears and tail. That's the only way to get him out from under the charm."

But Hiram, squinting up to assure himself that the calf was comfortable, pushed Mr. Gammon back and made him sit down on a pile of bean-poles.

"Better put your hat between your knees," he suggested, noting the way Mr. Gammon's thin knees were jigging. "You might knock a sliver off the bones, rappin' them together that way."

He lighted one of his long cigars, his shrewd eyes searching Mr. Gammon all the time.

"Now," said he, tipping down a battered wheelbarrow and sitting on it, "there's nothin' like gettin' down to cases. We're here official. The first selectman of this town is here. Go ahead, Cap'n Sproul, and put your questions."

"Ask 'em yourself," snorted the Cap'n, with just a flicker of resentful malice; "you're the witch expert. I ain't."

"Well," retorted Hiram, with an alacrity that showed considerable zest for the business in hand, "I never shirked duty. First, what's her name again—the woman that's doin' it all?"

"I want you to come and see—" began Mr. Gammon, apparently having his own ideas as to a witch-hunt, but Hiram shook the big cigar at him fiercely.

"We ain't got time nor inclination for inspectin' coffin-plates, wax-flowers, bewitched iron kittles, balky horses, and old ganders. Who is this woman and where does she live, and what's the matter with her?"

"She's Arizima Orff, and that's her house over the rise of that land where you can see the chimblys." Mr. Gammon was perfunctory in that reply, but immediately his little blue eyes began to sparkle and he launched out into his troubles. "There's them that don't believe in witches. I know that! And they slur me and slander me. I know it. I don't get no sympathy. I—"

"Shut up!" commanded the chief of the inquisition.

"They say I'm crazy. But I know better. Here I am with rheumaticks! Don't you s'pose I know where I got 'em? It was by standin' out all het up where she had hitched me after she'd rid' me to one of the witch conventions. She—"

"Say, you look here!" roared the old showman; "you stay on earth. Don't you try to fly and take us with you. There's the principal trouble in gettin' at facts," he explained, whirling on the Cap'n.

"Investigators don't get down to cases. Talk with a stutterer, and if you don't look sharp you'll get to stutterin' yourself. Now, if we don't look out, Gammon here will have us believin' in witches before we've investigated."

"You been sayin' right along that you did believe in 'em," grunted the first selectman.

"Northin' of the sort!" declared Hiram. "I was only showin' you that when you rose up and hollered that there never was any witches you didn't know what you were talkin' about."

While Cap'n Sproul was still blinking at him, trying to comprehend the exact status of Hiram's belief, that forceful inquisitor, who had been holding his victim in check with upraised and admonitory digit, resumed:

"Old maid or widder?"

"Widder."

"Did deceased leave her that farm, title clear, and well-fixed financially?"

"Yes," acknowledged Mr. Gammon.

"Now," Hiram leaned forward and wagged that authoritative finger directly under the other's case-knife nose, "what was it she done to you to make you get up this witch-story business about her? Here! Hold on!" he shouted, detecting further inclination on the part of Mr. Gammon to rail about his bedevilment. "You talk good Yankee common sense! Down to cases! What started this? You can't fool me, not for a minute! I've been round the world too much. I know every fake from a Patagonian cockatoo up to and including the ghost of Bill Beeswax. She done something to you. Now, what was it?"

Mr. Gammon was cowed. He fingered his dewlap and closed and unclosed his lips.

"Out with it!" insisted Hiram. "If you don't, me and the selectman will have you sued for slander."

"Up to a week ago," confessed Mr. Gammon, gazing away from the blazing eyes of Hiram into the placid orbs of the calf in the tree, "we was goin' to git married. Farms adjoined. She knowed me and I knowed her. I've been solemn since Mis' Gammon died, but I've been gittin' over it. We was goin' to jine farms and I was goin' to live over to her place, because it wouldn't be so pleasant here with Mis' Gammon—"

He hesitated, and ducked despondent head in the direction of the front yard.

"Well, seconds don't usually want to set in the front parlor window and read firsts' epitaphs for amusement," remarked Hiram, grimly. "What then?"

"Well, then all at once she wouldn't let me into the house, and she shooed me off'm her front steps like she would a yaller cat, and when I tried to find out about it that young Haskell feller that she's hired to do her chores come over here and told me that he wasn't goin' to stay there much longer, 'cause she had turned witch, and had put a cluck onto the cat when the old hen—"

"'Tend to cases! 'Tend to cases!" broke in Hiram, impatiently.

"And about that time the things began to act out round my place, and the Haskell boy told me that she was braggin' how she had me bewitched."

"And you believed that kind of infernal tomrot?" inquired the showman, wrathfully. Somewhat to the Cap'n's astonishment, Hiram seemed to be taking only a sane and normal view of the thing.

"I did, after I went over and taxed her with it, and she stood off and pointed her shotgun at me and said that yes, she was a witch, and if I didn't get away and keep away she would turn me into a caterpillar and kill me with a fly-spanker. There! When a woman says that about herself, what be ye goin' to do—tell her she's a liar, or be a gent and believe her?" Mr. Gammon was bridling a little.

Hiram looked at "Cheerful Charles" and jerked his head around and stared at the Cap'n as though hoping for some suggestion. But the selectman merely shook his head with a pregnant expression of "I told you so!"

Hiram got up and stamped around the tree to cover what was evidently momentary embarrassment. All at once he kicked at something in the grass, bent over and peered at it, looked up at the calf, then picked up the object on the ground and stuffed it deep into his trousers pocket.

"You said that chore feller's name was Haskell, hey?" he demanded, returning and standing over Mr. Gammon.

"Simmy Haskell," said the other.

"Well, now, what have you done to *him*?"

"Nothin'—never—no, sir—never nothin'!" insisted Mr. Gammon, with such utter conviction that Hiram forebore to question further. He whirled on his heel and started away toward the chimney that poked above the rise of land.

"Come along!" he called, gruffly, over his shoulder, and the two followed.

It was a trim little place that was revealed to them. A woman in a sunbonnet was on her knees near some plants in the cozy front yard, and a youth was wheeling apples up out of the orchard.

The youth set down his barrow and surveyed them with some curiosity as they came up to him, Hiram well ahead, looming with all his six feet two, his plug-hat flashing in the sun. Hiram did not pause to palter with the youth. He grabbed him by the back of the neck with one huge hand, and with the other tapped against the Haskell boy's nose the object he had picked up from the grass.

"Next time you put a man's calf up a tree look out that you don't drop your knife in the wrassle."

"'Tain't my knife!" gasped the accused.

"Lie to me, will ye? Lie to me—a man that's associated with liars all my life? Not your knife, when your name is scratched on the handle? And don't you know that two officers stood right over behind the stone wall and saw you do it? Because you wasn't caught in your cat-yowlin' round and your ox-chain foolishness and your other didoes, do you think you can fool a detective like me? You come along to State Prison! I *was* intendin' to let you off if you owned up and told all you know—but now that you've lied to me, come along to State Prison!"

There was such vengefulness and authority in the big man's visage that the Haskell boy wilted in unconditional surrender.

"He got me into the scrape. I'll tell on him. I don't want to go to State Prison," he wailed, and then confession flowed from him with the steady gurgle of water from a jug. "He come to me, and he says, says he, 'He won't ever be no kind of a boss for you. If he marries her you'll get fed on bannock and salt pork. He's sourer'n bonny-clabber and meaner'n pig-swill. Like enough he won't keep help, anyway, and will let everything go to rack and ruin, the same as he has on his own place. I'm the one to stick to,' says he. 'I've got a way planned, and all I need is your help and we'll stand together,' he says, 'and here's ten dollars in advance.' And I took it and done what he planned. I needed the money, and I done it. He says to me that we'll do things to him to make him act crazy, and we'll tell her that he's dangerous, and then you can tell him, says he, that she's turned witch, and is doin' them things to him; 'cause a man that has got his first wife buried in front of his doorstep is fool enough to believe most anything,' says he."

"Well," remarked Hiram, after a long breath, "this 'sezzer,' whoever he may be, when he got to sezzin', seems to have made up his mind that there was one grand, sweet song of love in this locality that was goin' to be sung by a steam-calliope, and wind up with boiler bustin'."

"Why in devilnation don't you ask him who 'twas that engineered it?" demanded Cap'n Sproul, his eyes blazing with curiosity.

"An official investigation," declared Hiram, with a relish he could not conceal, as he returned the Cap'n's earlier taunt upon that gentleman himself, "is not an old maids' quiltin'-bee, where they throw out the main point as soon's they get their hoods off, and then spend the rest of the afternoon talkin' it over. Things has to take their right and proper course in an official investigation. *I'm* the official investigator."

He turned on Mr. Gammon.

"What do you think now, old hearse-hoss? Have you heard enough to let you in on this? Or do you want to be proved out as the original old Mister Easymark, in a full, illustrated edition, bound in calf? So fur's I'm concerned, I've heard enough on that line to make me sick."

This amazing demolishment of his superstition left Mr. Gammon gasping. Only one pillar of that mental structure was standing. He grabbed at it.

"I didn't believe she was the witch till she told me so herself," he stammered. "She never lied to me. I believed what she told me with her own mouth."

The Haskell boy, still in the clutch of Hiram, evidently believed that the kind of confession that was good for the soul was full confession.

"I told her that the time you was dangerousest was when any one disputed with you about not havin' the witches. I told her that if you ever said anything she'd better join in and agree with you, and humor you, 'cause that's the only way to git along with crazy folks."

For the first time in many years color showed in the drab cheeks of the melancholy Mr. Gammon. Two vivid red spots showed that, after all, it was blood, not water, that flowed in his veins.

"Dod lather you to a fritter, you little freckle-faced, snub-nosed son of seco!" he yelped, shrilly. "I've been a mild and peaceable man all my life, but I'm a good mind to—I'm a good mind to—" He searched his meek soul for enormities of retribution, and declared: "I'm a good mind to skin you, hide, pelt, and hair. I'll cuff your ears up to a pick, any way!" But Hiram pushed him away when he advanced.

"There! That's the way to talk up, Gammon," he said, encouragingly. "You are showin' improvement. Keep on that way and you'll get to be quite a man. I was afraid you wasn't anything but a rusty marker for a graveyard lot. If you don't keep your back up *some* in this world, you're apt to get your front knocked in. But I can't let you lick the boy! This investigation is strictly official and according to the law, and he's turned State's evidence. It's the other critter that you want to be gettin' your muscle up for—the feller that was tryin' to get the widder and the property away from you. All the other evidence now bein' in, you may tell the court, my son, who was that 'sezzer.' You sha'n't be hurt!"

"It was Mister Batson Reeves, the second selectman," blurted the youth.

There are moments in life when language fails, when words are vain; when even a whisper would take the edge from a situation. Such a moment seemed that one when Hiram Look and Cap'n Sproul gazed at each other after the Haskell boy had uttered that name.

After a time Hiram turned, seized the boy by the scruff of his coat, and dragged him up to the front-yard fence, where the widow was gazing at them with increasing curiosity.

"Haskell boy," commanded Hiram, "tell her—tell her straight, and do it quick."

And when the confession, which went more glibly the second time, was concluded, the investigator gave the culprit a toss in the direction of the Gammon farm, and shouted after him: "Go get that calf down out of that apple-tree, and set down with him and trace out your family relationship. You'll probably find you're first cousins."

Mrs. Orff had sunk down weakly on a bed of asters, and was staring from face to face.

"Marm," said Hiram, taking off his plug hat and advancing close to the fence, "Cap'n Sproul and myself don't make it our business to pry into private affairs, or to go around this town saving decent wimmen from Batson Reeves. But we seem to have more or less of it shoved onto us as a side-line. You listen to me! Batson Reeves was the man that lied to the girl I was engaged to thirty years ago, and broke us up and kept us apart till I came back here and licked him, and saved her just in the nick of time. What do you think of a man of that stamp?"

"I didn't really like him as well—as well as—" quavered the widow, her eyes on the appealing orbs of Mr. Gammon; "but I was told I was in danger, and he wanted to be my protector."

"Protector!" sneered Hiram. "Since he's been a widderer he's been tryin' to court and marry every woman in the town of Smyrna that's got a farm and property. We know it. We can prove it. All he wants is money! You've just escaped by luck, chance, and the skin of your teeth from a cuss that northin' is too low for him to lay his hand to. What do you think of a man that, in order to make trouble and disgrace for his neighbors, will dress up in his dead wife's clothes and snoop around back doors and write anonymous letters to confidin' wimmen?"

"My Lawd!" gasped the widow.

"We caught him at it! So, as I say, you've escaped from a hyena. Now, Mr. Gammon only needs a wife like you to get him out of the dumps."

Mr. Gammon wiped tears from his cheeks and gazed down on her.

"Charles," she said, gently, "won't you come into the house for a few minits? I want to talk to you!"

But as Mr. Gammon was about to obey joyously, Hiram seized his arm.

"Just a moment," he objected. "We'll send him right in to you, marm, but we've got just a little matter of business to talk over with him."

And when they were behind the barn he took Mr. Gammon by his coat-collar with the air of a friend.

"Gammon," said he, "what are you goin' to do to him? Me and the Cap'n are interested. He'll be comin' here this evenin'. He'll be comin' to court. Now, what are you goin' to do?"

There was an expression on Mr. Gammon's face that no one had ever seen there before. His eyes were narrowed. His pointed tongue licked his lips. His thin hair bristled.

"What are you goin' to do to him?"

"Lick him!" replied Mr. Gammon. It was laconic, but it sounded like a rat-tail file on steel.

"You can do it!" said Hiram, cheerfully. "The Cap'n and I both have done it, and it's no trouble at all. I was in hopes you'd say that!"

"Lick him till his tongue hangs out!" said Mr. Gammon, with bitterer venom.

"That will be a good place to lay for him; right down there by the alders," suggested the Cap'n, pointing his finger.

"Yes, sir, lick him till his own brother won't know him." And Mr. Gammon clicked together his bony fists, as hard as flints.

"And that's another point!" said Hiram, hastily. "You've seen to-day that I'm a pretty shrewd chap to guess. I've been round the world enough to put two and two together. Makin' man my study is how I've got my property. Now, Gammon, you've got that writin' by Squire Alcander Reeves. When you said 'brother' it reminded me of what I've been ponderin'. Bat Reeves has been making the Widder Orff matter a still hunt. His brother wasn't on. When you went to the squire to complain, squire saw a chance to get the Cap'n into a law scrape—slander, trespass, malicious mischief—something! Them lawyers are ready for anything!"

"Reg'lar sharks!" snapped the selectman.

"Now," continued Hiram, "after you've got Bat Reeves licked to an extent that will satisfy inquirin' friends and all parties interested, you hand that writin' to him! It will show him that his blasted fool of a lawyer brother, by tryin' to feather his own nest, has lost him the widder and her property, got him his lickin', and put him into a hole gen'rally. Tell him that if it hadn't been for that paper drivin' us out here northin' would have been known."

Hiram put up his nose and drew in a long breath of prophetic satisfaction.

"And if I'm any judge of what 'll be the state of Bat Reeves's feelin's in general when he gets back to the village, the Reeves family will finish up by lickin' each other—and when they make a lawsuit out of that it will be worth while wastin' a few hours in court to listen to. How do you figger it, Cap'n?"

"It's a stem-windin', self-actin' proposition that's wound up, and is now tickin' smooth and reg'lar," said the Cap'n, with deep conviction. "They'll both get it!"

And they did.

Cap'n Aaron Sproul and Hiram Look shook hands on the news before nine o'clock the next morning.

XIX

Mr. Loammi Crowther plodded up the road. Mr. Eleazar Bodge stumped down the road.

They arrived at the gate of Cap'n Aaron Sproul, first selectman of Smyrna, simultaneously.

Bathed in the benignancy of bland Indian summer, Cap'n Sproul and his friend Hiram Look surveyed these arrivals from the porch of the Sproul house.

At the gate, with some apprehensiveness, Mr. Bodge gave Mr. Crowther precedence. As usual when returning from the deep woods, Mr. Crowther was bringing a trophy. This time it was a three-legged lynx, which sullenly squatted on its haunches and allowed itself to be dragged through the dust by a rope tied into its collar.

"You needn't be the least mite afeard of that bobcat," protested Mr. Crowther, cheerily; "he's a perfick pet, and wouldn't hurt the infant in its cradle."

The cat rolled back its lips and snarled. Mr. Bodge retreated as nimbly as a man with a peg-leg could be expected to move.

"I got him out of a trap and cured his leg, and he's turrible grateful," continued Mr. Crowther.

But Mr. Bodge trembled even to his mat of red beard as he backed away.

"Him and me has got so's we're good friends, and I call him Robert—Bob for short," explained the captor, wistfully.

"You call him off—that's what you call him," shouted Mr. Bodge. "I hain't had one leg chawed off by a mowin'-machine to let a cust hyeny chaw off the other. Git out of that gateway. I've got business here with these gents."

"So've I," returned Mr. Crowther, meekly; and he went in, dragging his friend.

"I done your arrunt," he announced to the Cap'n. "I cruised them timberlands from Dan to Beersheby, and I'm ready to state facts and figgers."

"Go ahead and state," commanded the Cap'n.

"I reckon it better be in private," advised the other, his pale-blue eyes resting dubiously on Hiram.

"I ain't got no secrets from him," said the Cap'n, smartly. "Break cargo!"

"You'll wish you heard it in private," persisted Mr. Crowther, with deep meaning. "It ain't northin' you'll be proud of."

"I'll run along, I guess!" broke in the old showman. "It may be something—"

"It ain't," snapped the Cap'n. "It's only about them timberlands that my wife owned with her brother, Colonel Gideon Ward. Estate wasn't divided when the old man Ward died, and since we've been married I've had power of attorney from my wife to represent her." His jaw-muscles ridged under his gray beard, and his eyes narrowed in angry reminiscence.

"We've had two annual settlements, me and her brother. First time 'twas a free fight—next time 'twas a riot—third time, well, if there had been a third time I'd have killed him. So I saved myself from State Prison by dividin' accordin' to the map, and then I sent Crowther up to look the property over. There ain't no secret. You sit down, Hiram."

"Considerin' the man, I should think you'd have done your lookin' over before you divided," suggested the showman. He scented doleful possibilities in Mr. Crowther's mien.

"If I'd done business with him fifteen minutes longer by the clock I'd have been in prison now for murder—and it would have been a bloody murder at that," blurted the Cap'n. "It had to be over and done with short and sharp. He took half. I took half. Passed papers. He got away just before I lost control of myself. Narrowest escape I ever had. All I know about the part I've got is that it's well wooded and well watered."

"It is," agreed Mr. Crowther, despondently. "It's the part where the big reservoir dam flows back for most twenty miles. You can sail all over it in a bo't, and cut toothpicks from the tops of the second-growth birch. He collected all the flowage damages. He's lumbered the rest of your half till there ain't northin' there but hoop poles and battens. All the standin' timber wuth anything is on his half. I wouldn't swap a brimstun' dump in Tophet for your half."

"How in the devil did you ever let yourself get trimmed that way?" demanded Hiram. "It's all right for ten-year-old boys to swap jack-knives, sight unseen, but how a man grown would do a thing like you done I don't understand."

"Nor I," agreed the Cap'n, gloomily. "I reckon about all I was thinkin' of was lettin' him get away before I had blood on my hands. I'm afraid of my own self sometimes. And it's bad in the family when you kill a brother-in-law. I took half. He took half. Bein' a sailorman, I reckoned that land was land, acre for acre."

"The only man I ever heard of as bein' done wuss," continued Mr. Crowther, "was a city feller that bought a quarter section of township 'Leven for a game-preserve, and found when he got up there that it was made up of Misery Bog and the south slope of Squaw Mountain, a ledge, and juniper bushes. The only game that could stay there was swamp-swogons, witherlicks, and doodywhackits."

"What's them?" inquired the Cap'n, as though he hoped that he might at least have these tenants on his worthless acres.

"Woods names for things that there ain't none of," vouchsafed Mr. Crowther. "You owe me for twenty-two days' work, nine shillin's a day, amountin' to—"

"Here! Take that and shut up!" barked the Cap'n, shoving bills at him. Then he wagged a stubby finger under Mr. Crowther's nose. "Now you mark well what I say to you! This thing stays right here among us. If I hear of one yip comin' from you about the way I've been done, I'll come round to your place and chop you into mincemeat and feed you to that animile there!"

"Oh, I'm ashamed enough for you so that I won't ever open my mouth," cried Mr. Crowther. He went out through the gate, dragging his sulky captive.

"And you needn't worry about me, neither," affirmed Mr. Bodge, who had been standing unnoted in the shadow of the woodbine.

"Of course," he continued, "I ain't got so thick with either of you gents as some others has in this place, never likin' to push myself in where I ain't wanted. But I know you are both gents and willin' to use them right that uses you right."

It was not exactly a veiled threat, but it was a hint that checked certain remarks that the Cap'n was about to address to the eavesdropper.

Mr. Bodge took advantage of the truce, and seated himself on the edge of the porch, his peg-leg sticking straight out in forlorn nakedness.

"Investments is resky things in these days, Cap'n Sproul. Gold-mines—why, you can't see through 'em, nor the ones that run 'em. And mark what has been done to you when you invested in the forest primeval! I knowed I was comin' here at just the right time.

I've got a wonderful power for knowin' them things. So I came. I'm here. You need a good investment to square yourself for a poor one. Here it is!" He pulled off his dented derby and patted his bald head.

"Skatin'-rink?" inquired the Cap'n, sarcastically.

"Brains!" boomed Mr. Bodge, solemnly. "But in these days brains have to be backed with capital. I've tried to fight it out, gents, on my own hook. I said to myself right along, 'Brains has got to win in the end, Bodge. Keep on!' But have they? No! Five hundred partunts, gents, locked up in the brains of Eleazar Bodge! Strugglin' to get out! And capital pooled against me! Ignoramuses foolin' the world with makeshifts because they've got capital behind 'em to boost them and keep others down—and Bodge with five hundred partunts right here waitin'." Again he patted the shiny sphere shoved above the riot of hair and whiskers.

The Cap'n scrutinized the surface with sullen interest.

"They'd better stay inside, whatever they are you're talkin' about," he growled. "They couldn't pick up no kind of a livin' on the outside."

"Gents, do you know what's the most solemn sound in all nature?" Mr. Bodge went on. "I heard it as I came away from my house. It was my woman with the flour-barrel ended up and poundin' on the bottom with the rollin'-pin to get out enough for the last batch of biscuit. The long roll beside the graves of departed heroes ain't so sad as that sound. I see my oldest boy in the dooryard with the toes of his boots yawed open like sculpins' mouths. My daughter has outgrown her dress till she has to wear two sets of wristers to keep her arms warm—and she looks like dressed poultry. And as for me, I don't dare to set down enough to get real rested, because my pants are so thin I'm afraid I can't coax 'em along through next winter. I've come to the place, gents, where I've give up. I can't fight the trusts any longer without some backin'. I've got to have somebody take holt of me and get what's in me out. I reelize it now. It's in me. Once out it will make me and all them round me rich like a—a—"

When Mr. Bodge halted for a simile Hiram grunted under his breath: "Like a compost heap."

"I was born the way I am—with something about me that the common run of men don't have. How is it my brains gallop when other brains creep? It's that mysterious force in me. Seein' is believin'. Proof is better than talkin'. Cap'n Sproul, you just take hold of one of my whiskers and yank it out. Take any one, so long's it's a good lengthy one."

His tone was that of a sleight-of-hand man offering a pack of cards for a draw.

The Cap'n obeyed after Mr. Bodge had repeated his request several times, shoving his mat of beard out invitingly.

Mr. Bodge took the whisker from the Cap'n's hand, pinched its butt firmly between thumb and forefinger and elevated it in front of his face. It stuck straight up. Then it began to bend until its tip almost touched his lips. A moment thus and it bent in the other direction.

"There!" cried Mr. Bodge, triumphantly. "Thomas A. Edison himself couldn't do that with one of his whiskers."

"You're right," returned Hiram, gravely. "He'd have to borrow one."

"A man that didn't understand electricity and the forces of nature, and that real brains of a genius are a regular dynamo, might think that I done that with my breath. But there is a strange power about me. All it needs is capital to develop it. You've got the capital, you gents. This ain't any far-away investment. It's right here at home. I'm all business when it comes to business." He stuck up a grimy finger. "You've got to concede the mysterious power because you've seen it for yourselves. Now you come over to my house with me and I'll show you a few inventions that I've been able to put into shape in spite of the damnable combination of the trusts."

He slid off the porch and started away, beckoning them after him with the battered derby.

"I've heard 'em buzz in my time, too," sneered Hiram, pushing back his plug hat, "but that hummin' is about the busiest yet. He could hold a lighted taller candle in his hand and jump off'm a roof and think he was a comet."

But the Cap'n did not seem to be disposed to echo this scorn.

"This here I've got may be only a notion, and it prob'ly is," he said, knotting his gray brows, "and it don't seem sensible. First sight of him you wouldn't think he could be used. But when I laid eyes on old Dot-and-carry-one there, and when he grabbed into this thing the way he did just as I was thinkin' hard of what Colonel Gid Ward has done to me, it came over me that I was goin' to find a use for him."

"How?" persisted the utilitarian Hiram.

"Don't have the least idea," confessed the Cap'n. "It's like pickin' up a stockin' full of wet mud and walkin' along hopin' that you'll meet the man you want to swat with it. I'm goin' to pick him up."

He stumped off the piazza and followed Mr. Bodge. And Hiram, stopping to relight his cigar, went along, too, reflecting that when a man has plenty of time on his hands he can afford to spend a little of it on the gratification of curiosity.

The first exhibits in the domain of Bodge were not cheering or suggestive of value. For instance, from among the litter in a tumble-down shop Mr. Bodge produced something in the shape of a five-pointed star that he called his "Anti-stagger Shoe."

"I saw old Ike Bradley go past here with a hard-cider jag that looped over till its aidges dragged on the ground," he explained. "I tied cross-pieces onto his feet and he went along all level. Now see how a quick mind like mine acts? Here's the anti-stagger shoe. To be kept in all city clubs and et cetry. Let like umbrellas. Five places in each shoe for a man to shove his foot. Can't miss it. Then he starts off braced front, sides, and behind."

Hiram sniffed and the Cap'n was pensive, his thoughts apparently active, but not concerned in any way with the "Anti-stagger Shoe."

The "Patent Cat Identifier and Introducer," exhibited in actual operation in the Bodge home, attracted more favorable attention from inspecting capital. Mr. Bodge explained that this device allowed a hard-working man to sleep after he once got into bed, and saved his wife from running around nights in her bare feet and getting cold and incurring disease and doctors' bills. It was an admitted fact in natural history, he stated, that the uneasy feline is either yowling to be let out or meowing on the window-sill to be let in. With quiet pride the inventor pointed to a panel in the door, hinged at the top. This permitted egress, but not ingress.

"An ordinary, cheap inventor would have had the panel swing both ways," said Mr. Bodge, "and he would have a kitchen full of strange cats, with a skunk or two throwed in for luck. You see that I've hinged a pane of winder-glass and hitched it to a bevelled stick that tips inward. Cat gets up on the sill outside and meows. Dog runs to the winder and stands up to see, and puts his paws on the stick because it's his nature for to do so. Pane tips in. If it's our cat, dog don't stop her comin' in. If it's a strange cat—br-r-r, wow-wow! Off she goes!"

Mr. Bodge noted with satisfaction the gleam of interest in capital's eyes.

"You can reckon that at least a million families in this country own cats—and the nature of cats and dogs can be depended on to be the same," said Mr. Bodge. "It's a self-actin' proposition, this identifier and introducer; that means fortunes for all concerned just as soon as capital gets behind it. And I've got five hundred bigger partunts wrasslin' around in my head."

But Cap'n Sproul continued to be absorbed in thought, as though the solution of a problem still eluded him.

"But if capital takes holt of me," proceeded Mr. Bodge, "I want capital to have the full layout. There ain't goin' to be no reserves, the same as there is with most of these cheatin' corporations these days. You come with me."

They followed him into a scraggly orchard, and he broke a crotched limb from a tree. With a "leg" of this twig clutched firmly in either hand he stumped about on the sward until the crotch suddenly turned downward.

"There's runnin' water there," announced the wizard, stabbing the soil with his peg-leg. "I can locate a well anywhere, any place. When I use willer for a wand it will twist in my hands till the bark peels off. You see, I'm full of it—whatever it is. I showed you that much with the whisker. I started in easy with you. It makes me dizzy sometimes to foller myself. I have to be careful and let out a link at a time, or I'd take folks right off'm their feet. Now you come with me and keep cool—or as cool as you can, because I'm goin' to tell you something that will give you sort of a mind-colic if you ain't careful how you take it in."

He pegged ahead of them, led the way around behind a barn that was skeow-wowed in the last stages of dilapidation, and faced them with excitement vibrating his streaming whiskers.

"This, now," he declared, "is just as though I took you into a national bank, throwed open the safe door, and said: 'Gents, help yourselves!'"

He drew a curious object out of the breast pocket of his faded jumper. It was the tip of a cow's horn securely plugged. Into this plug were inserted two strips of whalebone, and these he grasped, as he had clutched the "legs" of the apple-tree wand.

"One of you lay some gold and silver down on the ground," he requested. "I'd do it, but I ain't got a cent in my pocket."

Hiram obeyed, his expression plainly showing his curiosity.

When Mr. Bodge advanced and stood astride over the money, the cow's horn turned downward and the whalebone strips twisted.

"It's a divinin'-rod to find buried treasure," said Mr. Bodge; "and it's the only one in the world like it, because I made it myself, and I wouldn't tell an angel the secret of the stuff I've plugged in there. You see for yourself what it will do when it comes near gold or silver."

Hiram turned a cold stare on his wistful eagerness.

"I don't know what you've got in there, nor why it acts that way," said the showman, "but from what I know about money, the most of it's well taken care of by the men that own it; and just what good it's goin' to do to play pointer-dog with that thing there, and go round and flush loose change and savin's-banks, is more than I can figger."

Mr. Bodge merely smiled a mysterious and superior smile.

"Cap'n Sproul," said he, "in your seafarin' days didn't you used to hear the sailormen sing this?" and he piped in weak falsetto:

> "Oh, I've been a ghost on Cod Lead Nubble,
>   Sence I died—sence I died.
> I buried of it deep with a lot of trouble,
> And the chist it was in was locked up double,
> And I'm a-watchin' of it still on Cod Lead Nubble,
>   Sence I died—sence I died."

"It's the old Cap Kidd song," admitted the Cap'n, a gleam of new interest in his eyes.

"As a seafarin' man you know that there was a Cap'n Kidd, don't you?"

Cap'n Sproul wagged nod of assent.

"He sailed and he sailed, and he robbed, and he buried his treasure, ain't that so?"

"I believe that's the idea," said the Cap'n, conservatively.

"And it's still buried, because it ain't been dug up, or else we'd have heard of it. Years ago I read all that hist'ry ever had to say about it. I said then to myself, 'Bodge,' says I, 'if the treasure of old Cap Kidd is ever found, it will be you with your wonderful powers that will find it!' I always said that to myself. I know it now. Here's the tool." He shook the cow's horn under the Cap'n's nose.

"Why ain't you been down and dug it up?" asked Hiram, with cold practicality.

"Diggin' old Cap Kidd's treasure ain't like digging a mess of potaters for dinner, Mr. Look. The song says 'Cod Lead Nubble.' Old Cap Kidd composed that song, and he put in the wrong place just to throw folks off'm the track. But if I had capital behind me I'd hire a schooner and sail round them islands down there, one after the other; and with that power that's in me I could tell the right island the minute I got near it. Then set me ashore and see how quick this divinin'-rod would put me over that chist! But it's buried deep. It's goin' to take muscle and grit to dig it up. But the right crew can do it—and that's where capital comes in. Capital ain't ever tackled it right, and that's why capital ain't got hold of that treasure."

"I reckon I'll be movin' along," remarked Hiram, with resentment bristling the horns of his mustache; "it's the first time I ever had a man pick me out as a candidate for a gold brick, and the feelin' ain't a pleasant one."

But the Cap'n grasped his arm with detaining grip.

"This thing is openin' up. It ain't all clear, but it's openin'. I had instink that I could use him. But I couldn't figger it. It ain't all straightened out in my mind yet. But when you said 'gold brick' it seemed to be clearer."

Hiram blinked inquiringly at his enigmatic friend.

"It was what I was thinkin' of—gold brick," the Cap'n went on. "I thought that prob'ly you knew some stylish and reliable gold-bricker—havin' met same when you was travellin' round in the show business."

Replying to Mr. Look's indignant snort Cap'n Sproul hastened to say: "Oh, I don't mean that you had any gold-bricker friends, but that you knew one I could hire. Probably, though, you don't know of any. Most like you don't. I realize that the gold-bricker idea ain't the one to use. There's the trouble in findin' a reliable one. And even when the feller got afoul of him, the chances are the old land-pirut would steal the brick. This here"—jabbing thumb at Mr. Bodge—"is fresher bait. I believe the old shark will gobble it if he's fished for right. What's your idea?"

"Well, generally speakin'," drawled Hiram, sarcastically, "it is that you've got softenin' of the brain. I can't make head or tail out of anything that you're sayin'."

Cap'n Sproul waked suddenly from the reverie in which he had been talking as much to himself as to Hiram.

"Say, look here, you can understand this, can't you, that I've been done out of good property—buncoed by a jeeroosly old hunk of hornbeam?"

"Oh, I got bulletins on that, all right," assented Hiram.

"Well, from what you know of me, do you think I'm the kind of a man that's goin' to squat like a hen in a dust-heap and not do him? Law? To Tophet with your law! Pneumony, lightnin', and lawyers—

they're the same thing spelled different. I'm just goin' to do him, that's all, and instink is whisperin' how." He turned his back on the showman and ran calculating eye over Mr. Bodge.

"I don't hardly see how that old hair mattress there is goin' to be rung in on the deal," growled Hiram.

"Nor I," agreed the Cap'n, frankly; "not so fur as the details appear to me just now. But there's something about him that gives me hopes." He pulled out his wallet, licked his thumb, and peeled off a bill.

"Bodge, so fur's I can see now, you seem to be a good investment. I don't know just yet how much it is goin' to take to capitalize you, but here's ten dollars for an option. You understand now that I'm president of you, and my friend here is sekertary. And you're to keep your mouth shut."

Mr. Bodge agreed with effusive gratitude, and capital went its way. The inventor chased after them with thumping peg-leg to inquire whether he should first perfect the model of the "cat identifier," or develop his idea of an automatic chore-doer, started by the rooster tripping a trigger as he descended to take his matutinal sniff of air.

"You just keep in practise with that thing," commanded the Cap'n, pointing to the cow's horn.

"I don't see even yet how you are goin' to do it," remarked Hiram, as they separated a half-hour later at Cap'n Sproul's gate.

"Nor I," said the Cap'n; "but a lot of meditation and a little prayer will do wonders in this world, especially when you're mad enough."

XX

The night seemed to afford counsel, for the next day Cap'n Sproul walked into the dooryard of Colonel Gideon Ward with features composed to an almost startling expression of amiability. The Colonel, haunted by memories and stung by a guilty conscience, appeared at the door, and his mien indicated that he was prepared for instant and desperate combat.

At the end of a half-hour's discourse, wholly by the Cap'n, his face had lost a measure of its belligerency, but sullen fear had taken its place. For Cap'n Sproul's theme had been the need of peace and mutual confidence in families, forbearance and forgetfulness of injuries that had been mutual. The Cap'n explained that almost always property troubles were the root of family evils, and that as soon as property disputes were eliminated in his case, he at once had come to a realizing sense of his own mistakes and unfair attitude, and had come to make frank and manly confession, and to shake hands. Would the Colonel shake hands?

The Colonel shook hands apprehensively, bending back and ready to duck a blow. Would the Colonel consent to mutual forgiveness, and to dwell thereafter in bonds of brotherly affection? The Colonel had only voiceless stammerings for reply, which the Cap'n translated to his own satisfaction, and went away, casting the radiance of that startling amiability over his shoulder as he departed. Colonel Ward stared after the pudgy figure as long as it remained in sight, muttering his boding thoughts.

It required daily visits for a week to make satisfactory impress on the Colonel's mistrustful fears, but the Cap'n was patient. In the end, Colonel Ward, having carefully viewed this astonishing conversion from all points, accepted the amity as proof of the guileless nature of a simple seaman, and on his own part reciprocated with warmth — laying up treasures of friendship against that possible day of discovery and wrath that his guilty conscience suggested.

If Colonel Ward, striving to reciprocate, had not been so anxious to please Cap'n Sproul in all his vagaries he would have barked derisive laughter at the mere suggestion of the Captain Kidd treasure, to the subject of which the simple seaman aforesaid led by easy stages. The Colonel admitted that Mr. Bodge had located a well for him by use of a witch-hazel rod, but allowed that the buried-treasure proposition was too stiff batter for him to swallow. He did come at last to accept Cap'n Sproul's dictum that there was once a Captain Kidd, and that he had buried vast wealth somewhere—for Cap'n Sproul as a sailorman seemed to be entitled to the possession of authority on that subject. But beyond that point there was reservation that didn't fit with Cap'n Sproul's calculations.

"Blast his old pork rind!" confided the Cap'n to Hiram. "I can circle him round and round the pen easy enough, but when I try to head him through the gate, he just sets back and blinks them hog eyes at me and grunts. To get near him at all I had to act simple, and I reckon I've overdone it. Now he thinks I don't know enough to know that old Bodge is mostly whiskers and guesses. He's known Bodge longer'n I have, and Bodge don't seem to be right bait. I can't get into his wallet by first plan."

"It wasn't no kind of a plan, anyway," said Hiram, bluntly. "It wouldn't be stickin' him good and plenty enough to have Bodge unloaded onto him, just Bodge and nothin' else done. 'Twasn't complicated enough."

"I ain't no good on complicated plots," mourned Cap'n Sproul.

"You see," insisted Hiram, "you don't understand dealin' with jay nature the same as I do. Takes the circus business to post you on jays. Once in a while they'll bite a bare hook, but not often. Jays don't get hungry till they see sure things. Your plain word of old Cap Kidd and buried treasure sounds good, and that's all. In the shell-game the best operator lets the edge of the shell rest on the pea carelesslike, as though he didn't notice it, and then joggles it down over as if by accident; and, honest, the jay hates to take the money, it looks so easy! In the candy-game there's nothing doin' until the jay thinks he catches you puttin' a twenty-dollar bill into the package. Then look troubled, and try to stop him from buyin' that package! You ain't done anything to show your brother-in-law that Bodge ain't a blank."

The Cap'n turned discouraged gaze on his friend. "I've got to give it up," he complained. "I ain't crook enough. He's done me, and I'll have to stay done."

Hiram tapped the ashes from his cigar, musingly surveyed his diamond ring, and at last said: "I ain't a butter-in. But any time you get ready to holler for advice from friends, just holler."

"I holler," said the Cap'n, dispiritedly.

"Holler heard by friends," snapped Hiram, briskly. "Friends all ready with results of considerable meditation. You go right over and tell your esteemed relative that you're organizin' an expedition to discover Cap Kidd's treasure, and invite him to go along as member of your family, free gratis for nothin', all bills paid, and much obleeged to him for pleasant company."

"Me pay the bills?" demanded the Cap'n.

"Money advanced for development work on Bodge, that's all! To be taken care of when Bodge is watered ready for sale. Have thorough understandin' with esteemed relative that no shares in Bodge are for sale. Esteemed relative to be told that any attempt on the trip to buy into Bodge will be considered fightin' talk. Bodge and all results from Bodge are yours, and you need him along—esteemed relative—to see that you have a square deal. That removes suspicion, and teases at the same time."

"Will he go?" asked Cap'n Sproul, anxiously.

"He will," declared Hiram, with conviction. "A free trip combined with a chance of perhaps doin' over again such an easy thing as you seem to be won't ever be turned down by Colonel Gideon Ward."

At nine o'clock that evening Cap'n Sproul knocked at Hiram Look's front door and stumped in eagerly. "He'll go!" he reported. "Now let me in on full details of plan."

"Details of plan will be handed to you from time to time as you need 'em in your business," said Hiram, firmly. "I don't dare to load you. Your trigger acts too quick."

"For a man that is handlin' Bodge, and is payin' all the bills, I don't seem to have much to do with this thing," grunted the Cap'n, sullenly.

"I'll give you something to do. To-morrow you go round town and hire half a dozen men—say, Jackson Denslow, Zeburee Nute, Brad Wade, Seth Swanton, Ferd Parrott, and Ludelphus Murray. Be sure they're all members of the Ancient and Honorable Firemen's Association."

"Hire 'em for what?"

"Treasure-huntin' crew. I'll go with you. I'm their foreman, and I can make them keep their mouths shut. I'll show you later why we'll need just those kind of men."

The Cap'n took these orders with dogged resignation.

"Next day you'll start with Bodge and charter a packet in Portland for a pleasure cruise—you needin' a sniff of salt air after bein' cooped up on shore for so long. Report when ready, and I'll come along with men and esteemed relative."

"It sounds almighty complicated for a plot," said the Cap'n. In his heart he resented Hiram's masterfulness and his secretiveness.

"This ain't no timber-land deal," retorted Hiram, smartly, and with cutting sarcasm. "You may know how to sail a ship and lick Portygee sailors, but there's some things that you can afford to take advice in."

On the second day Cap'n Sproul departed unobtrusively from Smyrna, with the radiant Mr. Bodge in a new suit of ready-made clothes as his seat-mate in the train.

Smyrna perked up and goggled its astonishment when Hiram Look shipped his pet elephant, Imogene, by freight in a cattle-car, and followed by next train accompanied by various tight-mouthed members of the Smyrna fire department and Colonel Gideon Ward.

Cap'n Sproul had the topmast schooner *Aurilla P. Dobson* handily docked at Commercial Wharf, and received his crew and brother-in-law with cordiality that changed to lowering gloom when Hiram followed ten minutes later towing the placid Imogene, and followed by a wondering concourse of men and boys whom his triumphal parade through the streets from the freight-station had attracted. With a nimbleness acquired in years of touring the elephant came on board.

Cap'n Sproul gazed for a time on this unwieldy passenger, surveying the arrival of various drays laden with tackle, shovels, mysterious boxes, and baled hay, and then took Hiram aside, deep discontent wrinkling his forehead.

"I know pretty well why you wanted Gid Ward along on the trip. I've got sort of a dim idea why you invited the Hecly fire department; and perhaps you know what we're goin' to do with all that dunnage on them trucks. But what in the devil you're goin' to do with that cust-fired old elephant—and she advertisin' this thing to the four corners of God's creation—well, it's got my top-riggin' snarled."

"Sooner you get your crew to work loadin', sooner you'll get away from sassy questions," replied Hiram, serenely, wagging his head at the intrusive crowd massing along the dock's edge. And the Cap'n, impressed by the logic of the advice, and stung by the manner in which Hiram had emphasized "sassy questions," pulled the peak of his cap over his eyes, and became for once more in his life the autocrat of the quarter-deck.

An hour later the packet was sluggishly butting waves with her blunt bows in the lower harbor, Cap'n Sproul hanging to the weather-worn wheel, and roaring perfectly awful profanity at the clumsy attempts of his makeshift crew.

"I've gone to sea with most everything in the line of cat-meat on two legs," he snarled to Hiram, who leaned against the rail puffing at a long cigar with deep content, "but I'll be billy-hooed if I ever saw six men before who pulled on the wrong rope every time, and pulled the wrong way on every wrong rope. You take them and — and that elephant," he added, grimly returning to that point of dispute, "and we've got an outfit that I'm ashamed to have the Atlantic Ocean see me in company with."

"Don't let that elephant fuss you up," said Hiram, complacently regarding Imogene couched in the waist.

"But there ain't northin' sensible you can do with her."

Hiram cocked his cigar pertly.

"A remark, Cap'n Sproul, that shows you need a general manager with foresight like me. When you get to hoistin' dirt in buckets she'll be worth a hundred dollars an hour, and beat any steam-winch ever operated."

Again the Cap'n felt resentment boil sourly within him. This doling of plans and plot to him seemed to be a reflection on his intelligence.

"Reckon it's buried deep, do you?" inquired Colonel Ward, a flavor of satiric skepticism in his voice. He was gazing quizzically forward to where Mr. Bodge sat on the capstan's drumhead, his nose elevated with wistful eagerness, his whiskers flapping about his ears, his eyes straight ahead.

"It's buried deep," said Hiram, with conviction. "It's buried deep, because there's a lot of it, and it was worth while to bury it deep. A man like Cap Kidd wa'n't scoopin' out a ten-foot hole and buryin' a million dollars and goin' off and leavin' it to be pulled like a pa'snip by the first comer."

"A million dollars!" echoed the Colonel.

"Northin' less! History says it. There was a lot of money flyin' around the world in them days, and Cap Kidd knew how to get holt of it. The trouble is with people, Colonel, they forget that there was a lot of gold in the world before the 'Forty-niners' got busy."

"But Bodge," snorted the Colonel. "He—"

"Certain men for certain things," declared Hiram, firmly. "Most every genius is more or less a lunatic. It needed capital to develop Bodge. It's takin' capital to make Bodge and his idea worth anything. This is straight business run on business principles! Bodge is like one of them dirt buckets, like a piece of tackle, like Imogene there. He's capitalized."

"Well, he gets his share, don't he?" asked Colonel Ward, his business instinct at the fore.

"Not by a blame sight," declared Hiram, to the Cap'n's astonished alarm. "It would be like givin' a dirt bucket or that elephant a share."

When the Cap'n was about to expostulate, Hiram kicked him unobserved and went on: "I'm bein' confidential with you, Colonel, because you're one of the family, and of course are interested in seein' your brother-in-law make good. Who is takin' all the resks? The Cap'n. Bodge is only a hired man. The Cap'n takes all profits. That's business. But of course it's between us."

When Colonel Ward strolled away in meditative mood the Cap'n made indignant remonstrance.

"Ain't I got trouble enough on my hands with them six Durham steers forrads to manage without gettin' into a free fight with old

Bodge?" he demanded. "There ain't any treasure, anyway. You don't believe it any more'n I do."

"You're right!" assented Hiram.

"But Bodge believes it, and when it gets to him that' we're goin' to do him, you can't handle him any more'n you could a wild hyeny!"

"When you hollered for my help in this thing," said the old showman, boring the Cap'n with inexorable eye, "you admitted that you were no good on complicated plots, and put everything into my hands. It will stay in my hands, and I don't want any advice. Any time you want to operate by yourself put me and Imogene ashore and operate."

For the next twenty-four hours the affairs of the *Aurilla P. Dobson* were administered without unnecessary conversations between the principals.

On the afternoon of the second day Mr. Bodge, whom no solicitation could coax from his vigil on the capstan, broke his trance.

"That's the island," he shouted, flapping both hands to mark his choice. It wasn't an impressive islet. There were a few acres of sand, some scraggy spruces, and a thrusting of ledge.

Mr. Bodge was the first man into the yawl, sat in its bow, his head projected forward like a whiskered figurehead, and was the first on the beach.

"He's certainly the spryest peg-legger I ever saw," commented Hiram, admiringly, as the treasure-hunter started away, his cow's-horn diving-rod in position. The members of Hecla fire department, glad to feel land under their country feet once more, capered about on the beach, surveying the limited attractions with curious eyes. Zeburee Nute, gathering seaweed to carry home to his wife, stripped the surface of a bowlder, and called excited attention to an anchor and a cross rudely hacked into the stone.

"It's old Cap Kidd's mark," whispered Hiram to Colonel Ward. And with keen gaze he noted the Colonel's tongue lick his blue lips, and saw the gold lust beginning to gleam in his eyes.

Hiram was the only one who noted this fact: that, concealed under more seaweed, there was a date whose modernity hinted that the inscription was the work of some loafing yachtsman.

As he rose from his knees he saw Mr. Bodge pause on a hillock, arms rigidly akimbo, the point of the cow's horn directed straight down.

"I've found it!" he squealed. "It's here! Come on, come one, come all and dig, for God sakes!"

The excitement of those first few hours was too much for the self-control of Colonel Gideon Ward's avaricious nature. He hesitated a long time, blinking hard as each shovelful of dirt sprayed against the breeze. Then he grasped an opportunity when he could talk with Cap'n Sproul apart, and said, huskily:

"It's still all guesswork and uncertain, and you stand to lose a lot of expense. I know I promised not to talk business with you, but couldn't you consider a proposition to stand in even?"

The Cap'n glared on him severely.

"Do you think it's a decent proposition to step up to me and ask me to sell you gold dollars for a cent apiece? When you came on this trip you understood that Bodge was mine, and that he and this scheme wa'n't for sale. Don't ever mention it again or you and me'll have trouble."

And Colonel Ward went back to watch the digging, angry, lusting, and disheartened.

The next day the hole was far enough advanced to require the services of Imogene as bucket-lifter. That docile animal obligingly swam ashore, to the great admiration of all spectators.

On that day it was noted first that gloom was settling on the spirits of Mr. Bodge. The gloom dated from a conversation held very privately the evening before between Mr. Bodge and Colonel Ward.

Mr. Bodge, pivoting on his peg-leg, stood at the edge of the deepening hole with a doleful air that did not accord with his enthusiastic claims as a treasure-hunter. That night he had another conference with Colonel Ward, and the next day he stood beside the hole and muttered constantly in the confidential retirement of his whiskers. On the third day he had a murderous look in his eyes every time he turned them in the direction of Cap'n Sproul. On the night of the fourth day Hiram detected him hopping softly on bare foot across the cabin of the *Dobson* toward the stateroom of Cap'n Sproul. He carried his unstrapped peg-leg in his hand, holding it as he would a weapon. Detected, he explained to Hiram with guilty confusion that he was walking in his sleep. The next night, at his own request, he was left alone on the island, where he might indulge in the frailty of somnambulism without danger to any one.

Colonel Ward, having missed his usual private conference with Mr. Bodge that night, and betraying a certain uneasiness on that account, gobbled a hurried breakfast, took the dingy, and went ashore alone.

Cap'n Sproul and Hiram Look, stepping from the yawl upon the beach a half-hour later, saw the Colonel's gaunt frame outlined against the morning sun. He was leaning over the hole, hands on his knees, and appeared to be very intently engaged.

"There's something underhanded going on here, and I propose to find out what it is," growled the Cap'n.

"Noticed it, have you?" inquired Hiram, cheerfully.

"I notice some things that I don't talk a whole lot about."

"I'm glad you have," went on Hiram, serenely overlooking a possible taunt regarding his own reticence. "It's a part of the plot, and plot aforesaid is now ripe enough to be picked. Or, to put it another way, I figger that the esteemed relative has bit and has swallered the hook."

"Ain't it about time I got let in on this?" demanded the Cap'n, with heat.

With an air as though about to impart a vital secret, Hiram grasped the Cap'n's arm and whispered: "I'll tell you just what you've got to do to make the thing go. You say 'Yes' when I tell you to."

Then he hurried up the hill, Cap'n Sproul puffing at his heels and revolving venomous thoughts.

It was a deep hole and a gloomy hole, but when the two arrived at the edge they could see Mr. Bodge at the bottom. His peg-leg was unstrapped, and he held it clutched in both hands and brandished it at them the moment their heads appeared over the edge.

"And there you be, you robber!" he squalled. "You would pick cents off'm, a dead man's eyes, and bread out of the mouths of infants." He stopped his tirade long enough to suck at the neck of a black bottle.

"Come on! Come one, come all!" he screamed. "I'll split every head open. I'll stay here till I starve. Ye'll have to walk over my dead body to get it."

"Well, he's good and drunk, and gone crazy into the bargain," snorted the Cap'n, disgustedly.

"It's a sad thing," remarked Colonel Ward, his little, hard eyes gleaming with singular fires, and trying to compose his features. "I'm afraid of what may happen if any one tries to go down there."

"I'll come pretty near to goin' down into my own hole if I want to," blurted the Cap'n.

"I'll kill ye jest so sure's hell's a good place to thaw plumbin'," cried Mr. Bodge. "I've got ye placed. You was goin' to steal my brains. You was goin' to suck Bodge dry and laugh behind his back. You're an old thief and liar."

"There's no bald-headed old sosh that can call me names—not when I can stop it by droppin' a rock on his head," stated the Cap'n with vigor.

"You don't mean to say you'd hurt that unfortunate man?" inquired Colonel Ward. "He has gone insane, I think. He ought to be treated gently. I probably feel different about it than either of you, who are comparative strangers in Smyrna. But I've always known Eleazar Bodge, and I should hate to see any harm come to him. As it is, his brain has been turned by this folly over buried treasure." The Colonel tried to speak with calmness and dignity, but his tones were husky and his voice trembled. "Perhaps I can handle him better than any of the rest of you. I was talkin' with him when you came up."

"You all go away and leave me with Colonel Gid Ward," bawled Bodge. "He's the only friend I've got in the world. He'll be good to me."

"It's pretty bad business," commented Hiram, peering down into the pit with much apprehension.

"It's apt to be worse before it's over with," returned the Colonel.

And, catching a look in Hiram's eyes that seemed to hint at something, he called the showman aside.

"I can't talk with my brother-in-law," he began. "He seems to get very impatient with me when we try to talk business. But I've got a proposition to make, and perhaps I can make it through you."

Then, seeing that the Cap'n was bending malevolent gaze on them, he drew Hiram farther away, and they entered into spirited colloquy.

"It's this way," reported the showman, returning at last to the Cap'n, and holding him firmly by the coat lapel. "As you and I have talked it, you've sort of got cold feet on this treasure proposition." This was news to the Cap'n, but his eyelids did not so much as quiver. "Here you are now up against a man that's gone crazy and that's threatenin' to kill you, and may do so if you try to do more business with him. Colonel Ward says he's known him a good many years, and pities him in his present state, and, more than that, has got sort of interested in this Cap Kidd treasure business himself, and has a little money he'd like to spend on it—and to help Mr. Bodge. Proposition by Colonel Ward is that if you'll step out and turn over Mr. Bodge and this hole to him just as it stands he'll hand you his check now for fifteen thousand dollars, and"—the showman hastened to stop the Cap'n's amazed gasping by adding decisively— "as your friend and general manager of this expedition, and knowin' your feelin's pretty well, I've accepted and herewith hand you check. Members of Hecla fire company will please take notice of trade. Do I state it right, Colonel Ward?"

The Colonel, with high color mantling his thin cheeks, affirmed hoarsely.

"And, bein' induced to do this mostly out of regard for Mr. Bodge, he thinks it's best for us to sail away so that Mr. Bodge can calm himself. We'll send a packet from Portland to take 'em off. They would like to stay here and prospect for a few days. Right, Colonel Ward?"

The Colonel affirmed once more.

Casting one more look into the hole, another at his inexplicable brother-in-law, and almost incredulous gaze at the check in his hand, Cap'n Sproul turned and marched off down the hill. He promptly went on board, eager to get that check as far away from its maker as possible.

It was an hour later before he had opportunity of a word with Hiram, who had just finished the embarkation of Imogene.

"My Gawd, Hiram!" he gasped, "how did you skin this out of him?"

"I could have got twenty-five thousand just as quick," replied the showman. "You take a complicated plot like that, and when it does get ripe it's easy pickin'. When old Dot-and-carry got to pokin' around in that hole this mornin' and come upon the chist bound with iron, after scrapin' away about a foot of dirt, he jest naturally concluded he'd rather be equal partners with Colonel Gid Ward than be with you what I explained he was to the Colonel."

"Chist bound with iron?" demanded the Cap'n.

"Cover of old planks that Ludelphus and I patched up with strap iron down in the hold and planted after dark last night. Yes, sir, with old Bodge standin' there as he was to-day, and reportin' to Ward what he had under foot, I could have got ten thousand more out of esteemed relative. But I reckoned that fifteen thousand stood for quite a lot of profit on timber lands."

The Cap'n gazed aloft to see that the dingy canvas of the *Dobson* was drawing, and again surveyed the check.

"I reckon I'll cash it in before makin' any arrangements to send a packet out after 'em," he remarked.

After a few moments of blissful contemplation he said, with a little note of regret in his voice: "I wish you had let me know about that plankin'. I'd have liked to put a little writin' under it—something sarcastic, that they could sort of meditate on when they sit there in that hole and look at each other.

"It was certainly a complicated plot," he went on. "And it had to be. When you sell a bunch of whiskers and a hole in the ground for fifteen thousand dollars, it means more brain-work than would be needed in selling enough gold bricks to build a meetin'-house."

And with such and similar gratulatory communings they found their setting forth across the sunlit sea that day an adventuring full of rich contentment.

XXI

"She sails about like a clam-shell in a puddle of Porty Reek m'lasses," remarked Cap'n Aaron Sproul, casting contemptuous eye into the swell of the dingy mainsail, and noting the crawl of the foam-wash under the counter of the *Aurilla P. Dobson*.

But he could not infect Hiram Look with his dissatisfaction. The ex-circus man sat on the deck with his back against the port bulwark, his knees doubled high before his face as a support for a blank-book in which he was writing industriously. He stopped to lick the end of his pencil, and gazed at the Cap'n.

"I was just thinkin' we was havin' about as pleasant a sail as I ever took," he said. "Warm and sunny, our own fellers on board havin' a good time, and a complicated plot worked out to the queen's taste."

The Cap'n, glancing behind, noted that a certain scraggly island had once more slid into view from behind a wooded head. With his knee propped against the wheel, he surveyed the island's ridged backbone.

"Plot seems to be still workin'," he remarked, grimly. "If it was all worked they'd be out there on them ledges jumpin' about twenty feet into the air, and hollerin' after us."

"Let's whoa here and wait for 'em to show in sight," advised Hiram, eagerly. "It will be worth lookin' at."

"Hain't no need of slackin' sail," snorted the skipper. "It's about like bein' anchored, tryin' to ratch this old tin skimmer away from anywhere. You needn't worry any about our droppin' that island out of sight right away."

"For a man that's just got even with Colonel Gideon Ward to the tune of fifteen thousand dollars, and with the check in your pocket, you don't seem to be enjoyin' the comforts of religion quite as much as a man ought to," remonstrated Hiram.

"It's wadin' a puddle navigatin' this way," complained the Cap'n, his eyes on the penning shores of the reach; "and it makes me homesick when I think of my old four-sticker pilin' white water to her bowsprit's scroll and chewin' foam with her jumper-guys. Deep water, Hiram! Deep water, with a wind and four sticks, and I'd show ye!"

"There's something the matter with a man that can't get fun out of anything except a three-ring circus," said his friend, severely. "I'm contented with one elephant these days. It's all the responsibility I want." His eyes dwelt fondly on the placid Imogene, couchant amidships. Then he lighted a cigar, using his plug hat for a wind-break, and resumed his labors with the pencil.

"What be ye writin'—a novel or only a pome?" inquired Cap'n Sproul at last.

"Log," replied the unruffled Hiram. "This is the first sea trip I ever made, and whilst I don't know how to reeve the bowsprit or clew up the for'rad hatch, I know that a cruise without a log is like circus-lemonade without a hunk of glass to clink in the mix bowl. Got it up to date! Listen!"

He began to read, displaying much pride in his composition:

"September the fifteen. Got word that Cap'n Aaron Sproul had been cheated out of wife's interest in timber lands by his brother-in-law, Colonel Gideon Ward."

"What in Josephus's name has that got to do with this trip?" demanded the Cap'n, with rising fire, at this blunt reference to his humiliation.

"If it wa'n't for that we wouldn't be on this trip," replied Hiram, with serene confidence in his own judgment.

"Well, I don't want that set down."

"You can keep a log of your own, and needn't set it down." Hiram's tone was final, and he went on reading:

"Same date. Discovered Eleazar Bodge and his divinin'-rod. Bought option on Bodge and his secret of Cap'n Kidd's buried treasure on Cod Lead Nubble. September the fifteen to seventeen. Thought up plot to use Bodge to get even with Ward. September the twenty-three. Raised crew in Smyrna for cruise to Cod Lead, crew consistin' of men to be depended on for what was wanted—"

"Not includin' sailin' a vessel," sneered the Cap'n, squinting forward with deep disfavor to where the members of the Smyrna Ancient and Honorable Firemen's Association were contentedly fishing over the side of the sluggish *Dobson*. "Here, leave hands off'm that tops'l downhaul!" he yelled, detecting Ludelphus Murray slashing at it with his jack-knife. "My Gawd, if he ain't cut it off!" he groaned.

Murray, the Smyrna blacksmith, growled back something about not seeing what good the rope did, anyway.

Cap'n Sproul turned his back on the dim gleam of open sea framed by distant headlands.

"I'm ashamed to look the Atlantic Ocean in the face, with that bunch of barn-yarders aboard," he complained.

"Shipped crew," went on Hiram, who had not paused in his reading. "Took along my elephant to h'ist dirt. Found Cod Lead Nubble. Began h'istin' dirt. Dug hole twenty feet deep. Me and L. Murray made fake treasure-chist cover out of rotten planks. Planted treasure-chist cover. Let E. Bodge and G. Ward discover same, and made believe we didn't know of it. Sold out E. Bodge and all chances to G. Ward for fifteen thousand and left them to dig, promisin' to send off packet for them. Sailed with crew and elephant to cash check before G. Ward can get ashore to stop payment. Plot complicated, but it worked, and has helped to pass away time."

"That ain't no kind of a ship's log," objected the Cap'n, who had listened to the reading with an air too sullen for a man who had profited as much by the plot. "There ain't no mention of wind nor weather nor compass nor—"

"You can put 'em all in if you want to," broke in Hiram. "I don't bother with things I don't know anything about. What I claim is, here's a log, brief and to the point, and covers all details of plot. And I'm proud of it. That's because it's my own plot."

The Cap'n, propping the wheel with his knee, pulled out his wallet, and again took a long survey of Colonel Ward's check. "For myself, I ain't so proud of it," he said, despondently. "It seems sort of like stealin' money."

"It's a good deal like it," assented Hiram, readily. "But he stole from you first." He took up the old spy-glass and levelled it across the rail.

"That's all of log to date," he mumbled in soliloquy. "Now if I could see—"

He uttered an exclamation and peered into the tube with anxiety.

"Here!" he cried. "You take it, Cap'n. I ain't used to it, and it wobbles. But it's either them or gulls a-flappin'."

Cap'n Sproul's brown hands clasped the rope-wound telescope, and he trained its lens with seaman's steadiness.

"It's them," he said, with a chuckle of immense satisfaction. They're hoppin' up and down on the high ridge, and slattin' their arms in the air. It ain't no joy-dance, that ain't. I've seen Patagonian Injuns a war-dancin'. It's like that. They've got that plank cover pried up. I wisht I could hear what they are sayin'."

"I can imagine," returned Hiram, grimly. "Hold it stiddy, so's I can look. Them old arms of Colonel Gid is goin' some," he observed, after a pause. "It will be a wonder if he don't shake his fists off."

"There certainly is something cheerful about it—lookin' back and knowin' what they must be sayin'," observed the Cap'n, losing his temporary gloom. "I reckon I come by this check honest, after all, considerin' what he done to me on them timber lands."

"Well, it beats goin' to law," grinned Hiram. "Here you be, so afraid of lawyers—and with good reason—that you'd have let him get away with his plunder before you'd have gone to law—and he knew it when he done you. You've taken back what's your own, in your own way, without havin' to give law-shysters the biggest part for gettin' it. Shake!" And chief plotter and the benefited clasped fists with radiant good-nature. The Cap'n broke his grip in order to twirl the wheel, it being necessary to take a red buoy to port.

"We're goin' to slide out of sight of 'em in a few minutes," he said, looking back over his shoulder regretfully. "I wisht I had a crew! I could stand straight out through that passage on a long tack to port, fetch Half-way Rock, and slide into Portland on the starboard tack, and stay in sight of 'em pretty nigh all day. It would keep 'em busy thinkin' if we stayed in sight."

"Stand out," advised Hiram, eagerly. "We ain't in any hurry. Let's rub it into 'em. Stand out."

"With them pea-bean pullers to work ship?" He pointed to the devoted band of Smyrna fire-fighters, who were joyously gathering in with varying luck a supply of tomcod and haddock to furnish the larder inshore. "When I go huntin' for trouble it won't be with a gang of hoss-marines like that."

Hiram, as foreman of the Ancients, felt piqued at this slighting reference to his men, and showed it.

"They can pull ropes when you tell 'em to," he said. "Leastways, when it comes to brains, I reckon they'll stack up better'n them Portygees you used to have."

"I never pretended that them Portygees had any brains at all," said the Cap'n, grimly. "They come aboard without brains, and I took a belayin'-pin and batted brains into 'em. I can't do that to these critters here. It would be just like 'em to misunderstand the whole thing and go home and get me mixed into a lot of law for assaultin' 'em."

"Oh, if you're afraid to go outside, say so!" sneered Hiram. "But you've talked so much of deep water, and weatherin' Cape Horn, and—"

"Afraid? Me afraid?" roared the Cap'n, spatting his broad hand on his breast. "Me, that kicked my dunnage-bag down the fo'c's'le-hatch at fifteen years old? I'll show you whether I'm afraid or not."

He knotted a hitch around the spokes of the wheel and scuffed hastily forward.

"Here!" he bawled, cuffing the taut sheets to point his meaning, "when I get back to the wheel and holler 'Ease away!' you fellers get hold of these ropes, untie 'em, and let out slow till I tell you stop. And then tie 'em just as you find 'em."

They did so clumsily, Cap'n Sproul swearing under his breath, and at last the *Dobson* got away on the port tack.

"Just think of me—master of a four-sticker at twenty-seven—havin' to stand here in the face and eyes of the old Atlantic Ocean and yell about untyin' ropes and tyin' 'em up like I was givin' off orders in a cow-barn!"

"Well, they done it all right—and they done it pretty slick, so far as I could see," interjected Hiram.

"Done it!" sneered the Cap'n. "Eased sheets here in this puddle, in a breeze about stiff enough to winnow oats! Supposin' it was a blow, with a gallopin' sea! Me runnin' around this deck taggin' gool on halyards, lifts, sheets, and downhauls, and them hoss-marines

230

follerin' me up. Davy Jones would die laughin', unless some one pounded him on the back to help him get his breath."

Now that his mariner's nose was turned toward the sea once again after his two years of landsman's hebetude, all his seaman's instinct, all his seaman's caution, revived. His nose snuffed the air, his eyes studied the whirls of the floating clouds. There was nothing especially ominous in sight.

The autumn sun was warm. The wind was sprightly but not heavy. And yet his mariner's sense sniffed something untoward.

The *Dobson*, little topmast hooker, age-worn and long before relegated to the use of Sunday fishing-parties "down the bay," had for barometer only a broken affair that had been issued to advertise the virtues of a certain baking-powder. It was roiled permanently to the degree marked "Tornado."

"Yes," remarked Hiram, nestling down once more under the bulwark, after viewing the display of amateur activity, "of course, if you're afraid to tackle a little deep water once more, just for the sake of an outin', then I've no more to say. I've heard of railro'd engineers and sea-capt'ns losin' their nerve. I didn't know but it had happened to you."

"Well, it ain't," snapped the Cap'n, indignantly. And yet his sailor instinct scented menace. He couldn't explain it to that cynical old circus-man, intent on a day's outing. Had it not been for Hiram's presence and his taunt, Cap'n Sproul would have promptly turned tail to the Atlantic and taken his safe and certain way along the reaches and under shelter of the islands. But reflecting that Hiram Look, back in Smyrna, might circulate good-natured derogation of his mariner's courage, Cap'n Sproul set the *Dobson's* blunt nose to the heave of the sea, and would not have quailed before a tidal wave.

The Smyrna contingent hailed this adventuring into greater depths as a guarantee of bigger fish for the salt-barrel at home, and proceeded to cut bait with vigor and pleased anticipation.

Only the Cap'n was saturnine, and even lost his interest in the animated figures on distant Cod Lead Nubble, though Hiram could not drag his eyes from them, seeing in their frantic gestures the denouement of his plot.

Shortly after noon they were well out to sea, still on the port tack, the swells swinging underneath in a way that soothed the men of Smyrna rather than worried them. So steady was the lift and sweep of the long roll that they gave over fishing and snored wholesomely in the sun on deck. Hiram dozed over his cigar, having paid zestful attention to the dinner that Jackson Denslow had spread in the galley.

Only Cap'n Sproul, at the wheel, was alert and awake. With some misgivings he noted that the trawl fishers were skimming toward port in their Hampton boats. A number of smackmen followed these. Later he saw several deeply laden Scotiamen lumbering past on the starboard tack, all apparently intent on making harbor.

"Them fellers has smelt something outside that don't smell good," grunted the Cap'n. But he still stood on his way. "I reckon I've got softenin' of the brain," he muttered; "livin' inshore has given it to me. 'Cause if I was in my right senses I'd be runnin' a race with them fellers to see which would get inside Bug Light and to a safe anchorage first. And yet I'm standin' on with this old bailin'-dish because I'm afraid of what a landlubber will say to folks in Smyrna about my bein' a coward, and with no way of my provin' that I ain't. All that them hoss-marines has got a nose for is a b'iled dinner when it's ready. They couldn't smell nasty weather even if 'twas daubed onto their mustaches."

At the end of another hour, during which the crew of the *Dobson* had become thoroughly awake and aware of the fact that the coast-line was only a blue thread on the northern horizon, Cap'n Sproul had completely satisfied his suspicions as to a certain bunch of slaty cloud.

There was a blow in it—a coming shift of wind preceded by flaws that made the Cap'n knot his eyebrows dubiously.

"There!" he blurted, turning his gaze on Hiram, perched on the grating. "If you reckon you've got enough of a sail out of this, we'll put about for harbor. But I want it distinctly understood that I ain't sayin' the word 'enough.' I'd keep on sailin' to the West Injies if we had grub a-plenty to last us."

"There ain't grub enough," suggested Jackson Denslow, who came up from the waist with calm disregard of shipboard etiquette. "The boys have all caught plenty of fish, and we want to get in before dark. So gee her round, Cap'n."

"Don't you give off no orders to me!" roared the Cap'n. "Go back for'ard where you belong."

"That's the sense of the boys, just the same," retorted Denslow, retreating a couple of steps. "'Delphus Murray is seasick, and two or three of the boys are gettin' so. We ain't enlisted for no seafarin' trip."

"Don't you realize that we're on the high seas now and that you're talkin' mutiny, and that mutiny's a state-prison crime?" clamored the irate skipper. "I'd have killed a Portygee for sayin' a quarter as much. I'd have killed him for settin' foot abaft the gratin'—killed him before he opened his mouth."

"We ain't Portygees," rejoined Denslow, stubbornly. "We ain't no sailors."

"Nor I ain't liar enough to call you sailors," the Cap'n cried, in scornful fury.

"If ye want to come right down to straight business," said the refractory Denslow, "there ain't any man got authority over us except Mr. Look there, as foreman of the Smyrna Ancients and Honer'bles."

Mr. Denslow, mistaking the Cap'n's speechlessness for conviction, proceeded:

"We was hired to take a sail for our health, dig dirt, and keep our mouths shut. Same has been done and is bein' done—except in so far as we open 'em to remark that we want to get back onto dry ground."

Hiram noted that the Cap'n's trembling hands were taking a half-hitch with a rope's end about a tiller-spoke. He understood this as meaning that Cap'n Sproul desired to have his hands free for a moment. He hastened to interpose.

"We're goin' to start right back, Denslow. You can tell the boys for me."

"All right, Chief!" said the faithful member of the Ancients, and departed.

"We be goin' back, hey?" The Cap'n had his voice again, and turned on Hiram a face mottled with fury. "This firemen's muster is runnin' this craft, is it? Say, look-a-here, Hiram, there are certain things 'board ship where it's hands off! There is a certain place where friendship ceases. You can run your Smyrna fire department on shore, but aboard a vessel where I'm master mariner, by the wall-eyed jeehookibus, there's no man but me bosses! And so long as a sail is up and her keel is movin' I say the say!"

In order to shake both fists under Hiram's nose, he had surrendered the wheel to the rope-end. The *Dobson* paid off rapidly, driven by a sudden squall that sent her lee rail level with the foaming water. Those forward howled in concert. Even the showman's face grew pale as he squatted in the gangway, clutching the house for support.

"Cut away them ropes! She's goin' to tip over!" squalled Murray, the big blacksmith. Between the two options—to take the wheel and bring the clumsy hooker into the wind, or to rush forward and flail his bunglers away from the rigging—Cap'n Sproul shuttled insanely, rushing to and fro and bellowing furious language. The language had no effect. With axes and knives the willing crew hacked away every rope forward that seemed to be anything supporting a sail, and down came the foresail and two jibs. The Cap'n knocked down the two men who tried to cut the mainsail halyards. The next moment the *Dobson* jibed under the impulse of the mainsail, and the swinging boom snapped Hiram's plug hat afar into the sea, and left the showman flat on his back, dizzily rubbing a bump on his bald head.

For an instant Cap'n Sproul was moved by a wild impulse to let her slat her way to complete destruction, but the sailorman's instinct triumphed, and he worked her round, chewing a strand of his beard with venom.

"I don't pretend to know as much about ship managin' as you do," Hiram ventured to say at last, "but if that wa'n't a careless performance, lettin' her wale round that way, then I'm no judge."

He got no comment from the Cap'n.

"I don't suppose it's shipshape to cut ropes instead of untie 'em," pursued Hiram, struggling with lame apology in behalf of the others, "but I could see for myself that if them sails stayed up we were goin' to tip over. It's better to sail a little slower and keep right side up."

He knotted a big handkerchief around his head and took his place on the grating once more.

"What can we do now?" bawled Murray.

"You're the one that's issuin' orders 'board here now," growled the Cap'n, bending baleful gaze on the foreman of the Ancients. "Go for'ard and tell 'em to chop down both masts, and then bore some holes in the bottom to let out the bilge-water. Then they can set her on fire. There might be something them blasted Ancients could do to a vessel on fire."

"I don't believe in bein' sarcastic when people are tryin' to do the best they can," objected Hiram. He noted that the *Dobson* was once again setting straight out to sea. She was butting her snub nose furiously into swelling combers. The slaty bench of clouds had lifted into the zenith. Scud trailed just over the swaying masts. The shore line was lost in haze. "Don't be stuffy any longer, Cap'n," he pleaded. "We've gone fur enough. I give up. You are deep-water, all right!"

Cap'n Sproul made no reply. Suddenly catching a moment that seemed favorable, he lashed the wheel, and with mighty puffing and grunting "inched" in the main-sheet. "She ought to have a double reef," he muttered. "But them petrified sons of secos couldn't take in a week's wash."

"You can see for yourself that the boys are seasick," resumed Hiram, when the Cap'n took the wheel again. "If you don't turn 'round—"

"Mr. Look," grated the skipper, "I've got just a word or two to say right now." His sturdy legs were straddled, his brown hands clutched the spokes of the weather-worn wheel. "I'm runnin' this packet from now on, and it's without conversation. Understand? Don't you open your yap. And you go for'ard and tell them steer calves that I'll kill the first one that steps foot aft the mainmast."

There was that in the tones and in the skipper's mien of dignity as he stood there, fronting and defying once again his ancient foe, the ocean, which took out of Hiram all his courage to retort. And after a time he went forward, dragging himself cautiously, to join the little group of misery huddled in the folds of the fallen canvas.

"A cargo of fools to save!" growled Cap'n Sproul, his eyebrows knotted in anxiety. "Myself among 'em! And they don't know what the matter is with 'em. We've struck the line gale—that's what we've done! Struck it with a choppin'-tray for a bo't and a mess of rooty-baggy turnips for a crew! And there's only one hole to crawl out of."

XXII

The wind had shifted when it settled into the blow—a fact that the Cap'n's shipmates did not realize, and which he was too disgusted by their general inefficiency to explain to them. In his crippled condition, in the gathering night, he figured that it would be impossible for him to make Portland harbor, the only accessible refuge. The one chance was to ride it out, and this he set himself to do, grimly silent, contemptuously reticent. He held her nose up to the open sea, allowing her only steerageway, the gale slithering off her flattened sail.

The men who gazed on him from the waist saw in his resolution only stubborn determination to punish them.

"He's sartinly the obstinatest man that ever lowered his head at ye," said Zeburee Nute, breaking in on the apprehensive mumble of his fellows. "He won't stop at northin' when he's mad. Look what he's done in Smyrna. But I call this rubbin' it in a darn sight more'n he's got any right to do."

His lament ended in a seasick hiccough.

"I don't understand sailormen very well," observed Jackson Denslow; "and it may be that a lot of things they do are all right, viewed from sailorman standpoint. But if Cap Sproul wa'n't plumb crazy and off'm his nut them times we offered him honors in our town, and if he ain't jest as crazy now, I don't know lunatics when I see 'em."

"Headin' straight out to sea when dry ground's off that way," said Murray, finning feeble hand to starboard, "ain't what Dan'l Webster would do, with his intellect, if he was here."

Hiram Look sat among them without speaking, his eyes on his friend outlined against the gloom at the wheel. One after the other the miserable members of the Ancients and Honorables appealed to him for aid and counsel.

"Boys," he said at last, "I've been figgerin' that he's just madder'n blazes at what you done to the sails, and that as soon's he works his mad off he'll turn tail. Judgin' from what he said to me, it ain't safe to tackle him right away. It will only keep him mad. Hold tight for a little while and let's see what he'll do when he cools. And if he don't cool then, I've got quite a habit of gettin' mad myself."

And, hanging their hopes on this argument and promise, they crouched there in their misery, their eyes on the dim figure at the wheel, their ears open to the screech of the gale, their souls as sick within them as were their stomachs.

In that sea and that wind the progress of the *Dobson* was, as the Cap'n mentally put it, a "sashay." There was way enough on her to hold her into the wind, but the waves and the tides lugged her slowly sideways and backward. And yet, with their present sea-room Cap'n Sproul hoped that he might claw off enough to save her.

Upon his absorption in these hopes blundered Hiram through the night, crawling aft on his hands and knees after final and despairing appeal from his men.

"I say, Cap'n," he gasped, "you and I have been too good friends to have this go any further. I've took my medicine. So have the boys. Now let's shake hands and go ashore."

No reply from the desperate mariner at the wheel battling for life.

"You heard me!" cried Hiram, fear and anger rasping in his tones. "I say, I want to go ashore, and, damme, I'm goin'!"

"Take your shoes in your hand and wade," gritted the Cap'n. "I ain't stoppin' you." He still scorned to explain to the meddlesome landsman.

"I can carry a grudge myself," blustered Hiram. "But I finally stop to think of others that's dependent on me. We've got wives ashore, you and me have, and these men has got families dependent on 'em. I tell ye to turn round and go ashore!"

"Turn round, you devilish idjit?" bellowed the Cap'n. "What do you think this is—one of your circus wagons with a span of hosses hitched in front of it? I told you once before that I didn't want to be bothered with conversation. I tell you so ag'in. I've got things on my mind that you don't know anything about, and that you ain't got intellect enough to understand. Now, you shut up or I'll kick you overboard for a mutineer."

At the end of half an hour of silence—bitter, suffering silence— Hiram broke out with a husky shout.

"There ye go, Cap'n," he cried. "Behind you! There's our chance!"

A wavering red flare lighted the sky, spreading upward on the mists.

The men forward raised a quavering cheer.

"Ain't you goin' to sail for it?" asked Hiram, eagerly. "There's our chance to get ashore." He had crept close to the skipper.

"I s'pose you feel like puttin' on that piazzy hat of yourn and grabbin' your speakin'-trumpet, leather buckets, and bed-wrench, and startin' for it," sneered Cap'n Sproul in a lull of the wind. "In the old times they had wimmen called sirens to coax men ashore. But that thing there seems to be better bait of the Smyrna fire department."

"Do you mean to tell me that you ain't agoin' to land when there's dry ground right over there, with people signallin' and waitin' to help you?" demanded the showman, his temper whetted by his fright.

The Cap'n esteemed the question too senseless to admit any reply except a scornful oath. He at the wheel, studying drift and wind, had pretty clear conception of their whereabouts. The scraggly ridge dimly outlined by the fire on shore could hardly be other than Cod Lead, where Colonel Gideon Ward and Eleazar Bodge were languishing. It was probable that those marooned gentlemen had lighted a fire in their desperation in order to signal for assistance. The Cap'n reflected that it was about as much wit as landsmen would possess.

To Hiram's panicky mind this situation seemed to call for one line of action. They were skippered by a madman or a brute, he could not figure which. At any rate, it seemed time to interfere.

He crawled back again to the huddled group of the Ancients and enlisted Ludelphus Murray, as biggest and least incapacitated by seasickness.

They staggered back in the gloom and, without preface or argument, fell upon the Cap'n, dragged him, fighting manfully and profanely, to the companionway of the little house, thrust him down, after an especially vigorous engagement of some minutes, slammed and bolted the doors and shot the hatch. They heard him beating about within and raging horribly, but Murray doubled himself over, his knees against the doors, his body prone on the hatch.

His position was fortunate for him, for again the *Dobson* jibed, the boom of the mainsail slishing overhead. Hiram was crawling on hands and knees toward the wheel, and escaped, also. When the little schooner took the bit in her teeth she promptly eliminated the question of seamanship. It was as though she realized that the master-hand was paralyzed. She shook the rotten sail out of the bolt-ropes with a bang, righted and went sluggishly rolling toward the flare on shore.

"I don't know much about vessel managin'," gasped Hiram, "but seein' that gettin' ashore was what I was drivin' at; the thing seems to be progressin' all favorable."

Up to this time one passenger on the schooner appeared to be taking calm or tempest with the same equanimity. This passenger was Imogene, couched at the break of the little poop. But the cracking report of the bursting sail, and now the dreadful clamor of the imprisoned Cap'n Sproul, stirred her fears. She raised her trunk and trumpeted with bellowings that shamed the blast.

"Let him up now, 'Delphus!" shouted Hiram, after twirling the wheel vainly and finding that the *Dobson* heeded it not. "If there ain't no sails up he can't take us out to sea. Let him up before he gives Imogene hysterics."

And when Murray released his clutch on the hatch it snapped back, and out over the closed doors of the companionway shot the Cap'n, a whiskered jack-in-the-box, gifted with vociferous speech.

Like the cautious seaman, his first glance was aloft. Then he spun the useless wheel.

"You whelps of perdition!" he shrieked. "Lifts cut, mains'l blowed out, and a lee shore a quarter of a mile away! I've knowed fools, lunatics, and idjits, and I don't want to insult 'em by callin' you them names. You—"

"Well, if we are any crazier for wantin' to go ashore where we belong than you was for settin' out to cross the Atlantic Ocean in a night like this, I'd like to have it stated why," declared Hiram.

"Don't you know enough to understand that I was tryin' to save your lives by ratchin' her off'm this coast?" bellowed Cap'n Sproul.

"Just thought you was crazy, and think so now," replied the showman, now fully as furious as the Cap'n—each in his own mind accusing the other of being responsible for their present plight. "The place for us is on shore, and we're goin' there!"

"What do you suppose is goin' to become of us when she strikes?" bawled the Cap'n, clutching the backstay and leaning into the night.

"She'll strike shore, won't she? Well, that's what I want to strike. It'll sound good and feel good."

For such gibbering lunacy as this the master mariner had no fit reply. His jaws worked wordlessly. He kept his clutch on the backstay with the dizzy notion that this saved him from clutching some one's throat.

"You'd better begin to pray, you fellers," he cried at last, with a quaver in his tones. "We're goin' smash-ti-belter onto them rocks, and Davy Jones is settin' on extra plates for eight at breakfast to-morrer mornin'. Do your prayin' now."

"The only Scripture that occurs to me just now," said Hiram, in a hush of the gale, "is that 'God tempers the wind to the shorn lamb.'"

That was veritably a Delphic utterance at that moment, had Hiram only known it.

Some one has suggested that there is a providence that watches over children and fools. It is certain that chance does play strange antics. Men have fallen from balloons and lived. Other men have slipped on a banana skin and died. Men have fought to save themselves from destruction, and have been destroyed. Other men have resigned themselves and have won out triumphantly.

The doomed *Dobson* was swashing toward the roaring shore broadside on. The first ledge would roll her bottom up, beating in her punky breast at the same time. This was the programme the doleful skipper had pictured in his mind. There was no way of winning a chance through the rocks, such as there might have been with steerageway, a tenuous chance, and yet a chance. But the Cap'n decided with apathy and resignation to fate that one man could not raise a sail out of that wreck forward and at the same time heave her up to a course for the sake of that chance.

As to Imogene he had not reckoned.

Perhaps that faithful pachyderm decided to die with her master embraced in her trunk. Perhaps she decided that the quarter-deck was farther above water than the waist.

At any rate, curving back her trunk and "roomping" out the perturbation of her spirit, she reared on her hind-legs, boosted herself upon the roof of the house, and clawed aft. This auto-shifting of cargo lifted the bow of the little schooner. Her jibs, swashing soggily about her bow, were hoisted out of the water, and a gust bellied them. On the pivot of her buried stern the *Dobson* swung like a top just as twin ledges threatened her broadside, and she danced gayly between them, the wind tugging her along by her far-flung jibs.

In matter of wrecks, it is the outer rocks that smash; it is the teeth of these ledges that tear timbers and macerate men. The straggling remains are found later in the sandy cove.

But with Imogene as unwitting master mariner in the crisis, the schooner dodged the danger of the ledges by the skin of her barnacled bottom, spun frothing up the cove in the yeast of the waves, bumped half a dozen times as though searching suitable spot for self-immolation, and at last, finding a bed of white sand, flattened herself upon it with a racket of demolition—the squall of drawing spikes her death-wail, the boom of water under her bursting deck her grunt of dissolution.

The compelling impulse that drives men to close personal contact in times of danger had assembled all the crew of the schooner upon the poop, the distracted Imogene in the centre. She wore the trappings of servitude—the rude harness in which she had labored to draw up the buckets of dirt on Cod Lead, the straps to which the tackle had been fastened to hoist her on board the *Dobson*.

When the deck went out from under them, the elephant was the biggest thing left in reach.

And as she went sturdily swimming off, trunk elevated above the surges, the desperate crew of the *Dobson* grabbed at straps and dangling traces and went, too, towing behind her. Imogene could reach the air with the end of her uplifted trunk. The men submerged at her side gasped and strangled, but clung with the death-grip of drowning men; and when at last she found bottom and dragged herself up the beach with the waves beating at her, she carried them all, salvaged from the sea in a fashion so marvellous that Cap'n Aaron Sproul, first on his legs, had no voice left with which to express his sentiments.

He staggered around to the front of the panting animal and solemnly seized her trunk and waggled it in earnest hand-shake.

"You're a dumb animile," he muttered, "and you prob'ly can't have any idea of what I'm meanin' or sayin'. But I want to say to you, man to elephant, that I wouldn't swap your hind-tail—which don't seem to be of any use, anyway—for the whole Smyrna fire company. I'm sayin' to you, frank and outspoken, that I was mad when you first come aboard. I ask your pardon. Of course, you don't understand that. But my mind is freer. Your name ought to be changed to Proverdunce, and the United States Government ought to give you a medal bigger'n a pie-plate."

He turned and bent a disgusted stare on the gasping men dimly outlined in the gloom.

"I'd throw you back again," he snapped, "if it wa'n't for givin' the Atlantic Ocean the colic."

One by one they staggered up from the beach grass, revolved dizzily, and with the truly homing instinct started away in the direction of the fire-flare on the higher land of the island.

Of that muddled company, he was the only one who had the least knowledge of their whereabouts or guessed that those responsible for the signal-fire were Colonel Gideon Ward and Eleazar Bodge. He followed behind, steeling his soul to meet those victims of the complicated plot. An astonished bleat from Hiram Look, who led the column, announced them. Colonel Ward was doubled before the fire, his long arms embracing his thin knees. Eleazar Bodge had just brought a fresh armful of driftwood to heap on the blaze.

"We thought it would bring help to us," cried the Colonel, who could not see clearly through the smoke. "We've been left here by a set of thieves and murderers." He unfolded himself and stood up. "You get me in reach of a telegraph-office before nine o'clock to-morrow and I'll make it worth your while."

"By the long-horned heifers of Hebron!" bawled Hiram. "We've come back to just the place we started from! If you built that fire to tole us ashore here, I'll have you put into State Prison."

"Here they are, Bodge!" shrieked the Colonel, his teeth chattering, squirrel-like, in his passion. "Talk about State Prison to me! I'll have the whole of you put there for bunco-men. You've stolen fifteen thousand dollars from me. Where is that old hell-hound that's got my check?"

"Here are six square and responsible citizens of Smyrna that heard you make your proposition and saw you pass that check," declared Hiram, stoutly, awake thoroughly, now that his prized plot was menaced. "It was a trade."

"It was a steal!" The Colonel caught sight of Cap'n Sproul on the outskirts of the group. "You cash that check and I'll have you behind bars. I've stopped payment on it."

"Did ye telegraft or ride to the bank on a bicycle?" inquired the Cap'n, satirically. He came straight up to the fire, pushing the furious Colonel to one side as he passed him. Angry as Ward was, he did not dare to resist or attack this grim man who thus came upon him, dripping, from the sea.

"Keep out of the way of gentlemen who want to dry themselves," grunted the skipper, and he calmly took possession of the fire, beckoning his crew to follow him. The Colonel and Mr. Bodge were shut out from the cheering blaze.

The first thing Cap'n Sproul did, as he squatted down, was to pull out his wallet and inspect the precious check.

"It's pretty wet," he remarked, "but the ink ain't run any. A little dryin' out is all it needs."

And with Ward shouting fearful imprecations at him over the heads of the group about the fire, he proceeded calmly to warm the check, turning first one side and then the other to the blaze.

"If you try to grab that," bawled Hiram, who was squatting beside the Cap'n, eying him earnestly in his task, "I'll break in your head." Then he nudged the elbow of the Cap'n, who had remained apparently oblivious of his presence. "Aaron," he muttered, "there's been some things between us to-night that I wish hadn't been. But I'm quick-tempered, and I ain't used to the sea, and what I done was on the spur of the moment. But I've shown that I'm your friend, and I'll do more to show —"

"Hiram," broke in the Cap'n, and his tone was severe, "mutiny ain't easy overlooked. But considerin' that your elephant has squared things for you, we'll let it stand as settled. But don't ever talk about it. I'm havin' too hard work to control my feelin's."

And then, looking up from the drying check, he fixed the vociferous Colonel with flaming eyes.

"Did ye hear me make a remark about my feelin's?" he rasped. "Your business and my business has been settled, and here's the paper to show for it." He slapped his hand across the check. "I didn't come back here to talk it over." He gulped down his wrathful memory of the reasons that had brought him. "You've bought Bodge. You've bought Cap Kidd's treasure, wherever it is. You're welcome to Bodge and to the treasure. And, controllin' Bodge as you do, you'd better let him make you up another fire off some little ways from this one, because this one ain't big enough for you and me both." The Cap'n's tone was significant. There was stubborn menace there, also. After gazing for a time on Sproul's uncompromising face and on the check so tantalizingly displayed before the blaze, Colonel Ward turned and went away. Ten minutes later a rival blaze mounted to the heavens from a distant part of Cod Lead Nubble. Half an hour later Mr. Bodge came as an emissary. He brought the gage of battle and flung it down and departed instantly.

"Colonel Ward says for me to say to you," he announced, "that he'll bet a thousand dollars you don't dare to hand that check into any bank."

"And you tell him I'll bet five thousand dollars," bellowed the Cap'n, "that I not only dare to cash it, but that I'll get to a bank and do it before he can get anywhere and stop payment."

"It's a pretty fair gamble both ways," remarked Hiram, his sporting instincts awake. "You may know more about water and ways of gettin' acrost that, but if this wind holds up the old spider will spin out a thread and ride away on it. He's ga'nt enough!"

Cap'n Sproul made no reply. He sat before his fire buried in thought, the gale whipping past his ears.

Colonel Ward, after ordering the returned and communicative Bodge to shut up, was equally thoughtful as he gazed into his fire. Ludelphus Murray, after trying long and in vain to light a soggy pipeful of tobacco, gazed into the fire-lit faces of his comrades of the Ancients and Honorables of Smyrna and said, with a sickly grin:

"I wisht I knew Robinson Crusoe's address. He might like to run out and spend the rest of the fall with us."

But the jest did not cheer the gloom of the marooned on Cod Lead Nubble.

XXIII

Cap'n Aaron Sproul had forgotten his troubles for a time. He had been dozing. The shrewish night wind of autumn whistled over the ledges of Cod Lead Nubble and scattered upon his gray beard the black ashes from the bonfire that the shivering men of Smyrna still plied with fuel. The Cap'n sat upright, his arms clasping his doubled knees, his head bent forward.

Hiram Look, faithful friend that he was, had curled himself at his back and was snoring peacefully. He had the appearance of a corsair, with his head wrapped in the huge handkerchief that had replaced the plug hat lost in the stress and storm that had destroyed the *Aurilla P. Dobson*. The elephant, Imogene, was bulked dimly in the first gray of a soppy dawn.

"If this is goin' to sea," said Jackson Denslow, continuing the sour mutterings of the night, "I'm glad I never saw salt water before I got pulled into this trip."

"It ain't goin' to sea," remarked another of the Smyrna amateur mariners. "It's goin' ashore!" He waved a disconsolate gesture toward the cove where the remains of the *Dobson* swashed in the breakers.

"If any one ever gets me navigatin' again onto anything desp'ritter than a stone-bo't on Smyrna bog," said Denslow, "I hope my relatives will have me put into a insane horsepittle."

"Look at that!" shouted Ludelphus Murray. "This is a thunderation nice kind of a night to have a celebration on!"

This yelp, sounding above the somniferous monotone of grumbling, stirred Cap'n Sproul from his dozing. He snapped his head up from his knees. A rocket was streaking across the sky and popped with a sprinkling of colored fires. Another and another followed with desperate haste, and a Greek fire shed baleful light across the waters.

"Yes, sir," repeated Murray, indignantly sarcastic, "it's a nice night and a nice time of night to be celebratin' when other folks is cold and sufferin' and hungry."

"What's the matter?" asked Hiram, stirring in his turn.

The Cap'n was prompt with biting reply.

"One of your Smyrna 'cyclopedys of things that ain't so is open at the page headed 'idjit,' with a chaw of tobacker for a book-mark. If the United States Government don't scoop in the whole of us for maintainin' false beacons on a dangerous coast in a storm, then I miss my cal'lations, that's all!"

"That shows the right spirit out there," vouchsafed Hiram, his eyes kindling as another rocket slashed the sky. "Fireworks as soon as they've located us is the right spirit, I say! The least we can do is to give 'em three cheers."

But at this Cap'n Sproul staggered up, groaning as his old enemy, rheumatism, dug its claws into his flesh. He made for the shore, his disgust too deep for words.

"Me—me," he grunted, "in with a gang that can't tell the difference between a vessel goin' to pieces and a fireworks celebration! I don't wonder that the Atlantic Ocean tasted of us and spit us ashore. She couldn't stand it to drown us!"

When the others straggled down and gabbled questions at him he refused to reply, but stood peering into the lifting dawn. He got a glimpse of her rig before her masts went over. She was a hermaphrodite brig, and old-fashioned at that. She was old-fashioned enough to have a figure-head. It came ashore at Cap'n Sproul's feet as *avant-coureur* of the rest of the wreckage. It led the procession because it was the first to suffer when the brig butted her nose against the Blue Cow Reef. It came ashore intact, a full-sized woman carved from pine and painted white. The Cap'n recognized the fatuous smile as the figure rolled its face up at him from the brine.

"The old *Polyhymnia*!" he muttered.

Far out there was a flutter of sail, and under his palm he descried a big yawl making off the coast. She rode lightly, and he could see only two heads above her gunwale.

"That's Cap Hart Tate, all right," mused the Cap'n; "Cap Hart Tate gallantly engaged in winnin' a medal by savin' his own life. But knowin' Cap Hart Tate as well as I do, I don't see how he ever so far forgot himself as to take along any one else. It must be the first mate, and the first mate must have had a gun as a letter of recommendation!"

It may be said in passing that this was a distinctly shrewd guess, and the Cap'n promptly found something on the seas that clinched his belief. Bobbing toward Cod Lead came an overloaded dingy. There were six men in it, and they were making what shift they could to guide it into the cove between the outer rocks. They came riding through safely on a roller, splattered across the cove with wildly waving oars, and landed on the sand with a bump that sent them tumbling heels over head out of the little boat.

"Four Portygee sailors, the cook, and the second mate," elucidated Cap'n Sproul, oracularly, for his own information.

The second mate, a squat and burly sea-dog, was first up on his feet in the white water, but stumbled over a struggling sailor who was kicking his heels in an attempt to rise. When the irate mate was up for the second time he knocked down this sailor and then strode ashore, his meek followers coming after on their hands and knees.

"Ahoy, there, Dunk Butts!" called Cap'n Sproul, heartily.

But Dunk Butts did not appear to warm to greetings nor to rejoice over his salvation from the sea. He squinted sourly at the Cap'n, then at the men of Smyrna, and then his eyes fell upon the figurehead and its fatuous smile.

With a snarl he leaped on it, smashed his knuckles against its face, swore horribly while he danced with pain, kicked it with his heavy sea-boots, was more horribly profane as he hopped about with an aching toe in the clutch of both hands, and at last picked up a good-sized hunk of ledge and went at the smiling face with Berserker rage.

Cap'n Sproul had begun to frown at Butts's scornful slighting of his amiable greeting. Now he ran forward, placed his broad boot against the second mate, and vigorously pushed him away from the prostrate figure. When Butts came up at him with the fragment of rock in his grasp, Cap'n Sproul faced him with alacrity, also with a piece of rock.

"You've knowed me thutty years and sailed with me five, Dunk Butts, and ye're shinnin' into the wrong riggin' when ye come at me with a rock. I ain't in no very gentle spirits to-day, neither."

"I wasn't doin' northin' to you," squealed Butts, his anger becoming mere querulous reproach, for the Cap'n's eye was fiery and Butts's memory was good.

"You was strikin' a female," said Cap'n Sproul, with severity, and when the astonished Butts blazed indignant remonstrance, he insisted on his point with a stubbornness that allowed no compromise. "It don't make any difference even if it is only a painted figger. It's showin' disrespect to the sex, and sence I've settled on shore, Butts, and am married to the best woman that ever lived, I'm standin' up for the sex to the extent that I ain't seein' no insults handed to a woman—even if it ain't anything but an Injun maiden in front of a cigar-store."

Butts dropped his rock.

"I never hurt a woman, and I would never hurt one," he protested, "and you that's sailed with me knows it. But that blasted, grinnin' effijiggy there stands for that rotten old punk-heap that's jest gone to pieces out yender, and it's the only thing I've got to get back on. Three months from Turk's Island, Cap'n Sproul, with a salt cargo and grub that would gag a dogfish! Lay down half a biskit and it would walk off. All I've et for six weeks has been doughboys lolloped in Porty Reek. He kicked me when I complained." Butts shook wavering finger at the shred of sail in the distance. "He kept us off with the gun to-day and sailed away in the yawl, and he never cared whuther we ever got ashore or not. And the grin he give me when he done it was jest like the grin on that thing there." Again the perturbed Butts showed signs of a desire to assault the wooden incarnation of the spirit of the *Polyhymnia*.

"A man who has been abused as much as you have been abused at sea has good reason to stand up for your rights when you are abused the moment you reach shore," barked a harsh voice. Colonel Gideon Ward, backed by the faithful Eleazar Bodge, stood safely aloof on a huge bowlder, his gaunt frame outlined against the morning sky. "Are you the commander of those men?" he inquired.

"I'm second mate," answered Mr. Butts.

"You and your men are down there associatin' with the most pestilent set of robbers and land-pirates that ever disgraced a civilized country," announced the Colonel. "They robbed me of fifteen thousand dollars and left me marooned here on this desert island, but the wind of Providence blew 'em back, and the devil wouldn't have 'em in Tophet, and here they are. They'll have your wallets and your gizzards if you don't get away from 'em. I invite you over there to my fire, gentlemen. Mr. —"

"Butts," said the second mate, staring with some concern at the group about him and at the Cap'n, who still held his fragment of rock.

"Mr. Butts, you and your men come with me and I'll tell you a story that will —"

Hiram Look thrust forward at this moment. The ex-showman was not a reassuring personality to meet shipwrecked mariners. His big handkerchief was knotted about his head in true buccaneer style. The horns of his huge mustache stuck out fiercely. Mr. Butts and his timid Portuguese shrank.

"He's a whack-fired, jog-jiggered old sanup of a liar," bellowed this startling apparition, who might have been Blackbeard himself. "We only have got back the fifteen thousand that he stole from us."

These amazing figures dizzied Mr. Butts, and his face revealed his feelings. He blinked from one party to the other with swiftly calculating gaze. Looking at the angry Hiram, he backed away two steps. After staring at the unkempt members of the Smyrna fire department, ranged behind their foreman, he backed three steps more. And then reflecting that the man of the piratical countenance had unblushingly confessed to the present possession of the disputed fortune, he clasped his hands to his own money-belt and hurried over to Colonel Ward's rock, his men scuttling behind him.

"Don't you believe their lies," bellowed the Colonel, breaking in on Hiram's eager explanations of the timber-land deal and the quest of the treasure they had come to Cod Lead to unearth. "I'll take you right to the hole they sold to me, I'll show you the plank cover they made believe was the lid of a treasure-chest, I'll prove to you they are pirates. We've got to stand together." He hastened to Mr. Butts and linked his arm in the seaman's, drawing him away. "There's only two of us. We can't hurt you. We don't want to hurt you. But if you stay among that bunch they'll have your liver, lights, and your heart's blood."

Five minutes later the Ward camp was posted on a distant pinnacle of the island. Cap'n Sproul had watched their retreat without a word, his brows knitted, his fists clutched at his side, and his whole attitude representing earnest consideration of a problem. He shook his head at Hiram's advice to pursue Mr. Butts and drag him and his men away from the enemy. It occurred to him that the friendliest chase would look like an attack. He reflected that he had not adopted exactly the tactics that were likely to warm over the buried embers of friendship in Mr. Butts's bosom. He remembered through the mists of the years that something like a kick or a belaying-pin had been connected with Mr. Butts's retirement from the *Benn*.

And until he could straighten out in his mind just what that parting difficulty had been, and how much his temper had triumphed over his justice to Butts, and until he had figured out a little something in the line of diplomatic conciliation, he decided to squat for a time beside his own fire and ruminate.

For an hour he sat, his brow gloomy, and looked across to where Colonel Ward was talking to Butts, his arms revolving like the fans of a crazy windmill.

"Lord! Cap'n Aaron," blurted Hiram at last, "he's pumpin' lies into that shipmate of yourn till even from this distance I can see him swellin' like a hop-toad under a mullein leaf. I tell you, you've got to do something. What if it should come calm and you ain't got him talked over and they should take the boat and row over to the mainland? Where'd you and your check be if he gets to the bank first? You listen to my advice and grab in there or we might just as well never have got up that complicated plot to get even with the old son of a seco."

"Hiram," said the Cap'n, after a moment's deliberation, the last hours of the *Aurilla P. Dobson* rankling still, "sence you and your gang mutinied on me and made me let a chartered schooner go to smash I ain't had no especial confidence in your advice in crisises. I've seen you hold your head level in crisises on shore—away from salt water, but you don't fit in 'board ship. And this, here, comes near enough to bein' 'board ship to cut you out. I don't take any more chances with you and the Smyrna fire department till I get inland at least fifty miles from tide-water."

Hiram bent injured gaze on him.

"You're turnin' down a friend in a tight place," he complained. "I've talked it over with the boys and they stand ready to lick those dagos and take the boat, there, and row you ashore."

But his wistful gaze quailed under the stare the Cap'n bent on him. The mariner flapped discrediting hand at the pathetic half-dozen castaways poking among the rocks for mussels with which to stay their hunger.

"Me get in a boat again with that outfit? Why, I wouldn't ride acrost a duck pond in an ocean liner with 'em unless they were crated and battened below hatches." He smacked his hard fist into his palm. "There they straddle, like crows on new-ploughed land, huntin' for something to eat, and no thought above it, and there ain't one of 'em come to a reelizin' sense yet that they committed a State Prison offence last night when they mutinied and locked me into my own cabin like a cat in a coop. Now I don't want to have any more trouble over it with you, Hiram, for we've been too good friends, and will try to continner so after this thing is over and done with, but if you or that gang of up-country sparrer-hawks stick your fingers or your noses into this business that I'm in now, I'll give the lobsters and cunners round this island just six good hearty meals. Now, that's the business end, and it's whittled pickid, and you want to let alone of it!"

He struggled up and strode away across the little valley between the stronghold of Colonel Ward and his own hillock.

Colonel Ward stood up when he saw him approaching, and Butts, after getting busy with something on the ground, stood up, also. When the Cap'n got nearer he noted that Butts had his arms full of rocks.

"Dunk," called Cap'n Sproul, placatingly, pausing at a hostile movement, "you've had quite a long yarn with that critter there, who's been fillin' you up with lies about me, and now it's only fair that as an old shipmate you should listen to my side. I—"

"You bear off!" blustered Mr. Butts. "You hold your own course, 'cause the minute you get under my bows I'll give you a broadside that will put your colors down. You've kicked me the last time you're ever goin' to."

"I was thinkin' it was a belayin'-pin that time aboard the *Benn*," muttered the Cap'n. "I guess I must have forgot and kicked him." Then once again he raised his voice in appeal. "You're the first seafarin' man I know of that left your own kind to take sides with a land-pirut."

"You ain't seafarin' no more," retorted Mr. Butts, insolently. "Talk to me of bein' seafarin' with that crowd of jays you've got round you! You ain't northin' but moss-backs and bunko-men." Cap'n Sproul glanced over his shoulder at the men of Smyrna and groaned under his breath. "I never knowed a seafarin' man to grow to any good after he settled ashore. Havin' it in ye all the time, you've turned out a little worse than the others, that's all."

Mr. Butts continued on in this strain of insult, having the advantage of position and ammunition and the mind to square old scores. And after a time Cap'n Sproul turned and trudged back across the valley.

There was such ferocity on his face when he sat down by his fire that Hiram Look gulped back the questions that were in his throat. He recognized that it was a crisis, realized that Cap'n Sproul was autocrat, and refrained from irritating speech.

XXIV

By noon the sun shone on Cod Lead wanly between ragged clouds. But its smile did not warm Cap'n Sproul's feelings. Weariness, rheumatism, resentment that became bitterer the more he pondered on the loss of the *Dobson*, and gnawing hunger combined to make a single sentiment of sullen fury; the spectacle of Colonel Ward busy with his schemes on the neighboring pinnacle sharpened his anger into something like ferocity.

The wind had died into fitful breaths. The sea still beat furiously on the outer ledges of the island, but in the reach between the island and the distant main there was a living chance for a small boat. It was not a chance that unskilful rowers would want to venture upon, but given the right crew the Cap'n reflected that he would be willing to try it.

Evidently Mr. Butts, being an able seaman, was reflecting upon something of the same sort. The Portuguese sailors, the last one of the departing four dodging a kick launched at him by Mr. Butts, went down to the shore, pulled the abandoned dingy upon the sand, and emptied the water out of it. They fished the oars out of the flotsam in the cove. Then they sat down on the upturned boat, manifestly under orders and awaiting further commands.

"Then ye're goin' to let 'em do it, be ye?" huskily asked Hiram. "Goin' to let him get to the bank and stop payment on that check? I tell you the boys can get that boat away from 'em! It better be smashed than used to carry Gid Ward off'm this island."

But Cap'n Sproul did not interrupt his bitter ruminations to reply. He merely shot disdainful glance at the Smyrna men, still busy among the mussels.

It was apparent that Mr. Butts had decided that he would feel more at ease upon his pinnacle until the hour arrived for embarkation. In the game of stone-throwing, should Cap'n Sproul accept that gage of battle, the beach was too vulnerable a fortress, and, like a prudent commander, Mr. Butts had sent a forlorn hope onto the firing-line to test conditions. This was all clear to Cap'n Sproul. As to Mr. Butts's exact intentions relative to the process of getting safely away, the Cap'n was not so clear.

"Portygees!" he muttered over and over. "There's men that knows winds, tides, rocks, shoals, currents, compass, and riggin' that don't know Portygees. It takes a master mariner to know Portygees. It takes Portygees to know a master mariner. They know the language. They know the style. They get the idee by the way he looks at 'em. It's what he says and the way he says it. Second mates ain't got it. P'r'aps I ain't got it, after bein' on shore among clodhoppers for two years. But, by Judas Iscarrot, I'm goin' to start in and find out! Portygees! There's Portygees! Here's me that has handled 'em—batted brains into 'em as they've come over the side, one by one, and started 'em goin' like I'd wind up a watch! And a belayin'-pin is the key!"

He arose with great decision, buttoned his jacket, cocked his cap to an angle of authority on his gray hair, and started down the hill toward the boat.

"He's goin' to call in his bunko-men and take that boat," bleated Mr. Butts to Colonel Ward.

"Wild hosses couldn't drag him into a boat again with those human toadstools, and I've heard him swear round here enough to know it," scoffed the Colonel. "He's just goin' down to try to wheedle your sailors like he tried to wheedle you, and they're your men and he can't do it."

And in the face of this authority and confidence in the situation Mr. Butts subsided, thankful for an excuse to keep at a respectful distance from Cap'n Aaron Sproul.

That doughty expert on "Portygees" strode past the awed crew with an air that they instinctively recognized as belonging to the quarter-deck. Their meek eyes followed him as he stumped into the swash and kicked up two belaying-pins floating in the debris. He took one in each hand, came back at them on the trot, opening the flood-gates of his language. And they instinctively recognized that as quarter-deck, too. They knew that no mere mate could possess that quality of utterance and redundancy of speech.

He had a name for each one as he hit him. It was a game of "Tag, you're it!" that made him master, in that moment of amazement, from the mere suddenness of it. A man with less assurance and slighter knowledge of sailorman character might have been less abrupt—might have given them a moment in which to reflect. Cap'n Aaron Sproul kept them going—did their thinking for them, dizzied their brains by thwacks of the pins, deafened their ears by his terrific language.

In fifteen seconds they had run the dingy into the surf, had shipped oars, and were lustily pulling away—Cap'n Sproul in the stern roaring abuse at them in a way that drowned the howls of Mr. Butts, who came peltering down the hill.

But Hiram Look was even more nimble than that protesting seaman.

Before the little craft was fairly under way he plunged into the surf waist-deep and scrambled over the stern, nearly upsetting the Cap'n as he rolled in.

And Imogene, the elephant, a faithful and adoring pachyderm, pursued her lord and master into the sea.

Cap'n Sproul, recovering his balance and resuming his interrupted invective, was startled by the waving of her trunk above his head, and his rowers quit work, squealing with terror, for the huge beast was making evident and desperate attempts to climb on board and join her fleeing owner. It was a rather complicated crisis even for a seaman, accustomed to splitting seconds in his battling with emergencies. An elephant, unusual element in marine considerations, lent the complication.

But the old sea-dog who had so instantly made himself master of men now made himself master of the situation, before the anxious Imogene had got so much as one big foot over the gunwale. He picked up the late-arriving Jonah, and, in spite of Hiram's kicks and curses, jettisoned him with a splash that shot spray over the pursuing elephant and blinded her eyes.

"Row—row, you blue-faced sons of Gehenna, or she'll eat all four of you!" shrieked the Cap'n; and in that moment of stress they rowed! Rowed now not because Cap'n Sproul commanded—nor ceased from rowing because Mr. Butts countermanded. They rowed for their own lives to escape the ravening beast that had chased them into the sea.

Cap'n Sproul, watching his chance, took a small wave after the seventh big roller, let it cuff his bow to starboard, and made for the lee of Cod Lead, rounding the island into the reach. He was safely away and, gazing into the faces of the Portuguese, he grimly reflected that for impressed men they seemed fully as glad to be away as he. They rowed now without further monition, clucking, each to himself, little prayers for their safe deliverance from the beast.

It was not possible, with safety, to cut across the reach straight for the main, so the Cap'n quartered his course before the wind and went swinging down the seas, with little chance of coming soon to shore, but confident of his seamanship.

But that seamanship was not sufficient to embolden him into an attempt to dodge a steamer with two masts and a dun funnel that came rolling out from behind Eggemoggin and bore toward him up the reach. He was too old a sailor not to know that she was the patrol cutter of the revenue service; wind and sea forced him to keep on across her bows.

She slowed her engines and swung to give him a lee. Cap'n Sproul swore under his breath, cursed aloud at his patient rowers, and told them to keep on. And when these astonishing tactics of a lonely dingy in a raging sea were observed from the bridge of the cutter, a red-nosed and profane man, who wore a faded blue cap with peak over one ear, gave orders to lower away a sponson boat, and came himself as coxswain, as though unwilling to defer the time of reckoning with such recalcitrants.

"What in billy-be-doosen and thunderation do you mean, you weevil-chawers, by not coming alongside when signalled—and us with a dozen wrecks to chase 'longshore?" he demanded, laying officious hand on the tossing gunwale of the dingy.

"We're attendin' strictly to our own business, and the United States Govvument better take pattern and go along and mind its own," retorted Cap'n Sproul, with so little of the spirit of gratitude that a shipwrecked mariner ought to display that the cutter officer glared at him with deep suspicion.

"What were you mixed up in—mutiny or barratry?" he growled. "We'll find out later. Get in here!"

"This suits me!" said Cap'n Sproul, stubbornly.

The next moment he and his Portuguese were yanked over the side of the boat into the life-craft—a dozen sturdy chaps assisting the transfer.

"Let the peapod go afloat," directed the gruff officer. "It's off the *Polyhymnia*—name on the stern-sheets—evidence enough—notice, men!"

"I'm not off the *Polyhymnia*," protested Cap'n Sproul, indignantly. "I was goin' along 'tendin' to my own business, and you can't—"

"Business?" sneered the man of the faded blue cap. "I thought you were out for a pleasure sail! You shut up!" he snapped, checking further complaints from the Cap'n. "If you've got a story that will fit in with your crazy-man actions, then you can wait and tell it to the court. As for me, I believe you're a gang of mutineers!" And after that bit of insolence the Cap'n was indignantly silent.

The cutter jingled her full-speed bell while the tackle was still lifting the sponson boat.

"They're ugly, and are hiding something," called the man of the faded cap, swinging up the bridge-ladder. "No good to pump more lies out of them. We'll go where they came from, and we'll get there before we can ask questions and get straight replies."

Cap'n Sproul, left alone on the cutter's deck, took out his big wallet, abstracted that fifteen-thousand-dollar check signed by Gideon Ward, and seemed about to fling it into the sea.

"Talk about your hoodoos!" he gritted. "Talk about your banana skins of Tophet! Twice I've slipped up on it and struck that infernal island. Even his name written on a piece of paper is a cuss to the man that lugs it!"

But after hale second thought he put the check back into his wallet and the wallet into his breast pocket and buttoned his coat securely. And the set of his jaws and the wrinkling of his forehead showed that the duel between him and Colonel Ward was not yet over.

As the steamer with the dun smoke-stack approached Cod Lead he noted sourly the frantic signallings of the marooned. He leaned on the rail and watched the departure of the officer of the faded blue cap with his crew of the sponson boat. He observed the details of the animated meeting of the rescuers and the rescued. Without great astonishment he saw that Hiram, of all the others, remained on shore, leaning disconsolately against the protecting bulk of Imogene.

"It's most a wonder he didn't try to load that infernal elephant onto that life-boat," he muttered. "If I couldn't travel through life without bein' tagged by an old gob of meat of that size, I'd hire a museum and settle down in it."

Cap'n Sproul, still leaning on the rail, paid no attention to the snort that Colonel Ward emitted as he passed on his way to the security of the steamer's deck. He resolutely avoided the reproachful starings of the members of the Smyrna fire department as they struggled on board. Mr. Butts came last and attempted to say something, but retreated promptly before the Cap'n's fiendish snarl and clicking teeth.

"That man there, with the elephant, says he can't leave her," reported Faded Cap to the wondering group on the bridge.

"A United States cutter isn't sent out to collect menageries accompanied by dry-nurses," stated the commander. "What is this job lot, anyway—a circus in distress?"

"Says the elephant can swim out if we'll rig a tackle and hoist her on board. Says elephant is used to it."

Something in the loneliness of the deserted two on Cod Lead must have appealed to the commander. He was profane about it, and talked about elephants and men who owned them in a way that struck an answering chord in the Cap'n's breast. But he finally gave orders for the embarkation of Imogene, and after much more profanity and more slurs which Hiram was obliged to listen to meekly, the task was accomplished, and the cutter proceeded on her way along coast on further errands of mercy.

And then the Cap'n turned and gazed on Hiram, and the showman gazed on the Cap'n. The latter spoke first.

"Hiram," he said, "it ain't best for you and me to talk this thing over, just as it stands now—not till we get back to Smyrna and set down on my front piazzy. P'r'aps things won't look so skeow-wowed then to us as they do now. We won't talk till then."

But the captain of the cutter was not as liberal-minded. In the process of preparing his report he attempted to interview both the Cap'n and Colonel Ward at the same time in his cabin, and at the height of the riot of recriminations that ensued was obliged to call in some deck-hands and have both ejected. Then he listened to them separately with increasing interest.

"When you brought this family fight down here to sprinkle salt water on it," he said at last, having the two of them before him again, with a deck-hand restraining each, "you didn't get it preserved well enough to keep it from smelling. I don't reckon I'll stir it. It doesn't seem to be a marine disaster. The United States Government has got other things to attend to just now besides settling it. Listen!"

He held up a forefinger.

"Smyrna isn't so far away from the seashore but what I've had plenty of chances to hear of Colonel Gideon Ward and his general dealings with his neighbors. For myself, I'd rather have less money and a reputation that didn't spread quite so far over the edges. As for you, Cap'n Sproul, as a seaman I can sympathize with you about getting cheated by land-pirates in that timber-land deal and in other things. But as a representative of the Government I'm not going to help you make good to the extent of fifteen thousand dollars on a hole and a Cap Kidd treasure fake. Hands off for me, seeing that it's a matter strictly in the family! This cutter is due to round to in Portland harbor to-morrow morning a little after nine o'clock. I'll send the two of you in my gig to Commercial Wharf, see that both are landed at the same time, and then—well"—the commander turned quizzical gaze from one to the other with full appreciation of the situation—"it then depends on what you do, each of you, and how quick you do it."

The Cap'n walked out of the room, his hand on his breast pocket. Colonel Ward followed, closing and unclosing his long fingers as if his hands itched to get at that pocket.

At the first peep of dawn Cap'n Aaron Sproul was posted at the cutter's fore windlass, eyes straight ahead on the nick in the low, blue line of coast that marked the harbor's entrance. His air was that of a man whose anxiety could not tolerate any post except the forepeak. And to him there came Hiram Look with tremulous eagerness in his voice and the weight of a secret in his soul.

"I heard him and Butts talkin' last night, Cap'n Aaron," he announced. "It was Butts that thought of it first. The telefoam. 'Run into the first place and grab a telefoam,' says Butts. 'Telefoam 'em at the bank to stop payment. It will take him ten minutes to run up from the wharf. Let him think you're right behind him. He's got to go to the bank,' says Butts. 'He can't telefoam 'em to pay the check.'"

The Cap'n's hand dropped dispiritedly from his clutch at his pocket.

"I knowed something would stop me," he mourned. "The whole plot is a hoodoo. There I was fired back twice onto Cod Lead! Here he is, landin' the same time as I do! And when he stops that check it throws it into law—and I've got the laborin'-oar."

"It ain't throwed into law yet, and you ain't got no laborin'-oar," cried Hiram, with a chuckle that astonished the despondent Cap'n. "He can't telefoam!"

"Can't what?"

"Why, stayin' out in that rain-storm has give him the most jeeroosly cold there's been sence Aunt Jerushy recommended thoroughwort tea! It's right in his thro't, and he ain't got so much voice left as wind blowing acrost a bottle. Can't make a sound! The bank folks ain't goin' to take any one's say-so for him. Not against a man like you that's got thutty thousand dollars in the same bank, and a man that they know! By the time he got it explained to any one so that they'd mix in, you can be at the bank and have it all done."

"Well, he ain't got cold in his legs, has he?" demanded the Cap'n, failing to warm to Hiram's enthusiasm. "It stands jest where it has been standin'. There ain't no reason why he can't get to that bank as quick as I can. Yes, quicker! I ain't built up like an ostrich, the way he is."

"Well," remarked Hiram, after a time, "a fair show and an even start is more'n most folks get in this life—and you've got that. The boss of this boat is goin' to give you that much. So all you can do is to take what's given you and do the best you can. And all I can do is stay back here and sweat blood and say the only prayer that I know, which is 'Now I lay me down to sleep.'"

And after this bit of consolation he went back amidships to comfort the hungry Imogene, who had been unable to find much in the cuisine of a revenue cutter that would satisfy the appetite of elephants.

At half-past nine in the forenoon the cutter swept past Bug Light and into the inner harbor. Hardly had the steamer swung with the tide at her anchorage before the captain's gig was proceeding briskly toward Commercial Wharf, two men rowing and the man of the faded blue cap at the helm. The antagonists in the strange duello sat back to back, astraddle a seat. At this hateful contact their hair seemed fairly to bristle.

"Now, gents," said Faded Cap, as they approached the wharf, "the skipper said he wanted fair play. No scrougin' to get out onto the ladder first. I'm goin' to land at the double ladder at the end of the wharf, and there's room for both of you. I'll say 'Now!' and then you start."

"You fellers are gettin' a good deal of fun out this thing," sputtered Cap'n Sproul, angrily, "but don't you think I don't know it and resent it. Now, don't you talk to me like you were startin' a foot-race!"

"What is it, if it ain't a foot-race?" inquired Faded Cap, calmly. "They don't have hacks or trolley-cars on that wharf, and you'll either have to run or fly, and I don't see any signs of wings on you."

Colonel Ward did not join in this remonstrance. He only worked his jaws and uttered a few croaks.

When the gig surged to the foot of the ladder, Colonel Ward attempted a desperate play, and an unfair one. He was on the outside, and leaped up, stepped on Cap'n Sproul, and sprang for the ladder. The Cap'n was quick enough to grab his legs, yank him back into the boat, and mount over him in his turn. The man of the faded cap was nearly stunned by Ward falling on him, and the rowers lost their oars.

When the Colonel had untangled himself from the indignant seamen and had escaped up the ladder, Cap'n Sproul was pelting up the wharf at a most amazing clip, considering his short legs. Before Ward had fairly gathered himself for the chase his fifteen-thousand-dollar check and the man bearing it had disappeared around a corner into the street.

But the squat and stubby old sailor stood little show in a foot-race with his gaunt and sinewy adversary. It was undoubtedly Colonel Ward's knowledge of this that now led him to make the race the test of victory instead of depending on an interpreter over the telephone. A little more than a block from the wharf's lane he came up with and passed his adversary. Men running for trolley-cars and steamboats were common enough on the busy thoroughfare, and people merely made way for the sprinters.

But when Colonel Ward was a few lengths ahead of the Cap'n, the latter made use of an expedient that the voiceless Colonel could not have employed even if he had thought of it.

With all the force of his seaman's lungs he bellowed: "Stop thief!" and pounded on behind, reiterating the cry vociferously. At first he had the pursuit all to himself, for bystanders merely ducked to one side. But earnest repetition compels attention, and attention arouses interest, and interest provokes zeal. In a little while a dozen men were chasing the Colonel, and when that gentleman went lashing around the corner into Congress Street he—by an entirely natural order of events—ran into a policeman, for the policeman was running in the opposite direction to discover what all that approaching hullabaloo was about.

Cap'n Sproul, prudently on the outskirts of the gathering crowd, noted with rising hope that the policeman and the Colonel were rolling over each other on the ground, and that even when officious hands had separated them the facial contortions of the voiceless tyrant of Smyrna were not making any favorable impression on the offended bluecoat.

Cap'n Sproul started away for the bank at a trot. But he began to walk when he heard the policeman shout: "Aw, there's enough of ye'r moonkey faces at me. Yez will coome along to th' station, and talk it on yer fingers to th' marshal!"

At the bank door the Cap'n halted, wiped his face, composed his features, set on his cap at an entirely self-possessed angle, and then marched in to the wicket.

"Will you have this transferred to your account, Captain Sproul?" inquired the teller, with the deference due to a good customer.

The Cap'n anxiously bent a stubbed finger around a bar of the grating. Sudden anxiety as to leaving the money there beset him. After his perils and his toils he wanted to feel that cash—to realize that he had actually cashed in that hateful check.

"I'll take the real plasters," he said, huskily; "big ones as you've got. I—I want to pay for some vessel property!" He reflected that the few hundreds that the loss of the ancient *Dobson* called for lifted this statement out of the cheap level of prevarication.

When he hurried out of the bank with various thick packets stowed about his person, he headed a straight course for the police-station.

In the marshal's office he found Colonel Gideon Ward, voiceless, frantic, trembling—licking at the point of a stubby lead-pencil that had been shoved into his grasp, and trying to compose his soul sufficiently to write out some of the information about himself, with which he was bursting.

"There ain't no call for this man to write out the story of his life," declared Cap'n Sproul, with an authority in his tones and positiveness in his manner that did not fail to impress the marshal. "He is my brother-in-law, he is Colonel Gideon Ward, of Smyrna, a man with more'n a hundred thousand dollars, and any one that accuses him of bein' a thief is a liar, and I stand here to prove it."

And to think there was no one present except the Colonel to appreciate the cryptic humor of that remark!

The Cap'n avoided the demoniacal gaze that Ward bent on him and disregarded the workings of that speechless mouth. Sproul shoved his hand deep into his trousers pocket and pulled out a roll of bills on which the teller's tape had not been broken. At this sight the Colonel staggered to his feet.

"Here!" cried the Cap'n, shoving money into the hand of the officer who had made the arrest. "There's something to pay for your muddy clothes. Now you'd better go out and find the man that started all this touse about a leadin' citizen. I'll sue this city as a relative of his if you don't let him go this minute."

And they let him go, with an apology that Colonel Ward treated with perfectly insulting contempt.

Cap'n Sproul faced him on the street outside the prison, standing prudently at guard, for he perfectly realized that just at that moment Colonel Gideon Ward had all the attributes of a lunatic.

"You can see it bulgin' all over me," said the Cap'n, "all tied up in bundles. I don't say my way was the best way to get it. But I've got it. I suppose I might have gone to law to get it, but that ain't my way. Of course you can go to law to get it back; but for reasons that you know just as well as I, I'd advise you not to—and that advice don't cost you a cent."

For a full minute Colonel Ward stood before him and writhed his gaunt form and twisted his blue lips and waggled his bony jaws. But not a sound could he utter. Then he whirled and signalled a trolley-car and climbed on board. With intense satisfaction the Cap'n noted that the car was marked "Union Station."

"Well, home is the best place for him," muttered the Cap'n; "home and a flaxseed poultice on his chist and complete rest of mind and body. Now I'll settle for that schooner, hunt up Hime Look and that pertickler and admirin' friend of his, that infernal elephant, and then I reckon I'll—eraow-w-w!" he yawned. "I'll go home and rest up a little, too."

That repose was not disturbed by Colonel Gideon Ward. The Colonel had decided that affairs in his timber tracts needed his attention during that autumn.

XXV

Events do bunch themselves strangely, sometimes.

They bunched in Smyrna as follows:

1. The new monument arrived for Batson Reeves's graveyard lot in which was interred the first Mrs. Reeves; monument a belated arrival.

2. The announcement was made that Batson Reeves had at last caught a new wife in the person of Widow Delora Crymble, wedding set for Tuesday week.

3. Dependence Crymble, deceased husband of Delora, reappeared on earth. This latter event to be further elaborated.

Cap'n Aaron Sproul, first selectman of Smyrna, on his way from his home to the town office, found several men leaning on the graveyard fence, gazing over into the hallowed precincts of the dead with entire lack of that solemnity that is supposed to be attached to graveyards. It was on the morning following the last stroke of work on the Reeves monument.

The Reeves monument, a wholly unique affair, consisted of a life-sized granite figure of Mr. Reeves standing on a granite pedestal in the conventional attitude of a man having his photograph taken. His head was set back stiffly, the right foot was well advanced, and he held a round-topped hat in the hook of his elbow.

On the pedestal was carved:

ERECTED TO THE MEMORY OF

LOANTHA REEVES,

WIFE OF BATSON REEVES, ACCORDING TO HER LAST REQUEST.

It may be said in passing that Mrs. Reeves, having entertained a very exalted opinion of Mr. Reeves during life, left a portion of her own estate in the hands of trustees in order that this sentinel figure should stand guard above her in the sunshine and the rain. The idea was poetic. But Cap'n Sproul, joining the hilarious group at the graveyard fence, noted that some gruesome village humorist had seriously interfered with the poetic idea. Painted on a planed board set up against the monument was this:

I'm Watching Here Both Night and Day,
So Number One Can't Get Away.

"That's kind o' pat, Cap'n, considerin' he's goin' to get married to Number Two next week," suggested one of the loungers.

Cap'n Sproul scowled into the grin that the other turned on him.

"I ain't got any regard for a human dogfish like Bat Reeves," he grunted, his heart full of righteous bitterness against a proclaimed enemy, "but as first selectman of this town I don't stand for makin' a comic joke-book out of this cemetery." He climbed over the fence, secured the offending board and split it across his broad toe. Then with the pieces under his arm he trudged on toward the town office, having it in his mind to use the board for kindling in the barrel stove.

One strip he whittled savagely into shavings and the other he broke into fagots, and when the fire was snapping merrily in the rusty stove he resumed a labor upon which he had been intent for several days. Predecessors in office had called it "writing the town report." Cap'n Sproul called it "loggin' the year's run."

A pen never did hang easy in the old shipmaster's stiff fingers. The mental travail of this unwonted literary effort wrung his brain. An epic poet struggling with his masterpiece could not have been more rapt. And his nerves were correspondingly touchy. Constable

Zeburee Nute, emerging at a brisk trot from the town office, had a warning word of counsel for all those intending to venture upon the first selectman's privacy. He delivered it at Broadway's store.

"Talk about your r'yal Peeruvian tigers with eighteen rings on their tails! He's settin' there with his hair standin' straight up and ink on his nose and clear to his elbows, and he didn't let me even get started in conversation. He up and throwed three ledger-books and five sticks of wood at me, and—so I come away," added Mr. Nute, resignedly. "I don't advise nobody to go in there."

However, the warning delivered at Broadway's store did not reach a certain tall, thin man; for the tall, thin man stalked straight through the village and up to the door inscribed "Selectman's Office." In his hand he carried a little valise about as large as a loaf of yeast bread. The shrewish December wind snapped trousers about legs like broom-handles. Black pads were hugged to his ears by a steel strip that curved behind his head, and he wore a hard hat that seemed merely to perch insecurely on his caput instead of fit. Constable Nute, getting a glimpse of him through the store-window, remarked that with five minutes and a razor-strop he could put a shaving edge on the stranger's visage, but added promptly when he saw him disappear into the town office that some one could probably get a job within the next five minutes honing the nicks out of that edge.

Cap'n Sproul was just then absorbed in a task that he hated even worse than literary composition. He was adding figures. They were the items for road bills, and there were at least two yards of them on sheets of paper pasted together, for nearly every voter in town was represented. The Cap'n was half-way up one of the columns, and was exercising all his mental grip to hold on to the slowly increasing total on which he was laboriously piling units.

"I am always glad to meet a man who loves figgers," remarked the stranger, solemnly. He set his valise on the table and leaned over the Cap'n's shoulder. "I have wonderful faculty for figgers. Give me a number and I'll tell you the cube of it instantly, in the snap of a finger."

Cap'n Sproul merely ground his teeth and shoved his nose closer to the paper. He did not dare to look up. His whole soul was centred in effort to "walk the crack" of that column.

"I could do it when I was fifteen—and that was fifty years ago," went on the thin man.

The enunciation of those figures nearly put the Cap'n out of commission, but with a gulp and after a mental stagger he marched on.

"Now give me figgers—tens or hundreds," pleaded the stranger. "I'll give you the cube in one second—the snap of a finger. Since I see you hesitate, we'll take sixteen—a very simple factor. Cube it!" He clacked a bony finger into an osseous palm and cried: "Four thousand and ninety-six!"

That did it!

"Ninety-six," repeated the Cap'n, dizzily; realizing that he had bounced off the track, he rose, kicked his chair out from under him and shoved a livid and infuriated visage into the thin man's face.

"Whang-jacket your gor-righteously imperdence!" he bellowed, "what do you mean by stickin' that fish-hawk beak of your'n into my business and make me lose count? Get to Tophet out of here!"

The stranger calmly removed his ear-pads and gazed on the furious selectman with cold, gray and critical eyes.

"Your suggestion as to destination is not well considered," he said. "There is no hell. There is no heaven. I practically settled that point the first time I died. The—"

Cap'n Sproul, without especial attention to this astonishing announcement, was provoked beyond control by this stranger's contemptuous stare. He grabbed up an ash-stick that served him for a stove-poker.

"Get out of here," he repeated, "or I'll peg you down through this floor like a spike!"

But the thin man simply gazed at him mournfully and sat down.

"Havin' been killed three times—three times—dead by violent means," he said, "I have no fear of death. Strike me—I shall not resist."

Even a bashi-bazouk must have quailed before that amazing declaration and that patient resignation to fate. Cap'n Sproul looked him up and down for many minutes and then tucked the smutty ash-stick under the stove.

"Well, what insane horsepittle did you get out of by crawlin' through the keyhole?" he demanded.

"Oh, I am not insane," remonstrated the thin man. "It is always easy for fools in this world to blat that insult when a man announces something that they don't understand. A man that knows enough to be selectman of Smyrna hadn't ought to be a fool. I hope you are not. But you mustn't blat like a fool."

Cap'n Sproul could not seem to frame words just then.

"The first time I died," pursued his remarkable guest, "I was frozen to death." He pulled up his trousers and showed a shank as shrunken as a peg-leg. "All the meat came off. The second time I died, a hoss kicked me on the head. The third time, a tree fell on me. And there is no hell—there is no heaven. If there had been I'd have gone to one place or the other."

"If I was runnin' either place you wouldn't," said the Cap'n, sourly.

The thin man crossed his legs and was beginning to speak, but the first selectman broke in savagely: "Now look here, mister, this ain't either a morgue, a receivin'-tomb, nor an undertaker's parlor. If you want to get buried and ain't got the price I'll lend it to you. If you want to start over again in life I'll pay for havin' your birth-notice put into the newspaper. But you want to say what you do want and get out of here. I've got some town business to 'tend to, and I ain't got any time to spend settin' up with corpses."

Again the man tried to speak. Again the Cap'n interrupted. "I ain't disputin' a thing you say," he cried. "I'm admittin' everything, 'cause I haven't got time to argue. You may have been dead nine times like a cat. I don't care. All is, you go along. You'll find accommodations at the tavern, the graveyard, or the town farm, whichever hits you best. I'm busy."

But when he pulled his paper of figures under his nose again, the thin man tapped his fleshless digit on the table.

"You're the first selectman, aren't you?" he demanded.

"That's what I be," returned the Cap'n, smartly.

"Well, then, you got to pay attention to town business when it is put before you. I've come here on town business. I used to live in this town."

"Was you buried here or was your remains taken away?" inquired the Cap'n, genially, hoping that satire might drive out this unwelcome disturber.

"Oh, I died all three times after I left this town," said the thin man, in matter-of-fact tones. "What I'm comin' at is this: my father gave the land to this town to build the school-house on out in the Crymble district. Deed said if the building was ever abandoned for school purposes for five years running, land and buildin' came back to estate. I came past that school-house to-day and I see it hasn't been used."

"We don't have school deestricks any more," explained the Cap'n. "We transport scholars to the village here. That's been done for six years and over."

"Then I claim the school-house and land," declared the thin man.

"You do, hey?"

"I do. I've got tired of travellin' round over this world, and I'm goin' to settle down. And that school-house is the only real estate I've got to settle down in. I'll keep bach' hall there."

"Who in thunderation are you, anyway?" demanded Cap'n Sproul, propping himself on the table and leaning forward belligerently.

"My name is Dependence Crymble," replied the other, quietly. "My father was Hope-for-grace Crymble. Odd names, eh? But the Crymbles were never like other folks."

Cap'n Sproul sat down hard in his chair and goggled at the thin man.

"Say, look-here-you," he gasped at last. "There never could be more'n one name like Dependence Crymble in this world. I ain't a native here and I don't know you from Adam. But is your wife the Widow Delora Crymble—I mean, was she—oh, tunk-rabbit it, I reckon I'm gettin' as crazy as you are!"

"I'm not insane," persisted the other. "I'm Dependence Crymble, and I married Delora Goff. I've been away from here twenty years, but I guess the old residents will recognize me, all right."

"But," declared the Cap'n, floundering for a mental footing, "it's always been said to me that Dependence Crymble died off—away somewhere."

"I've already told you I died," said the thin man, still mild but firm. "That's right, just as you've heard it."

"There's a stone in the graveyard to you," went on the Cap'n, clawing his stubby fingers into his bristle of hair, "and they've always called her 'Widder Crymble' and"—he stood up again and leaned forward over the table in the attitude of Jove about to launch a thunderbolt and gasped—"she's goin' to get married to Bat Reeves, Tuesday of next week—and he's the most infernal scalawag in this town, and he's took her after he's tried about every other old maid and widder that's got property."

The thin man did not even wince or look astonished. His querulous mouth only dropped lower at the corners.

"I don't care who marries her. She's a widder and can marry any one she's got a mind to. I didn't come back here to mix in. She's welcome to the property I left her. There was a will. It's hers. I've been administered on according to law. All I want is that school-house back from the town. That's mine by law."

Cap'n Sproul sat down once more.

"Well," he said at last, with some indignation, "if you was dead and wanted to stay dead and leave a widder and property and let her get married again, and all that—what in the name of the yaller-bellied skate-fish have ye come ghostin' round here for to tip everything upside down and galley-west after it's been administered on and settled? And it gets town business all mixed up!"

The thin man smiled a wistful smile.

"The poet says: 'Where'er we roam, the sky beneath, the heart sighs for its native heath.' That's the sentiment side of it. But there's a practical side. There's the school-house. It was worth passing this way to find out whether the town had abandoned it—and I reckoned it had, and I reckoned right. I have presentiments that come true. I reckoned that probably the relict would put a stone in the graveyard for me. I have a presentiment that I shall die twice more, staying dead the fifth time I pass away. That will be here in this town, and the gravestone won't be wasted."

While the first selectman was still trying to digest this, the thin man opened his valise. He took out a nickel plate that bore his name.

"This is my casket-plate," he explained, forcing the grisly object into the resisting hands of the Cap'n. "Friends ordered it for me the first time I died. I've carried it with me ever since."

"It must be a nice way of passin' a rainy Sunday," said the Cap'n, sarcastically, pushing the plate back across the table; "set and look at that and hum a pennyr'yal hymn! It's sartinly a rollickin' life you're leadin', Mister Crymble."

Mr. Crymble did not retort. On the contrary he asked, mildly, gazing on the scattered sheets of paper containing the selectman's efforts at town-report composition, "Do you write poetry, sir?"

"Not by a—by a—" gasped the Cap'n, seeking ineffectually for some phrase to express his ineffable disgust.

"I was in hopes you did," continued Mr. Crymble, "for I would like a little help in finishing my epitaph. I compose slowly. I have worked several years on this epitaph, but I haven't finished it to suit me. What I have got done reads":

He unfolded a dirty strip of paper and recited:

"There is no sting in death;
  Below this stone there lies
  A man who lost his mortal breath
  Three times—"

Mr. Crymble looked up from the paper.

"I have thought of 'And death defies.' But that might sound like boasting."

"End it up, 'And still he lies,'" growled Cap'n Sproul. But the thin man meekly evaded the sarcasm.

"That would be a repetition of the rhyme," he objected. "I see you were right when you said you did not write poetry."

"P'r'aps I ain't no poet," cried the Cap'n, bridling. "But I'm the first selectman of this town, and I've got considerable to do with runnin' it and keepin' things straightened out. You may be dead, but you ain't buried yet. I've got two errunts for you. You go hunt up Bat Reeves and tell him that the weddin' next Tuesday is all off, and for good reasons—and that you're one of the reasons, and that there are nine others just as good but which you haven't got time to repeat. Then you go home to your wife and settle down, throw away that coffin-plate, tear up that epitaph, and stop this dyin' habit. It's a bad one to get into."

"I won't do any such thing," returned the prodigal, stubbornly. "I lived fifteen years with a woman that wouldn't let me smoke, busted my cider jug in the cellar, jawed me from sun-up till bedtime, hid my best clothes away from me like I was ten years old, wouldn't let me pipe water from the spring, and stuck a jeroosly water-pail under my nose every time I showed in sight of the house. I haven't died three times, all by violent means, not to stay dead so far's she's concerned. Now you tell me where to get the key to that school-house and I'll move in."

For the first time in their conversation Mr. Crymble dropped his meek manner. His little eyes blazed. His drooping mouth snarled and his yellow teeth showed defiantly. Cap'n Sproul always welcomed defiance. It was the thin man's passive resignation at the beginning of their acquaintance that caused the Cap'n to poke the ash-stick back under the stove. Now he buttoned his pea-jacket, pulled his hat down firmly, and spat first into one fist and then the other.

"You can walk, Crymble, if you're a mind to and will go quiet," he announced, measuring the other's gaunt frame with contemptuous eye. "I'd rather for your sake that the citizens would see you walkin' up there like a man. But if you won't walk, then I'll pick you up and stick you behind my ear like a lead-pencil and take you there."

"Where?"

"To your house. Where else should a husband be goin' that's been gallivantin' off for twenty years?"

And detecting further recalcitrancy in the face of his visitor, he pounced on him, scrabbled up a handful of cloth in the back of his coat, and propelled him out of doors and up the street. After a few protesting squawks Mr. Crymble went along.

An interested group of men, who had bolted out of Broadway's store, surveyed them as they passed at a brisk pace.

"By the sacred codfish!" bawled Broadway, "if that ain't Dep Crymble! How be ye, Dep?"

Mr. Crymble lacked either breath or amiability. He did not reply to the friendly greeting. Cap'n Sproul did that for him enigmatically. "He's back from paradise on his third furlough," he cried.

"And bound to hell," mourned Mr. Crymble, stumbling along before the thrust of the fist at his back.

XXVI

The Crymble place was a full half mile outside the village of Smyrna, but Cap'n Sproul and his victim covered the distance at a lively pace and swung into the yard at a dog-trot. Batson Reeves was just blanketing his horse, for in his vigorous courtship forenoon calls figured regularly.

"My Gawd!" he gulped, fronting the Cap'n and staring at his captive with popping eyes, "I knowed ye had a turrible grudge agin' me, Sproul, but I didn't s'pose you'd go to op'nin' graves to carry out your spite and bust my plans."

"He didn't happen to be anchored," retorted the Cap'n, with cutting reference to the granite statue in Smyrna's cemetery. "Ahoy, the house, there!"

Mrs. Crymble had been hastening to the door, the sound of her suitor's wagon-wheels summoning her. A glimpse of the tall figure in the yard, secured past the leaves of the window geraniums, brought her out on the run.

Mrs. Delora Crymble, whose natural stock of self-reliance had been largely improved by twenty years of grass-widowhood, was not easily unnerved.

But she staggered when searching scrutiny confirmed the dreadful suspicion of that first glimpse through the geraniums. For precaution's sake Cap'n Sproul still held Mr. Crymble by the scrabbled cloth in the back of his coat, and that despairing individual dangled like a manikin. But he braced his thin legs stubbornly when the Cap'n tried to push him toward the porch.

"If married couples are goin' to act like this on judgment mornin'," muttered the mediator, "it will kind o' take the edge off'm the festivities. Say, you two people, why don't you hoorah a few times and rush up and hug and kiss and live happy ever after?"

But as soon as Mrs. Crymble could get her thin lips nipped together and her hands on her hips she pulled herself into her accustomed self-reliant poise.

"It's you, is it, you straddled-legged, whittled-to-a-pick-ed northin' of a clothes-pin, you? You've sneaked back to sponge on me in your old age after runnin' off and leavin' me with a run-down farm and mortgidge! After sendin' me a marked copy of a paper with your death notice, and after your will was executed on and I wore mournin' two years and saved money out of hen profits to set a stun' in the graveyard for you! You mis'sable, lyin' 'whelp o' Satan!"

"There wa'n't no lie to it," said Mr. Crymble, doggedly. "I did die. I died three times—all by violent means. First time I froze to death, second—"

"Let up on that!" growled the Cap'n, vigorously shaking Mr. Crymble. "This ain't no dime-novel rehearsal. It's time to talk business!"

"You bet it's time to talk business!" affirmed the "widow." "I've paid off the mortgidge on this place by hard, bone labor, and it's willed to me and the will's executed, and now that you've been proved dead by law, by swanny I'll make you prove you're alive by law before you can set foot into this house."

"And I'll go and buy the law for you!" cried Batson Reeves, stripping the blanket off his horse. "I'll drive straight to my brother Alcander's law office, and he'll find law so that a hard-workin' woman can't be robbed of her own."

"Oh, he'll find it, all right!" agreed the Cap'n, sarcastically. "And if he don't find it ready-made he'll gum together a hunk to fit the case. But in the mean time, here's a man—" he checked himself and swung Mr. Crymble's hatchet face close to his own. "How much money have you got?" he demanded. "Have you come back here strapped?"

"I ain't got any money," admitted Mr. Crymble, "but I own a secret how to cure stutterin' in ten lessons, and with that school-house that—"

"You don't dock in any school-house nor you don't marine railway into our poorhouse, not to be a bill of expense whilst I'm first selectman," broke in Cap'n Sproul with decision. "That's official, and I've got a license to say it."

"You think you've got a license to stick your nose into the business of every one in this town because you're first selectman," roared Reeves, whipping out of the yard; "but I'll get a pair of nippers onto that old nose this time."

"Here's your home till further orders," said the Cap'n, disregarding the threat, "and into it you're goin'."

He started Mr. Crymble toward the steps.

Mrs. Crymble was pretty quick with the door, but Cap'n Sproul was at the threshold just in time to shove the broad toe of his boot between door and jamb. His elbows and shoulders did the rest, and he backed in, dragging Mr. Crymble, and paid no attention whatever to a half-dozen vigorous cuffs that Mrs. Crymble dealt him from behind. He doubled Mr. Crymble unceremoniously into a calico-covered rocking-chair, whipped off the hard hat and hung it up, and took from Mr. Crymble's resisting hands the little valise that he had clung to with grim resolution.

"Now, said Cap'n Sproul, you are back once more in your happy home after wanderin's in strange lands. As first selectman of this town I congratulate you on gettin' home, and extend the compliments of the season." He briskly shook Mr. Crymble's limp hand—a palm as unresponsive as the tail of a dead fish. "Now," continued the Cap'n, dropping his assumed geniality, "you stay here where I've put you. If I catch you off'm these primises I'll bat your old ears and have you arrested for a tramp. You ain't nothin' else, when it comes to law. I'm a hard man when I'm madded, Crymble, and if I start in to keelhaul you for disobeyin' orders you'll—" The Cap'n did not complete the sentence, but he bent such a look on the man in the chair that he trembled through all his frail length.

"I wisht I could have stayed dead," whimpered Mr. Crymble, thoroughly spirit-broken.

"It might have been better all around," agreed the Cap'n, cheerfully. "But I ain't no undertaker. I'm a town official, sworn to see that paupers ain't poked off onto the taxpayers. And if you want to keep out of some pretty serious legal trouble, Mis' Crymble, you'll mind your p's and q's—and you know what I mean!"

Feeling a little ignorant of just what the law was in the case, Cap'n Sproul chose to make his directions vague and his facial expression unmistakable, and he backed out, bending impartial and baleful stare on the miserable couple.

When he got back to the town office he pen-printed a sign, "Keep Out," tacked it upon the outer door, set the end of his long table against the door for a barricade, and fell to undisturbed work on the figures. And having made such progress during the day that his mind was free for other matters in the evening, he trudged over to Neighbor Hiram Look's to smoke with the ex-showman and detail to that wondering listener the astonishing death-claims of the returned Mr. Crymble.

"Grampy Long-legs, there, may think he's dead and may say he's dead," remarked Hiram, grimly, "but it looks to me as though Bat Reeves was the dead one in this case. He's lost the widder."

Cap'n Sproul turned luminous gaze of full appreciation on his friend.

"Hiram," he said, "we've broke up a good many courtships for Reeves, you and me have, but, speakin' frankly, I'd have liked to see him get that Crymble woman. If she ain't blood kin to the general manager of Tophet, then I'm all off in pedigree, I don't blame

Crymble for dyin' three times to make sure that she was a widder. If it wasn't for administerin' town business right I'd have got him a spider-web and let him sail away on it. As it is, I reckon I've scared him about twenty-four hours' worth. He'll stick there in torment for near that time. But about noon to-morrow he'll get away unless I scare him again or ball-and-chain him with a thread and a buckshot."

"I'm interested in freaks," said Hiram, "and I'll take this case off your hands and see that the livin' skeleton don't get away until we decide to bury him or put him in a show where he can earn an honest livin'. Skeletons ain't what they used to be for a drawin'-card, but I know of two or three punkin circuiters that might take him on."

In view of that still looming incubus of the unfinished town report, Cap'n Sproul accepted Hiram's offer with alacrity.

"It ain't that I care so much about the critter himself," he confided, "but Bat Reeves has got his oar in the case, and by to-morrow the whole town will be watchin' to see which gets the upper hands."

"I'll camp there," promised Hiram, "and I don't reckon they can do old dead-and-alive to any great extent whilst I've got my eye on 'em."

Cap'n Sproul barricaded his door again the next day and disregarded ordinary summons at the portal. But along in the afternoon came one who, after knocking vainly, began to batter with fists and feet, and when the first selectman finally tore open the door with full determination to kick this persistent disturber off the steps, he found Hiram Look there. And Hiram Look came in and thumped himself into a chair with no very clearly defined look of triumph on his face.

"He ain't dead again, is he?" demanded Cap'n Sproul, apprehensively.

"No, he ain't, and that's where he loses," replied the old showman. He chafed his blue nose and thumped his feet on the floor to warm them. It was plain that he had been long exposed to the December wind.

"Law," announced Hiram, "has got more wrinkles in it than there are in a fake mermaid's tail. Do you know what kind of a game they've gone to work and rigged up on your friend, the human curling-tongs? The widder has got him to doin' chores again. It seems that she was always strong on keepin' him doin' chores. He's peckin' away at that pile of wood that's fitted and lays at the corner of the barn. He's luggin' it into the woodshed, and three sticks at a time make his legs bend like corset whalebones. Looks like he's got a good stiddy job for all winter—and every once in a while she comes out and yaps at him to prod him up."

"Well, that gets him taken care of, all right," said the Cap'n, with a sigh of relief.

"Yes, he's taken care of," remarked Hiram, dryly. "But you don't understand the thing yet, Cap'n. On top of that woodpile sets Bat Reeves, lappin' the end of a lead-pencil and markin' down every time old water-skipper there makes a trip."

"Well, if it amuses him, it takes care of him, too," said the Cap'n.

"Looks innercent, childlike, and sociable, hey?" inquired the showman, sarcastically. "Well, you just listen to what I've dug up about that. Bat Reeves has bought the strip of ground between the woodpile and the shed door by some kind of a deal he's rigged up with the widder, and with Alcander Reeves advisin' as counsel. And he's got a stake set in the middle of that piece of ground and on that stake is a board and on that board is painted: 'Trespassing Forbidden on Penalty of the Law.' And him and that woman, by Alcander Reeves's advice, are teaming that old cuss of a husband back and forth acrost that strip and markin' down a trespass offence every time he lugs an armful of wood."

The Cap'n blinked his growing amazement.

"And the scheme is," continued Hiram, "to have old law shark of an Alcander, as trial justice, sentence the livin' skeleton on each separate trespass offence, fine and imprisonment in default of payment. Why, they've got enough chalked down against him now to make up a hundred years' sentence, and he's travellin' back and forth there as innercent of what they're tryin' to do as is the babe unborn."

"Can they do any such infernal thing as that in law?" demanded the Cap'n.

"Blamed if I know. But I never see northin' yet they couldn't do in law, if they see you comin' and got the bind on you."

"Law!" roared Cap'n Sproul, clacking his hard fist on the table rim. "Law will tie more knots in a man's business than a whale can tie in a harpoon-line. There ain't no justice in it—only pickin's and stealin's. Why, I had a mate once that was downed on T wharf in Bos'n and robbed, and they caught the men, and the mate couldn't give witness bonds and they locked him up with 'em, and the men got away one night and wa'n't ever caught, and the result was the mate served a jail sentence before they got his bonds matter fixed. It was just the same as a jail sentence. He had to stay there."

Hiram was fully as doleful in regard to the possibilities of the law.

"Once they get old Soup-bone behind bars on them trespass cases," he said, "he'll stay there, all right. They'll fix it somehow—you needn't worry. I reckon they'll be arrestin' him any minute now. They've got cases enough marked down."

"We'll see about that," snapped the Cap'n.

He buttoned his jacket and hurried into Hiram's team, which was at the door. And with Hiram as charioteer they made time toward the Crymble place. Just out of the village they swept past Constable

Zeburee Nute, whose slower Dobbin respectfully took the side of the highway.

"Bet ye money to mushmelons," mumbled Hiram as they passed, "he's got a warrant from old Alcander and is on his way to arrest."

"I know he is," affirmed the Cap'n. "Every time he sticks that old tin badge on the outside of his coat he's on the war-path. Whip up, Hiram!"

From afar they spied the tall figure of Dependence Crymble passing wraithlike to and fro across the yard.

"Thirty days per sashay!" grunted Hiram. "That's the way they figger it."

Batson Reeves would have scrambled down from the top of the woodpile when he saw Cap'n Sproul halt Crymble in his weary labor and draw him to one side. But Hiram suggested to Mr. Reeves that he better stay up, and emphasized the suggestion by clutching a stick of stove-wood in each hand.

"Crymble," huskily whispered the Cap'n, "I put ye here out of a good meanin'—meanin' to keep ye out of trouble. But I'm afraid I've got ye into it."

"I told ye what she was and all about it," complained Mr. Crymble, bitterly.

"It ain't 'she,' it's—it's—" The Cap'n saw the bobbing head of Nute's Dobbin heaving into sight around distant alders. "All is, you needn't stay where I put ye."

Mr. Crymble promptly dropped the three sticks of wood that he was carrying.

"But I don't want you to get too far off till I think this thing over a little," resumed the Cap'n. "There ain't no time now. You ought to know this old farm of your'n pretty well. You just go find a hole and crawl into it for a while."

"I'll do it," declared Mr. Crymble, with alacrity. "I knew you'd find her out. Now that you're with me, I'm with you. I'll hide. You fix 'em. 'Tend to her first." He grabbed the Cap'n by the arm. "There's a secret about that barnyard that no one knows but me. Blind his eyes!"

He pointed to Mr. Reeves. There was no time to delve into Mr. Crymble's motives just then. There was just time to act. The blank wall of the ell shut off Mrs. Crymble's view of the scene. Constable Nute was still well down the road. There was only the basilisk Mr. Reeves on the woodpile. Cap'n Sproul grabbed up a quilt spread to air behind the ell, and with a word to Hiram as he passed him he scrambled up the heap of wood. Hiram followed, and the next moment they had hoodwinked the amazed Mr. Reeves and held him bagged securely in the quilt.

The Cap'n, with chin over his shoulder, saw Mr. Crymble scuff aside some frozen dirt in a corner of the barnyard, raise a plank with his bony fingers and insert his slender figure into the crevice disclosed, with all the suppleness of a snake. The plank dropped over his head, and his hiding-place was hidden. But while he and Hiram stood looking at the place where Mr. Crymble had disappeared, there sounded a muffled squawk from the depths, there was the dull rumble of rocks, an inward crumbling of earth where the planks were, a puff of dust, and stillness.

"Gawd A'mighty!" blurted Hiram, aghast, "a dry well's caved in on him."

"I told him to find a hole and crawl into it," quavered the Cap'n, fiddling trembling finger under his nose, "but I didn't tell him to pull the hole in after him."

Mr. Reeves, left free to extricate himself from the quilt, bellowed to Mrs. Crymble and addressed the astonished Nute, who just then swung into the yard.

"They murdered that man, and I see 'em do it!" he squalled, and added, irrelevantly, "they covered my head up so I couldn't see 'em do it."

Mrs. Crymble, who had been dignifiedly keeping the castle till the arrival of the constable, swooped upon the scene with hawk-like swiftness.

"This day's work will cost you a pretty penny, Messers Look and Sproul," she shrilled. "Killin' a woman's husband ain't to be settled with salve, a sorry, and a dollar bill, Messers Sproul and Look."

"I reckon we're messers, all right," murmured the Cap'n, gazing gloomily on the scene of the involuntary entombment of the three-times-dead Crymble. "I couldn't prove that he was ever dead in his life, but there's one thing I've seen with my own eyes. He acted as his own sexton, and that's almost as unbelievable as a man's comin' back to life again."

"I ain't lookin' for him to come back this last time," remarked Hiram, with much conviction; "unless there's an inch drain-pipe there and he comes up it like an angleworm. Looks from this side of the surface as though death, funeral service, interment, and mournin' was all over in record time and without music or flowers."

Batson Reeves brought the crowd.

It was plainly one of the opportunities of his life.

The word that he circulated, as he rattled down to Broadway's store and back, was that Cap'n Sproul and Hiram Look had attacked him with murderous intent, and that after he had bravely fought them off they had wantonly grabbed Mr. Dependence Crymble, jabbed him down a hole in the ground and kicked the hole in on him.

"I've always vowed and declared they was both lunatics," cried the returning Mr. Reeves. He darted accusatory finger at the disconsolate pair where they stood gazing down upon the place of Crymble's sepulture. "They was hatchin' a plot and I busted it, and now this is what they've done for revenge. And I'll leave it to Mis' Crymble herself, who stands there and who saw it all."

Mrs. Crymble was in a state of mind to take the cue promptly, and affirmed the charge with an inspirational wealth of detail and a ferocity of shrill accusation that took effect on the crowd in spite of the lack of logic. In moments of excitement crowds are not discriminating. The Cap'n and Hiram gazed with some uneasiness on the lowering faces.

"They beat his brains out, gents," she screamed—"beat the brains out of the husband that had just come home to me after roamin' the wide world over. Hang 'em, I say! And I'll soap the clothes-line if you'll do it!"

"Ain't she a hell-cat, though!" muttered Hiram.

"When I think of what I was tryin' to make that poor critter do," said Cap'n' Sproul, absent-mindedly kicking a loosened clod into the hole, "I'm ashamed of myself. I reckon he's better off down there than up here. I don't wish him back."

"If accused wish to say anything in their own defence it will be heard," declaimed Squire Alcander, advancing from the gathering throng. "Otherwise, Constable Nute will—"

"Constable Nute will keep his distance from me," roared Cap'n Sproul, "or he'll get his everlastin' come-uppance. I can stand a certain amount of dum foolishness, and I serve notice that I've had full amount served out. Now you loafers standin' round gawpin, you grab anything that will scoop dirt and get to work diggin' here."

"I don't propose to have no bill of expense run up on me," announced Mrs. Crymble, "I've paid out for him all I'm goin' to, and I got done long ago."

"Bereaved and lovin' widder heard, neighbors and friends," said the Cap'n, significantly. "Now go ahead, people, and believe what she says about us, if you want to! Get to work here."

"You sha'n't stir a shovelful of that dirt," declared Mrs. Crymble. "You'll claim day's wages, every one of you."

"Wages is cheaper in Chiny," said the Cap'n satirically. "You can cable round and have him dug out from that side if you want to. But I'm tellin' you right here and now that he's goin' to be dug out from one side or the other."

"He's dead and he's buried, ain't he?" demanded Reeves, rallying to the support of the widow. "What more is there to do?"

"Go down to the graveyard and get that stone of his and set it here," replied Cap'n Sproul, with bitter sarcasm. "Go somewhere to get out of my way here, for if you or any other human polecat, male or female"—he directed withering glance at Mrs. Crymble—"gets in my way whilst I'm doin' what's to be done, if we ain't heathen, I'll split 'em down with this barn shovel." He had secured the implement and tossed out the first shovelful.

There were plenty of willing volunteers. They paid no attention to the widow's reproaches. All who could, toiled with shovels. Others lifted the dirt in buckets. At the end of half an hour Cap'n Sproul, who was deepest in the hole, uttered a sharp exclamation.

"By the mud-hoofed mackinaw!" he shouted, waving his shovel to command silence, "if he ain't alive again after bein' killed the fourth time!"

Below there was a muffled "tunk-tunk-tunk!" It was plainly the sound of two rocks clacking together. It was appealing signal.

Ten minutes later, furious digging brought the rescuers to a flat rock, part of the stoning of the caved-in well. In its fall it had lodged upon soil and rocks, and when it was raised, gingerly and slowly, they found that, below in the cavern it had preserved, there sat Mr. Crymble, up to his shoulders in dirt.

"If some gent will kindly pass me a chaw of tobacker," he said, wistfully, "it will kind of keep up my strength and courage till the rest of me is dug up."

When he had been lifted at last to the edge of the well he turned dull eyes of resentment on Mrs. Crymble.

"I wish there'd been a hole clear through to the Sandwich Isle or any other heathen country," he said, sourly. "I'd have crawled there through lakes of fire and seas of blood."

She lifted her voice to vituperate, but his last clinch with death seemed to have given Mr. Crymble a new sense of power and self-reliance. He hopped up, gathered a handful of rocks and made at his Xantippe. His aim was not too good and he did not hit her, but he stood for several minutes and soulfully bombarded the door that she slammed behind her in her flight.

Then he came back and gathered more rocks from the scene of his recent burial. He propped his thin legs apart, brandished a sizable missile, and squalled defiance.

"I've just died for the fourth time—killed by a well cavin' in on me. There ain't no hell where I've been. And if there's any man here that thinks he can shove me back into this hell on earth"—he shook his fist at the house and singled Cap'n Sproul with flaming eye—"now is the time for him to try to do it."

"There ain't nobody goin' to try to do it," said the Cap'n, coming up to him with frankly outstretched hand. He patted the rocks gently from the arms of the indignant Mr. Crymble. "As a gen'ral thing I stand up for matrimony and stand up for it firm—but I reckon I didn't understand your case, Crymble. I apologize, and we'll shake hands on it. You can have the school-house, and I'll do more'n that— I'll pay for fixin' it over. And in the mean time you come up to my house and make me a good long visit."

He shoved ingratiating hand into the hook of the other's bony elbow and led him away.

"But I want my valise," pleaded Mr. Crymble.

"You leave that coffin-plate and epitaph with her," said the Cap'n, firmly. "You're in for a good old age and don't need 'em. And they may cheer up Mis' Crymble from time to time. She needs cheerin' up."

Hiram Look, following them out of the yard, yanked up the trespass sign and advanced to Batson Reeves and brandished it over his head.

"Gimme it!" he rasped.

"What?" quavered Reeves.

"That paper I stood here and watched you makin' up. Gimme it, or I'll peg you like I peg tent-pegs for the big tent."

And Reeves, having excellent ideas of discretion, passed over the list of trespasses. He did not look up at the windows of the Crymble house as he rode away with his brother, the squire. And what was significant, he took away with him the neck-halter that, for convenience' sake on his frequent calls, he had left hanging to the hitching-post in the Crymble yard for many weeks.

XXVII

At last the Women's Temperance Workers' Union of Smyrna became thoroughly indignant, in addition to being somewhat mystified.

Twice they had "waited on" Landlord Ferd Parrott, of the Smyrna tavern—twelve of them in a stern delegation—and he had simply blinked at them out of his puckery eyes, and pawed nervously at his weazened face, and had given them no satisfaction.

Twice they had marched bravely into the town office and had faced Cap'n Aaron Sproul, first selectman, and had complained that Ferd Parrott was running "a reg'lar rum-hole." Cap'n Sproul had nipped his bristly beard and gazed away from them at the ceiling, and said he would see what could be done about it.

Mrs. Aaron Sproul, a devoted member of the W.T.W.'s, was appointed a committee of one to sound him, and found him, even in the sweet privacy of home, so singularly embarrassed and uncommunicative that her affectionate heart was disturbed and grieved.

Then came Constable Zeburee Nute into the presence of the town's chief executive with a complaint.

"They're gittin' worse'n hornicks round me," he whined, "them Double-yer T. Double-yers. Want Ferd's place raided for licker. But I understood you to tell me—"

"I hain't told you northin' about it!" roared the Cap'n, with mighty clap of open palm on the town ledger.

"Well, you hain't give off orders to raid, seize and diskiver, libel and destroy," complained the officer.

"What be you, a 'tomatom that don't move till you pull a string, or be you an officer that's supposed to know his own duty clear, and follow it?" demanded the first selectman.

"Constables is supposed to take orders from them that's above 'em," declared Mr. Nute. "I'm lookin' to you, and the Double-yer T. Double-yers is lookin' to you."

"Well, if it's botherin' your eyesight, you'd better look t'other way," growled the Cap'n.

"Be I goin' to raid or ain't I goin' to raid?" demanded Constable Nute. "It's for you to say!"

"Look here, Nute," said the Cap'n, rising and aiming his forefinger at the constable's nose as he would have levelled a bulldog revolver, "if you and them wimmen think you're goin' to use me as a pie-fork to lift hot dishes out of an oven that they've heated, you'd better leave go—that's all I've got to say."

"You might just as well know it's makin' talk," ventured the constable, taking a safer position near the door. A queer sort of embarrassment that he noted in the Cap'n's visage emboldened him. "You know just as well as I do that Ferd Parrott has gone and took to sellin' licker. Old Branscomb is goin' home tea-ed up reg'lar, and Al Leavitt and Pud Follansby and a half a dozen others are settin' there all times of night, playin' cards and makin' a reg'lar ha'nt of it. If Ferd ain't shet up it will be said"—the constable looked into the snapping eyes of the first selectman and halted apprehensively.

"It ain't that I believe any such thing, Cap'n Sproul," he declared at last, breaking an embarrassing silence. "But here's them wimmen takin' up them San Francisco scandals to study in their Current Events Club, and when the officers here don't act when complaint is made about a hell-hole right here in town, talk starts, and it ain't complimentary talk, either. Pers'n'ly, I feel like a tiger strainin' at his chain, and I'd like orders to go ahead."

"Tiger, hey?" remarked the Cap'n, looking him up and down. "I knowed you reminded me of something, but I didn't know what, before. Now, if them wimmen—" he began with decision, but broke off to stare through the town-office window. Mr. Nute stepped from the door to take observation, too.

Twelve women in single file were picking their way across the mushy street piled with soft March snow.

"Reckon the Double-yer T. Double-yers is goin' to wait on Ferd ag'in to give him his final come-uppance," suggested the constable. "Heard some talk of it yistiddy."

The Smyrna tavern into which they disappeared was a huge hulk, relic of the old days when the stage-coaches made the village their headquarters. The storms of years had washed the paint from it; it had "hogged" in the roof where the great square chimney projected its nicked bulk from among loosened bricks scattered on the shingles; and from knife-gnawed "deacon-seat" on the porch to window-blind, dangling from one hinge on the broad gable, the old structure was seedy indeed.

"I kind of pity Ferd," mumbled the constable, his faded eyes on the cracked door that the last woman had slammed behind her. "Hain't averaged to put up one man a week for five years, and I reckon he's had to sell rum or starve."

Cap'n Sproul made no observation. He still maintained that air of not caring to discuss the affairs of the Smyrna tavern. He stared at the building as though he rather expected to see the sides tumble out or the roof fly up, or something of the sort.

He did not bestow any especial attention on his friend Hiram Look when the ex-circus man drove up to the hitching-post in front of the town house with a fine flourish, hitched and came in.

"Seems that your wife and mine have gone temperancin' again to-day with the bunch," remarked Hiram, relighting his cigar. "I don't know what difference it makes whether old Branscomb and the other soshes round here get their ruin in an express-package or help Ferd to a little business. They're bound to have it, anyway."

"That ain't the p'int," protested Constable Nute, stiffly, throwing back his coat to display his badge. "Ferd Parrott's breakin' the law, and it hurts my feelin's as an officer to hear town magnates and reprusentative citizens glossin' it over for him."

The Cap'n stared at him balefully but did not trust himself to retort. Hiram was not so cautious. He bridled instantly and insolently.

"There's always some folks in this world ready to stick their noses into the door-crack of a man's business when they know the man ain't got strength to slam the door shut on 'em. Wimmen's clubs is all right so long as they stick to readin' hist'ry and discussin' tattin', but when they flock like a lot of old hen turkeys and go to peckin' a man because he's down and can't help himself, it ain't anything but persecution—wolves turnin' on another one that's got his leg broke. I know animiles, and I know human critters. Them wimmen better be in other business, and I told my wife so this mornin'."

"So did I," said Cap'n Sproul, gloomily.

"And mine up at me like a settin' hen."

"So did mine," assented the Cap'n.

"Gave me a lecture on duties of man to feller man."

"Jest the same to my house."

"Have any idea who's been stuffin' their heads with them notions?" inquired Hiram, malevolently.

"Remember that square-cornered female with a face harder'n the physog of a wooden figurehead that was here last winter, and took 'em aloft and told 'em how to reef parli'ment'ry law, and all such?" asked the Cap'n. "Well, she was the one."

"You mind my word," cried Hiram, vibrating his cigar, "when a wife begins to take orders from an old maid in frosted specs instead of from her own husband, then the moths is gettin' ready to eat the worsted out of the cardboard in the motto 'God bless our home!'"

"Law is law," broke in the unabashed representative of it, "and if the men-folks of this town ain't got the gumption to stand behind an officer—"

"Look here, Nute," gritted the Cap'n, "I'll stand behind you in about two seconds, and I'll be standin' on one foot, at that! Don't you go to castin' slurs on your betters. Because I've stood some talk from you to-day isn't any sign that I'm goin' to stand any more."

Now the first selectman had the old familiar glint in his eyes, and Mr. Nute sat down meekly, returning no answer to the Cap'n's sarcastic inquiry why he wasn't over at the tavern acting as convoy for the Temperance Workers.

Two minutes later some one came stamping along the corridor of the town house. The office door was ajar, and this some one pushed it open with his foot.

It was Landlord Ferd Parrott. In one hand he carried an old glazed valise, in the other a canvas extension-case, this reduplication of baggage indicating a serious intention on the part of Mr. Parrott to travel far and remain long. His visage was sullen and the set of his jaws was ugly. Mr. Parrott had eyes that turned out from his nose, and though the Cap'n and Hiram were on opposite sides of the room it seemed as though his peculiar vision enabled him to fix an eye on each at the same time.

"I'm glad I found you here both together," he snarled. "I can tell you both at one whack. I ain't got northin' against you. You've used me like gents. I don't mean to dump you, nor northin' of the sort, but there ain't anything I can seem to do. You take what there is—this here is all that belongs to me." He shook the valises at them. "I'm goin' to git out of this God-forsaken town—I'm goin' now, and I'm goin' strong, and you're welcome to all I leave, just as I leave it. For the first time in my life I'm glad I'm a widderer."

After gazing at Mr. Parrott for a little time the Cap'n and Hiram searched each the other's face with much interest. It was apparent that perfect confidence did not exist between them on some matters that were to the fore just then.

"Yours," said Mr. Parrott, jerking a stiff nod to the Cap'n, "is a morgidge on house and stable and land. Yours," he continued, with another nod at Hiram, "is a bill o' sale of all the furniture, dishes, liv'ry critters and stable outfit. Take it all and git what you can out of it."

"This ain't no way to do—skip out like this," objected Hiram.

"Well, it's *my* way," replied Mr. Parrott, stubbornly, "and, seein' that you've got security and all there is, I don't believe you can stop me."

Mr. Parrott dropped his valises and whacked his fists together.

"If the citizens of this place don't want a hotel they needn't have a hotel," he shrilled. "If they want to turn wimmen loose on me to run me up a tree, by hossomy! I'll pull the tree up after me."

"Look here, Ferd," said the Cap'n, eagerly, forgetting for the moment the presence of Constable Nute, "those wimmen might gabble a little at you and make threats and things like that—but—but—there isn't anything they can do, you understand!" He winked at Mr. Parrott. "You know what I told you!"

But Mr. Parrott was in no way swayed or mollified.

"They *can't'* do anything, can't they?" he squealed. "They've been into my house and knocked in the head of a keg of Medford rum, and busted three demijohns of whiskey, and got old Branscomb to sign the pledge, and scared off the rest of the boys. Now they're goin' to hire a pung, and a delegation of three is goin' to meet every train with badges on and tell every arrivin' guest that the Smyrna tavern is a nasty, wicked place, and old Aunt Juliet Gifford and her two old-maid girls are goin' to put up all parties at half-price. They *can't* do anything, hey! them wimmen can't? Well, that's what they've done to date—and if the married men of this place can't keep their wives to home and their noses out of my business, then Smyrna can get along without a tavern. I'm done, I say. It's all yours." Mr. Parrott tossed his open palms toward them in token of utter surrender, and picked up his valises.

"You can't shove that off onto us that way," roared Hiram.

"Well, your money is there, and you can go take it or leave it," retorted the desperate Mr. Parrott. "You'd better git your money where you can git it, seein' that you can't very well git it out of my hide." And the retiring landlord of Smyrna tavern stormed out and plodded away down the mushy highway.

Constable Nute gazed after him through the window, and then surveyed the first selectman and Hiram with fresh and constantly increasing interest. His tufty eyebrows crawled like caterpillars, indicating that the thoughts under them must be of a decidedly stirring nature.

"Huh! That's it, is it?" he muttered, and noting that Cap'n Sproul seemed to be recovering his self-possession, he preferred not to wait for the threats and extorted pledge that his natural craftiness scented. He dove out.

"Where be ye goin' to?" demanded Hiram, checking the savage rush of the Cap'n.

"Catch him and make him shet his chops about this, if I have to spike his old jaws together."

"It ain't no use," said Hiram, gloomily, setting his shoulders against the door. "You'd only be makin' a show and spectacle in front of the wimmen. And after that they'd squat the whole thing out of him, the same as you'd squat stewed punkin through a sieve." He bored the Cap'n with inquiring eye. "You wasn't tellin' me that you held a morgidge on that tavern real estate." There was reproach in his tones.

"No, and you wasn't tellin' me that you had a bill of sale of the fixin's and furniture," replied the Cap'n with acerbity. "How much did you let him have?"

"Fifteen hunderd," said Hiram, rather shamefacedly, but he perked up a bit when he added: "There's three pretty fair hoss-kind."

"If there's anything about that place that's spavined any worse'n them hosses it's the bedsteads," snorted the other capitalist. "He's beat you by five hundred dollars. If you should pile that furniture in the yard and hang up a sign, 'Help yourself,' folks wouldn't haul it off without pay for truckin'."

"Le's see!" said Hiram, fingering his nose, "was it real money or Confederate scrip that *you* let him have on *your* morgidge?"

"Thutty-five hunderd ain't much on the most central piece of real estate in this village," declared the Cap'n, in stout defence.

"It's central, all right, but so is the stomach-ache," remarked Hiram, calmly. "What good is that land when there ain't been a buildin' built in this town for fifteen years, and no call for any? As for the house, I'll bet ye a ten-cent cigar I can go over there and push it down—and I ain't braggin' of my strength none, either."

The Cap'n did not venture to defend his investment further. He stared despondently through the window at the seamed roof and weather-worn walls that looked particularly forlorn and dilapidated on that gray March day.

"I let him have money on it when the trees was leaved out, and things look different then," he sighed.

"And I must have let him have it when I was asleep and dreamin' that Standard Ile had died and left his money to me," snorted the showman. "I ain't blamin' you, Cap, and you needn't blame me, but the size of it is you and me has gone into partnership and bought a tavern, and didn't know it. If they had let Parrott alone he might have wiggled out of the hole after a while."

"It ain't wuth a hoorah in a hen-pen if it ain't run as a tavern," stated the Cap'n. "I ain't in favor of rum nor sellin' rum, and I knew that Ferd was sellin' a little suthin' on the sly, but he told me he was goin' to repair up and git in some summer boarders, and I was lettin' him work along. There ain't much business nor look-ahead to wimmen, is there?" he asked, sourly.

"Not when they bunch themselves in a flock and get to squawkin'," agreed his friend.

"I don't know what they are doin' over there now," averred the first selectman, "but before they set fire to it or tear the daylights out, and seein' as how it's our property accordin' to present outlook, I reckon we'd better go over and put an eye on things. They prob'ly think it belongs to Ferd."

"Not since that bean-pole with a tin badge onto it got acrost there with its mouth open," affirmed Hiram, with decision, "and if he ain't told 'em that we bought Ferd out and set him up in the rum business, he's lettin' us out easier than I figger on."

The concerted glare of eyes that fairly assailed them when they somewhat diffidently ventured into the office of the tavern indicated that Hiram was not far off in his "figgerin'." The embarrassed self-consciousness of Constable Nute, staring at the stained ceiling, told much. The indignant eyes of the women told more.

Mr. Parrott's brother was a sea-captain who had sent him "stuffed" natural-history curios from all parts of the world, and Mr. Parrott had arranged a rather picturesque interior. Miss Philamese Nile, president of the W.T.W.'s, stood beneath a dusty alligator that swung from the ceiling, and Cap'n Sproul, glancing from one to the other, confessed to himself that he didn't know which face looked the most savage.

She advanced on him, forefinger upraised.

"Before you go to spreadin' sail, marm," said the Cap'n, stoutly, "you'd better be sure that you ain't got holt of the down-haul instead of the toppin'-lift."

"Talk United States, Cap'n Sproul," snapped Miss Nile. "You've had your money in this pit of perdition here, you and Hiram Look, the two of you. As a town officer you've let Ferd Parrott fun a cheap, nasty rum-hole, corruptin' and ruinin' the manhood of Smyrna, and you've helped cover up this devilishness, though we, the wimmen of this town, have begged and implored on bended knee. Now, that's plain, straight Yankee language, and we want an answer in the same tongue."

Neither the Cap'n nor Hiram found any consolation at that moment in the countenances of their respective wives. Those faces were very red, but their owners looked away resolutely and were plainly animated by a stern sense of duty, bulwarked as they were by the Workers.

"We've risen for the honor of this town," continued Miss Nile.

"Well, stay up, then!" snorted the short-tempered Hiram. "Though as for me, I never could see anything very handsome in a hen tryin' to fly."

"Do you hear that?" shrilled Miss Nile. "Aren't you proud of your noble husband, Mis' Look? Isn't he a credit to the home and an ornament to his native land?"

But Hiram, when indignant, was never abashed.

"Wimmen," said he, "has their duties to perform and their place to fill—all except old maids that make a specialty of 'tending to other folks' business." He bent a withering look on Miss Nile. "Cap'n Sproul and me ain't rummies, and you can't make it out so, not even if you stand here and talk till you spit feathers. We've had business dealin's with Parrott, and business is business."

"And every grafter 'twixt here and kingdom come has had the same excuse," declared the valiant head of the Workers. "Business or no business, Ferd Parrott is done runnin' this tavern."

"There's a point I reckon you and me can agree on," said Hiram, sadly. He gazed out to where the tracks of Mr. Parrott led away through the slush.

"And it's the sense of the women of this place that such a dirty old ranch sha'n't disgrace Smyrna any longer."

"You mean—"

"I mean shut up these doors—nail 'em—and let decent and respectable women put up the folks who pass this way—put 'em up in a decent and respectable place. That's the sense of the women."

"And it's about as much sense as wimmen show when they get out of their trodden path," cried Hiram, angrily. "You and the rest of ye think, do ye, that me and Cap'n Sproul is goin' to make a present of five thousand dollars to have this tavern stand here as a Double-yer T. Double-yer monnyment? Well, as old Bassett said, skursely, and not even as much as that!"

"Then I'd like to see the man that can run it," declared the spokeswoman with fine spirit. "We're going to back Mis' Gifford. We're going to the train to get custom for her. We're going to warn every one against this tavern. There isn't a girl or woman in twenty towns around here who'll work in this hole after we've warned 'em what it is. Yes, sir, I'd like to see the man that can run it!"

"Well, you look at him!" shouted Hiram, slapping his breast. He noted a look of alarm on the Cap'n's face, and muttered to him under his breath: "You ain't goin' to let a pack of wimmen back ye down, be ye?"

"How be we goin' to work to run it?" whispered the Cap'n.

"That ain't the p'int now," growled Hiram. "The p'int is, we're goin' to run it. And you've got to back me up."

"Hiram!" called his wife, appealingly, but he had no ears for her.

"You've made your threats," he stormed, addressing the leader of the Workers. "You haven't talked to us as gents ought to be talked to. You haven't made any allowances. You haven't shown any charity. You've just got up and tried to jam us to the wall. Now, seein' that your business is done here, and that this tavern is under new management, you'll be excused to go over and start your own place."

He opened the door and bowed, and the women, noting determination in his eyes, began to murmur, to sniff spitefully, and to jostle slowly out. Mrs. Look and Mrs. Sproul showed some signs of lingering, but Hiram suggested dryly that they'd better stick with the band.

"We'll be man and wife up home," he said, "and no twits and no hard feelin's. But just now you are Double-yer T. Double-yers and we are tavern-keepers—and we don't hitch." They went.

"Now, Nute," barked Hiram, when the constable lingered as though rather ashamed to depart with the women, "you get out of here and you stay out, or I'll cook that stuffed alligator and a few others of these tangdoodiaps here and ram 'em down them old jaws of yours." Therefore, Constable Nute went, too.

XXVIII

Moved by mutual impulse, Hiram and the Cap'n plodded through the deserted tavern, up-stairs and down-stairs. When they went into the kitchen the two hired girls were dragging their trunks to the door, and scornfully resisted all appeals to remain. They said it was a nasty rum-hole, and that they had reputations to preserve just as well as some folks who thought they were better because they had money. Fine hand of the W.T.W.'s shown thus early in the game of tavern-keeping! There were even dirty dishes in the sink, so precipitate was the departure.

In the stable, the hostler, a one-eyed servitor, with the piping voice, wobbly gait, and shrunken features of the "white drunkard," was in his usual sociable state of intoxication, and declared that he would stick by them. He testified slobberingly as to his devotion to Mr. Parrott, declared that when the women descended Mr. Parrott confided to him the delicate task of "hiding the stuff," and that he had managed to conceal quite a lot of it.

"Well, dig it up and throw it away," directed Hiram.

"Oh, only a fool in the business buries rum," confided the hostler. "I've been in the rum business, and I know. They allus hunts haymows and sullers. But I know how to hide it. I'm shrewd about them things."

"We don't want no rum around here," declared the showman with positiveness.

The hostler winked his one eye at him, and, having had a rogue's long experience in roguery, plainly showed that he believed a command of this sort to be merely for the purpose of publication and not an evidence of good faith.

"And there won't be much rum left round here if we only let him alone," muttered Hiram as he and the Cap'n walked back to the house. "I only wisht them hired girls had as good an attraction for stayin' as he's got."

"Look here, Hiram," said the Cap'n, stopping him on the porch, "it's all right to make loud talk to them Double-yer T. Double-yers, but there ain't any sense in makin' it to each other. You and me can't run this tavern no more'n hen-hawks can run a revival. Them wimmen—
"

"You goin' to let them wimmen cackle for the next two years, and pass it down to their grandchildren how they done us out of all the money we put in here—two able-bodied business men like we be? A watch ain't no good only so long's it's runnin', and a tavern ain't, either. We've got to run this till we can sell it, wimmen or no wimmen—and you hadn't ought to be a quitter with thutty-five hunderd in it."

But there was very little enthusiasm or determination in the Cap'n's face. The sullenness deepened there when he saw a vehicle turn in at the tavern yard. It was a red van on runners, and on its side was inscribed:

T. BRACKETT,

TINWARE AND YANKEE NOTIONS.

He was that round-faced, jovial little man who was known far and wide among the housewives of the section as "Balm o' Joy Brackett," on account of a certain liniment that he compounded and dispensed as a side-line. With the possible exception of one Marengo Todd, horse-jockey and also far-removed cousin of Mrs. Sproul, there was no one in her circle of cousins that the Cap'n hated any more cordially than Todd Ward Brackett. Mr. Brackett, by cheerfully hailing the Cap'n as "Cousin Aaron" at every opportunity, had regularly added to the latter's vehemence of dislike.

The little man nodded cheery greeting to the showman, cried his usual "Hullo, Cousin Aaron!" to the surly skipper, bobbed off his van, and proceeded to unharness.

"Well," sighed Hiram, resignedly, "guest Number One for supper, lodgin', and breakfast—nine shillin's and hossbait extry. 'Ev'ry little helps,' as old Bragg said when he swallowed the hoss-fly."

"There ain't any Todd Ward Brackett goin' to stop in *my* tavern," announced the Cap'n with decision. Mr. Brackett overheard and whirled to stare at them with mild amazement. "That's what I said," insisted Cap'n Sproul, returning the stare. "Ferd Parrott ain't runnin' this tavern any longer. We're runnin' it, and you nor none of your stripe can stop here." He reflected with sudden comfort that there was at least one advantage in owning a hotel. It gave a man a chance at his foes.

"You're *runnin'* it, be you?" inquired Mr. Brackett, raising his voice and glancing toward Broadway's store platform where loafers were listening.

"That's what we be," shouted the Cap'n.

"Well, I'm glad to hear that you're really *runnin'* it—and that it ain't closed," said Mr. Brackett, "'cause I'm applyin' here to a public house to be put up, and if you turn me away, havin' plenty of room and your sign up, by ginger, I'll sue you under the statute and law made and pervided. I ain't drunk nor disorderly, and I've got money to pay—and I'll have the law on ye if ye don't let me in."

Mention of the law always had terrifying effect on Cap'n Sproul. He feared its menace and its intricacies. It was his nightmare that law had long been lying in wait on shore for him, and that once the land-sharks got him in their grip they would never let go until he was sucked dry.

"I've got witnesses who heard," declared Mr. Brackett, waggling mittened hand at the group on the platform. "Now you look out for yourself!"

He finished unharnessing his horse and led the animal toward the barn, carolling his everlasting lay about "Old Hip Huff, who went by freight to Newry Corner, in this State."

"There's just this much about it, Cap," Hiram hastened to say; "me 'n' you have got to run the shebang till we can unlo'd it. We can't turn away custom and kill the thing dead. I'll 'tend the office, make the beds, and keep the fires goin'. You—you—" He gazed at the Cap'n, faltering in his speech and fingering his nose apprehensively.

"Well, me what?" snapped the ex-master of the *Jefferson P. Benn*. But his sparkling eyes showed that he realized what was coming.

"You've allus been braggin'," gulped Hiram, "what a dabster you was at cookin', havin' been to sea and—"

"Me—*me?*" demanded the Cap'n, slugging his own breast ferociously. "Me put on an ap'un, and go out there, and kitchen-wallop for that jimbedoggified junacker of a tin-peddler? I'll burn this old shack down first, I will, by the—"

But Hiram entered fervent and expostulatory appeal.

"If you don't, we're sendin' that talkin'-machine on legs off to sue and get damages, and report this tavern from Clew to Hackenny, and spoil our chances for a customer, and knock us out generally."

He put his arm about the indignant Cap'n and drew him in where the loafers couldn't listen, and continued his anxious coaxings until at last Cap'n Sproul kicked and stamped his way into the kitchen, cursing so horribly that the cat fled. He got a little initial satisfaction by throwing after her the dirty dishes in the sink, listening to their crashing with supreme satisfaction. Then he proceeded to get supper.

It had been a long time since he had indulged his natural taste for cookery. In a half-hour he had forgotten his anger and was revelling in the domain of pots and pans. He felt a sudden appetite of his own for the good, old-fashioned plum-duff of shipboard days, and started one going. Then gingercake—his own kind—came to his memory. He stirred up some of that. He sent Hiram on a dozen errands to the grocery, and Hiram ran delightedly.

"I'll show you whether I can cook or not," was the Cap'n's proud boast to the showman when the latter bustled eagerly in from one of his trips. He held out a smoking doughnut on a fork. "There ain't one woman in ten can fry 'em without 'em soakin' fat till they're as heavy as a sinker."

Hiram gobbled to the last mouthful, expressing his admiration as he ate, and the Cap'n glowed under the praise.

His especial moment of triumph came when his wife and Mrs. Look, adventuring to seek their truant husbands, sat for a little while in the tavern kitchen and ate a doughnut, and added their astonished indorsement. In the flush of his masterfulness he would not permit them to lay finger on dish, pot, or pan.

Hiram served as waiter to the lonely guest in the dining-room, and was the bearer of several messages of commendation that seemed to anger the Cap'n as much as other praise gratified him.

"Me standin' here cookin' for that sculpin!" he kept growling.

However, he ladled out an especially generous portion of plum-duff—the climax of his culinary art—and to his wrathful astonishment Hiram brought it back untasted.

"Mebbe it's all right," he said, apologetically, "but he was filled full, and he said it was a new dish to him and didn't look very good, and—"

The Cap'n grabbed the disparaged plum-duff with an oath and started for the dining-room.

"Hold on!" Hiram expostulated; "you've got to remember that he's a guest, Cap. He's—"

"He's goin' to eat what I give him, after I've been to all the trouble," roared the old skipper.

Mr. Brackett was before the fire in the office, hiccuping with repletion and stuffing tobacco into the bowl of his clay pipe.

"Anything the matter with that duff?" demanded the irate cook, pushing the dish under Mr. Brackett's retreating nose. "Think I don't know how to make plum-duff—me that's sailed the sea for thutty-five years?"

"Never made no such remarks on your cookin'," declared the guest, clearing his husky throat in which the food seemed to be sticking.

"Hain't got no fault to find with that plum-duff?"

"Not a mite," agreed Mr. Brackett, heartily.

"Then you come back out here to the table and eat it. You ain't goin' to slander none of my vittles that I've took as much trouble with as I have with this."

"But I'm full up—chock!" pleaded Mr. Brackett. "I wisht I'd have saved room. I reckon it's good. But I ain't carin' for it."

"You'll come out and eat that duff if I have to stuff it down your thro't with the butt of your hoss-whip," said the Cap'n with an iciness that was terrifying. He grabbed the little man by the collar and dragged him toward the dining-room, balancing the dish in the other hand.

"I'll bust," wailed Mr. Brackett.

"Well, that bump will make a little room," remarked Cap'n Sproul, jouncing him down into a chair.

He planted one broad hand on the table and the other on his hip, and stood over the guest until the last crumb of the duff was gone, although Mr. Brackett clucked hiccups like an overfed hen. The Cap'n felt some of his choler evaporate, indulging in this sweet act of tyranny.

Resentment came slowly into the jovial nature of meek Todd Ward Brackett. But as he pushed away from the table he found courage to bend baleful gaze on his over-hospitable host.

"I've put up at a good many taverns in my life," he said, "and I'm allus willin' to eat my fair share of vittles, but I reckon I've got the right to say how much!"

"If you're done eatin'," snapped the Cap'n, "get along out, and don't stay round in the way of the help." And Mr. Brackett retired, growling over this astonishing new insult.

He surveyed the suspended alligator gloomily, as he stuffed tobacco into his pipe.

"Better shet them jaws," he advised, "or now that he's crazy on the plum-duff question he'll be jamming the rest of that stuff into you."

"You can't say outside that the table ain't all right or that folks go away hungry under the new management," remarked Hiram, endeavoring to palliate.

"New management goin' to inorg'rate the plum-duffin' idee as a reg'lar system?" inquired Mr. Brackett, sullenly. "If it is, I'll stay over to-morrow and see you operate on the new elder that's goin' to supply the pulpit Sunday—pervidin' he stays here."

Hiram blinked his eyes inquiringly. "New elder?" he repeated.

"Get a few elders to put up here," suggested Mr. Brackett, venomously, "and new management might take a little cuss off'm the reppytation of this tavern." And the guest fell to smoking and muttering.

Even as wisdom sometimes falls from the mouths of babes, so do good ideas occasionally spring from careless sarcasm.

After Mr. Brackett had retired Hiram discussed the matter of the impending elder with Cap'n Sproul, the Cap'n not warming to the proposition.

"But I tell you if we can get that elder here," insisted Hiram, "and explain it to him and get him to stay, he's goin' to look at it in the right light, if he's got any Christian charity in him. We'll entertain him free, do the right thing by him, tell him the case from A to Z, and get him to handle them infernal wimmen. Only an elder can do it. If we don't he may preach a sermon against us. That'll kill our business proposition deader'n it is now. If he stays it will give a tone to the new management, and he can straighten the thing out for us."

Not only did Cap'n Sproul fail to become enthusiastic, but he was so distinctly discouraging that Hiram forbore to argue, feeling his own optimistic resolution weaken under this depressing flow of cold water.

He did not broach the matter the next morning. He left the Cap'n absorbed and busy in his domain of pots, set his jaws, took his own horse and pung, and started betimes for the railroad-station two miles away. On the way he overtook and passed, with fine contempt for their podgy horse, a delegation from the W.T.W.'s.

On the station platform they frowned upon him, and he scowled at them. He realized that his only chance in this desperate venture lay in getting at the elder first, and frisking him away before the women had opportunity to open their mouths. A word from them might check operations. And then, with the capture once made, if he could speed his horse fast enough to allow him an uninterrupted quarter of an hour at the tavern with the minister, he decided that only complete

paralysis of the tongue could spoil his plan.

Hiram, with his superior bulk and his desperate eagerness, had the advantage of the women at the car-steps. He crowded close. It was the white-lawn tie on the first passenger who descended that did the business for Hiram. In his mind white-lawn ties and clergymen were too intimately associated to admit of error. He yanked away the little man's valise, grabbed his arm, and rushed him across the platform and into the pung's rear seat. And the instant he had scooped the reins from the dasher he flung himself into the front seat and was away up the road, larruping his horse and ducking the snow-cakes that hurtled from the animal's hoofs.

"Look here! I—I—" gasped the little man, prodding him behind.

"It's all right, elder!" bellowed Hiram. "You wait till we get there and it will be made all right. Set clus' and hold on, that's all now!"

"But, look here, I want to go to Smyrna tavern!"

"Good for you!" Hiram cried. "Set clus' and you'll get there!" It seemed, after all, that ill repute had not spread far. His spirits rose, and he whipped on at even better speed.

"If this isn't life or death," pleaded the little man, "you needn't hurry so." Several "thank-you-marms" had nearly bounced him out.

"Set clus'," advised the driver, and the little man endeavored to obey the admonition, clinging in the middle of the broad seat.

Hiram did not check speed even on the slope of the hill leading into the village, though the little man again lifted voice of fear and protest. So tempestuous was the rush of the pung that the loafers in Broadway's store hustled out to watch. And they saw the runners strike the slush-submerged plank-walk leading across the square, beheld the end of the pung flip, saw the little man rise high above the seat with a fur robe in his arms and alight with a yell of mortal fright in the mushy highway, rolling over and over behind the vehicle.

Helping hands of those running from the store platform picked him up, and brought his hat, and stroked the slush out of his eyes so that he could see Hiram Look sweeping back to recover his passenger.

"You devilish, infernal jayhawk of a lunatic!" squealed the little man. "Didn't I warn you not to drive so fast?"

Hiram's jaw dropped at the first blast of that irreligious outbreak. But the white-lawn tie reassured him. There was no time for argument. Before those loafers was no fit place. He grabbed up the little man, poked him into the pung, held him in with one hand and with the other drove furiously to the tavern porch. With equal celerity he hustled him into the office.

"You ain't in any condition to talk business jest now till you're slicked off a little, elder," he began in tones of abject apology.

"You bet your jeeroosly life I'm not!" cried the little man in a perfect frenzy of fury.

Again Hiram opened his mouth agitatedly, and his eyebrows wrinkled in pained surprise. Yet once more his eyes sought the white tie and his hand reached for the little man's arm, and, feeling at a loss just then for language of explanation, he hurried him up-stairs and into a room whose drawn curtains masked some of its untidiness.

"You wash up, elder," he counselled. "I won't let anybody disturb you, and then whatever needs to be explained will be all explained. Don't you blame me till you know it all." And he backed out and shut the door.

He faced the Cap'n at the foot of the stairs. The Cap'n had been watching intently the ascent of the two, and had gathered from the little man's scuffles and his language that he was not a particularly enthusiastic guest.

"They come hard, but we must have 'em, hey?" he demanded, grimly. "This is worse than shanghaiing for a Liverpool boardin'-house, and I won't—"

"S-s-s-sh!" hissed Hiram, flapping his hand. "That's the elder."

"An elder? A man that uses that kind of language?"

"He's had good reason for it," returned Hiram, fervently. "It's stout talk, but I ain't blamin' him." He locked the outside door. "Them Double-yer T. Double-yers will be flockin' this way in a few minutes," he said, in explanation, "but they'll have to walk acrost me in addition to the doormat to get him before I've had my say."

But even while he was holding the unconvinced Cap'n by the arm and eagerly going over his arguments, once more they heard the treading of many feet in the office. There were the W.T.W.'s in force, and they had with them a tall, gaunt man; and the presence of Mrs. Look and Mrs. Sproul, flushed but determined, indicated that the citadel had been betrayed from the rear.

"I present to you Reverend T. Thayer, gents," said the president, icily, "and seein' that he is field-secretary of the enforcement league, and knows his duty when he sees it clear, he will talk to you for your own good, and if it don't do you good, I warn you that there will be something said from the pulpit to-morrow that will bring down the guilty in high places."

"The elder!" gasped Hiram, whirling to gaze aghast at the Cap'n. Then he turned desperate eyes up at the ceiling, where creaking footsteps sounded. "Who in the name o' Jezebel—" he muttered.

Above there was a sort of spluttering bark of a human voice, and the next moment there was a sound as of some one running about wildly. Then down the stairs came the guest, clattering, slipping, and falling the last few steps as he clung to the rail. His eyes were shut tight, his face was dripping, and he was plaintively bleating over and over: "I'm poisoned! I'm blind!"

Hiram ran to him and picked him up from where he had fallen. His coat and vest were off, and his suspenders trailed behind him. One sniff at his frowsled hair told Hiram the story. The little man's topknot was soppy with whiskey; his face was running with it; his eyes were full of it. And the next moment the doubtful aroma had spread to the nostrils of all. And the one-eyed hostler and liquor depository, standing on the outskirts of the throng that he had solicitously followed in, slapped palm against thigh and cried: "By Peter, that's the gallon I poured in the water-pitcher and forgot where I left it!"

"Didn't I tell you and command you and order you to throw away all the liquor round this place, you one-eyed sandpipe?" demanded Hiram, furiously.

"There was a lot of hidin' done in a hurry when they come down on Ferd," pleaded the hostler, "and I forgot where I hid that gallon!"

The little man had his smarting eyes open. "Whiskey?" he mumbled, dragging his hand over his hair and sniffing at his fingers.

"You heard what that renegade owned up to," shouted Hiram, facing the women. "I gave him his orders. I give him his orders now. You jest appoint your delegation, wimmen! Don't you hold me to blame for rum bein' here. You foller that man! And if he don't show you where every drop is hid and give it into your hands to spill, I'll—I'll—" He paused for a threat, cast his eyes about him, and tore down the alligator from the ceiling, seized it by the stiff tail and poised it like a cudgel. "I'll meller him within an inch of his life."

"That sounds fair and reasonable, ladies," said the clergyman, "though, of course, we don't want any violence."

"I'm always fair and reasonable," protested Hiram, "when folks come at me in a fair and reasonable way. You talk to them wimmen, elder, about bein' fair and reasonable themselves, and then lead 'em back here, and you'll find me ready to pull with 'em for the good of this place, without tryin' to run cross-legged or turn a yoke or twist the hames."

When the reformers had departed on the heels of the cowed hostler, Hiram surveyed with interest the little man who was left alone with them.

"I—I—reckon I've got a little business to talk over with you," faltered the old showman, surveying him ruefully. The little man took a parting sniff at his finger-tips.

"You think, do you, that you've got over being driven up and that now you can stop flying and perch a few minutes?" inquired the little man with biting irony.

"I'll 'tend to your case now jest as close as I can," returned Hiram, meekly.

"Well," proceeded the little man, after boring Hiram and then the Cap'n for a time with steely eyes, "I happened to run across one Ferdinand Parrott on the train, and he seemed to have what I've been looking for, a property that I can convert into a sanitarium. My name is Professor Diamond, and I am the inventor of the Telauto—"

But Hiram's curiosity did not extend to the professor's science.

"The idee is," he broke in, eagerly, "did Ferd Parrott say anything about a morgidge and bill of sale bein' on this property, and be you prepared to clear off encumbrances?"

"I am," declared the professor promptly.

"Then you take it," snapped Hiram, with comprehensive sweep of his big hand. He kicked the alligator into the fireplace, took down his overcoat and shrugged his shoulders into it. "Get your money counted and come 'round to town office for your papers."

While he was buttoning it the Reverend Thayer returned, leading the ladies of the Women's Temperance Workers, Miss Philamese Nile at his side. But Hiram checked her first words.

"You talk to him after this," he said, with a chuck of his thumb over his shoulder toward the professor. "Speakin' for Cap'n Aaron Sproul and myself, I take the liberty to here state that we are now biddin' farewell to the tavern business in one grand tableau to slow music, lights turned low and the audience risin' and singin' 'Home, Sweet Home'." He strode out by the front way, followed by Mrs. Look.

"Had you just as soon come through the kitchen with me?" asked the Cap'n in a whisper as he approached his wife. "I'm goin' to do up what's left of that plum-duff and take it home. It kind o' hits my tooth!"

XXIX

Mr. Aholiah Luce, of the Purgatory Hollow section of Smyrna, stood at bay on the dirt-banking of his "castle," that is, a sagged-in old hulk of a house of which only the L was habitable.

He was facing a delegation of his fellow-citizens, to wit: Cap'n Aaron Sproul, first selectman of the town; Hiram Look, Zeburee Nute, constable; and a nervous little man with a smudge of smut on the side of his nose—identity and occupation revealed by the lettering on the side of his wagon:

T. TAYLOR

STOVES AND TINWARE

VIENNA

Mr. Luce had his rubber boots set wide apart, and his tucked-in trousers emphasized the bow in his legs. With those legs and his elongated neck and round, knobby head, Mr. Luce closely resembled one of a set of antique andirons.

"You want to look out you don't squdge me too fur in this," said Mr. Luce, warningly. "I've been squdged all my life, and I've 'bout come to the limick. Now look out you don't squdge me too fur!"

He side-stepped and stood athwart his door, the frame of which had been recently narrowed by half, the new boarding showing glaringly against the old. When one understood the situation, this new boarding had a very significant appearance.

Mr. Luce had gone over into Vienna, where his reputation for shiftiness was not as well known, and had secured from Mr. T. Taylor, recently set up in the stove business, a new range with all modern attachments, promising to pay on the instalment plan. Stove once installed, Mr. Luce had immediately begun to "improve" his mansion by building a new door-frame too narrow to permit the exit of the stove. Then Mr. Luce had neglected to pay, and, approached by replevin papers, invoked the statute that provides that a man's house cannot be ripped in pieces to secure goods purchased on credit.

Constable Nute, unable to cope with the problem, had driven to Smyrna village and summoned the first selectman, and the Cap'n had solicited Hiram Look to transport him, never having conquered his sailor's fear of a horse.

"It ain't goin' to be twitted abroad in Vienny nor any other town that we let you steal from outsiders in any such way as this," declared the first selectman, once on the ground. "Folks has allus cal'lated on your stealin' about so much here in town in the run of a year, and haven't made no great fuss about it. But we ain't goin' to harbor and protect any general Red Rover and have it slurred against this town. Take down that scantlin' stuff and let this man have his stove."

"You can squdge me only so fur and no furder," asserted Luce, sullenly, holding down his loose upper lip with his yellow teeth as though to keep it from flapping in the wind. Within the mansion there was the mellow rasp of a tin of biscuit on an oven floor, the slam of an oven door, and Mrs. Luce appeared dusting flour from her hands. All who knew Mrs. Luce knew that she was a persistent and insistent exponent of the belief of the Millerites—"Go-uppers," they called the sect in Smyrna.

"I say you've got to open up and give this man his property," cried Cap'n Sproul, advancing on them.

"Property? Who talks of property?" demanded Mrs. Luce, her voice hollow with the hollowness of the prophet. "No one knows the day and the hour when we are to be swept up. It is near at hand. We shall ride triumphant to the skies. And will any one think of property and the vain things of this world then?"

"Prob'ly not," agreed the Cap'n, sarcastically, "and there won't be any need of a cook-stove in the place where your husband will fetch up. He can do all his cookin' on a toastin'-fork over an open fire — there'll be plenty of blaze."

"Don't squdge me too fur," repeated Mr. Luce, clinging to the most expressive warning he could muster just then.

"It's full time for that critter to be fetched up with a round turn," muttered Constable Nute, coming close to the elbow of the first selectman, where the latter stood glowering on the culprit. "I reckon you don't know as much about him as I do. When his mother was nussin' him, a helpless babe, he'd take the pins out'n her hair, and they didn't think it was anything but playin'. Once he stole the specs off'm her head whilst she was nappin' with him in her arms, and jammed 'em down a hole in the back of the rockin'-chair. Whilst old Doc Burns was vaccinatin' him — and he wa'n't more'n tew years old — he got Doc's watch."

"Those things would kind of give you a notion he'd steal, give him a fair chance," commented Hiram, dryly.

"He's stole ever since — everything from carpet tacks to a load of hay," snapped the constable, "till folks don't stop to think he's stealin'. He's got to be like rats and hossflies and other pests — you cuss 'em, but you reckon they've come to stay."

"I've abated some of the nuisances in this town," stated the Cap'n, "and I cal'late I'm good for this one, now that it's been stuck under my nose. Why haven't you arrested him in times past, same as you ought to have done?"

"Wasn't any one who would swear out complaints," said the constable. "He's allus been threatenin' what kairosene and matches would do to barns; and it wouldn't be no satisfaction to send 'Liah Luce to State Prison — he ain't account enough. It wouldn't pay the loser for a stand of buildin's — havin' him there."

Cap'n Sproul began to understand some of the sane business reasons that guaranteed the immunity of Aholiah Luce, so long as he stuck to petty thieving. But this international matter of the town of Vienna seemed to the first selectman of Smyrna to be another sort of proposition. And he surveyed the recalcitrant Mr. Luce with malignant gaze.

"I've never seen you backed down by nobody," vouchsafed the admiring constable, anxious to shift his own responsibility and understanding pretty well how to do it. "I've allus said that if there was any man could run this town the way it ought to be run you was the man to do it."

Cap'n Sproul was not the kind to disappoint the confident flattery of those who looked up to him. He buttoned his pea-jacket, and set his hat firmly on his head. Mr. Luce noted these signs of belligerency and braced his firedog legs.

"It's the meek that shall inherit, ye want to remember that!" croaked Mrs. Luce. "And the crowned heads and the high and mighty—where will they be then?"

"They won't be found usin' a stolen cook-stove and quotin' Scriptur'," snorted the Cap'n in disgust.

"It ain't been stole," insisted Mr. Luce. "It was bought reg'lar, and it can't be took away without mollywhackin' my house—and I've got the law on my side that says you can't do it."

Cap'n Sproul was close to the banking.

"Luce," he said, savagely, "I ain't out here to-day to discuss law p'ints nor argy doctrines of religion. You've got a stove there that belongs to some one else, and you either pay for it or give it up. I'm willin' to be fair and reasonable, and I'll give you fifteen seconds to pay or tear down that door framework."

But neither alternative, nor the time allowed for acceptance, seemed to please Mr. Luce. In sudden, weak anger at being thus cornered after long immunity, he anathematized all authority as 'twas vested in the first selectman of Smyrna. Several men passing in the highway held up their horses and listened with interest.

Emboldened by his audience, spurred to desperate measures, Mr. Luce kicked out one of his rubber boots at the advancing Cap'n. The Cap'n promptly grasped the extended leg and yanked. Mr. Luce came off his perch and fell on his back in the mud, and Constable Nute straddled him instantly and held him down. With an axe that he picked up at the dooryard woodpile, Cap'n Aaron hammered out the new door-frame, paying no heed to Mr. Luce's threats or Mrs. Luce's maledictions.

"I don't know the law on it, nor I don't care," he muttered between his teeth as he toiled. "All I know is, that stove belongs to T. Taylor, of Vienny, and he's goin' to have it."

And when the new boarding lay around him in splinters and the door was wide once more, he led the way into the kitchen.

"You undertake to throw that hot water on me, Mis' Luce," he declared, noting what her fury was prompting, "and you'll go right up through that roof, and it won't be no millennium that will boost you, either."

The stove man and Hiram followed him in and the disinterested onlookers came, too, curiosity impelling them. And as they were Smyrna farmers who had suffered various and aggravating depredations by this same Aholiah Luce, they were willing to lend a hand even to lug out a hot stove. The refulgent monarch of the kitchen departed, with the tin of biscuit still browning in its interior, passed close to the cursing Mr. Luce, lying on his back under Nute's boring knee, and then with a lusty "Hop-ho! All together!" went into T. Taylor's wagon.

Mr. Luce, freed now as one innocuous, leaped up and down in a perfect ecstasy of fury. "You've squdged me too fur. You've done it at last!" he screamed, with hysteric iteration. "You've made me a desp'rit' outlaw."

"Outlaw! You're only a cheap sneak-thief!"

"That's right, Cap'n Sproul," remarked the constable. "He can't even steal hens till it's dark and they can't look at him. If they turned and put their eye on him he wouldn't dare to touch 'em."

"I don't dast to be an outlaw, hey?" shrieked Mr. Luce. The vast injury that had been done him, this ruthless assault on his house, his humiliation in public, and now these wanton taunts, whipped his weak nature into frenzy. Cowards at bay are the savagest foes. Mr. Luce ran amuck!

Spurring his resolution by howling over and over: "I don't dast to be an outlaw, hey? I'll show ye!" he hastened with a queer sort of stiff-legged gallop into the field, tore away some boarding, and descended into what was evidently a hiding-place, a dry well. A moment, and up he popped, boosting a burden. He slung it over his shoulder and started toward them, staggering under its weight. It was a huge sack, with something in it that sagged heavily.

"Nice sort of an outlaw he'll make—that woodchuck!" observed Constable Nute with a cackle of mirth.

The first selectman and his supporters surveyed the approach of the furious Mr. Luce with great complacency. If Mr. Luce had emerged with a shot-gun in his fist and a knife in his teeth he might have presented some semblance of an outlaw. But this bow-legged man with a sack certainly did not seem savage. Hiram offered the humorous suggestion that perhaps Mr. Luce proposed to restore property, and thereby causing people to fall dead with astonishment would get his revenge on society.

"I warned ye and you wouldn't listen," screamed the self-declared pariah. "I said there was such a thing as squdgin' me too fur. Ye didn't believe it. Now mebbe ye'll believe that!"

He had halted at a little distance from them, and had set down his sack. He dove into it and held up a cylinder, something more than half a foot long, a brown, unassuming cylinder that certainly didn't have anything about its looks to call out all the excitement that was convulsing Mr. Luce.

"Pee-ruse that!" squealed he. "*There's* a lead-pencil that will write some news for ye." He shook the cylinder at them. "And there's plenty more of 'em in this bag." He curled his long lip back. "Daminite!" he spat. "I'll show ye whuther I'm an outlaw or not."

"And I know where you stole it," bawled one of the bystanders indignantly. "You stole all me and my brother bought and had stored for a season's blastin'. Constable Nute, I call on you to arrest him and give me back my property."

"Arrest me, hey?" repeated Mr. Luce. In one hand he shook aloft the stick of dynamite, with its dangling fuse that grimly suggested the detonating cap at its root. In the other hand he clutched a bunch of matches. "You start in to arrest me and you'll arrest two miles straight up above here, travellin' a hundred miles a minit."

"There ain't any grit in him, Nute," mumbled Cap'n Sproul. "Jest give a whoop and dash on him."

"That sounds glib and easy," demurred the prudent officer, "but if that man hasn't gone clean loony then I'm no jedge. I don't reckon I'm goin' to charge any batteries."

"You'll do what I tell you to! You're an officer, and under orders."

"You told me once to take up Hiram Look's el'funt and put her in the pound," remonstrated the constable. "But I didn't do it, and I wasn't holden to do it. And I ain't holden to run up and git blowed to everlastin' hackmetack with a bag of dynamite."

"Look here, Nute," cried the Cap'n, thoroughly indignant and shifting the contention to his officer—entirely willing to ignore Mr. Luce's threats and provocations—"I haven't called on you in a tight place ever in my life but what you've sneaked out. You ain't fit for even a hog-reeve. I'm going to cancel your constable appointment, that's what I'll do when I get to town hall."

"I'll do it right now," declared the offended Mr. Nute, unpinning his badge. "Any time you've ordered me to do something sensible I've done it. But el'funts and lunatics and dynamite and some of the other jobs you've unlo'ded onto me ain't sensible, and I won't stand for 'em. You can't take me in the face and eyes of the people and rake me over." He had noted that the group in the highway had considerably increased. "I've resigned."

Mr. Luce was also more or less influenced and emboldened and pricked on by being the centre of eyes. As long as he seemed to be expected to give a show, he proposed to make it a good one. His flaming eyes fell on T. Taylor, busy over the stove, getting it ready for its journey back to Vienna. Mr. Taylor, happy in the recovery of his property, was paying little attention to outlaws or official disputes. He had cleaned out the coals and ashes, and having just now discovered the tin of biscuit, tossed it away. This last seemed too much for Mr. Luce's self-control.

"I don't dast to be an outlaw, hey?" he cried, hoarsely. "That stove is too good for me, is it? My wife's biskits throwed into the mud and mire!"

He lighted the fuse of the dynamite, ran to the team and popped the explosive into the stove oven and slammed the door. Then he flew to his sack, hoisted it to his shoulder and staggered back toward the dry well.

At this critical juncture there did not arise one of those rare spirits to perform an act of noble self-sacrifice. There have been those who have tossed spluttering bombs into the sea; who have trodden out hissing fuses. But just then no one seemed to care for the exclusive and personal custody of that stick of dynamite.

All those in teams whipped up, yelling like madmen, and those on foot grabbed on behind and clambered over tailboards. Cap'n Sproul, feeling safer on his own legs than in Hiram's team, pounded away down the road with the speed of a frantic Percheron. And in all this panic T. Taylor, only dimly realizing that there was something in his stove that was going to cause serious trouble, obeyed the exhortations screamed at him, cut away his horse, straddled the beast's back and fled with the rest.

The last one in sight was Mrs. Luce, who had shown serious intentions of remaining on the spot as though she feared to miss anything that bore the least resemblance to the coming of the last great day. But she suddenly obeyed her husband, who was yelling at her over the edge of the hole, and ran and fell in by his side.

Missiles that screamed overhead signalized to the scattered fugitives the utter disintegration of T. Taylor's stove. The hearth mowed off a crumbly chimney on the Luce house, and flying fragments crushed out sash in the windows of the abandoned main part. Cap'n Sproul was the first one to reappear, coming from behind a distant tree. There was a hole in the ground where T. Taylor's wagon had stood.

"Daminite!" screamed a voice. Mr. Luce was dancing up and down on the edge of his hole, shaking another stick of the explosive. "I'll show ye whuther I'm an outlaw or not! I'll have this town down on its knees. I'll show ye what it means to squdge me too fur. I give ye fair warnin' from now on. I'm a desp'rit' man. They'll write novels about me before I'm done. Try to arrest me, will ye? I'll take the whole possy sky-hootin' with me when ye come." He was drunk with power suddenly revealed to him.

He lifted the sack out of the hole and, paying no heed to some apparent expostulations of Mrs. Luce, he staggered away up the hillside into the beech growth, bowed under his burden. And after standing and gazing for some time at the place where he disappeared, the first selectman trudged down the road to where Hiram was waiting for him, soothing his trembling horse.

"Well," said the old showman, with a vigorous exhalation of breath to mark relief, "get in here and let's go home. Accordin' to my notion, replevinin' and outlawin' ain't neither sensible or fashionable or healthy. Somethin' that looked like a stove-cover and sounded like a howlaferinus only just missed me by about two feet. That critter's dangerous to be let run loose. What are you goin' to do about him?"

"Ketch him," announced the Cap'n, sturdily.

"Well," philosophized Hiram, "smallpox is bad when it's runnin' round loose, but it's a blastnation sight worse when it's been ketched. You're the head of the town and I ain't, and I ain't presumin' to advise, but I'd think twice before I went to runnin' that bag o' dynamite into close corners. Luce ain't no account, and no more is an old hoss-pistol, but when a hoss-pistol busts it's a dangerous thing to be close to. You let him alone and mebbe he'll quiet down."

But that prophecy did not take into account the state of mind of the new outlaw of Smyrna.

XXX

At about midnight Cap'n Sprou, snoring peaceably with wide-open mouth, snapped upright in bed with a jerk that set his teeth into his tongue and nearly dislocated his neck. He didn't know exactly what had happened. He had a dizzy, dreaming feeling that he had been lifted up a few hundred feet in the air and dropped back.

"Land o' Goshen, Aaron, what was it?" gasped his wife. "It sounded like something blowing up!"

The hint steadied the Cap'n's wits. 'Twas an explosion—that was it! And with grim suspicion as to its cause, he pulled on his trousers and set forth to investigate. An old barn on his premises, a storehouse for an overplus of hay and discarded farming tools, had been blown to smithereens and lay scattered about under the stars. And as he picked his way around the ruins with a lantern, cursing the name of Luce, a far voice hailed him from the gloom of a belt of woodland: "I ain't an outlaw, hey? I don't dast to be one, hey? You wait and see."

About an hour later, just as the selectman was sinking into a doze, he heard another explosion, this time far in the distance—less a sound than a jar, as of something striking a mighty blow on the earth.

"More dynamite!" he muttered, recognizing that explosive's down-whacking characteristic. And in the morning Hiram Look hurried across to inform him that some miscreant had blown up an empty corn-house on his premises, and that the explosion had shattered all the windows in the main barn and nearly scared Imogene, the elephant, into conniptions. "And he came and hollered into my bedroom window that he'd show me whuther he could be an outlaw or not," concluded the old showman. "I tell you that critter is dangerous, and you've got to get him. Instead of quietin' down he'll be growin' worse."

The Skipper and the Skipped

There were eleven men in Smyrna, besides Zeburee Nute, who held commissions as constables, and those valiant officers Cap'n Sproul called into the first selectman's office that forenoon. He could not tell them any news. The whole of Smyrna was ringing with the intelligence that Aholiah Luce had turned outlaw and was on the rampage.

The constables, however, could give Selectman Sproul some news. They gave it to him after he had ordered them to surround Mr. Luce and take him, dynamite and all. This news was to the effect that they had resigned.

"We've talked it over," averred Lycurgus Snell, acting as spokesman, "and we can't figger any good and reeliable way of gittin' him without him gittin' us, if he's so minded, all in one tableau, same to be observed with smoked glasses like an eclipse. No, s'r, we ain't in any way disposed to taller the heavens nor furnish mince-meat funerals. And if we don't git him, and he knows we're takin' action agin' him, he'll come round and blow our barns up—and we ain't so well able to stand the loss as you and Mr. Look be."

"Well, if you ain't about the nearest to knot-holes with the rims gone off'm 'em of anything I ever see," declared the Cap'n, with fury, "may I be used for oakum to calk a guano gunlow!"

"If you think it's a job to set any man to, you'd better go and do it yourself," retorted Snell, bridling. "You know as well as I do, s'leckman, that so long as 'Liah has been let alone he's only been a plain thief, and we've got along with him here in town all right—onpleasant and somewhat expensive, like potater-bugs. But you seem to have gone to pushin' him and have turned him from potater-bug into a royal Peeruvian tiger, or words to that effect, and I don't see any way but what you'll have to tame him yourself. There's feelin' in town that way, and people are scart, and citizens ain't at all pleased with your pokin' him up, when all was quiet."

"Citizens ruther have it said, hey, that we are supportin' a land-pirut here in this town, and let him disgrace us even over in Vienny?" demanded the Cap'n.

"Which was wuss?" inquired Mr. Snell, serenely. "As it was or as it is?"

Then the ex-constables, driven forth with contumely, went across to the platform of Broadway's store, and discussed the situation with other citizens, finding the opinion quite unanimous that Cap'n Sproul possessed too short a temper to handle delicate matters with diplomacy. And it was agreed that Aholiah Luce, weak of wit and morally pernicious, was a delicate matter, when all sides were taken into account.

To them appeared Aholiah Luce, striding down the middle of the street, with that ominous sack on his shoulder.

"Be I an outlaw, or ain't I?" he shouted over and over, raising a clamor in the quiet village that brought the Cap'n out of the town house. "Arrest me, will ye? When ye try it there won't be nothin' left of this town but a hole and some hollerin'."

He walked right upon the store platform and into the store, and every one fled before him. Broadway cowered behind his counter.

"Put me up a fig o' tobacker, a pound of tea, quart o' merlasses, ten pounds of crackers, hunk o' pork, and two cans of them salmons," he ordered.

In past years Mr. Luce had always slunk into Broadway's store apologetically, a store-bill everlastingly unpaid oppressing his spirits. Now he bellowed autocratic command, and his soul swelled when he saw Broadway timorously hastening to obey.

"I'll show 'em whuther I'm an outlaw or not," he muttered. "And I wisht I'd been one before, if it works like this. The monarch of the

Injies couldn't git more attention," he reflected, as he saw the usually contemptuous Broadway hustling about, wrapping up the goods.

He saw scared faces peering in at him through the windows. He swung the sack off his shoulder, and bumped it on the floor with a flourish.

"My Lord-amighty, be careful with that!" squawked Broadway, ducking down behind the counter.

"You 'tend to business and make less talk, and you won't git hurt," observed Mr. Luce, ferociously. He pointed at the storekeeper the stick of dynamite that he carried in his hand. And Mr. Broadway hopped up and bestirred himself obsequiously.

"I don't know whuther I'll ever pay for these or not," announced Mr. Luce, grabbing the bundles that Broadway poked across the counter as gingerly as he would feed meat to a tiger. He stuffed them into his sack. "I shall do jest as I want to about it. And when I've et up this grub in my lair, where I propose to outlaw it for a while, I shall come back for some more; and if I don't git it, along with polite treatment, I'll make it rain groc'ries in this section for twenty-four hours."

"I didn't uphold them that smashed in your door," protested the storekeeper, getting behind the coffee-grinder.

"I've been squdged too fur, that's what has been done," declared Mr. Luce, "and it was your seleckman that done it, and I hold the whole town responsible. I don't know what I'm li'ble to do next. I've showed *him*—now I'm li'ble to show the town. I dunno! It depends."

He went out and stood on the store platform, and gazed about him with the air of Alexander on the banks of the Euphrates. For the first time in his lowly life Mr. Luce saw mankind shrink from before him. It was the same as deference would have seemed to a man who had earned respect, and the little mind of Smyrna's outlaw whirled dizzily in his filbert skull.

"I don't know what I'll do yit," he shouted, hailing certain faces that he saw peering at him. "It was your seleckman that done it—and a seleckman acts for a town. I reckon I shall do some more blowin' up."

He calmly walked away up the street, passing Cap'n Sproul, who stood at one side.

"I don't dast to be an outlaw, hey?" jeered Mr. Luce.

"You don't dare to set down that sack," roared the selectman. "I'll pay ye five hundred dollars to set down that sack and step out there into the middle of that square—and I call on all here as witnesses to that offer," he cried, noting that citizens were beginning to creep back into sight once more. "Five hundred dollars for you, you bow-legged hen-thief! You sculpin-mouthed hyena, blowing up men's property!"

"Hold on," counselled Mr. Luce. "You're goin' to squdgin' me ag'in. I've been sassed enough in this town. I'm goin' to be treated with respect after this if I have to blow up ev'ry buildin' in it."

"It ain't safe to go to pokin' him up," advised Mr. Nute from afar. "I should think you'd 'a' found that out by this time, Cap'n Sproul."

"I've found out that what ain't cowards here are thieves,'" roared the Cap'n, beside himself, ashamed, enraged at his impotence before this boastful fool and his grim bulwark. His impulse was to cast caution to the winds and rush upon Luce. But reflection told him that, in this flush of his childish resentment and new prominence, Luce was capable of anything. Therefore he prudently held to the side of the road.

"The next time I come into this village," said Mr. Luce, "I don't propose to be called names in public by any old salt hake that has pounded his dollars out of unfort'nit' sailors with belayin'-pins. I know your record, and I ain't afeard of you!"

"There'll be worse things happen to you than to be called names."

"Oh, there will, hey?" inquired Mr. Luce, his weak passion flaming. "Well, lemme give you jest one hint that it ain't safe to squdge me too fur!"

He walked back a little way, lighted the fuse of the stick of dynamite that he carried, and in spite of horrified appeals to him, cast over the shoulders of fleeing citizens, he tossed the wicked explosive into the middle of the square and ran.

In the words of Mr. Snell, when he came out from behind the watering-trough: "It was a corn-cracker!"

A half-hour later Mr. Nute, after sadly completing a canvass of the situation, headed a delegation that visited Cap'n Sproul in the selectman's office, where he sat, pallid with rage, and cursing.

"A hundred and seventeen lights of glass," announced Mr. Nute, "includin' the front stained-glass winder in the meetin'-house and the big light in Broadway's store. And it all happened because the critter was poked up agin'—and I warned ye not to do it, Cap'n."

"Would it be satisfactory to the citizens if I pulled my wallet and settled the damage?" inquired the first selectman, with baleful blandness in his tones.

Mr. Nute did not possess a delicate sense of humor or of satire. He thoughtfully rubbed his nose.

"Reely," he said, "when you git it reduced right down, that critter ain't responsible any more'n one of them dynamite sticks is responsible, and if it hadn't been for you lettin' him loose and then pokin' him, contrary to warnin', them hundred and seventeen lights of glass wouldn't—"

"Are there any left?" asked Cap'n Sproul, still in subdued tones.

"About as many more, I should jedge," replied Mr. Nute.

"Well, I simply want to say," remarked the Cap'n, standing up and clinching his fists, "that if you ever mention responsibility to me again, Nute, I'll take you by the heels and smash in the rest of that glass with you—and I'll do the same with any one else who don't know enough to keep his yawp shut. Get out of here, the whole of you, or I'll begin on what glass is left in this town house."

They departed silently, awed by the menace of his countenance, but all the more bitterly fixed in their resentment.

That night two more hollow "chunks" shook the ground of Smyrna, at intervals an hour separated, and morning light showed that two isolated barns had been destroyed.

Mr. Luce appeared in the village with his sack, quite at his ease, and demanded of Broadway certain canned delicacies, his appetite seeming to have a finer edge to correspond with his rising courage. He even hinted that Broadway's stock was not very complete, and that some early strawberries might soften a few of the asperities of his nature.

"I ain't never had a fair show on eatin'," he complained to the apprehensive storekeeper. "It's been ten years that my wife ain't got me a fair and square meal o' vittles. She don't believe in cookin' nothin' ahead nor gettin' up anything decent. She's a Go-upper and thinks the end of the world is li'ble to come any minit. And the way I figger it, not havin' vittles reg'lar has give me dyspepsy, and dyspepsy has made me cranky, and not safe to be squdged too fur. And that's the whole trouble. I've got a hankerin' for strorb'ries. They may make me more supple. P'raps not, but it's wuth tryin'."

He tossed the cans into his sack in a perfectly reckless manner, until Broadway was sick and hiccuping with fear. "Love o' Lordy," he pleaded, "don't act that way. It's apt to go off—go off any time. I know the stuff better'n you do—I've dealt in it. Ain't I usin' you square on goods?"

"Mebbe so," admitted Mr. Luce. "Fur's you know, you are. But the trouble with me is my disposition. It ain't been made supple yet. If you've got in stock what my appetite craves I may be more supple next time I come."

He dug a tender strip out of the centre of a hanging codfish, and walked out. Parading his ease of spirits and contempt for humanity in general, he stood on the platform and gnawed at the fish and gazed serenely on the broken windows.

"I done it," he mumbled, admiringly. "I showed 'em! It won't take much more showin', and then they'll let me alone, and I'll live happy ever after. Wonder is I hadn't reelized it before. Tail up, and everybody stands to one side. Tail down, and everybody is tryin' to kick you. If it wa'n't for that streak in human nature them devilish trusts that I've heard tell of couldn't live a minit." He saw men standing afar and staring at him apprehensively. "That's right, ding baste ye," he said, musingly, "look up to me and keep your distance! It don't make no gre't diff'runce how it's done, so long as I can do it."

And after further triumphant survey of the situation, he went away.

"Hiram," said Cap'n Sproul, with decision, turning from a long survey of Mr. Luce's retreating back through a broken window of the town house, "this thing has gone jest as far as it's goin'."

"Well," declared the showman with some bitterness, "to have them that's in authority stand round here and let one bow-legged lunatic blow up this whole town piecemeal ain't in any ways satisfyin' to the voters. I hear the talk, and I'm givin' it to you straight as a friend."

"I've got my plan all made," said the first selectman. "I want you as foreman to call out the Ancient and Honer'ble Firemen's Association and have 'em surround them woods, and we'll take him."

"We will, hey?" demanded Hiram, pushing back his plug hat and squinting angrily. "What do you think that firemen's association is for, anyway?"

"Never knew it to do anything but eat free picnics and give social dances," retorted the Cap'n. "I didn't know but it was willin' to be useful for once in its life."

"Slur noted!" said Hiram, with acerbity. "But you can't expect us to pull you out of a hole that you've mismanaged yourself into. You needn't flare, now, Cap'n. It's been mismanaged, and that's the sentiment of the town. I ain't twittin' you because I've lost property. I'm talkin' as a friend."

"That's twice this mornin' you've passed me that 'friend' handbill," raged the selectman. "Advertisin' yourself, be ye? And then leavin' me in the lurch! This is a friendly town, that's what it is. Constables, voters, firemen, and you yourself dump the whole burden of this onto me, and then stand back and growl at me! Well, if this thing is up to me alone and friendless and single-handed, I know what I'm goin' to do!" His tone had the grate of file against steel.

"What?" inquired his friend with interest.

"Get a gun and go out and drop that humpbacked old Injy-cracker!"

But Hiram protested fervently.

"Where would you shoot him?" he cried. "You don't know where to find him in them woods. You'd have to nail him here in the village, and besides its bein' murder right in the face and eyes of folks, you'd put a bullet into that sack o' dynamite and blow ev'ry store, meetin'-house, and school-house in Smyrna off'm the map. You give that up, or I'll pass the word and have you arrested, yourself, as a dangerous critter."

He went away, still protesting as long as he was in hearing.

Cap'n Sproul sat despondent in his chair, and gazed through the broken window at other broken windows. Ex-Constable Nute presented himself at the pane outside and said, nervously chewing tobacco: "I reckon it's the only thing that can be done now, Cap'n. It seems to be the general sentiment."

With a flicker of hope irradiating his features, Cap'n Sproul inquired for details.

"It's to write to the President and get him to send down a hunk of the United States Army. You've got to fight fire with fire."

Without particular display of passion, with the numb stolidity of one whose inner fires have burned out, the selectman got up and threw a cuspidor through the window at his counsellor, and then seated himself to his pondering once more.

That afternoon Mrs. Aholiah Luce came walking into the village, spent, forlorn, and draggled. She went straight to the town office, and seated herself in front of the musing first selectman.

"I've come to call on for town help," she said. "I haven't got scrap nor skred to eat, and northin' to cook it with. You've gone to work and put us in a pretty mess, Mister S'leckman. Makin' my husband an outlaw that's took to the woods, and me left on the chips!"

The Cap'n surveyed her without speaking—apparently too crushed to make any talk. In addition to other plagues, it was now plain that he had brought a pauper upon the town of Smyrna.

"So I call on," she repeated, "and I need a whole new stock of groc'ries, and something to cook 'em with."

And still the Cap'n did not speak. He sat considering her, his brows knitted.

"I'm a proud woman nat'rally," she went on, "and it's tough to have to call on 'cause the crowned heads of earth has oppressed the meek and the lowly."

Cap'n Sproul trudged across the room, and took down a big book inscribed "Revised Statutes." He found a place in the volume and began to read in an undertone, occasionally looking over his specs at her.

"It's as I thought it was," he muttered; "when one member of a family, wife or minor children, call on for town aid, whole family can be declared paupers till such time as, and so forth." He banged the big book shut. "Interestin' if true—and found to be true. Law to use as needed. So you call on, do you, marm?" he queried, raising his voice. "Well, if you're all ready to start for the poor-farm, come along."

"I ain't goin' onto no poor-farm," she squealed. "I call on, but I want supplies furnished."

"Overseer of the poor has the say as to what shall be done with paupers," announced the Cap'n. "I say poor-farm. They need a good, able-bodied pauper woman there, like you seem to be. The other wimmen paupers are bedridden."

"My husband will never let me be took to the poorhouse and kept there."

"Oh, there ain't goin' to be any trouble from that side. You're right in line to be a widder most any time now."

"Be you goin' to kill 'Liah?" she wailed.

"It will be a self-actin' proposition, marm. I ain't got any very special grudge against him, seein' that he's a poor, unfortunate critter. I'm sorry, but so it is." He went on with great appearance of candor. "You see, he don't understand the nature of that stuff he's luggin' round. It goes off itself when it gets about so warm. It's comin' warmin' weather now—sun gettin' high—and mebbe next time he starts for the village the bust will come."

"Ain't any one goin' to warn him?"

"I can't find it's set down in my duties, marm; and from the acts of the gen'ral run of cowards in this town I don't reckon any one else will feel called on to get near enough to him to tell him. Oh no! He'll fire himself like an automatic bomb. Prob'ly to-morrow. By the looks of the sky it's goin' to be a nice, warm day."

She backed to the door, her eyes goggling.

"I ain't got any hard feelin's at all, marm. I pity you, and here's a ten-dollar bill that I'll advance from the town. I reckon I'll wait till after you're a widder before I take you to the poorhouse."

She clutched the bill and ran out. He watched her scurry down the street with satisfaction wrinkling under his beard. "It was a kind of happy idee and it seems to be workin'," he observed. "I've allus thought I knew enough about cowards to write a book on 'em. We'll see!"

That night there were no alarms in Smyrna. Cap'n Sproul, walking to his office the next forenoon, mentally scored one on the right side of his calculations.

When he heard Mr. Luce in the village square and looked out on him, he scored two, still on the right side. Mr. Luce bore his grisly sack, but he did not carry a stick of dynamite in his hand.

"Goin' to put my wife in the poorhouse, hey?" he squalled.

Cap'n Sproul scored three. "She got at him and unloaded!" he murmured. "And it fixed him, if I know cowards."

"She's goin' to be a widder, hey? I'm afeard o' daminite, hey? I'll show ye!" He swung the sack from his shoulder, and held it up in both hands for the retreating populace to see. "I jest as soon flam this whole thing down here in the ro'd. I jest as soon kick it. I jest as soon set on it and smoke my pipe. I'm an outlaw and I ain't afeard of it. You use me right and let my wife alone, or I'll show ye."

Cap'n Sproul, sailor-habit always strong with him, had for a long time kept one of his telescopes hanging beside a window in the town office. He took this down and studied the contour of the bumps that swelled Mr. Luce's sack. His survey seemed to satisfy him. "Tone of his talk is really enough—but the shape of that bag settles it with me."

The next moment all of Smyrna that happened to be in sight of the scene gasped with horror on beholding the first selectman walk out of the town house and stalk directly across the square toward the dynamiter.

"You go back," screamed Mr. Luce, "or I'll flam it!"

But no longer was Mr. Luce's tone dauntless and ferocious. The Cap'n's keen ear caught the coward's note of querulousness, for he had heard that note many times before in his stormy association with men. He chuckled and walked on more briskly.

"I'll do it—I swear I will!" said Mr. Luce, but his voice was only a weak piping.

In spite of itself Smyrna stopped, groaned, and squatted where it stood when Mr. Luce swung the sack and launched it at the intrepid selectman. As he threw it, the outlaw turned to run. The Cap'n grabbed the sack, catapulted it back, and caught the fleeing Mr. Luce squarely between the shoulders; and he went down on his face with a yell of pain. The next moment Smyrna saw her first selectman kicking a bleating man around and around the square until the man got down, lifted up his hands, and bawled for mercy.

And when Smyrna flocked around, the Cap'n faced them, his fist twisted in Mr. Luce's collar.

The Skipper and the Skipped

"This critter belongs in State Prison, but I ain't goin' to send him there. He's goin' onto our poor-farm, and he's goin' to work for the first time in his life, and he'll keep to work till he works up some of the bill he owes this town. He's a pauper because his wife has called on. But I ain't dependin' on law. I'm runnin' this thing myself. I've shown ye that I can run it. And if any of you quitters and cowards have got anything to say why my sentence won't be carried out, now is the time to say it."

He glowered into their faces, but no one said anything except Zeburee Nute, who quavered: "We allus knowed you was the smartest man that ever came to this town, and—"

"Close that mouth!" yelped Cap'n Sproul. "It's worse than an open hatch on a superphosphate schooner."

"You dare to leave that town farm, you or your wife either," the selectman went on, giving Mr. Luce a vigorous shake, "and I'll have you in State Prison as quick as a grand jury can indict. Nute, you hitch and take him down there, and tell the boss he's to work ten hours a day, with one hour's noonin', and if he don't move fast enough, to get at him with a gad."

Mr. Luce, cowed, trembling, appealing dumbly for sympathy, was driven away while the first selectman was picking up the sack that still lay in the village square. Without a moment's hesitation he slit it with his big knife, and emptied its contents into a hole that the spring frosts had left. Those contents were simply rocks.

"In the name of Joanthus Cicero!" gasped Broadway, licking his dry lips. "How did you figger it?"

The Cap'n finished kicking the sack down into the hole beside the rocks, clacked shut his knife-blade, and rammed the knife deep into his trousers pocket.

"When you critters here in town get to be grown up to be more than ten years old," he grunted, surveying the gaping graybeards of

Smyrna, "and can understand man's business, I may talk to you. Just now I've got something to attend to besides foolishness."

And he trudged back into the town house, with his fellow-citizens staring after him, as the populace of Rome must have stared after victorious Cæsar.

XXXI

For some weeks the town of Smyrna had been witnessing something very like a bear-baiting.

Cap'n Aaron Sproul, first selectman, again played the rôle of the bear, as he had on occasions previous.

They had stalked him; they had flanked him; they had surrounded him; they had driven him to centre; he was at bay, bristling with a sullen rage that was excusable, if viewed from the standpoint of an earnest town officer. Viewed from the standpoint of the populace, he was a selfish, cross-grained old obstructionist.

Here was the situation: By thrift and shrewd management he had accumulated during his reign nearly enough funds to pay off the town debt and retire interest-bearing notes. He had proposed to make that feat the boast and the crowning point of his tenure of office. He had announced that on a certain day he would have a bonfire of those notes in the village square. After that announcement he had listened for plaudits. What he did hear were resentful growls from taxpayers who now discovered that they had been assessed more than the running expenses of the town called for; and they were mad about it. The existence of that surplus seemed to worry Smyrna. There were many holders of town notes for small amounts, a safe investment that paid six per cent. and escaped taxation. These people didn't want to be paid. In many cases their fathers had loaned the money to the town, and the safe and sound six per cent. seemed an heirloom too sacred to be disturbed.

Cap'n Sproul's too-zealous thrift annoyed his townsmen. To have the town owe money made individual debtors feel that owing money was not a particularly heinous offence. To have the town free of debt might start too enterprising rivalry in liquidation.

Therefore, for the first time in his life, Consetena Tate found one of his wild notions adopted, and gasped in profound astonishment at the alacrity of his townsmen. Consetena Tate had unwittingly stumbled upon a solution of that "surplus" difficulty. He wasn't thinking of the surplus. He was too utterly impractical for that. He was a tall, gangling, effeminate, romantic, middle-aged man whom his parents still supported and viewed with deference as a superior personality. He was Smyrna's only literary character.

He made golden weddings gay with lengthy epics that detailed the lives of the celebrants; he brought the dubious cheer of his verses to house-warmings, church sociables, and other occasions when Smyrna found itself in gregarious mood; he soothed the feelings of mourners by obituary lines that appeared in print in the county paper when the mourners ordered enough extra copies to make it worth the editor's while. Added to this literary gift was an artistic one. Consetena had painted half a dozen pictures that were displayed every year at the annual show of the Smyrna Agricultural Fair and Gents' Driving Association; therefore, admiring relatives accepted Mr. Tate as a genius, and treated him as such with the confident prediction that some day the outside world would know him and appreciate him.

A flicker of this coming fame seemed to dance on Consetena's polished brow when he wrote a piece for the county paper, heralding the fact that Smyrna was one hundred years old that year.

Mr. Tate, having plenty of leisure to meditate on those matters, had thought of this fact before any one else in town remembered it. He wrote another article urging that the town fittingly celebrate the event. The Women's Temperance Workers discussed the matter and concurred. It would give them an opportunity to have a tent-sale of food and fancy-work, and clear an honest penny.

The three churches in town came into the project heartily. They would "dinner" hungry strangers in the vestries, and also turn an honest penny. The Smyrna Ancient and Honorable Firemen's Association, Hiram Look foreman, was very enthusiastic. A celebration would afford opportunity to parade and hold a muster.

The three uniformed secret societies in town, having an ever-lurking zest for public exhibition behind a brass-band, canvassed the prospect delightedly. The trustees of the Agricultural Fair and Gents' Driving Association could see a most admirable opening for a June horse-trot.

In fact, with those inducements and with motives regarding the "surplus" spurring them on secretly, all the folks of Smyrna rose to the occasion with a long, loud shout for the celebration—and suggested that the "surplus" be expended in making a holiday that would be worth waiting one hundred years for.

After that shout, and as soon as he got his breath, the voice of First Selectman Aaron Sproul was heard. He could not make as much noise as the others, but the profusion of expletives with which he garnished his declaration that the town's money should not be spent that way made his talk well worth listening to.

It was then that the bear-baiting began.

Every society, every church, every organization in town got after him, and Hiram Look—a betrayal of long friendship that touched the Cap'n's red anger into white heat—captained the whole attack.

The final clinch was in the town office, the Cap'n at bay like the boar in its last stronghold, face livid and hairy fists flailing the scattered papers of his big table. But across the table was Hiram Look, just as intense, the unterrified representative of the proletariat, his finger jabbing the air.

"That money was paid into the treasury o' this town by the voters," he shouted, "and, by the Sussanified heifer o' Nicodemus, it can be spent by 'em! You're talkin' as though it was your own private bank-account."

"I want you to understand," the Cap'n shouted back with just as much vigor—"it ain't any jack-pot, nor table-stakes, nor prize put up for a raffle. It's town money, and I'm runnin' this town."

"Do you think you're an Emp'ror Nero?" inquired Hiram, sarcastically. "And even that old cuss wa'n't so skin-tight as you be. He provided sports for the people, and it helped him hold his job. Hist'ry tells you so."

"There ain't any hist'ry about this," the selectman retorted with emphasis. "It's here, now, present, and up to date. And I can give you the future if you want any predictions. That money ain't goin' to be throwed down a rat-hole in any such way."

"Look here, Cap'n Sproul," said the showman, grinding his words between his teeth, "you've been talkin' for a year past that they'd pushed this job of selectman onto you, and that you didn't propose to hold it."

"Mebbe I did," agreed the Cap'n. "Most like I did, for that's the way I feel about it."

"Then s'pose you resign and let me take the job and run it the way it ought to be run?"

"How would that be—a circus every week-day and a sacred concert Sundays? Judging from your past life and your present talk I don't reckon you'd know how to run anything any different!" This taunt as to his life-work in the show business and his capability stirred all of Hiram's venom.

"I've come here to tell ye," he raged, "that the citizens of this town to a man want ye to resign as first selectman, and let some one in that don't wear brustles and stand with both feet in the trough."

"That's just the reason I won't resign—because they want me to," returned the Cap'n with calm decisiveness. "They got behind me when I wasn't lookin', and picked me up and rammed me into this office, and I've been wantin' to get out ever since. But I'll be cussed if I'll get out, now that they're tryin' to drive me out. I'm interested enough now to stay."

"Say, did you ever try to drive a hog?" demanded the irate old circus-man.

"Yes," said the Cap'n, imperturbably, "I'm tryin' it now—tryin' to drive a whole litter of 'em away from the trough where they want to eat up at one meal what it's taken me a whole year to scrape together."

Persiflage of this sort did not appear to be accomplishing anything. Hiram relieved his feelings by a smacking, round oath and stamped out of the town-house.

As they had done once before in the annals of his office, the other two selectmen made a party with Sproul's opposers. They signed a call for a special town-meeting. It was held, and an uproarious *viva-voce* vote settled the fate of the surplus. In the rush of popular excitement the voters did not stop to reflect on the legal aspects of the question. Law would not have sanctioned such a disposal of town money, even with such an overwhelming majority behind the movement. But Cap'n Sproul still held to his ancient and ingrained fear of lawyers. He remained away from the meeting and let matters take their course.

Hiram, still captain of the revolutionists, felt his heart grow softer in victory. Furthermore, Cap'n Sproul, left outside the pale, might conquer dislike of law and invoke an injunction.

The next morning, bright and early, he trudged over to the first selectman's house and bearded the sullen autocrat in his sitting-room. He felt that the peace of the Cap'n's home was better suited to be the setting of overtures of friendship than the angular interior of the town office.

"Cap," he said, appealingly, "they've gone and done it, and all the sentiment of the town is one way in the matter. What's the use of buckin' your own people as you are doin'? Get onto the band-wagon along with the rest of us. It's goin' to be a good thing for the town. It will bring a lot of spenders in here that day. They'll leave money here. It will be a good time all 'round. It will give the town a good name. Now, that money is goin' to be spent! I've made you chairman of the whole general committee—as first selectman. You'll have the principal say as to how the money is goin' to be spent. As long's it's goin' to be spent that ought to be some satisfaction to you."

"You take that money—you and your gang of black-flaggers that has captured this town on the high seas—and you rub it onto your carkisses where it will do the most good," snorted the Cap'n. "Light cigars with it—feed it to your elephant—send it up in a balloon—I don't give a kihooted dam what you do with it. But don't you try to enlist me under the skull and cross-bones!"

After this unpromising fashion did the conference begin. It was in progress at noon—and Hiram remained to dinner. Breaking bread with a friend has a consolatory effect—that cannot be denied. When they were smoking after dinner, the first selectman grudgingly consented to take charge of spending the money. He agreed finally with Hiram that with him—the Cap'n—on the safety-valve, mere wasteful folderols might be avoided—and the first selectman had seen enough of the temper of his constituents to fear for consequences should they get their hands into the treasury when he was not standing by.

"Now," said Hiram, in conclusion, "the committee is well organized. There's a representative from each of the societies in town to act with you and advise."

"I'd ruther try to steer a raft of lashed hen-coops from here to Bonis Airs and back, under a barkentine rig," snapped the Cap'n. "I know the kind o' critters they be. We won't get nowhere!"

"I had to put 'em onto the committee," apologized the people's representative. "But, you see, you and the secretary will do practically all the work. All you've got to do is just to make 'em think they're workin'. But you and the secretary will be the whole thing."

"Who is this secretary that I've got to chum with?" demanded the Cap'n, suspiciously.

"You see"—Hiram choked and blinked his eyes, and looked away as he explained—"it sort of had to be done, to please the people, because he's the feller that thought it up—and he's the only lit'ry chap we've got in town, and he—"

Cap'n Sproul got up and held his pipe away from his face so that no smoke-cloud could intervene.

"Do you mean to tell me," he raved, "that you've gone to work and pinned me into the same yoke with that long-legged cross between a blue heron and a monkey-wrench that started this whole infernal treasury steal?"

"Consetena—" began Hiram.

The Cap'n dashed his clay pipe upon the brick hearth and ground the bits under his heel.

"I ain't any hand to make love to Portygee sailors," he cried; "I don't believe I could stand it to hold one on my knee more'n half an hour at a time. I don't like a dude. I hate a land-pirut lawyer. But a critter I've al'ays reckoned I'd kill on sight is a grown man that writes portry and lets his folks support him. I've heard of that Concert—whatever his name is—Tate. I ain't ever wanted to see him. I've been afraid of what might happen if I did. Him and me run this thing together? Say, look here, Hiram! You say a few more things like that to me and I shall reckon you're tryin' to give me apoplexy and get rid of me that way!"

Hiram sighed. His car of hopes so laboriously warped to the top summit of success had been sluiced to the bottom. But he understood the temper of the populace of Smyrna in those piping days better than Cap'n Sproul did. Consetena Tate was not to be put aside with a wave of the hand.

Hiram began again. At first he talked to deaf ears. He even had to drown out contumely. But his arguments were good! Consetena Tate could write the many letters that would be necessary. There were many organizations to invite to town, many prominent citizens of the county to solicit, for the day would not shine without the presence of notables. There was all the work of that sort to be done with the delicate touch of the literary man—work that the Cap'n could not do. Mr. Tate had earned the position—at least the folks in town thought he had—and demanded him as the man through whom they could accomplish all epistolary effects.

In the end Hiram won the Cap'n over even to this concession. The Cap'n was too weary to struggle farther against what seemed to be his horrid destiny.

"I'll have him at town office to-morrow mornin'," declared Hiram, grabbing at the first growl that signified submission. "You'll find him meek and humble and helpful—I know you will." Then he promptly hurried away before the Cap'n revived enough to change his mind.

Cap'n Sproul found his new secretary on the steps of the town office the next morning, and scowled on him. Mr. Tate wore a little black hat cocked on his shaggy mane, and his thin nose was blue in the crisp air of early May. He sat on the steps propping a big portfolio on his knees. His thin legs outlined themselves against his baggy trousers with the effect of broomsticks under cloth.

He arose and followed the sturdy old seaman into the office. He sat down, still clinging to the portfolio, and watched the Cap'n build a fire in the rusty stove. The selectman had returned no answer to the feeble attempts that Mr. Tate had made to open conversation.

"Far asunder your life aims and my life aims have been, Cap'n Sproul," observed the secretary at last. "But when ships hail each other out of the darkness—"

"Three-stickers don't usually luff very long when they're hailed by punts," grunted the old skipper.

"There is a common ground on which all may meet," insisted Mr. Tate; "I frequently inaugurate profitable conversations and lay the foundations of new friendships this way: Who are your favorite poets?"

"Say, now, look here!" blurted the Cap'n, coming away from the stove and dusting his hard hands together; "you've been rammed into my throat, and I'm havin' pretty blamed hard work to swallow you. I may be able to do it if you don't daub on portry. Now, if you've got any idea what you're here for and what you're goin' to do, you get at it. Do you know?"

"I had ventured upon a little plan," said Mr. Tate, meekly. "I thought that first of all I would arrange the literary programme for the day, the oration, the poem, the various addresses, and I already have a little schedule to submit to you. I have a particular request to make, Cap'n Sproul. I wish that you, as chairman of the committee, would designate me as poet-laureate of the grand occasion."

"You can be any kind of a pote you want to," said the selectman, promptly. "And I'll tell you right here and now, I don't give a continental thunderation about your programmy or your speech-makers—not even if you go dig up old Dan'l Webster and set him on the stand. I didn't start this thing, and I ain't approvin' of it. I'm simply grabbin' in on it so that I can make sure that the fools of this town won't hook into that money with both hands and strew it galley-west. That's me! Now, if you've got business, then 'tend to it! And I'll be 'tendin' to mine!"

It was not an encouraging prospect for a secretary who desired to be humble and helpful. Cap'n Sproul busied himself with a little pile of smudgy account-books, each representing a road district of the town. He was adding "snow-bills." Mr. Tate gazed forlornly on the fiercely puckered brow and "plipping" lips, and heard the low growl of profanity as the Cap'n missed count on a column and had to start over again. Then Mr. Tate sighed and opened his portfolio. He sat staring above it at the iron visage of the first selectman, who finally grew restive under this espionage.

"Say, look-a-here, Pote Tate," he growled, levelling flaming eyes across the table, "if you think you're goin' to set there lookin' at me like a Chessy cat watchin' a rat-hole, you and me is goin' to have trouble, and have it sudden and have it vi'lent!"

"I wanted to ask you a question—some advice!" gasped the secretary.

"Haven't I told you to pick out your business and 'tend to it?" demanded the Cap'n, vibrating his lead-pencil.

"But this is about spending some money."

"Well, mebbe that's diff'runt." The selectman modified his tone. "Go ahead and stick in your paw! What's this first grab for?" he asked, resignedly.

"To make my letters official and regular," explained Mr. Tate, "I've got to have stationery printed with the names of the committee on it—you as chairman, per Consetena Tate, secretary."

"Go across to the printin'-office and have some struck off," directed the selectman. "If havin' some paper to write on will get you busy enough so't you won't set there starin' me out of countenance, it will be a good investment."

For the next few days Mr. Tate was quite successful in keeping himself out from under foot, so the Cap'n grudgingly admitted to Hiram. He found a little stand in a corner of the big room and doubled himself over it, writing letters with patient care. The first ones he ventured to submit to the Cap'n before sealing them. But the chairman of the committee contemptuously refused to read them or to sign. Therefore Mr. Tate did that service for his superior, signing: "Capt. Aaron Sproul, Chairman. Per Consetena Tate, Secretary." He piled the letters, sealed, before the Cap'n, and the latter counted them carefully and issued stamps with scrupulous exactness. Replies came in printed return envelopes; but, though they bore his name, Cap'n Sproul scornfully refused to touch one of them. The stern attitude that he had assumed toward the Smyrna centennial celebration was this: Toleration, as custodian of the funds; but participation, never!

During many hours of the day Mr. Tate did not write, but sat and gazed at the cracked ceiling with a rapt expression that made the Cap'n nervous. The Cap'n spoke of this to Hiram.

"That feller ain't right in his head," said the selectman. "He sets there hours at a time, like a hen squattin' on duck-eggs, lookin' up cross-eyed. I was through an insane horsepittle once, and they had patients there just like that. I'd just as soon have a bullhead snake in the room with me."

"He's gettin' up his pome, that's all," Hiram explained. "I've seen lit'ry folks in my time. They act queer, but there ain't any harm in 'em."

"That may be," allowed the Cap'n, "but I shall be almighty glad when this centennial is over and I can get Pote Tate out of that corner, and put the broom and poker back there, and have something sensible to look at."

Preparations for the great event went on smartly. The various societies and interests conferred amicably, and the whole centennial day was blocked out, from the hundred guns at early dawn to the last sputter of the fireworks at midnight. And everything and every one called for money; money for prizes, for souvenirs for entertainment of visitors, for bands, for carriages—a multitude of items, all to be settled for when the great event was over. If Cap'n Sproul had hoped to save a remnant of his treasure-fund he was soon undeceived. Perspiring over his figures, he discovered that there wouldn't be enough if all demands were met. But he continued grimly to apportion.

One day he woke the poet out of the trance into which he had fallen after delivering to his chairman a great pile of sealed letters to be counted for stamps.

"What do I understand by all these bushels of epistles to the Galatians that you've been sluicin' out?" he demanded. "Who be they, and what are you writin' to 'em for? I've been lookin' over the names that you've backed on these envelopes, and there isn't one of 'em I ever heard tell of, nor see the sense in writin' to."

Mr. Tate untangled his twisted legs and came over to the table, quivering in his emotion.

"Never heard of them? Never heard of them?" he repeated, gulping his amazement. He shuffled the letters to and fro, tapping his thin finger on the superscriptions. "Oh, you must be joking, Captain Sproul, dear sir! Never heard of the poets and orators and *savants* whose names are written there? Surely, 'tis a joke."

"I ain't feelin' in no very great humorous state of mind these days," returned the Cap'n with vigor. "If you see any joke in what I'm sayin' you'd better not laugh. I tell ye, I never heard of 'em! Now you answer my question."

"Why, they are great poets, authors, orators—the great minds of the country. They—"

"Well, they ain't all mind, be they? They're hearty eaters, ain't they? They'll want three square meals when they get here, won't they? What I want to know now is, how many thousands of them blasted grasshoppers you've gone to work and managed to tole in here to be fed? I'm just wakin' up to the resks we're runnin', and it makes me sweat cold water." He glanced apprehensively at the papers bearing his computations.

"All the replies I have received so far have been regrets," murmured Mr. Tate, sorrowfully. "I took the greatest names first. I was ambitious for our dear town, Captain. I went directly to the highest founts. Perhaps I looked too high. They have all sent regrets. I have to confess that I have not yet secured the orator of the day nor any of the other speakers. But I was ambitious to get the best."

"Well, that's the first good news I've heard since we started on this lunatic fandango," said the Cap'n, with soulful thanksgiving. "Do you think there's any in this last mess that 'll be li'ble to come if they're asked?"

"I have been gradually working down the scale of greatness, but I'm afraid I have still aimed too high," confessed Mr. Tate. "Yet the effort is not lost by any means." His eyes kindled. "All my life, Captain Sproul, I have been eager for the autographs of great men—that I might gaze upon the spot of paper where their mighty hands have rested to write. I have succeeded beyond my fondest dreams. I have a collection of autograph letters that make my heart swell with pride."

"So that's how you've been spendin' the money of this town— writin' to folks that you knew wouldn't come, so as to get their autographs?"

He touched the point better than he realized. Poet Tate's face grew paler. After his first batch of letters had brought those returns from the regretful great he had been recklessly scattering invitations from the Atlantic to the Pacific—appealing invitations done in his best style, and sanctioned by the aegis of a committee headed by "Captain Sproul, Chairman." Such unbroken array of declinations heartened him in his quest, and he was reaping his halcyon harvest as rapidly as he could.

"I was going to put them on exhibition at the centennial, and make them the great feature of the day," mumbled the poet, apologetically.

"So do! So do!" advised the Cap'n with bitter irony. "I can see a ramjam rush of the people away from the tub-squirt, right in the middle of it, to look at them autographs. I can see 'em askin' the band to stop playin' so that they can stand and meditate on them letters. It'll bust up the hoss-trot. Folks won't want to get away from them letters long enough to go down to the track. I wish I'd 'a' knowed this sooner, Pote Tate. Take them letters and your pome, and we wouldn't need to be spendin' money and foolin' it away on the other kind of a programmy we've got up! Them Merino rams from Vienny, Canaan, and surroundin' towns that 'll come in here full of hell and hard cider will jest love to set down with you and study autographs all day!"

Mr. Tate flushed under the satire by which the Cap'n was expressing his general disgust at Smyrna's expensive attempt to celebrate. He exhibited a bit of spirit for the first time in their intercourse.

"The literary exercises ought to be the grand feature of the day, sir! Can a horse-trot or a firemen's muster call attention to the progress of a hundred years? I fear Smyrna is forgetting the main point of the celebration."

"Don't you worry any about that, Pote," snapped the selectman. "No one round here is losin' sight of the main point. Main point is for churches and temperance workers and wimmen's auxiliaries to sell as much grub as they can to visitors, and for citizens to parade round behind a brass-band like mules with the spring-halt, and to spend the money that I had ready to clear off the town debt. And if any one thinks about the town bein' a hundred years old, it'll be next mornin' when he wakes up and feels that way himself. You and me is the losin' minority this time, Pote. I didn't want it at all, and you want it something diff'runt." He looked the gaunt figure up and down with a little of the sympathy that one feels for a fellow-victim. Then he gave out stamps for the letters. "As long as it's got to be spent, this is about the innocentest way of spendin' it," he muttered.

XXXII

As the great occasion drew nearer, Mr. Tate redoubled his epistolary efforts. He was goaded by two reasons. He had not secured his notables for the literary programme; he would soon have neither excuse nor stamps for collecting autographs. He descended into the lower levels of genius and fame. He wound up his campaign of solicitation with a stack of letters that made the Cap'n gasp. But the chairman gave out the stamps with a certain amount of savage satisfaction in doing it, for some of the other hateful treasury-raiders would have to go without, and he anticipated that Poet Tate, suggester of the piracy, would meet up with proper retribution from his own ilk when the committee in final round-up discovered how great an inroad the autograph-seeker had made in the funds. The Cap'n had shrewd fore-vision as to just how Smyrna would view the expenditure of money in that direction.

For the first time, he gazed on his secretary with a sort of kindly light in his eyes, realizing and relishing the part that Consetena was playing. On his own part, Poet Tate welcomed this single gleam of kindly feeling, as the Eskimo welcomes the first glimpse of the vernal sun. He ran to his portfolio.

"I have it finished, Captain!" he cried. "It is the effort of my life. To you I offer it first of all—you shall have the first bloom of it. It begins"—he clutched the bulky manuscript in shaking hands—"it begins:

"Ethereal Goddess, come, oh come, I pray,
    And press thy fingers, on this festal day,
    Upon my fevered brow and—"

"May I ask what you're settin' about to do, there?" inquired Cap'n Sproul, balefully.

"It is my poem! I am about to read it to you, to offer it to you as head of our municipality. I will read it to you."

The Cap'n waited for the explanation patiently. He seemed to want to make sure of the intended enormity of the offence. He even inquired: "How much do you reckon there is of it?"

"Six thousand lines," said Mr. Tate, with an author's pride.

"Pote Tate," he remarked, solemnly, "seein' that you haven't ever been brought in very close touch with deep-water sailors, and don't know what they've had to contend with, and how their dispositions get warped, and not knowin' my private opinion of men-grown potes, you've set here day by day and haven't realized the chances you've been takin'. Just one ordinary back-handed wallop, such as would only tickle a Portygee sailor, would mean wreaths and a harp for you! Thank God, I haven't ever forgot myself, not yet. Lay that pome back, and tie them covers together with a hard knot."

The Cap'n's ominous calm, his evident effort to repress even a loud tone, troubled Poet Tate more than violence would have done. He took himself and his portfolio away. As he licked his stamps in the post-office he privately confided to the postmistress his conviction that Cap'n Sproul was not exactly in his right mind at all times, thus unconsciously reciprocating certain sentiments of his chairman regarding the secretary's sanity.

"I don't think I'll go back to the office," said Mr. Tate. "I have written all my letters. All those that come here in printed envelopes for Captain Sproul I will take, as secretary."

At the end of another ten days, and on the eve of the centennial, Mr. Tate had made an interesting discovery. It was to the effect that although genius in the higher altitudes is not easily come at, and responds by courteous declinations and regrets, genius in the lower levels is still desirous of advertising and an opportunity to shine, and can be cajoled by promise of refunded expenses and lavish entertainment as guest of the municipality.

The last batch of letters of invitation, distributed among those lower levels of notability, elicited the most interesting autograph letters of all; eleven notables accepted the invitation to deliver the oration of the day; a dozen or so announced that they would be present and speak on topics connected with the times, and one and all assured Captain Aaron Sproul that they thoroughly appreciated his courtesy, and looked forward to a meeting with much pleasure, and trusted, etc., etc.

Poet Tate, mild, diffident, unpractical Poet Tate, who in all his life had never been called upon to face a crisis, did not face this one.

The bare notion of going to Cap'n Aaron Sproul and confessing made his brain reel. The memory of the look in the Cap'n's eyes, evoked by so innocent a proposition as the reading of six thousand lines of poetry to him, made Mr. Tate's fluttering heart bang against his ribs. Even when he sat down to write a letter, making the confession, his teeth chattered and his pen danced drunkenly. It made him so faint, even to put the words on paper, that he flung his pen away.

A more resourceful man, a man with something in his head besides dreams, might have headed off the notables. But in his panic Poet Tate became merely a frightened child with the single impulse to flee from the mischief he had caused. With his poem padding his thin chest, he crept out of his father's house in the night preceding the great day, and the blackness swallowed him up. Uneasy urchins in the distant village were already popping the first firecrackers of the celebration. Poet Tate groaned, and fled.

Cap'n Aaron Sproul arrived at the town office next morning in a frame of mind distinctly unamiable. Though his house was far out of the village, the unearthly racket of the night had floated up to him— squawking horns, and clanging bells, and exploding powder. The hundred cannons at sunrise brought a vigorous word for each reverberation. At an early hour Hiram Look had come over, gay in his panoply as chief of the Ancient and Honorables, and repeated his insistent demand that the Cap'n ride at the head of the parade in an imported barouche, gracing the occasion as head of the municipality.

"The people demand it," asseverated Hiram with heat. "The people have rights over you."

"Same as they had over that surplus in the town treasury, hey?" inquired the Cap'n. "What's that you're luggin' in that paper as though 'twas aigs?"

"It's one of my plug hats that I was goin' to lend you," explained his friend, cheerily. "I've rigged it up with a cockade. I figger that we can't any of us be too festal on a day like this. I know you ain't no ways taken to plug hats; but when a man holds office and the people look to him for certain things, he has to bow down to the people. We're goin' to have a great and glorious day of this, Cap," he cried, all his showman's soul infected by gallant excitement, and enthusiasm glowing in his eyes. It was a kind of enthusiasm that Cap'n Sproul's gloomy soul resented.

"I've had consid'able many arguments with you, Hiram, over this affair, first and last, and just at present reck'nin' I'm luggin' about all the canvas my feelin's will stand. Now I won't wear that damnation stove-funnel hat; I won't ride in any baroosh; I won't make speeches; I won't set up on any platform. I'll simply set in town office and 'tend to my business, and draw orders on the treasury to pay bills, as fast as bills are presented. That's what I started out to do, and that's all I will do. And if you don't want to see me jibe and all go by the board, you keep out of my way with your plug hats and barooshes. And it might be well to inform inquirin' friends to the same effect."

He pushed away the head-gear that Hiram still extended toward him, and tramped out of the house and down the hill with his sturdy sea-gait. Dodging firecrackers that sputtered and banged in the highway about his feet, and cursing soulfully, he gained the town office and grimly sat himself down.

He knew when the train from down-river and the outside world had arrived by the riotous accessions to the crowds without in the square. Firemen in red shirts thronged everywhere. Men who wore feathered hats and tawdry uniforms filled the landscape. He gazed on them with unutterable disgust.

A stranger awakened him from his reverie on the vanities of the world. The stranger had studied the sign

SELECTMEN'S OFFICE

and had come in. He wore a frock coat and shiny silk hat, and inquired whether he had the pleasure of speaking to Captain Aaron Sproul, first selectman of Smyrna.

"I'm him," said the Cap'n, glowering up from under knotted eyebrows, his gaze principally on the shiny tile.

"I was just a little surprised that there was no committee of reception at the station to meet me," said the stranger, in mild rebuke. "There was not even a carriage there. But I suppose it was an oversight, due to the rush of affairs to-day."

The Cap'n still scowled at him, not in the least understanding why this stranger should expect to be carted into the village from the railroad.

"I will introduce myself. I am Professor William Wilson Waverley, orator of the day; I have had some very pleasant correspondence with you, Captain Sproul, and I'm truly glad to meet you face to face."

"You've got the advantage of me," blurted the Cap'n, still dense. "I never heard of you before in my life, nor I never wrote you any letter, unless I got up in my sleep and done it."

With wonderment and some irritation growing on his face, the stranger pulled out a letter and laid it before the Cap'n.

The selectman studied it long enough to see that it was an earnest invitation to honor the town of Smyrna with a centennial oration, and that the town would pay all expenses; and the letter was signed, "Captain Aaron Sproul, First Selectman and Chairman of Committee, Per Consetena Tate, Secretary."

"I never saw that before," insisted the Cap'n.

"Do you mean that you disown it?"

"No, I reckon it's all official and regular. What I just said about not havin' seen it before might have sounded a little queer, but there's an explanation goes with it. You see, it's been this way. I—"

But at that moment fully a score of men filed into the office, all of them with set faces and indignant demeanors. The Cap'n was not well posted on the breed of literati, but with half an eye he noted that these were not the ordinary sort of men. There were more silk hats, there were broad-brimmed hats, there was scrupulousness in attire, there was the disarray of Bohemianism. And it was plainly evident that these later arrivals had had word of conference with each other. Each held a "Per Consetena Tate" letter in his hand.

"I have met with some amazing situations in my time—in real life and in romance," stated a hard-faced man who had evidently been selected as spokesman. "But this seems so supremely without parallel that I am almost robbed of expression. Here are ten of us, each having the same identical letter of invitation to deliver the oration of the day here on this occasion."

"Ten, did you say? Eleven," said the first-comer. "Here is my letter."

"And the others have invitations to deliver discourses," went on the spokesman, severely. "As your name is signed to all these letters, Captain Aaron Sproul, first selectman of Smyrna, perhaps you will deign to explain to us what it all means."

Cap'n Sproul arose and then sat down; arose and sat down again. He tried to speak, but only a husky croak came forth. Something seemed to have crawled into his throat—something fuzzy and filling, that would not allow language to pass.

"Here are more than twenty prominent men, seduced from their manifold duties, called away up here to satisfy the rural idea of a joke—or, at least, I can see no other explanation," proceeded the hard-faced man. "It might be remarked in passing that the joke will be an expensive one for this town. Eleven distinguished men called here to deliver one oration in a one-horse town!"

The Cap'n did not like the bitter irony of his tone, and recovered his voice enough to say,

"You might cut the cards or spit at a crack, gents, to see which one does deliver the oration." But the pleasantry did not evoke any smile from that disgusted assemblage.

"It is safe to say that after this hideous insult not one of us will speak," declared one of the group. "But I for one would like some light on the insane freak that prompted this performance. As you are at the head of this peculiar community, we'd like you to speak for it."

Somewhat to his own surprise, Cap'n Sproul did not find in himself any especially bitter animosity toward Mr. Tate, just then, search his soul as he might.

These "lit'ry fellows," cajoled by one of their own ilk into this unspeakable muddle, were, after all, he reflected, of the sort he had scorned with all his sailor repugnance to airs and pretensions. Cap'n Sproul possessed a peculiarly grim sense of humor. This indignant assemblage appealed to that sense.

"Gents," he said, standing up and propping himself on the table by his knuckles, "there are things in this world that are deep mysteries. Of course, men like you reckon you know most everything there is to be known. But you see that on the bottom of each letter you have, there are the words: 'Per Consetena Tate.' There's where the mystery is in this case."

"I imagine it isn't so deep a mystery but that we can understand it if you will explain," said the spokesman, coldly.

"There's where you are mistaken," declared the Cap'n. "It would take a long time to tell you the inside of this thing, and even then you wouldn't know which, what, or whuther about it." In his heart Cap'n Sproul was resolved that he would not own up to these strangers the part his own negligence had played. He reflected for his consolation that he had not projected the centennial celebration of Smyrna. It occurred to him with illuminating force that he had pledged himself to only one thing: to pay the bills of the celebration as fast as they were presented to him. Consetena Tate was the secretary the town had foisted on his committee. Consetena Tate had made definite contracts. His lips twisted into a queer smile under his beard.

"Gents," he said, "there isn't any mystery about them contracts, however. This town pays its bills. You say no one of you wants to orate? That is entirely satisfactory to me—for I ain't runnin' that part. I'm here to pay bills. Each one of you make out his bill and receipt it. Then come with me to the town treasurer's office."

The tumultuous throngs that spied Cap'n Sproul leading that file of distinguished men to Broadway's store—Broadway being treasurer of Smyrna—merely gazed with a flicker of curiosity and turned again to their sports, little realizing just what effect that file of men was to have on the financial sinews of those sports. Cap'n Sproul scarcely realized it himself until all the returns were in. He simply hoped, that's all! And his hopes were more than justified.

"My Gawd, Cap'n," gasped Odbar Broadway when the notables had received their money and had filed out, "what does this mean? There ain't more'n a hundred dollars left of the surplus fund, and there ain't any of the prizes and appropriations paid yet! Who be them plug-hatters from all over God's creation, chalkin' up railroad fares agin us like we had a machine to print money in this town?"

"Them vouchers is all right, ain't they?" demanded the Cap'n. "Them vouchers with letters attached?"

"Yes, they be," faltered the treasurer.

"So fur as who strangers may be, you can ask Pote Consetena Tate, secretary, about that. They're lit'ry gents, and he's done all the official business with them."

Broadway stared at him, and then began to make some hasty figures.

"See here, Cap'n," he said, plaintively, "there's just about enough of that fund left to settle the committee bill here at my store. Have I got to share pro raty?"

"Pay yourself and clean it out. I'll countersign your bill," declared the chairman, cheerfully. "If there ain't any fund, I can go home. I'm infernal sick of this hellitywhoop noise."

And he trudged back up the hill to the quietude of his farm, with deep content.

He had been some hours asleep that night when vigorous poundings on his door awoke him, and when at last he appeared on his piazza he found a large and anxious delegation of citizens filling his yard.

"Cap'n," bleated one of the committee, "Broadway says there ain't any money to pay prizes with."

"Vouchers is all right. Money paid on contracts signed by your official secretary, that you elected unanimous," said the Cap'n, stoutly.

"We know it," cried the committeeman, "but we don't understand it."

"Then hunt up the man that made the contracts—Pote Tate," advised the selectman. "All the business I've done was to pay out the money. You know what stand I've took right along."

"We know it, Cap'n, and we ain't blamin' you—but we don't understand, and we can't find Consetena Tate. His folks don't know where he is. He's run away."

"Potes are queer critters," sighed the Cap'n, compassionately. He turned to go in.

"But how are we goin' to get the money to pay up for the sports, the fireworks, and things?"

"Them that hires fiddlers and dances all day and night must expect to pay said fiddlers," announced the Cap'n, oracularly. "I reckon you'll have to pass the hat for the fiddlers."

"If that's the case," called the committeeman, heart-brokenly, "won't you put your name down for a little?"

"Since I've had the rheumatiz I ain't been any hand at all to dance," remarked the Cap'n, gently, through the crack of the closing door.

And they knew what he meant, and went away down the hill, as sober as the cricket when he was departing from the door of the thrifty ant.

XXXIII

First Selectman Sproul halted for a few moments on the steps of the town house the next morning in order to gaze out surlily on the leftovers of that day of celebration. Smyrna's village square was unsightly with a litter of evil-smelling firecracker remnants, with torn paper bags, broken canes, dented tin horns and all the usual flotsam marking the wake of a carnival crowd.

Constable Nute came tramping to him across this untidy carpeting and directed his attention to the broken windows in the town house and in other buildings that surrounded the square.

"Actions of visitin' firemen, mostly," explained the constable, gloomily. "Took that way of expressin' their opinion of a town that would cheat 'em out of prize-money that they came down here all in good faith to get. And I don't blame 'em to any great extent."

"Nor I, either," agreed the Cap'n with a readiness that surprised Mr. Nute. "A town that doesn't pay its bills ought to be ashamed of itself."

The constable backed away a few steps and stared at this amazing detractor.

"I paid bills prompt and honest just as long as there was any money to pay 'em with," the Cap'n went on. "There's nothin' on *my* conscience."

"Yes, but who did you pay the money to?" complained Nute, voicing the protest of Smyrna. "The least you could have done was to make them plug-hatters share pro raty with the fire-company boys—and the fire-company boys furnished the show; them plug-hatters didn't."

"It's always been my rule to pay a hundred cents on the dollar, and I paid the hundred cents so long as the cash lasted. Go hunt up your

Pote Tate if you want to know why the plug-hatters had a good claim."

"He's back, Tate is, and we made him explain, and this town had no business in givin' a cussed fool like him so much power. If I had cut up the caper he has I'd have stayed away, but he's back for his folks to support him some more. He didn't even have gumption enough to beg vittles."

"Well, this town has had a hearty meal, and all is I hope it won't feel hungry for celebrations till it's time for the next centennial," observed the Cap'n. "There's one thing about this affair that I'm goin' to praise—it was hearty and satisfyin'. It has dulled the celebratin' appetite in this town for some time." He went into town office.

The constable followed and laid a paper before him. It was a petition of citizens for a special town-meeting; and there being a sufficient number of names on the paper, it became a matter of duty for Cap'n Sproul to call the meeting prayed for.

He quietly proceeded to draw up the necessary notice. Nute evidently expected that the Cap'n would promptly understand the meaning of the proposed meeting and would burst into violent speech. But the selectman hummed an old sea chanty while he hunted for a blank, and smiled as he penned the document.

"Committee has been to Squire Alcander Reeves to get some law on the thing," proceeded Nute, disappointed by this lack of interest in affairs. "Reeves says that since the show was advertised as a town shindig the town has got to stand behind and fid up for the money that's shy. Says it ain't supposed to fall on the committees to pay for what the town's beholden for."

"Let 'em go ahead and settle it to suit all hands," remarked the first selectman, amiably. "As the feller used to sing in the dog-watch:

"'Says Jonah, addressin' the whale, "I wish
You'd please take notice that I like fish."
Says the whale to Jonah, "It's plain to see
That you are goin' to agree with me."'"

A considerable gathering of the taxpayers of Smyrna had been waiting on the platform of Odbar Broadway's store for the first selectman to appear and open the town office. Hiram Look had marshalled them there. Now he led them across the square and they filed into the office.

The Cap'n did not look up until he had finished his work on the notice. He handed the paper to Nute with orders to post it after the signatures of the two associate selectmen had been secured.

Then to his surprise Hiram Look received an extremely benignant smile from the Cap'n.

"You ain't objectin' any to the special town-meetin', then?" inquired Hiram, losing some of his apprehensiveness.

"I'm callin' it as quick as the law will let me—and happy to do so," graciously returned the first selectman.

Hiram took off his tall hat with the air of one who has been invited to remain, after anticipating violent rebuff.

"You know, don't you, what the voters want this special meetin' for?"

"Sartin sure," cried the Cap'n. "Got to have money to square up bills and take the cuss off'm this town of welchin' on a straight proposition to outsiders who came down here all in good faith after prizes."

"Exactly," cried Hiram, glowing. "Didn't I always tell you, boys, that though Cap'n Aaron Sproul might be a little gruff and a bit short, sea-capt'in fashion, he was all right underneath?"

There was a mumble of assent.

"There ain't a first selectman in this State that has shown any more science in handlin' his job than Cap'n Aaron Sproul of this town."

"When you come to remember back how he's grabbed in and taken the brunt every time there's been anything that needed to be handled proper, you've got to admit all what you've said, Mr. Look," assented another of the party.

"We know now that it was by Tate forgin' your name and runnin' things underhanded that the town got into the scrape it did," Hiram went on. "Them bills had to be paid to keep outsiders slingin' slurs at us. You done just right. The town will have to meet and vote more money to pay the rest of the bills. But probably it won't come as hard as we think. What I was goin' to ask you, Cap'n Sproul, was whether there ain't an overplus in some departments? We can use that money so far's it'll go."

"Pauper department has something extry," stated the first selectman, dryly. "I was thinkin' of buyin' a new furnace for the poor-farm, but we can let the paupers shiver through another winter so's to pay them squirtin' prizes to the firemen."

"We don't want to do anything that ain't just accordin' to Hoyle," said Hiram, flushing a little, for he sensed the satire. "We'll meet and vote the money and then we can sit back and take comfort in thinkin' that there's just the right man at the head of town affairs to economize us back onto Easy Street." He was eager to flatter. "This town understands what kind of a man it wants to keep in office. I take back all I ever said about opposin' you, Cap'n."

"And that's the general sentiment of the town," affirmed Odbar Broadway.

The face of the first selectman did not indicate that he was especially gratified.

"That is to say," he inquired grimly, "after I've fussed, figured, and struggled for most of two years to save money and pay off the debts of this town and have had the cash yanked away from me like honey out of a hive, I'm supposed to start in all over again and do a similar job for this town on a salary of sixty dollars a year?"

"We don't feel you ought to put it just that way," objected Hiram.

"That's the way it suits me to put it. You can do it to me once—you have done it—but this is where this partickler little busy bee stops makin' honey for the town of Smyrna to lap up at one mouthful. That special town-meetin' comes along all handy for me. You notice I ain't objectin' to havin' it held."

Constable Nute, who had been looking puzzled ever since the selectman had signed the call for the meeting, perked up with the interest of one who is about to hear a mystery explained.

"For," the Cap'n went on, "I was goin' to call one on my own hook so that I can resign this office. I serve notice on you now that when this town touches dock at that meetin' I step ashore with my little dunnage bag on my back."

"The town won't let you do it," blazed Hiram.

"I was shanghaied aboard. You want to be careful, all of ye, how you gather at the gangway when I start to walk ashore! It's fair warnin'. Take heed of it!"

There was an expression on his weather-worn countenance that checked further expostulation. Hiram angrily led them out after a few muttered expletives.

"I've heard of contrary tantryboguses in my time," stated Broadway when they were back at his store, "but that feller over there has got all of 'em backed into the stall. This town better wake up. We've let ourselves be bossed around by him as though Smyrna was rigged out with masts and sails and he was boss of the quarter-deck. Give me a first selectman that has got less brustles."

It was the first word of a general revolt. It is the nature of man to pretend that he does not desire what he cannot get. The voters of Smyrna took that attitude.

On the eve of the projected town-meeting Hiram Look strolled over to call on his friend Sproul. The latter had been close at home for days, informing his loyal wife that for the first time since he had settled ashore he was beginning to appreciate what peace and quiet meant.

"I don't know how it happened," he informed Hiram, "how I ever let myself be pull-hauled as much as I've been. Why, I haven't had time allowed me to stop and consider what a fool and lackey I was lettin' 'em make of me. When I left the sea I came ashore with a hankerin' for rest, comfort, and garden sass of my own raisin', and I've been beatin' into a head wind of hoorah-ste-boy ever since. From now on I'll show you a man that's settled down to enjoy life!"

"That's the right way for you to feel," affirmed Hiram. "You take a man that holds office and the tide turns against him after a while. It's turned against you pretty sharp."

"Don't see how you figger that," returned the Cap'n with complacency. "I'm gettin' out just the right time. Time to leave is when they're coaxin' you to stay. If I'd stayed in till they got to growlin' around and wantin' to put me out I'd have to walk up and down in this town like Gid Ward does now—meechin' as a scalt pup. That's why I'm takin' so much personal satisfaction in gettin' out—they want to keep me in."

"You ought to travel out around this town a little," returned his friend, grimly. "The way they're talkin' now you'd think they was goin' to have bonfires and a celebration when they get rid of you. Hate to hurt your feelin's, but I'm only reportin' facts, and just as they're talkin' it. Bein' a friend I can say it to your face."

The Skipper and the Skipped

The expression of bland pride faded out of Cap'n Sproul's face. For a moment he seemed inclined to doubt Hiram's word in violent terms. A few words did slip out.

The old showman interrupted him.

"Go out and sound the pulse for yourself. I never lied to you yet. You've cuffed the people around pretty hard, you'll have to admit that. Take a feller in politics that undertakes to boss too much, and when the voters do turn on him they turn hard. They've done it to you. They're glad you're goin' out. You couldn't be elected hog-reeve in Smyrna to-day."

The Cap'n glared at him, voiceless for the moment.

"I know it hurts, but I'm tellin' you the truth," Hiram went on, remorselessly. "If they don't stand up and give three cheers in town-meetin' to-morrow when you hand in your resignation I'll be much surprised."

"Who's been lyin' about me?" demanded the first selectman.

"It ain't that way at all! Seems like the town sort of woke up all of a sudden and realized it didn't like your style of managin'. The way you acted when the delegation came to you put on the finishin' touch. Now, Aaron, you don't have to take my word for this. Prob'ly it doesn't interest you—but you can trot around and find out for yourself, if it does."

The first selectman, his eyes gleaming, the horn of gray hair that he twisted in moments of mental stress standing straight up, rose and reached for his hat.

"Mutiny on me, will they?" he growled. "We'll jest see about that!"

"Where are you goin', Aaron?" asked the placid Louada Murilla, troubled by his ireful demeanor.

"I'm goin' to find out if this jeebasted town is goin' to kick me out of office! They'll discover they haven't got any Kunnel Gid Ward to deal with!"

"But you said you were out of politics, Aaron!" Dismay and grief were in her tones. "I want you for myself, husband. You promised me. I don't want you to go back into politics."

"I hain't ever been out of politics yet," he retorted. "And if there are any men in this town that think I'm down and out they'll have another guess comin'."

He marched out of the house, leaving his visiting friend in most cavalier fashion.

Hiram stared after him, meditatively stroking his long mustache.

"Mis' Sproul," he said at last, "you take muddy roads, wet grounds, balky animils, fool rubes, drunken performers, and the high price of lemons, and the circus business is some raspy on the general disposition. But since I've known your husband I've come to the conclusion that it's an angel-maker compared with goin' to sea."

"You had no business tellin' him what you did," complained the wife. "You ought to understand his disposition by this time."

"I ought to, but I see I don't," acknowledged the friend. He scrubbed his plug hat against his elbow and started for the door. "I'd been thinkin' that if ever I'd run up against a man that really wanted to shuck office that man was your husband. I reckoned he really knew what he wanted part of the time."

"Can't you go after him and make him change his mind back?" she pleaded.

"The voters of this town will attend to that. I was tellin' him the straight truth. If he don't get it passed to him hot off the bat when he tackles 'em, then I'm a sucker. You needn't worry, marm. He'll have plenty of time to 'tend to his garden sass this summer."

It was midnight when Cap'n Sproul returned to an anxious and waiting wife. He was flushed and hot and hoarse, but the gleam in his eye was no longer that of offended pride and ireful resolve. There was triumph in his glance.

"If there's a bunch of yaller dogs think they can put me out of office in this town they'll find they're tryin' to gnaw the wrong bone," he declared hotly.

"But you had told them you wouldn't take the office—you insisted that you were going to resign—you said—"

"It didn't make any diff'runce what I said—when I said it things was headed into the wind and all sails was drawin' and I was on my course. But you let some one try to plunk acrost my bows when I'm on the starboard tack, and have got right of way, well, more or less tophamper is goin' to be carried away—and it won't be mine."

"What have you done, Aaron?" she inquired with timorous solicitude.

"Canvassed this town from one end to the other and by moral suasion, the riot act, and a few other things I've got pledges from three-quarters of the voters that when I pass in my resignation to-morrow they'll vote that they won't accept it and will ask me to keep on in office for the good of Smyrna. This town won't get a chance to yoke me up with your brother Gid and point us out as a steer team named 'Down and Out!' He's 'Down' but I ain't 'Out' yet, not by a dam—excuse me, Louada Murilla! But I've been mixin' into politics and talkin' political talk."

"And I had so hoped you were out of it," she sighed, as she followed him to their repose.

She watched him make ready and depart for town hall the next morning without comment, but the wistful look in her eyes spoke volumes. Cap'n Sproul was silent with the air of a man with big events fronting him.

She watched the teams jog along the highway toward the village. She saw them returning in dusty procession later in the forenoon — signal that the meeting was over and the voters were returning to their homes.

In order to beguile the monotony of waiting she hunted up the blank-book in which she had begun to write "The Life Story of Gallant Captain Aaron Sproul." She read the brief notes that she had been able to collect from him and reflected with bitterness that there was little hope of securing much more data from a man tied up with the public affairs of a town which exacted so much from its first selectman.

Upon her musings entered Cap'n Sproul, radiant, serene. He bent and kissed her after the fashion of the days of the honeymoon.

"Whew!" he whistled, sitting down in a porch chair and gazing off across the blue hills. "It's good to get out of that steam and stew down in that hall. I say, Louada Murilla, there ain't in this whole world a much prettier view than that off acrost them hills. It's a good picture for a man to spend his last days lookin' at."

"I'm afraid you aren't going to get much time to look at it, husband." She fondled her little book and there was a bit of pathos in her voice.

"Got all the time there is!"

There was a buoyancy in his tones that attracted her wondering attention.

"They wouldn't accept that resignation," he said with great satisfaction. "It was unanimous. Them yaller dogs never showed themselves. Yes, s'r, unanimous, and a good round howl of a hurrah at that! Ought to have been there and seen the expression on Hiram's face! I reckon I've shown him a few things in politics that will last him for an object-lesson."

"I suppose they'll want to keep you in for life, now," she said with patient resignation. "And I had so hoped—"

She did not finish. He looked at her quizzically for a little while and her expression touched him.

"I was intendin' to string the agony out and keep you on tenter-hooks a little spell, Louada Murilla," he went on. "But I hain't got the heart to do it. All is, they wouldn't accept that resignation, just as I've told you. It makes a man feel pretty good to be as popular as that in his own town. Of course it wasn't all love and abidin' affection—I had to go out last night and temper it up with politics a little—but you've got to take things in this world just as they're handed to you. I stood up and made a speech and I thanked 'em— and it was a pretty good speech."

He paused and narrowed his eyes and dwelt fondly for a moment on the memory of the triumph.

"But when you're popular in a town and propose to spend your last days in that town and want to stay popular and happy and contented there's nothin' like clinchin' the thing. So here's what I done there and then, Louada Murilla: I praised up the voters of Smyrna as bein' the best people on earth and then I told 'em that, havin' an interest in the old town and wantin' to see her sail on full and by and all muslin drawin' and no barnacles of debt on the bottom, I'd donate out of my pocket enough to pay up all them prizes and purses contracted for in the celebration—and then I resigned again as first selectman. And I made 'em understand that I meant it, too!"

"Did they let you resign?" she gasped.

"Sure—after a tussle! But you see I'd made myself so popular by that time that they'd do anything I told 'em to do, even to lettin' me resign! And there's goin' to be a serenade to me to-night, Hiram Look's fife and drum corps and the Smyrna Ancients leadin' the parade. Last thing I done down-town was order the treat."

He nested his head in his interlocked fingers and leaned back.

"Louada Murilla, you and me is goin' to take solid comfort from now on—and there's nothin' like bein' popular in the place where you live." He glanced sideways at the little blank-book.

"We've been kind of neglectin' that, hain't we, wife? But we're goin' to have a good, long, cozy, chatty time together now! Make a note of this: One time when I was eleven days out from Boston with a cargo of woodenware bound to Australia, we run acrost a—"

THE END

CPSIA information can be obtained
at www.ICGtesting.com
Printed in the USA
LVHW030737120121
676263LV00002B/38